THREE DAYS OF SUMMER

C. J. Allan

First published in 2020 by the Centre for Connected Practice, Manchester, UK (www.c4cp.net)

C.J. Allan © 2020

Three Days of Summer

ISBN 978-1-9163008-0-4

All rights reserved. The author has asserted her rights to be identified as the author of this work in accordance with the Copyright, Designs and Patents Act 1988.

Printed and bound by Imprint Digital, Exeter, UK
Book production, cover design, and typesetting in 12pt Minion Pro, by Raven Books, UK
Proofread by George Kirkpatrick

Praise for C. J. Allan's first book, *Gerald and Breena & Rose*

"Here in one volume are two short novels dew-fresh in themes and very readable."
Daily Mirror

"Catherine Allan has written two unusual stories which bite off attention with sharp, compact-concrete economy."
Sunday Times

"This book is beautifully written, with penetrating insights and evoking pictures in the mind as one reads."
Church Times

"The two novellas have a deceptively simple clarity and directness and (for a new writer) a remarkable authority ... the impressive thing is the core of psychological or even anthropological toughness they conceal."
Guardian

"Allan has the steady ripple of the story-teller."
Books and Bookman

"C. J. Allan here provides us with a sympathetic and adult view of childhood."
Oxford Mail

ACKNOWLEDGEMENTS

With thanks to Sarah Bird, Editorial Consultant, for her encouragement and work on the book, and to Maggie Taylor-Sanders and the team at Raven Books who have kindly and graciously prepared the files for publication. Phil Barton, Catherine's son-in-law, having read the manuscript and believed in it, oversaw the publishing project through from start to finish and provided the front cover and interior design motif. Nóra Barton Kettleborough, C.J. Allan's granddaughter, contributed editorial work and support to Phil in the publishing process. Her daughter, Helena Mary, who found the manuscripts and has cajoled, supported and organised to ensure *Three Days of Summer* is published. Allan óg, her son, to whom this book is dedicated, who looks after C.J. Allan so well and so faithfully that she lives to see her book published. Finally, with thanks, Nóra, Catherine's sister, her brothers-in-law Tómas and Phil, granddaughters Merry and Ita and the rest of Catherine's family in Ireland, England and America, both living and dead, who are so dear to her.

ABOUT THE AUTHOR

C.J. (Catherine) Allan was born in Ireland in 1930. Part of a close and gifted family of six daughters and one son, she grew up by the Atlantic Ocean, which remained forever an inspiration for her. Following six happy years in a convent boarding school, she won a scholarship to University College Galway to study history through Irish and English. Whilst working at Butlins Holiday Camp in Filey, North Yorkshire, to earn money in the summer holidays, she met her future husband, Allan John Kettleborough. They were married in 1954 and had two children, a girl and a boy. In the 1960s, her husband was organising the Daily Mirror's Children's Literary Competition which put them in contact with some of the leading creative writers of the day. Together Catherine and Allan walked on the downs outside Brighton and by the sea, sharing their common passion for reading, literature and writing. Catherine's first book *Gerald and Breena & Rose* was published in 1967 by Faber & Faber. *Three Days of Summer* was completed in 1974 and around that time Allan wrote *A Human Face*, which Catherine edited. Catherine wrote one further book, *Never Be a Stranger*. C. J. Allan's beloved husband Allan sadly died in 1979 and the books remained unpublished.

Three Days of Summer appears in time for Catherine's 90th birthday, so that sometimes, in the face of all the odds, life can turn around again.

In Loving Memory
of
Allan John Kettleborough,
C. J. Allan's brother Jacky, sisters Ita, Moira, Helena and Brid,
and Brid's husband Eamonn.

Dedicated to her son,
Allan óg Kettleborough,
with immense gratitude.

CHAPTER 1

It was about an hour before sunset on a July evening. With her two dogs for companions, Breena was going for a walk up to the lake. She had started out on a much shorter walk to her friend's house; but had looked up and seen the sunbeams strike higher and higher on the small steep fields that led nearly half-way up the mountain, and turned off on impulse towards the lake. At that moment when she turned off, the sunlight striking on the high fields above seemed to bring them very near. She could believe that all she had to do was take one good run, and she would be up there. And the birds in the hedges and thorn trees all around, they were singing, singing! Breena could only wonder at them, as she had so often done before on summer evenings. To be able to sing themselves to sleep in that way, and know nothing of the strange power their singing had to make her so restless…

Many of them were probably already asleep, after they had urged her out and on into the summer evening, and made even the thought of any kind of rest distasteful to her.

Now the sunlight lit up the lowest mountain ridge, behind which the lake was hidden. Down here on the lower ground where Breena still was, the fields were fast losing the fresh greens and yellows the sun had gilded them with. They were ageing a thousand years every minute. Their blanched, brittle bones were showing up under their skins. It was easy to believe now that they were millions of years old. And yet, Breena thought, tomorrow morning they would look younger than she did herself, after this long hurried walk to the lake.

She was making for the lake not by the usual easy footpath but by a way she liked better; a way that branched off through heather and furze and ferns to the low ridge that hid the lake. As she left the fields behind and the hill got steeper, she reached out for clumps of fern and heather to ease her climb. In that way she eventually reached the top of the ridge and allowed herself to look freely about. All the wild landscape of mountain and water below struck her with a fresh and powerful impact.

As usual her first impression shocked her into sinking back and clutching hard at the thick strands of heather around her. Under the shallow of this ridge and the basalt cliffs of the mountain at the back, the lake below was swallowed up in darkness. For a moment it seemed that up here she teetered precariously on the very edge of nothingness. Below there was only blackness, a great abyss that reached down and down into the terrifying bowels of the world. Her heart lurched, she sat back, panting and holding hard to the heather. Then her vision adjusted itself to the change in the light, and she could make out the brown shining of the water below. She sat for some time looking down, then called to the dogs and began to ease herself down the steep slope towards the lake. She leant well back on her heels and held on to the ferns and heather to save herself from going too quickly.

As she went down, the shadows of the ridge and the cliffs retreated, until by the time she reached the water's edge the lake was as bright as the sky it reflected. How intensely, in those first few moments by the lake, she experienced two emotions as different as all the contrasts of dark and light around her. First there was a feeling of kinship with this secret place, so that her very breathing quietened to be in harmony with it. But there was also an ache at its strangeness – its utter carelessness of her and what she was. She knew that whether she came or went the brown water would be shining down here, the big furze bushes glooming like savages over the bright stones at the water's edge... In between the furze the grass would still be as green – the emerald-green 'fairy' grass that you stepped on at your peril. And all around and above the peaks and crags would still be plumping themselves out with cushiony shadows before they leaned against the sky, so concerned they seemed for its tender gleaming.

The only sound this place could hold, the sound of the river at the back falling into its underground channel, was one Breena's ears had grown accustomed to while she was still climbing the ridge. It was the jealous voice of the lake. Even now at her present age of nearly eighteen it could stir in her echoes of the strange terrors she had felt when she first heard it. Folklore had it you could hear human cries in it – the voices of the lost Danaan people, who had been driven by the Celts to take refuge under these mountains. As she listened to the sound of the water she could well believe that their despairing cries could be heard in it. And also, the sound brought back the sharp tang of the memory of her own childhood, of her first walk to this lake in the strange summer after her father's collapse and death and the break-up of her old home. She could recall very vividly what a long, long trek over heather and moorland the journey from the town had seemed that day... Endless, because the town was not yet home, not yet a place she could long to get back to.

A sense of the strangeness of this place, of its indifference to herself, even its malevolence, was growing on her. And she knew that the dogs, inferior as she ranked them to herself, felt it too. Their blood was warm like her own, and everything in this place was cold, cold. She looked across the water at the basalt cliffs and the peaks and crags of the mountain above, and all at once found it easy to imagine that they were tensed in a chill and evil watchfulness. Some lines she had come across the week before began to form themselves on her lips:

> *... No familiar shapes*
> *Remain, no pleasant images of trees*
> *Of sea or sky, no colours of green fields;*
> *But huge and mighty forms, that do not live*
> *Like living men, move slowly through the mind...*

With that she knew it was time to go. She made a sudden decision, turned swiftly to her left and began to run along the flat ground by the water's edge, between the furze bushes and over the fairy grass. The dogs bounded to her side at once with obvious relief. She was now making her way under the lee of the ridge she had climbed on her way up, towards the point at the northern end of the lake where the footpath began. She was taking the footpath home as a matter of course, not only because it led past her friend Kitty's house, where she still intended to call in, but because the lake was always for her the climax of the walk.

When she came out from under the shadow of the ridge and turned left again onto the footpath, it was to find herself staring straight into the red-gold face of the sun. It was resting its chin on one of the peaks of the Maurcappagh mountain range across the valley, and was still brilliant enough to put a golden glitter on the wild grass and rocks and heather around her up here. But directly below it the whole depth of the Maurcappagh mountains, with the little town she had come from at its foot, lay deep in shadow. She could barely make out the roofs and chimney tops of the town. For a few moments she stood still, looking across the valley. The mountains were behind her now: the Tobar mountains of the secret lake, and across the valley the higher mountains of the Maurcappagh range. Between and beyond these the sea.

Now the sun had dipped behind the horseshoe curve of the Maurcappagh range. For a few minutes the light was very pure. Cows and sheep in the fields could be seen clearly for miles around. Dark-clad men passing from one door to another in farm buildings away down to left or right of the valley seemed to be within hailing distance. The long grey glimmer of Church Street, far below in the town, looked like a continuation of the footpath; a place that could be reached in ten minutes or so by putting on a downhill spurt of speed into the wind.

She came out of the high fields into a stretch of open bogland. With the heavy rain the week before, the stepping-stones that usually marked the way through this bad stretch were lost under mud. Now she had to climb the fence that bordered the field and walk along there. She clambered up, urging the dogs on before her.

She had set out for the lake this evening much later than ever before. Now as she made her way along the high fence she saw how the street-lamps in the town below came more and more into prominence with the fading of the light in the sky. She hated it when this happened. It was not merely that the street-lamps made the countryside around seem darker and the way before her harder to distinguish. The after-sunset glow in the sky had this effect too, and she did not dislike it. No; something more happened when the street-lamps began to govern the dusk. All at once a sharp division was made in the landscape. The place where the street-lamps shone suddenly began to seem very cosy, warm, and pleasant. While a dreary gloom spread out by contrast over the rest of the countryside. Once or twice she stopped and turned back to stare at the Tobar mountains where the lake was. Finally, she saw behind her only a mass of darkness; mountains and sky merged together. And now all at once she was struck by the chill sound of the evening winds. How they seemed to come at her with a rush out of the thickening dusk, hissing in the furze, moaning over the bogland, shaking the sedges on the fence with a hungry sound! She was wearing only a light sweater over her dress; she had intended when she first came out to go only as far as Kitty's house. And now here she was in the dusk and cold, trudging along this high fence, with the night winds rising – their howl, their speed, and their bite getting keener every minute.

She began to think with longing of Kitty's house. What a fuss they would make of her when she told them that she had been up as far as the lake! And how warm the kitchen would be! She was able to imagine that room so clearly, how it would look when she went in with the dogs and was made to sit down in the old rocking chair by the fire while Kitty prepared hot drinks, that she began to lose herself in a daze of longing to be there, to be already in it, to be sitting by the stove talking at ease with Kitty and, of course, her brother Maurice.

But all the time the mechanical part of her brain was occupied with the way before her. A small copse of mountain ash marked the place where the bogland ended and she could jump down from the fence and strike to the right across a couple of fields to rejoin the footpath. She abandoned herself now to running along in a curious kind of wind-beaten haze, all her thoughts sunk into one desire to get this foolish, lonesome, impulsive trek over as soon as possible and to be back amongst the warmth and people again. In this dazed, half-blind way she kept up the going as best she could, always running fastest when the dogs were beside her, stopping the moment she missed them and calling out, a lonely cry in the cold and gloom, until they came back to her. She scarcely bothered to note where she was going. The track glimmered palely before her in the dusk. She followed it blindly. She halted, called their names impatiently. This time it took them longer than usual to return to her. And as she waited, hugging herself for warmth, she became aware of unexpected shapes around her. A fence, trees, a hillock to her left, lights far nearer than they should be; these in some vague manner penetrated her daze. Suddenly she was again in full possession of her senses, or thought she was. 'Where am I? Where can I have blundered to?' were the questions she asked herself as she swung rather wildly about, trying to place herself. It was almost as if she had woken out of a dream to find herself in a strange country. After a moment of perplexity and confusion she ran up the hillock to see about her.

The dogs came back. She felt rather than saw them. She was staring down with painful concentration on what had come clearly into view as she climbed the little hill. There below her stood a house. But not her friend's house; not the house she had been hurrying all this time to reach. 'Oh, no!' An involuntary cry escaped her. The dogs growled and pressed close against her. No, it was another and far different house. A house that to find here in her path at this time of evening made her blood rock in a wild see-saw of astonishment and dread. It was the house she had lived in as a child; the house that as a child she had left behind. Nearly a hundred miles from the place it should stand. Yet here it was, here before her it stood again, transported into her path by what unknown, what incomprehensible powers? Oh what was it, what was it that could make such a thing possible?

Then for a few seconds, a few seconds only, she was again a child. Her thoughts swayed back amongst the shadowed questionings and savage beliefs of childhood. She thought to herself, the lake, it could only be the lake! The folklore of the lake flashed through her mind; stories she had made fun of about the envious beings who bided their time up there and suddenly, swiftly, monstrously, revenged themselves on their mockers.

Only for a few seconds the illusion lasted. And then the cloud in her brain cleared away. She saw that it was indeed Kitty and Maurice's house that was there below her. At the same time too she realised with sweet relief that she was no longer a child, at the mercy of fierce and incomprehensible emotions. With the easing of her heartbeats she stared even more intently at the house, trying to understand what had caused her first reaction of terror. All at once she saw what it was. The house before her blazed with light. Not a window in all its untidy, rambling structure but carried its own pale or flame-like glow. And behind the windows, shadows of hurrying or frightened people seemed to move along the walls. So long ago – how long ago? – she had once come dreaming around a corner in the dusk and seen... She had seen, disastrously lit up in the same way, the house of her childhood on the night of her father's sudden death.

She found that she was standing about fifty yards from the house, above it on higher ground, at the corner of the orchard. Further up along the path, over-eagerness had made her blind. In her haste she had missed the gate to the right of the pathway that led into the yard. The dogs, of course, had turned in at the gate, expecting her to follow. That was why they had taken so long to come back. Now, standing very still, her hands resting warm on the dogs' necks as they stood one on either side of her, she stared at the lighted-up windows and tried to fight the impulse that urged her to turn again and run, to turn back to the path and not to stop running until she reached home. The most likely explanation, she told herself, was that some kind of impromptu party was in progress. She strained to hear some sound – of laughter, or gay talking. But all she could hear was the furious rustling of the night wind in the trees of the orchard.

She hesitated. For a moment she believed that she had argued herself into doing the usual, sensible, normal thing. She believed that she was going to walk back along the footpath as far as the gate and turn in towards the house. But the dogs were growling low in their throats; and dogs had a sixth sense. If they, always her companions and guardians on long walks, were afraid why shouldn't she be? The next moment, on a sudden impulse, she began to run, away from the house, down the path that led to the road and the first houses of the town. As she ran she told herself that it was an act of pure cowardice that she wasn't even going to attempt to excuse herself. She had run away, that was all.

Her thoughts now fastened on some words that had come into her head while she was still staring at the lighted-up windows of the house. She began to repeat them over and over again, doggedly forcing all her attention on them. '*All things remain in God. All things remain in God...*' What were they, she asked herself? Words out of a poem. But what poem? What did it matter? The only thing that mattered was to keep on running and to keep saying them, so that she need not think of anything else. She kept her face turned to the right as she ran; towards the lights of the town, very welcome now. By contrast field and sky seemed to be made of the same dark texture. Above her head when she looked up she saw a dark, rough-furred covering over the world. There seemed to be the same roughness under her feet when they touched the ground. But as far as she could, she kept her thoughts concentrated on the five words out of the poem. *All things remain in God.*

CHAPTER 2

Breena came at last to the road and the first houses of the town. She called to the dogs to come to heel, and did her best to smooth back her hair with her hands. At the big hotel by the corner people were eating out on the terrace, protected from the wind by a curved wall of stone and glass, on what must have seemed to them a balmy summer's evening. She walked slowly past, for the pleasure of hearing their voices and watching the little red lamps that winked on their tables.

Because it was a Saturday night doors were open on every side, there was an air of leisure and lazy talk. She could see the figures of people coming and going in the square further on, she could hear singing from a bar on the other side of the street. Then she saw a group of women coming out of one of the open doors ahead and she hurried to reach them. If anything had happened, if the scurry behind the lighted windows of Kitty's house had been seen by her and not imagined, she felt sure that rumours would already have got about. These women would no doubt be discussing them. But the slow way they turned and greeted her as she reached them, the calmness of their expressions, their smiles that half invited her to stop and join in their gossip, only exasperated her. She gave them a brief, 'Good evening!' and quickened her pace again and hurried on into the square.

She wanted to be home. She half-promised herself that as soon as she had reached home and said a few words with everybody and got back her sense of proportion, she would return to the house she had run away from. But next time she would approach it along the streets and not through the fields… Now she was coming up to the church, she had reached the corner, home was in sight. There were no lights to be seen in the front of the house. She thought to herself, they must all be round at the back. She began to run again.

She reached the house, hurried round it into Main Street, and pushed open the side-gate. Softly, almost secretly, and whispering to the dogs to be quiet, she tip-toed across the yard to the window of the stock-room and peeped in. Everything she saw at that first glance helped and comforted her. *All things remain in God*, was still running through her head. It seemed to her as she looked in that the words had come to her as a preparation for what she saw here. There was continuity in this place, 'things remaining'. 'Home' she had come to call it and home it truly had become. And she knew it was as much as she herself as any of those people in there who helped to give meaning to that word. Within the last few years she had become the focal personality of this house. A strange chance, that, surely…

She leaned against the wall, gasping, getting her breath back, and at the same time letting a kind of ease, a kind of grateful happiness take her over. The dogs sat obediently at her feet, and she stooped down and stroked and patted them lovingly. She was in that state of heightened sensitivity when many salient images of her life began to pass through her head, not singly, in stately procession, but four or five abreast, so that she was only just aware of them as they passed.

There was a picture of herself on the evening she first came here. A picture taken from inside her, as it were, so that it looked tight and strained, the way she felt. Then images of her mother's face, smiling, smiling, on the starched white pillows at the hospital… The blue-robed nun with the huge, high white hat that used to make Breena wonder how she could get through doorways. Incongruously and vividly, a picture of the big bowl of fruit jelly and ice-cream they had given her the night she first came to this house; food she didn't want and had to clamp her lips over and let slide down, down, until it felt like snakes in her throat. And then the memory of the faces of the people here, all very old and queer, as they had seemed to her when she first saw them! She took another peep now through the half-closed shutters. There were four people in there. One of them, Mrs Regan – dear old Hannah – had come with her from her old home to this house. *Her* face had always been familiar and dear. But the other three! Breena had to draw back from the window and lean against the wall again and find relief in a quick smile to herself. She was remembering – she still could remember very clearly – how very queer and old those other three faces in there had seemed to her the first time she saw them.

She continued to lean against the wall for some time, absolutely relaxed, not even bothering to look in through the window any more. In sheer laziness the line, *All things remain in God* ran again through her head. And then she thought once more what an unexpected pattern her life had taken; how strange it was that she should be leaning here tonight against this particular wall in the dusk. It seemed to her now that her coming here in the first place was a little bit like a shotgun wedding. Only after several years had passed would anybody venture to pronounce that the thing had been a success. But how very far away that bad old time seemed at this moment! And how wonderful to be nearly eighteen years of age, when everything could be dealt with by herself, when even the sharpest dread could be reasoned away or run away from by herself alone, with no fear of interference from older, slower, so-called wiser people.

Now she walked away from the wall and in a soft tone of relief called to the dogs to follow her to their shed at the upper end of the T-shaped house. A minute later she was back in the yard and going through the small door in the angle of the house into the corridor. By now she had given up all thought of returning to Kitty and Maurice's house. She had decided that this was a bit of folly best put behind her. Tomorrow morning, in the daylight, she would probably tell Kitty and Maurice about it, as a joke.

As she pushed open the stock-room door a foolishly big smile grew on her face, she just couldn't help it. The four people in the room glanced up at her with smiles and various questions and exclamations.

'So you're back!'

'You're a bit late!'

'Are you alone?'

'Didn't Kitty or Maurice feel like a stroll tonight then?'

Still smiling hugely she told them, 'I didn't go to Kitty's after all. I went up to the lake.'

And she closed the door and leant back against it to enjoy the effect of this announcement.

'Up to the lake?'

'At this time of night?'

'Tssch! Tssch!'

'Not alone, surely?'

Most of the volubility came from her left, from the big scrubbed deal table in the corner, from where Hannah and 'Aunt' Ursula were (aunt by courtesy; Ursula was a woman who liked to hear Breena call her 'Aunt Ursula'; but she had no blood claim to this title and in fact, if her age were taken into account, was more like Breena's grandmother than her aunt). Now Hannah and this Aunt Ursula were sitting side by side, looking up with amused interest from what could only be a new knitting pattern they had been studying. Breena, however, had aimed her information at the other end of the room. But the person whose reactions she was most concerned with was giving her very little satisfaction. He only raised his eyebrows and smiled. And his smile told her that if she were to announce on the spot that she had just come back from a visit to the moon, instead of

| 21

a paltry walk to the lake, he would still refuse to be impressed. She went across the room towards him.

'Uncle John, did you hear? I've just been up to the lake. On my own. At this time of night.'

'Yes. I heard.'

She had been calling him Uncle John for seven years now – for convenience's sake to begin with, and then out of a kind of affectionate necessity. But as far as blood-relationship went, he was only a second cousin of her father's.

He was sitting on the long bench behind the stove, with Thady beside him. They were smoking their pipes and stretching their legs. In front of them, by the stove, their two tankards of Guinness were gently mulling. Their faces wore almost identical expressions of half-suppressed, half-indulgent welcome, and this made them look for the moment almost like brothers. They made room for her on the bench between them.

'Anything more like a pair of Red Indian chieftains I have never seen in my life,' she told them as she sat down.

At moments like this she was strongly aware of a kind of behaviour that was forced on her by her position in the house. She had already come to terms with it by giving it to herself the somewhat pat name of 'juvenility'. She thought of it in her own mind as the price she had to pay, here in her second home, for being a general favourite, and for her complete freedom in certain vital directions. And the very fact that she was able to define and analyse this behaviour removed all the sting from it, in her own estimation. She believed that she was master of it. Now at the age of nearly eighteen she at least understood what was happening to her. No longer, as in childhood, was she the victim of vague and powerful emotions that angered or frightened her simply because they were beyond her understanding. No; this 'juvenility' was a thing she could keep consciously before her. She had placed it, named it, and was fully aware of it as a form of behaviour that was necessary while she remained in this house. She believed that therefore it could do neither herself nor anybody else in this house any harm. She believed, rather, that the very pleasure and relaxation of moments like the present depended on spontaneous, childlike reactions from herself. And perhaps she could always be 'juvenile' with Uncle John. Perhaps she owed it to him. She need not trouble him with her growing up processes which she could exercise with people of her own age.

Uncle John and Thady were talking about the fishing. Breena had already heard from three or four different sources that day that the sprat were coming all round the coast, with the usual shoals of mackerel close on their tails. But when Uncle John asked, 'I s'pose you've heard about the sprat?' she pretended complete ignorance, realising in her present sensitive, shamed mood how much pleasure it would give him to tell the story to fresh ears. Uncle John asked:

'You didn't meet Sean Mor then, in the square?'

'No. Has he just been here?'

'Yes, indeed. He was telling us that at low tide this morning the strand at Maurcappagh was littered with sprat, and the mackerel were in as far as the point, packed together like sardines. He claims that he caught a score o' mackerel in half a minute from the Boar Rock, just by lowering a canvas bag into the water.'

Breena didn't quite know how to take this. There was a note she did not like in Uncle John's voice. Coarseness was not too strong a word for it. Sean Cappagh, or Sean Mor as everybody called him because of his height, was the oldest member of their family. They were all Cappaghs, Uncle John, Breena herself, Thady, Kitty and Maurice, though only very distantly related. And in Uncle John's voice now there was a mocking dismissal of the old man, Sean Mor, whom Breena herself liked greatly. However, just as she had learned to stave off any silly resentment on her own account by inventing the concept of 'juvenility', so she had also taught herself to recognise on the instant, and limit, and hedge off as far as possible, this occasional coarseness of Uncle John's towards other people. She edged round the subject now by exclaiming:

'So the mackerel are in at Maurcappagh!' And she turned to Thady and asked him eagerly, 'D'you think they'll last out until tomorrow and give us a good day's fishing?'

Nearly every fine Sunday between May and October they went fishing from the jetty at Maurcappagh, where Thady still kept in use the boat he had helped his father and uncles to make when he was growing up. But Uncle John remarked:

'Now that the mackerel have caught a glimpse of Sean Mor, no doubt they'll get sense and beat it quickly back to the open sea.'

'Oh, I hope not!'

She said it too quickly, a little too childishly eager, knowing that she had failed to turn the subject and already racking her brains how to try again. But help came unexpectedly from the other side of the room. Ursula looked up from her knitting and called across:

'Breena, I wonder if you'd mind very much getting the tea? Hannah and myself seem to have got ourselves into a bit of a mess here. We... '

Breena jumped up at once. 'Of course I'll get it!' Not only was she delighted to escape any further quips at Sean Mor, but it eased her to think she could make herself useful, she felt so ashamed and chastened from her recent cowardly panic in the fields.

She went out and turned left along the corridor into the kitchen. The tray was already set. All she had to do was boil the kettle and make the tea. Now that she was alone again, however, her thoughts reverted once more to what she had seen in the fields, Kitty and Maurice's house all lit up in that queer way. She reflected uneasily that she ought to tell Uncle John what she had seen. Because the house whose windows had blazed above the darkening fields was the house of Uncle John's brother. Kitty was Uncle John's real niece – unlike Breena – whose nieceship was an honorary one. And though it was a long time now since Breena had stopped thinking of Kitty and Maurice as relatives of Uncle John's rather than as her own friends, yet at this present moment, as she moved about the kitchen, she was very conscious of the connection between the two families, and of Uncle John's right to be told what she had seen. And because she couldn't yet even begin to forgive herself for running away, because the shock of her first glimpse of the house, that had jolted her back into childhood, was still vivid in her mind, she just couldn't understand how she was able to keep it all back. Why, usually she was only too anxious to get things like that off her chest! Usually, the more ashamed she was of anything she had done, the more ready she was to speak about it to Uncle John. Only after he had forgiven her did she find it possible to forgive herself and to forget all about it.

The kettle began to whistle. She sighed heavily as she picked up the tea caddy. She was thinking that Ursula too had a right to hear the story, and could be trusted to take a real interest in it. Breena sighed again, even more heartily, struggling with her thoughts. Surely it was the very closeness of the tie between the two families that made any confession or revelation on her own part unnecessary now? It was precisely because she had found everybody so calm here when she arrived back that she had taken it for granted nothing very serious had happened at the other house.

She took up the tray and went through into the next room. Rather warily she put down the tray on the big table and began to pour out the tea. In her present mood it was more than a pleasure, it was an assuagement, to be given charge of the tea-tray. She took great care to suit Ursula's and Hannah's tastes in sugar and milk as she filled the cups. She even heartily wished that she understood something about knitting, so that she could help them. And that was a very self-sacrificing thing. Because usually the very sight of a knitting pattern was enough to make her fingers twitch nervously like knitting needles. One thing she had sworn she would never learn to do; she would never learn to knit.

She was just about to hand out the tea when she saw that Hannah was getting up from the table.

'What's the matter?' Breena asked. 'Have I forgotten something? If so, I can easily run next door and fetch it.'

'You've forgotten something alright. You've forgotten to get yourself a proper supper. Since you've been all the way up to the lake, you'll need something more than a biteen o' cake on your plate there.'

Breena gave her a whole-hearted smile of sudden discovery. 'Yes, Hannah, I *am* hungry. Ravenous. But until this moment I just didn't think.'

'No,' Hannah interrupted tartly, moving towards the door, 'somehow when it comes to taking a bit o' trouble, your powers o' thinking make quite a habit of deserting you.'

'But what about your tea, Hannah?' Breena called after her. No good. She was already on the other side of the door.

Hannah was Breena's old name for Mrs Regan, her first childish attempt at pronouncing her first name, Aine. There was a friendship between them that went back as far as Breena could remember. However, as in all cases of true friendship, allowances had to be made now and again for bouts of plain speaking. Now with Hannah's cup of tea in her hand, Breena said a little ruefully to Ursula:

'I'd better drink it myself, though there's too much sugar in it for me. If I took it to her in the kitchen, she wouldn't drink it, I know well. She'd present to be too busy.'

Ursula put down her knitting. 'Maybe one of the men…?' she suggested. Then she raised her voice and called across the room to Uncle John in a very precise, delicate, considerate tone of voice:

'John… John. There's a cup of tea to spare here. Would you like it?'

Across the room Breena saw Uncle John smile, lift his tankard and take a sip out of it, and then hold it up towards Ursula. Sufficient answer to an offer of tea, by any standards. A second or two later,

Thady made the same gesture. Ursula expressed her opinion of it in the almost comic tone she always used to Uncle John; a tone in which there was both humility and self-respect, consideration for Uncle John and a gentle but proud assertion of her own dignity and usefulness.

'Oh, John… John!' was what she said, 'it puzzles me how you can bring yourself to drink that stuff, you and Thady!'

Breena could not help smiling into Hannah's cup of tea. There really was something quite comic about Ursula's relationship with Uncle John. She was not his wife, but his wife's sister. However, she was far more about the house than her sister Peggy, Uncle John's wife, who had a profession of her own. As far as management of the house and shop were concerned, it was Ursula, rather than Doctor Peggy, who acted as wife to Uncle John. But everything was maintained on such a high level, there was such innocence and good manners in Ursula's bearing towards her brother-in-law, that it was obvious to everybody she never experienced the slightest qualm about her position in the house. She was needed in this house, she was useful here, she was always busy; this was therefore the station in life God had expressly created for her.

Hannah came in with Breena's supper. There was some home-made bread and butter, slices of pink, succulent home-cooked ham, a big square of curly-crusted, juicy apple cake. Breena spoke her thanks at some length as she jumped up to pour out fresh tea. Nothing was said about the first cup, which had been swallowed by now.

Then the knitting pattern was spread out again, Ursula's knitting needles began to click. Breena backed down the table a little, then stopped and looked wistfully across the room. Her heart lifted to see that Uncle John and Thady were watching her, showing plainly by their looks that they expected her to go and sit with them again by the stove. As she crossed the room towards them she had such a moment's keen sense of pleasure at being here, at being 'home' again after her long walk and fright in the lonesome fields, that like with pain itself she went tense against a recurrence of that fright.

'D'you want to show us how clever you are?' Thady challenged her amiably as she sat down. 'Well, then, tell us what we've just been talking about. We'll give you three guesses.'

She saw that it was time to fall again into her juvenile role. She assumed easily enough the saucy, knowing look that two years, or even eighteen months before, would have been her natural expression.

'No need for three guesses,' she told them pertly. 'Let me see… ' She paused and looked searchingly from one to the other. 'When I went out you were talking about the mackerel playing at Maurcappagh. From that you would naturally have gone on to talk about boats – then about seines, then about more boats and of course the men to work them. Sean Mor and… h'mmn! The only thing that's left for me to ask now is – when will this… err… transaction take place?'

She pronounced 'transaction' in such a peculiar way that Thady took it up and repeated it with relish, and Uncle John gave a snort of laughter. Her guess, since the time of year was right for it, was that they had been planning to go on a haul. Sean Mor had just been in – that was another clue. She knew that these hauls ('haul' was the local name for the night-time netting of fish) were against the law, and therefore very attractive to men like Thady and Uncle John, who still had a bit of the devil left in them. For these expeditions Sean Mor always provided the second boat, together with the seine and two or three young neighbours from beyond the Pass to act as look-outs against the police.

She saw that Uncle John and Thady were enjoying her deductions, so she went on to announce in an airy tone:

'Of course if the term "transaction" doesn't suit you, I can easily provide the exact word.'

Uncle John began, 'If I were you, I...' but a fit of coughing stopped him. As he put his handkerchief to his mouth and turned away, Breena's glance met Thady's. The look of concern on Thady's face made her stand up on a sudden impulse and pick up Uncle John's pipe from the bench, where he had just put it down. Then, under cover of going to refill her glass of milk, she took the pipe with her across to the table and hid it amongst the plates on the tray. She had come to hate this old pipe. She could not understand why Uncle John refused to see the harm it was doing him. Six months before he had been ordered to give up smoking. But he had only compromised and changed from cigarettes to a pipe. Her private view, the deduction she had drawn from watching him smoke a pipe for six months, was that a pipe, much used and tobacco stained as it was, must be far more harmful than cigarettes, which were at least fresh each time.

She brought back her refilled glass and sat down again on the bench. She knew Uncle John knew that she had taken away his pipe. But in this matter she exercised a kind of moral blackmail over him; he would never openly acknowledge to her how badly he needed his pipe.

She had just settled herself back in her seat when the telephone began to ring in the corridor outside. At the first harsh sound of it her hands started to tremble and she had to carefully lower her glass of milk to the floor. She became conscious of the throbbing of her heart. She realised then that since she first came into the room she had not once completely relaxed. Everything that had taken place had been at surface level. All the time she had been privately waiting for some sequel to what she had seen.

For a moment all the homeliness of the room she sat in was blotted out. In her imagination she was back in the dark and cold of the fields, staring down at the blazing windows of Kitty's house. Then her consciousness returned to the room; she became aware of faces turned towards her inquiringly. She understood how puzzled they must be that she had not jumped up at once to answer the

| 29

phone. They were always teasing her about the quick way she ran to answer the phone, expecting that every call would be for herself. Now she wanted to get up, an intense curiosity had taken possession of her. At the same time she was almost sick with nervousness; she was afraid to rise for fear she would fall back again.

And all the time, outside, the grating, tormenting sound went on and on. Slowly, painfully, she turned her head. 'Thady,' she whispered beseechingly, 'will you please… ?' Thady stood up and went out. The ringing stopped.

She knew that Uncle John was still watching her. She thought it as good a time as any to attempt an explanation. She blurted out; 'On my way back from the lake I came by the footpath, past Kitty's house. And I saw… I saw…'

'What did you see?' he encouraged her gently.

Thady appeared at the door. 'Can you come here a moment?' he asked Uncle John in his usual mild tones. Then before Breena could get a proper look at his face he had stepped back once more into the corridor. Uncle John closed the door as he went out.

Breena picked up her glass of milk and began to sip it mechanically. By very dint of reaction, a common-sense point of view was beginning to assert itself. More than likely, she told herself, it was Sean Mor on the phone now. If she had guessed right about the haul, then it stood to reason that Sean Mor must have hurried away from here to consort with his friends, many of whom would be in town tonight, Saturday night. Then as soon as they had all agreed on the look-outs and the manning of the boats and so on, and only a suitable date was left to be thrashed out, it was only natural that they should ring up Uncle John and let him know.

Yet, for all that, she could not help straining to hear what was going on outside. She was too far away from the door, however. The spurting, humming sound of the stove; the clicking of needles and exclamatory remarks at the other side of the room; made it impossible to be sure what it was she heard, or whether she heard anything at all. At last she found it impossible to sit still any longer. She put down her glass and jumped impulsively to her feet.

Her quick movements attracted the attention of Ursula, who called across the room, 'What can have happened to the men? What's keeping them I wonder?'

Very relieved to be able to discuss the matter, Breena hurried across the room, talking as she went.

'That's what I'm very curious to find out. D'you think that could have been Sean Mor on the phone just now? With all that that infers?'

'Well… it's possible,' Ursula said. 'Sean Mor was here for well over an hour. The three of them were talking together for a long time out in the yard.'

Now Hannah too had looked up and was smiling at Breena. 'You should have been quicker on your feet, girl, and answered the phone yourself. Why did you let Thady get there first?'

Breena understood this as a reference to her own vaunted ambition to be in on the next haul, no matter how secretly it was planned. Ursula and Hannah thought this a great joke, and egged her on, Hannah especially.

'You've let them get ahead of you again, girl,' she teased her now. 'I'd say you haven't much time to lose if you don't want to be out of the running altogether.'

'Yes I should have been quicker,' Breena agreed smiling. Of course that was all there was to worry about, whether or not she was going to be in on the next haul! 'Wish me luck!' she said lightly as she turned away towards the door.

The light was on in the corridor, but neither Uncle John nor Thady were to be seen. For a moment she stood uncertainly outside the door, her hand still on the knob. Across the way the big padlocks on the barred doors of the two sections of the shop were swollen out by their own shadows. The main hall, to her right where she stood with her back to the door, was in darkness. She turned the

| 31

other way, towards the kitchen. From there some narrow open stairs led up to the first floor and to the sitting room. She went quickly through the kitchen, up the stairs and knocked at the door of the sitting room. If Uncle John and Thady had seen fit to withdraw here for a discussion about the haul, then at least she could go in and give herself a chance to judge from their reactions what was afoot.

There was no answer to her knock and she opened the door of the sitting room and switched on the light. But at once she switched it off again and stood there petrified. Its quick flashing had shown her Uncle John seated at the table with his elbows on the table and his face pressed into his hands. For a few seconds she was absolutely incapable of movement. Total darkness seemed to follow that moment's glaring of the light. Yet she continued to see Uncle John, his image impressed on her mind. She stood there fixed in a strange state of intensity when perception and emotion seemed to be one and the same thing.

She knew that in a moment she must turn, that somehow she must step out and close the door with the utmost quietness. But it seemed almost impossible that he had neither heard her nor seen the light. She had no choice but to wait, to give him a chance to speak if he wished. And as she stood there, her wits were scattered for a moment by a faint sound that came out of the gloom ahead of her. At first she was not quite sure what kind of sound it was. She was not even sure that she had not made it herself. Then she heard it again and realised that it was coming from the table, from Uncle John, and that he was crying.

Afterwards she was quite unable to think clearly about what happened next. At the time she did not think at all. It never entered her head that she was intruding, that she had no right to be here, that Uncle John might wish her away. A passion of concern for him took her over. A thousand instances of his kindness towards herself crowded her mind. She stepped quickly forward. What words she could use for comfort, even how to make known her presence, she did not know. She hurried up to where he was and bent over him. The next moment a word she had no idea of uttering had slipped out of her mouth. She heard it with fresh force as though it had come from somebody else. But she knew that she herself was guilty of it.

'Father!'

It pulled her up. She crouched, shrank there in the darkness, in an agony of self-consciousness. The flow of love and pity that had made her forget herself was quite cut off. It seemed to her that she must have shrieked that word aloud. Oh, when Uncle John looked up, how could she explain it? Crouching, she waited for him to lift his head. When she thought about it afterwards it seemed that absolute, total darkness still surrounded her. But that was impossible. There must have been a strong glimmering of light from the windows. At any rate she knew where Uncle John was, she had gone straight towards him.

She waited; she had no means of knowing how long. And then somehow she began to back away. With infinite care she took herself out of the room. Afterwards she seemed to remember that it took her a long time to get the door closed without making a sound. Only then, safe on the other side of the door, did she understand that the cry she had uttered could not have got through to Uncle John – any more than the flashing of the light had done. He inhabited now a far country. Or… maybe she had only spoken that word in a whisper, or only thought it in her own mind. She stood for a moment by the high, narrow window of the corridor and looked down into Main Street. There were three men standing by the street lamp at the corner. She knew that if she were to lean forward and listen she would be able to hear what they were saying. But she turned away and began to go quickly and noiselessly down the corridor, guiding herself by trailing her left hand against the wall. She did not switch on the light; she walked very quickly. There was a sharp fear in her mind that Uncle John would come out of the sitting room and catch sight of her before she turned the corner.

When she came to the turn of the house, to the landing where the main staircase came up, it seemed to her that she had run far enough. She felt tired and an old habit reasserted itself. She went down half a dozen steps and then sat down on the stairs.

CHAPTER 3

Breena was sitting now in a kind of twilight. In front of her was the high, narrow window above the fanlight of the main front door. Its old-fashioned coloured panes caught gleams of pure red and yellow and green from the street lamps outside. This was familiar and comforting. And sitting here on the stairs was no act limited to this moment. From the time she was a child she had liked sitting on stairs. Since she first came to the house she had sat down on this particular step many times. It seemed a satisfying and comforting thing to do now…

She leaned back against the wall. Idle, pleasant pictures of other times she had sat on these stairs began to pass through her head. During her first year here she often used to sit reading on this step. She had enjoyed the privacy of being up here. And at the same time there was the pleasure of knowing that she could run down at any moment and join the bustle of comings and goings down below. Here on this step, again and again, she had tried to read *Master Humphrey's Clock*, which had been given to her as a school prize during her first year at the convent school in the town. She had never succeeded in getting into the story; its ramblings had somehow always become dreamily lost in the ramblings of footsteps down below. But then one day she had looked up from trying to read it and found the big clock on the wall opposite, leaning forward from its place, hanging its foolish old round yellow face over the banister, and watching her with an expression of good-natured inquisitiveness. She was startled and delighted. Any day at all after that, she had only to look up suddenly from her book to catch the old clock staring at her. Soon she was struck by the way its wheezy ticking always seemed to get very slow and deliberate – with a sense of its own importance – as soon as it was sure of her attention. Sometimes indeed the boastful slowness of its voice became so marked that she began to fear its vanity would one day be the death of it.

She could just dimly make out the clock now, and its ticking seemed to slow down in the old way and comfort her. But all the time some part of her mind was acutely occupied with the present. All at once she tensed herself; she had caught some vibration of sound even before she heard the opening of the sitting room door. Uncle John was coming out. For a moment she sat ready to run again if necessary. Then she heard Uncle John cross the corridor and go down the kitchen stairs. She heard the hopeful yapping of the dogs as he reached the outer kitchen door and began to cross the grass towards the gate that led to the garage. Thady, she surmised, was already out there waiting… She heard the car start up.

She felt no curiosity about what had happened or where they were going; she had seen Uncle John's brother's house all lit up; she had seen Uncle John with his face pressed into his hands, crying. It did not occur to her at that moment to question her inner certainty of what these things might mean. She understood the only thing that could have happened to make Uncle John cry – and the fact that he had stayed here to cry and not hurried away at once to the other house told her the whole story.

So attuned was she to everything that had relevance to this situation that when the stamping of heavy footsteps began outside in the square she caught the sound at once, through all the other noises out there. To be heard from that distance it could only be Dr Peggy, Uncle John's wife; the woman Breena had never called 'Aunt' even in the spirit of throwing a friendly rope into the darkness. She listened, straining all her attention. Soon she heard the dogs again, then Dr Peggy's voice calling from the kitchen, 'Ursula, Hannah!' It did not occur to her to move, to go down and join them. She knew very well that when she failed to appear they would take it for granted that she had already gone on with Uncle John & Thady to the other house. She heard the excitement of their voices from the kitchen. She was too far off to be able to distinguish their words. After a few minutes she heard once more the barking of dogs and knew that the three had left the house by the kitchen door.

She surprised herself then by standing up at once and hurrying back along the corridor into the sitting room. The three windows of this room overlooked the square (it was possible on summer evenings to look down from this room into the square as at a play, and even, when the windows were open, to hear clearly what was being said by the people who moved about below). She was astonished now to see how far the three had got in the short time since she had heard them go out. Led by Dr Peggy, who pounded on in front in her impatient, forward-pitching walk, they had already reached the corner by the church.

Now she stood a little back from the window so that nobody from the square could look up and see her. Her glance returned every other minute to focus on the corner by the church. She told herself that she could not possibly be waiting for anybody; that nobody at the other house would have a thought to spare for *her* at this particular time. Yet she continued to stand there. She was listening also for the sound of the telephone from below.

Her attention wandered for a moment; when she looked out again Maurice was below in the square, moving quickly so that he was already some way across it. She stared hard to make sure that it was really Maurice. When she thought about it afterwards, she could make little sense of what she did next. She turned at once from the window and ran on tip-toe through the sitting room and down the kitchen stairs to the outer kitchen door. She found it on

| 37

the latch as she had expected. They had gone out in too much of a hurry to think of locking it.

Swiftly she snapped down the lock and then ran back up the kitchen stairs and sat at the top, where the stairs opened on to the corridor. She had turned on no lights, but had guided herself by touch, with the sureness of familiarity, through the gloom of the kitchen and the stairs.

Maurice was already at the side-gate. She heard the dogs' low growling give place to friendly yapping as he called on them by name. She heard him try the kitchen door and then begin to knock at it, softly at first, then quite loudly. Then, as far as she could account for it afterwards, she continued to sit there at the top of the stairs, through a period of time when only her sense of hearing seemed active, and her very breathing and the beating of her heart seemed to depend on it. All the time the vibrations from the knocking seemed extraordinarily prolonged. It seemed impossible that she could merely continue to sit up here listening and not go down and open the door. Yet that was precisely what she did.

But at last the knocking stopped. She experienced intense relief. She had scarcely begun to relax again however, to decide that she could stand up, when her nerves were assailed by a new and even more harrowing sound; the shrill keening of the electric bell by the front door – the door of the main hall, where the old clock was. It made her start to her feet. Helplessly she pressed her fingers against her ears. Then she took them away again and found that the ringing had stopped. She drew one deep, deep, easeful breath. The next moment, however, she heard the knocking begin again, this time at the small door in the angle of the house; her own special door, across the hall from her bedroom, which was on the ground floor.

Her feelings reached a climax of exasperation. A peculiar kind of courage – that might also be called anger or even hate – took her over. Impossible, impossible to remain up here any longer! She went quickly down the stairs, hardly conscious that she moved in the dark, so sure was she in her movements, so intent on getting outside. Maurice must be stopped before he decided to climb over the garage wall. Maurice must be made to stop; he must be made to go away.

She opened the kitchen door and stepped out on the grass. She heard two tentative inviting barks from the dogs. She heard a car passing by on the other side of the wall. She stood very still and listened. She could hear no sound of knocking. 'Maurice?' she called softly into the shadows of the angle of the house. Swiftly she crossed the grass as far as the garage wall and called 'Maurice…?' once more. There was no answer. She realised that the silence around her was complete. Maurice had gone away.

Only then did she reflect on what she had done. She could only ask herself helplessly: 'Why did I run down and lock the door against Maurice? – How could I, Breena, have done such a thing?' She began to understand that it was an act of pure impulse, powered by some deep necessity that was beyond the reach of reflection or will. Suddenly she felt very wretched. A confused and groping sense of more than one kind of identity tucked away under her skin made her stand there very still, staring into the gloom over the garage wall, feeling only dismay and fear of herself.

Once more she was back in her imagination at the corner of the orchard above Kitty's house, looking down at the lit-up windows. At the same time the words she had repeated over and over as she fled from that house came back into her head: *All things remain in God*! All at once she thought she recognised those words. Excitement took the place of wretchedness inside her. Swiftly she turned and ran back across the grass into the kitchen, and hurried down the corridor into her room. She crossed at once to the window and closed and bolted the shutters. This was an old house, there were wooden shutters with iron bolts inside every window. Usually she slept with window and shutters open, but suddenly now the thought of this made her shiver.

For a few seconds she stood absolutely still, listening to faint creakings and rustlings in the distance of the corridor, and to a more ominous, muffled, burring sound in the narrow passage outside her room. She felt sure she had never heard this sound before. It was almost as if somebody were standing drawn up against the wall out there, trying hard to control the panting of his breath in the darkness. With that all kinds of silly and ugly fancies threatened to take her over. She listened again. Now the sounds she could hear from outside took on their proper significance. They were only the asthmatic rumblings of an old house; sounds she had never before taken note of, because she had never before been alone in the house in the silence of the night.

And now what had brought her in here in the first place returned to mind. Her excitement came back. She went to the special shelf where she kept her best books. She took down the newest of them, still in its own box (it had been given to her as a present the Christmas before). After some trouble, because she could not recollect either the title or the first line of the poem, she found the verse she wanted.

Before their eyes a house
That from childhood stood
Uninhabited, ruinous,
Suddenly lit up
From door to top:
All things remain in God.

In a secret and deep way that she could not yet begin to understand, these words calmed and comforted her. Somewhat disjointedly and wonderingly she read them again until she knew them by heart – as she always did now with any verse that had meaning for her. Then she read the other verses, making no conscious effort to learn them, but sounding each word and staring at it until it seemed to be written on a page in her mind rather than in the book before her.

After a while she was able to stand up and unbolt the shutters and open the window. The dogs heard her and barked hopefully and excitedly. She spoke to them a moment, encouraging them, enjoying the comfort of their nearness and watchfulness. She knew that she was still alone in the house. Nobody had yet come back. But now she felt no dismay. She had the poem to repeat to herself as she got ready for bed. By the time she was finally ready, the creakings and grumblings of the old house-boards on every side seemed to fuse in her mind into the sound of the poem she had just learned.

CHAPTER 4

The birds woke her in the morning. For a while she lay listening dreamily as they sang, 'Get up, get up, get up!' Her singing-birds she called them, the big thrushes and blackbirds and robins she often fed from her window, and who had such a power of carolling in their throats. As she listened to them now, only half-awake as yet, no memory of last night came for some time to disturb her ease. Her eyelids fluttered open a moment, she became aware of the beautiful shadowed dawn light in the room. Her one window faced eastwards and caught the first of the morning light. She felt the fresh air on her face above the warmth of the bedclothes and thought, 'In a moment I must get up.' But she really had no intention of doing so for some time yet. She lay there in a very pleasant, warm trance, letting half-formed wisps of thoughts drift in and out of her head. Sleep was so very enjoyable, she thought… How very unfair that nobody was ever given the chance to enjoy it. How stupid that when you should be enjoying it you were asleep, and knew nothing about it. Then you woke up, and just as you begun to realise what you had missed, you were expected to get up…

All the time the fresh air on her face, the gradually increasing light, and the insistent voices of the birds, were breaking in on her languor. She thought, that was a blackbird now, the sweetest singer of them all, perched, it must be, on top of the fuchsia bush to the right of the window. There was so much gladness in his voice that she too began to feel the excitement of the new day that was beginning. Another day! Why was she lying lumpishly here when she could be up and out in it, the first person in the town to be moving about in the freshly-made dawn? And now, by no means awake as yet, not wishing to be so, but beginning to wish that she could wish to be awake, she stretched and yawned with drowsy pleasure.

Now, with her growing wakefulness, came, as it had come every morning for the past month, the realisation that this was the summer of her freedom. She had left school at last, all the caged-in slavery of school was over... This was the summer she had been looking forward to for at least two years. It was nearly a month now since the last day of the exams, yet each morning when she woke up she experienced this same keen feeling of delight that the shadow-world of school was behind her, and real life had begun at last. This time last year she used to think 'Next summer...' – and at one time she had a calendar with over two hundred days still to be crossed off before the end of the exams. Now – oh, let her lie here very still and savour all the freedom and excitement of it! Now 'next summer' was here at last. She could only ask herself, was she still asleep? Could it really be possible that, for the first time since she could properly remember, there would be no school to go back to in September? No more bells, no more awful mornings when she hadn't done some particular piece of homework, and her heart sickened to see the teacher of that subject come into the room. The most hateful thing about school, she thought drowsily now, was the way clocks and bells ruled the day. And that was part and parcel of the next most hateful thing; the way they were always being hustled in a herd away from a favourite teacher and a favourite subject, and expected still to be cheerful, responsive, and polite. Could it possibly be all over? School standards had ruled her life so far. Even in holiday time there had been reading to do. But now, now... the first, and she had no doubt of it, the worst, phase of her life was over. Could anything ever again be worse than school?

All that studying, that forcing of interest, the cramp in her hand at exam time, the smell of old books and ink. No, in the future she could at least choose her subjects and her interests. School was over and done with, all that long agony of obedience and effort. What heady relish in the moment that thought could bring, what joy in looking forward to the future! She smiled; sleepily still, but with full awareness of what she was smiling at. School was over. How often in the past month had she experienced the conflict that was going on inside her now; the battle between the deliciousness of sleep and the excitement of full wakefulness. Of course the outcome depended on the sun, and not on herself at all, she told herself now with drowsy cunning. Whether she got up now or went back to sleep again depended entirely on the sun.

So she waited with eyes closed, in dreamy languor, for the sun to decide the issue. Growing brightness from the window beat on her eyelids. Soon the sun would be up. She thought back on the sunny mornings during the past month, when those bright sunbeams on her face had her out of bed in a frenzy of restlessness that was completely new, peculiar to the fresh joy of this summer. Without thinking about it at all, her limbs moving of their own accord it seemed, she would be up and dressed and climbing out through her window and over the garage wall to free the dogs. Usually then she turned down Main Street, the quickest way out to the open fields.

And five times already during the past fortnight – since she first told Maurice how the sunlight on her face got her out of bed on sunny mornings – she had looked up from the end of Main Street to see another figure running down the fields towards her. Maurice, with his long morning-shadow leaping before him! On those sunny mornings when they met, they either made for the lake across the valley, up the sloping fields towards the Tobar mountains, or began to climb one of the peaks of the Maurcappagh range directly above the town. Up and up they clambered then, until they were striding the crests against the coldest, hungriest winds out of the great Atlantic. And oh! How brilliant were those mornings.

And now her thoughts, which had drifted in easy languor towards the recollection of those early walks with Maurice, were pulled up by the thought of him, and began to circle uneasily about his name. Maurice…? What was it about Maurice she must remember? All at once she was fully awake and sitting up in bed. Last night! She remembered it all; her long walk, her panic when she stared down and saw lights in every window of Maurice's house; her cry of 'Father!' and that extraordinary thing, herself sitting in the darkness at the top of the stairs while Maurice knocked and rang at the door below.

After that she felt too thoroughly uncomfortable to remain in bed one moment longer. The bathroom and lavatory were upstairs, and she tried to move with great quietness. She had barely got back to her own room, however, when she heard quick footsteps in the corridor. The door opened, Ursula's head appeared cautiously round it.

'Breena! I thought I heard you. What have you got up at this hour for?'

'I, I… The sun was so bright, I just felt like getting up.'

They exchanged a long look. And as always when Breena looked properly at Ursula she was struck by her beauty; the serene, inward-shining, bone-gleaming beauty of a good woman who has grown old. Even when she was a child Ursula's eyes could not have been more blue than they were now. Her white hair brushed back in silky waves from her face, was also very lovely. Just looking at Ursula's face made Breena's mood swing round to the point when she was suddenly ashamed of what she now thought of as her 'hysterical' behaviour of the night before. The conclusions she had come to, merely on the evidence of her own memories!

'But why are *you* up?' she demanded of Ursula in turn. 'Is there anything wrong? Has anything happened?'

| 45

Ursula appeared to hesitate. Then she said in her usual gentle, low voice:

'I suppose I'd better tell you. You'll have to hear it any way and it may as well be from me.'

'Yes?' Breena said, 'Yes?' She was still looking full at Ursula.

'When we went out last night,' Ursula went on rather hurriedly, 'we had no idea that you had gone to bed. We thought you had already gone on in the car to the other house, with Thady and your Uncle John.'

'Yes?' Breena said again.

Then Ursula told her. As she spoke, Breena felt a queer kind of hollowness in her head, in which Ursula's words seemed to reverberate like the sound of waters in a cave. To be so right after all! To have guessed so accurately what had happened, on such slender evidence! Or could the evidence in any way be called slender? There was certain knowledge that, if acquired early enough, seeped into your blood; seeped into the blood stream that fed your nerves and your brain, and ever after that influenced your every judgement.

It was true then, that Uncle John's brother, his twin brother Jeremy, Kitty and Maurice's father, was dead. He had died of a heart attack at about half past ten last night. He had died alone, in his own room upstairs, where he had gone to fetch a book he was reading. Nobody knew exactly at what moment he had died. He had given no cry. There was no sound of falling, no exclamation of fear, no call for help. It was his wife (Ursula and Dr Peggy's sister) who found him. She followed him upstairs after he had been gone for some time, to see what was taking him so long. Her foot struck softly against him before she turned on the light, and at once she gave a loud shriek of fright. She knew it was a body her foot had touched, but she thought it was a mouse or even a rat there in the darkness, and she was disgusted and afraid. Afterwards, when they turned on the lights, they found him sitting on the floor, just inside the door, slumped low, yet with some suggestion of control in his attitude.

'He must have had some few seconds of warning,' Ursula was saying now, still in her low, controlled tones, though tears poured down her face. 'It seems he had time to sit down deliberately; he didn't fall – Oh God save us all from a sudden death! – But I'm sure he was ready to face his Judgement. He was a good man.' She paused a moment then went on in a voice scarcely louder than a whisper: 'I can't understand it, Breena. Anybody else would have used that last few seconds to cry out for help. Oh may God help us all in our last agony! Can you imagine what went through his mind at the end, alone up there in the dark?'

Breena backed to the chair behind her and sat down. She had heard enough. She thought to herself: in all decency talk should end at a certain point. But Ursula seemed unable to help herself. She repeated again:

'May God help us all in our last agony! – What I can't stop thinking about, Breena, what I can't stop asking myself, is why he had to go upstairs at that moment? Why did God in all His mercy allow him to go upstairs and die alone like that? What went through his head at the last moment? Why didn't he call out?'

Breena gritted her teeth. The thought crossed her mind: 'He didn't call out because there was so much pain in his heart there was nothing left to call out with. It wasn't courage that kept him quiet. It was pain. He had no time to think of anything except pain!'

Ursula was crossing herself and repeating once more: 'May God save us all from a sudden death! Oh may God help us all in our last agony!' Then in a changed voice, in a tone of great kindness, she went on: 'But I shouldn't have told you like this, Breena, so early in the morning. I've made you think of things it does you no good to think of, especially alone down here. Won't you come up with me now to my room, and lie down for a while on my bed?'

'Oh no, thank you Aunt Ursula. I'm quite all right. And I'm glad you told me. I'm glad that I know.'

'Well, at least you must go back to bed at once. I insist on that.

It can't be much after half past five. There's no sense in wandering about brooding on things at this hour of morning. I'll bring you a cup of tea. Hannah and myself have just been having a quiet cup together. We've just got back from the other house.'

Breena stood up at once and went back to her bed and jumped into it. It seemed the only way to make Ursula go away. Her thoughts had fastened again on the matter that had worried her last night; how soon had Uncle John been summoned. After Ursula went out she remembered suddenly and very clearly that she had glanced up at the clock on the stock-room wall the time she went to refill her glass, after she had taken away Uncle John's pipe. Just after twenty past eleven it was then. So they had waited nearly an hour before they phoned to this house. Was Uncle John the last person whose presence was needed?

Ursula came back with the tea. 'I've made you a fresh cup all of your own. And I'd better tell you that it's later than I thought. It's just turned half past six. Thank God for that, say I. The night's been long enough, heaven knows.'

Her lips smiled slightly, nervously, as she spoke. They were the only part of her face that showed strain. Above the twitching lips her vivid blue eyes were full of kindness. They made Breena feel ashamed – she wasn't quite sure of what. They often had that effect on her nowadays. She thanked Ursula for the tea in a very wordy manner, protesting that she could easily have got up and made it for herself.

'Now what would be the point of your getting up to make tea, when I'm already up? As it is, you can drink it here at your ease. Then you can have a little snooze, and soon after that it will be time to get up and get dressed for Mass.'

After Ursula went out Breena slipped out of bed again, and sipped her tea standing at the window. It had never been the custom in the house to have anything to eat before early Mass, because they were all in the habit of going to Holy Communion. Time passed very slowly as Breena stood there ay the window. She put on her watch and stared at the second hand as it went round the small inner dial. It gave her an ache, it moved so slowly. She felt her consciousness appeal to it from all directions, as if she had become the figures on the face of the watch. Then she remembered last night's poem, and with a thrill of real excitement turned to the table where she had left the book. She opened it at the page marked and began to repeat the poem. She checked it a verse at a time, half fearing that she had forgotten it, yet, even before she began, expecting to feel astonished and humiliated if even one word of it escaped her.

It turned out as she had hoped. Every word of the poem was impressed on her memory. She became aware, though only in a vague, unsatisfactory manner, that finding the poem and learning it by heart had in some subtle way changed her experience of last night. How, though? She puzzled over it, and had scarcely begun to do so when she heard the first bell ringing for early Mass. She decided to get dressed then at once and go across to the church, although there was more than half an hour still to go. She liked sitting in the church in the early mornings.

CHAPTER 5

In Main Street, on the other side of the high gate, there was not a soul to be seen. But when Breena turned into the sunny, rather windy square, she saw a number of old people already walking slowly along the pavement towards the church. At once then she stepped off the pavement and made obliquely across the square. She had no desire to speak to anybody just yet, and so break up the dreamy, reflective mood the poem had left in her.

This church which she now entered had been built within the past two years and was much larger than the old one. In the early mornings it was full of shadows. There was coldness too, but not a coldness that warped in a physical way. Coolness it must be called, rather, a condition of spaciousness. It impelled one towards serenity and calm reflection.

Breena went to her favourite seat in one of the side aisles and knelt down in the shadows. The other people who already knelt here and there were also absorbed by the shadows. The sounds they made, the footsteps, coughs, shufflings, whispered greetings and prayers, were caught up in the echoes from the vaulted roof and lost all human distinctness. They became a continuous murmur, a faint drone, a strange cry. She sat back and closed her eyes and savoured this familiar, distinctive sound. It was 'the voice of those crying in the wilderness'.

More and more people began to come in. She opened her eyes and saw the sunlight streaming in through the high, blue-toned windows of the nave. It made a shimmering ceiling that illumined the heads and shoulders of the people below. She was suddenly surprised to see how many people had come into the church since she herself had sat back and closed her eyes. It seemed that most of the town and half the countryside had turned out for this early Mass. Her thoughts drifted… It was always a good sign for the weather when so many people turned out for early Mass. So many people could hardly be mistaken! Her heart lifted in sudden happiness. Today the sunshine was going to last. It was going to be a lovely day.

Then the priest, Father Hennessey, came out and Mass began. She opened her missal and tried to keep all her attention on the Mass. She had not quite been able to keep her thoughts from straying to Maurice and Kitty and their family while she was waiting; she knew they must be somewhere here in the church. They always came to first Mass. Now she felt intense shyness at the thought of being noticed by any of them; she pressed further into the shadow of the nearby pillar. All the time too she was trying hard to think only of the prayers of the Mass, and to keep herself free from all distractions.

But then, a minute or two before the Epistle, when she had got a little ahead of Father Hennessey and was looking towards the altar and waiting, she thought she caught a glimpse of the black cartwheel hat Kitty's mother usually wore at Mass. There was something else too; something that before she could stop herself had her staring hard in the direction of that familiar hat. Yes! Her first impression was right, outrageous as it had seemed. There they were, the whole family sitting together in the main aisle, only one pew down from the Communion rails. Her astonishment was very great. You never saw families sitting all together like that nowadays. Since the building of the new church there were no more family pews. People just knelt down where they wished when they entered the church.

| 51

Again and again, in spite of herself, her glance was drawn back to the family. Uncle John was not there, nor was Jerry, Uncle Jeremy's eldest son. But Jerry's wife, Eileen, was there; and Kitty, Maurice, their mother, Hugh, Mrs Hugh, Ursula, Dr Peggy… Again and again she named them to herself as her glance swept over them.

And now that Breena had seen where the family were, she noticed that a great many other people in the church were also aware of it, and were turning to stare at them. But surely they had invited those prying glances, by sitting all together like that? It was the last thing in the world she would have expected them to do. She felt the tension in the church – or was it merely her own tension? Suddenly she had a vision of the family as strangers, and she did not like what she saw. Father Hennessey was in the middle of the announcements, but she slipped to her knees again, buried her face in her hands and pressed her fingers against her ears. The word 'life' was in her mind, together with its strange complement and opposite, 'death'. She tried to think about both concepts, to meditate on them until she had thought herself free of any further involvement with that family posturing there in such a distasteful way.

She was able to keep herself from any further glances at the family until Mass was over. During the Last Gospel she poised herself so that she could slip quickly past her neighbour and out of the side door the moment Father Hennessey turned away from the altar. But he surprised her, and arrested her attention by turning round towards the congregation again at the end of the Mass, and coming out to the top of the steps, while the altar-boys remained kneeling behind. Father Hennessey began to talk to the people.

Breena sat up to listen. In his hesitating, gentle way, Father Hennessey was telling them that this first Mass today had been offered up 'for the repose of the soul of our dear neighbour who died suddenly last night'. Then in very simple language, with pauses between every phrase that maybe gave them time for their own memories, he began to speak in praise of the dead man. 'How many of ye listening to me now did he bring into the world? How many of ye thought of him as a man always there to help others, but never needing help himself?' She leant her shoulder against the pillar to her right and let her thoughts dwell on what she could remember of Uncle John's brother. In her mind pictures of him formed – hovered and grew stronger and faded again – against a hazy background of liking and regret.

The pauses between Father Hennessey's words were getting longer. He was obviously coming to the end of what he had to say to them. 'Look up now… , let ye all look up at the sunlight that's streaming in through the windows above yer heads. It's going to be a beautiful day… Mass is over… In a few minutes' time we'll all be going home to our breakfasts. But before we go, let us all kneel down together here and say a De Profundis in the name of our dear neighbour. And while we say it let us think – let us think deeply – of the gift of life which we are all here enjoying at this moment. Let us think too of the way we are all of us, both living and dead, bound together in the Communion of Saints.'

He knelt down there on the top step and led off the De Profundis. He led it off in Latin, and for a moment he was on his own. Then the prayer swelled as the congregation came in to join him. The prayer ended. Father Hennessey stood up and gave the blessing. Now the unusual stillness all around arrested her attention. She glanced to the right and saw that there was movement only in one part of the church – that was along the pew where Kitty and Maurice and their family were sitting. Evidently by tacit consent, and sincere affection for the dead man, the congregation was sitting back to allow the dead man's family to pass first out of the church.

Breena sat back and like everybody else watched the procession – the progress, rather – of the bereaved family into the aisle. Then with a queer little pang she found herself looking at Maurice, who was behind Mrs Hugh. She had time only to see that his face was very white, that he was hanging his head, before an instinctive dislike of the way she was staring, gaping, spying on them, took her over, and she shrank behind the pillar and stopped looking.

Soon the family had reached the porch. People were swarming into the aisles on every side to follow them out. Breena thought it best not to move just yet, but to wait until the crush died down. She settled herself well back in her seat and challenged herself to put Kitty and Maurice and their family completely out of her thoughts. She decided to spend the time going back over what she called her 'resolutions'; the attempts she made each morning to order her conduct.

The aisles were clear by now, but her latest resolutions – she had promised herself firstly not to read a book for her own pleasure for two whole days and secondly to be careful not to drift off into reverie when others were talking, but to listen attentively – had made her thoughtful, and she remained in her place a little while longer. When she finally got to her feet her thoughts had reached that state of perfect balance when she no longer wanted anything, not even that the day should continue fine. And she reflected that to want nothing, to be empty of all the agitation of desire and hope, was more than happiness. It was freedom.

CHAPTER 6

Three doors opened out of the church, but the pathways from all three converged on the gravel sweep in front of the main gates. Breena crossed from her side-aisle into the nave, so that she came out of the part of the sweep nearest the gate. Scarcely had she taken one step across the gravel, however, when what she saw before her made her stop short and then instinctively step back again into the shadow of the doorway.

The bereaved family had managed to get no further than the middle of the sweep. There, evidently, their path had been blocked by people who pressed in on them from every side to offer sympathy for their loss. After a moment's hesitation, she only drew further back into the shadow of the doorway and watched them. The balmy day and the strong sunlight seemed to have put a restraint on everybody. The voices she could hear were little more than soft murmurs. What had to be said at such a time was laid down, a simple phrase that long custom had turned: 'I'm sorry for your trouble.' That, and the handclasp that went with it, took only a moment. People were continually giving place to one another. Dappled by the shadows from the trees above, they all moved so softly it seemed to Breena that only the leaves above moved, and the people were still. The sound of voices was lost in the gentle rustlings from the trees. She watched from the shadow of the doorway and for a moment was fascinated by what she saw. It was like a beautiful and restrained dance the people performed in honour of the dead man.

She decided then that it would be wrong, for herself at any rate, to go up to the family here. And with that she stepped out again on the gravel and with lowered glance made to go quickly past them towards the gate. As she drew level with the family, however, a number of people stepped aside and she was forced to look up in order to be able to keep out of their way. She found herself looking straight at Kitty, and she was shocked by what she saw. Kitty's veil had slipped a little sideways so that her face was clearly visible. Now Breena saw that it was marked with red weals under the eyes as if somebody had struck her there and that she was crying helplessly, without reserve or control; and at once she knew that Kitty could never have been responsible for that showy grouping in the church. Impulsively she went up to Kitty and caught her by the hand.

'Kitty, darling, come away. You're in no fit state to be here. I'll take you home.'

Kitty's hand clutched blindly back at hers. 'Yes, yes. I want to go home.'

But as Breena guided her past the crowd she realised that there could be no question of walking home with Kitty. People would be coming up to them all along the street; Kitty's plight would be worse than ever. What they needed was a car. She looked around for somebody whom she could ask for help. Almost immediately she caught sight of Thady, who was standing with some men under the trees by the gate.

'Wait here a moment,' she whispered to Kitty, and began to run across the grass towards Thady. He stepped forward from amongst the other men to meet her.

'Thady, have you your car anywhere handy? Can you drive Kitty home?'

'The car's across by the house, as usual. But 't won't take more than a few minutes to get it over here, will that do?'

'Oh, yes, Thady! We'll wait at the back of where Kitty is standing now, out of the way. If you just draw up by the gate.'

But Thady had already moved off. She ran back to Kitty, stepping unceremoniously between three old women, who in that short space of time had gathered round her.

'Kitty, come on over here!'

She drew Kitty to the back of the gravel sweep, well out of the way, and explained in a whisper about Thady and the car. In a surprisingly short time she heard footsteps behind her, she heard Maurice's voice:

'Thady's car is waiting outside, just beyond the gate.'

She wheeled round gratefully. What was implied in this little bit of information: that Maurice had seen her take Kitty away from the family group; that he had observed everything that had passed since, made her say in a very warm tone: 'Thank you, Maurice. We'll go out at once.' But as soon as she saw the curious, wide, almost impersonal way he was looking at her, she felt more than a little put out, and dropped her glance. He looked so thin and white-faced in his dark suit and black tie, she felt a kind of chill. Into her mind came that queer vision of herself sitting in the dark at the top of the stairs last night. Until now she had been able to fight it off in one way or another all morning. But here with Maurice standing before her, watching her with his wide, strained look, she felt again a stab of fear for herself because she had it in her to behave in such a preposterous way, and also a feeling of concern for Maurice. So obviously he believed that she had let him down last night! It proved beyond her power, however, to deal with the situation just now. She could think of nothing whatever to say that might melt that frozen look from his face. So after a moment's hesitation she turned uneasily away and moved off with Kitty.

When they reached the gate they found Thady standing by his car, looking eagerly around for them. He helped Kitty in and went quickly round to the driver's seat. Then Breena saw that he had opened the door behind for herself; taking it for granted that she would want to sit in at the back and go home with Kitty. But as soon as she caught sight of the jumble of fishing gear that was strewn across the back seat: frames of age-darkened lines, dirty boxes and hooks and weights, fishscale-spattered canvas bags and wooden boxes, she drew back with a helpless gesture of distaste. She was wearing her best linen suit, her new hat and white gloves.

'Are you in?' came Thady's voice. Then when she made no answer he twisted round in his seat to see what she was up to. She saw his glance take it all in; the way she was staring at the littered seat, and even, it seemed to her, the thoughts she was thinking at this very moment about his littered old car. She felt that any slight made against the car now after she had directly requested the use of it would be doubly resented. She stammered:

'I… I was just thinking I had better run across home, and change these clothes. They… they're not comfortable. I… '

'All right, then,' Thady's mild voice interrupted her, 'if you're not getting in, would you mind closing the door?'

She did so mechanically, then just in time remembered and opened it again so that she could say urgently to Kitty:

'I'll be along as soon as ever I can. But you can see… I must go and change these… '

Thady gave her no time to finish. As she felt the car move off from under her hand, just giving her time to bang the door shut, she understood that she had made too much of this business of wanting to change her clothes. She stood a moment staring rather wistfully after the car. She very much feared that she had hurt Thady's feelings.

All the same… if she had gone off in the car with Kitty, there could be no guarantee that she would get a chance to speak to Maurice again today, though she was going to his house. His look when he came up to tell them about Thady's car was not one that promised he would seek her out again. At the same time, he *had* approached her there. So now it was up to her. Suddenly she decided to take her courage in both hands and turn round and find him and speak to him again. She turned; saw him at once standing not very far behind, and very deliberately walked up to him.

'Maurice…'

One glance at his face, one further quick impression of his strained, white look, and her wits deserted her again; she could think of nothing appropriate to say. She dropped her glance. This was the first time she had ever been at a loss with Maurice, and she felt it keenly. She found herself looking above his collar at the prominent vein in his neck.

Then she seized on the necessity to say something about his father. She was beginning, 'I'm sorry…' when he broke in impulsively in a low voice:

'I know, I know. There's no need to say anything more about that.'

She stared at his neck and waited for him to go on, to say something more. But he seemed to be waiting too. After a painful silence, during which she racked her brains in vain for some helpful remark, he asked her in an abrupt and uncertain way, still speaking very low:

'Breena, what happened last night? Where were you when I came to the house?'

A very strong temptation to lie, to say something ordinary and sensible, came to her then. But she was afraid to lie, simply afraid to. She firmly believed that once you resorted to lying you were finished. So she mumbled in a low voice:

'When you knocked, I was in the house…'

'You mean you heard me?'

'Yes.'

'And you didn't open the door?'

That, she pretended to believe, could hardly be a question. But when she made no answer he went a stage further:

'Why didn't you open it?'

Sparse – that was the way his voice sounded… She answered as firmly as she could:

'I think that I… I must have been afraid to answer it.'

'Afraid of me? Breena, girl, that's funny.'

Every question he asked seemed to beat her down into a lower stage of humility. She wasn't even looking at the vein in his neck now. Quite suddenly, she had had more than enough of that, and she lifted her head with an impatient gesture and looked him straight in the eye. At once then she realised that she had misjudged his tone and his whole attitude. His face was no longer so white and strained, he had flushed a little. Evidently he too found it a relief to be having this matter out with her. At the same time he was giving her a look that she had never quite had from him before. It was only lately that they had both surfaced out of the awkwardness and involuntary slightings of adolescence. But she recognised his look at once and accepted it for her own. Beyond gratitude and guilt, her very own.

After she had met his look for only a few seconds she spoke his name impulsively, 'Maurice!' and made a sign to him to step a little further out into the square, so that they would be out of hearing of the people who passed behind on the pavement. Then with an intense feeling of relief, speaking very quickly, she began to tell him about the evening before. The only thing she left out was the way she had come on Uncle John in the sitting room and that cry out of her own childhood that she could not yet face, but must put by for some future time.

Never once while she was speaking did his glance wander from her face. She had the encouragement of knowing that at least he found what she was saying interesting, and maybe even accepted it as an explanation. When she had finished – and it took an astonishingly short time, the words tumbled out so quickly – he smiled at her, and then she realised that she too was smiling, with a feeling of relief that was like pure, warm, childlike happiness.

'Well, what a queer tale!' Maurice commented when she paused at last, breathless. 'And just like you! Well! After all that, I'm not surprised that you didn't feel up to opening the door to me.'

'Maurice… you don't think it was all so very odd, then?'

'Odd? No odder than going off to the lake on your own, at that time of evening. Why didn't you call in, and ask myself or Kit to go with you? You promised to call in, you know.'

'Yes, I know. And I meant to, at first. You must understand that. But somehow it became a sort of challenge, to go up to the lake on my own, in that light.'

'Challenge! We've spoken before about those challenges of yours.'

He said all this in a teasing, half-smiling way that made her feel very thankful to him. She heard him go on:

'Breena, my advice now, for what it's worth, is not to waste another thought on it all. Say to yourself it was a kind of dream, that was all. You were very tired.'

'Maurice, I'm sorry! How selfish of me to get us talking like this today, when… '

'Not selfish,' he broke in hastily. 'From my point of view, a very welcome change of subject. Anyway it was I started you talking. By the way, why didn't you go home with poor old Kit in Thady's car? I felt sure you would. Then we could have talked over there later on.'

Breena didn't quite feel up to telling him that it was very much the uncertainty of getting a chance to speak to him 'over there' that had kept her from stepping into Thady's car. Instead she began to explain to him about the state of the car. He smiled at her description of the littered back seat. When she had finished he made the unexpected comment:

'So Thady still intends to go out to Maurcappagh today, in spite of the wake. I thought he would. I've never known him to miss a fine Sunday at Maurcappagh yet. And the mackerel are still playing out there today; I heard somebody talking about it just now as I passed.'

'Of course! So that's why he had all the fishing gear strewn about. But I didn't think that today... '

At that moment, without any warning whatever, a low, curt voice whipped in over their shoulders, startling them out of their private world, making them both swerve round, sharply, foolishly. Hugh, Maurice's eldest brother, was standing behind them.

'Maurice! Breena! Everybody's staring at you. You ought to be ashamed, standing here talking and laughing like this today. I've been trying to attract your attention for the past five minutes.'

'Oh, Hugh, we weren't laughing,' Breena was horrified at the idea. 'I was just explaining to Maurice... '

But Hugh cut her off by saying sharply: 'Come along, Maurice. The car is waiting for you.'

Evidently he did not think it worth his while to reply to Breena, or take any notice whatever of what she had said. With a final curt, authoritative, 'Come along at once,' to Maurice, and not even a glance in Breena's direction, he turned on his heel and strode off. They both looked after him, in Breena's case rather anxiously and helplessly.

She glanced quickly up at Maurice's face, and saw that he had flushed deeply. She looked hastily away again. She could see Hugh's car, with most of the women of the family amongst the group standing round it.

She saw Hugh reach his car. He turned and called across in a strong, though now quite patient and even friendly tone:

'Maurice! Are you coming then?'

'That tone of voice is for the benefit of everybody standing around,' Maurice said under his breath to Breena. 'I'd better go. Otherwise he'll begin to blame you as well.'

'He's already doing that, judging by the way he ignored me just now. I'd say he must have noticed how I took Kitty off.'

'Then he should be grateful to you.'

They had begun to walk towards Hugh and the car. At the corner Breena stopped. She glanced up once more at Maurice's face and judged it best to leave him then.

'You'll be round the house very shortly?' he asked, seeing that she intended to go no further.

'Yes.'

With that she left him, and turned to make her way home. It was necessary to take some care in crossing the square as just now cars were pulling out and turning round every minute. Also today she had to keep her glances under strict control. She knew that there were a good many people about who were doing their best to attract her attention. A greeting – or in some cases even a look – would be enough to bring the thicker-skinned gossips to her side, asking all sorts of questions about last night, about Uncle John, the two families…

Already in her life she had experienced this sort of curiosity to the extent that she had come to think of it as something innocent and ruthless; a force of nature, like the gales or the storms of the sea. The only way to beat it was to keep out of its path. She knew that by means of it was spun, in nearly every house in the town, a kind of magic that formed an invisible connection between every individual person in it. She also knew that in most people's opinion there was no point in living in a small town unless you could practise this enjoyable sort of magic over the lives of other people.

Now as she left the square behind and turned right into Main Street she slowed down a little so as not to flurry the dogs with a quick approach to the side-gate. Once they had recognised her step they would refrain from barking, she knew. What she wanted was to slip quietly into her room and get rid of her clothes; then to get out again immediately and go across to the other house.

CHAPTER 7

Breena had reached the high wooden side-gate. As she opened it warily and stepped inside she saw that the outer door of the kitchen stood open, as it usually did on sunny mornings. The next thing she saw was Hannah, who was moving into full view to do something at the sink under the window. At the same time she caught a whiff of the bacon that was frying for breakfast. Alas! Breakfast after all, food in spite of everything! What a thing it was to be middle-aged… She closed the gate noiselessly and then stood hesitating for a few seconds, waiting for Hannah to look up and catch sight of her. The moments passed, however, and Hannah failed to look up. Breena then made a bet with fate and began to tiptoe across the open doorway towards her own small door in the angle of the house.

Her luck held. She got across to her own door and opened it softly and stepped across the hall. The first thing she did when she got into her room was to kick off her high heels. Then she went to the wardrobe and after some hesitation chose a dark blue cotton dress to change into. It was an old dress, but the only dark coloured one she had.

She was nearly ready. She finished tying her sandals and hurried out into the hall and across the corridor. Today this looked full of shadows, rather forbidding. The only light filtered through at second hand, from the high windows of the main hall.

She went quickly down the corridor. In a minute or two she could make out in the gloom the big padlocks on the barred doors of the two sections of the shop. There was also in her mind an image of them as she had seen them the night before, when she hurriedly left the stock-room to find out where Uncle John and Thady had gone. She came up to the stock-room door and saw at once that the usual bar and padlocks across this door were missing. She tried the handle. The door yielded before her at once. She switched on the light and saw that, yes! The tray was still there on the big table. The cups and saucers still stood where Ursula and Hannah had been sitting last night before they ran out in such a flurry. She darted forward to the table and pushed aside the plates on the tray. Yes, that too was still there. Uncle John's pipe!

She picked it up and hurried to the door. But just as she was reaching out to switch off the light her glance fell on the bar that usually secured this door. It lay down by the skirting board, near her right foot. She stared at it. Yes, here lay the bar, but where was the padlock? How very odd that she had no idea where the padlocks of this door were kept when not in use! She stood there in a kind of trance, picturing to herself what Uncle John would most likely have done yesterday if he had found this stock-room door unbarred and unlocked. Then all at once she closed the door with an impatient gesture and went quickly back along the corridor to the main hall, where she sat down on the bottom step of the stairs. Yes! Without a doubt she had some idea of how Uncle John would have behaved yesterday. But today… ?

She stared down into the stained, charred bowl of the pipe. Six – no, seven months old this ancient-looking pipe was. She had been with Uncle John when he bought it at Moran's in January, that time when they all wanted him to give up smoking altogether. But he had said no. For the sake of peace, he told them, he was willing to give up cigarettes; but he was an old man and an old man deserved at least a pipe. And yet today he was over there without it. All because she, she! in a fit of conceited juvenility had taken it on herself to… Well, certainly it was her duty now to see that he got back his pipe as soon as possible. But she had an equal duty to ensure that he got it back from somebody who – unlike herself in the sitting-room last night – would not intrude on his… his right of loneliness.

It seemed to her as she sat there that she caught some sounds from the landing above; faint rustlings of cloth, tinklings of glass. Could it possibly be Ursula? But why this sudden hope that the responsibility of Uncle John's pipe would now be lifted from her shoulders by the almost miraculous appearance of Ursula on the landing above? Yet… She did hope. She stood up and listened intently. It was either a mouse stirring up there, or Ursula doing something at the altar in the corner, where she always kept fresh flowers and a red Sacred Heart burning before the holy pictures.

Swiftly Breena began to ascend the stairs, clutching the pipe to her. At the turn of the stairs she paused to look up at the round yellow foolish face of the old clock. Then her heart gave some kind of nervous lurch as she became aware of another face staring down at her over the railings from above. She swerved round sharply. It was, of course, Ursula's face. And what other face could she have been expecting? Where could her thoughts have wandered to?

Yet it was somehow very pleasant to hear Ursula saying in the most matter-of-fact way possible: 'Oh it's you, Breena! I could hear you wandering about below. I was wondering what you were doing. Come on up here, will you? What do you think of this?'

Breena took the rest of the stairs two at a time. 'Aunt Ursula!' she called out in an urgent, impulsive tone that pulled Ursula up short as she was leading the way back to the altar. With something of a conjurer's aplomb, then Breena produced Uncle John's pipe from behind her back and held it out in full view. At the same time in a rush of speech she was explaining, half explaining, how she had found the pipe on the tray in the stock-room. Even while she was still speaking Ursula took the pipe out of her hand; took it with a greedy, pouncing gesture that expressed far more clearly than any words how delighted she was at this chance to do her brother-in-law a service.

'You can set your mind at rest at once about this pipe,' she said fervently as soon as Breena stopped. 'I'll be going across to the other house the moment I've finished here, and I'll see that your Uncle John has it as soon as possible after I get in.'

Her tone, her actions – she was now polishing the pipe with a piece of rag she held in her hand – gave Breena a moment's very clear insight into the meagreness of her pleasures. She could not doubt but that within the next hour or so the pipe would be discreetly conveyed into Uncle John's presence, wrapped up in brown paper probably, and with its flavour enhanced by a dab of furniture polish round the charred top of the bowl.

Now Ursula had gone on to explain: 'Oh, goodness! So we went out last night and left the stock-room door unlocked. But of course we did, and no wonder too... All the same, isn't it surprising that Thady didn't come straight back from Mass to check on things, like he does every Sunday?'

Breena thought it best to keep quiet about the part she herself had played in Thady's non-appearance; she wanted no further complications. Ursula was upset about the stock-room she could see; but certainly not as much as she would have been yesterday. In fact, the stock-room had already been dismissed with a comfortable, 'The moment I'm finished here I'll go down and see to it, on my way over to the other house... But tell me, what d'you think of this?'

They were now standing in front of the altar.

'D'you like this new cloth?' Ursula wanted to know. 'Come a bit closer. Take a good look at it. Feel it.'

Breena did so, and saw in detail the changes that had been made at the altar; the white lace cloth that usually covered it had been replaced by a special purple mourning cloth, and a fresh picture had been hung behind the Sacred Heart lamp. Ursula was explaining:

'... in honour of poor Jeremy. He's the patron saint of medicine... Saint Fiacre... It will remind us all to say an aspiration for Jeremy every time we pass by...'

Breena looked and listened and looked again, and tried hard to make the right comments. The second resolution she had made after Mass was very much in her thoughts – not to go off in a dream during the course of conversation with certain people. Ursula was of course the principal person concerned in this resolution. And now, after she had listened for a while with all her might, a sense of the mystery of Ursula's nature took her over and kept her rooted to the spot.

Ursula was now talking about the picture, which was obviously an old one, one of her treasures. Breena, however, had never seen it before – it depicted a thinly drawn, pale face, coloured in worn shades of brown, very like the colours of Uncle John's pipe. The face looked faded and sad, but the hands, which were crossed low down over the breast, in the bottom part of the picture, startled Breena as soon as her glance fell on them. They looked so incongruously flexible and alive against the shadowy outline of the rest of the body that she got a little excited and drew Ursula's attention to them, not altogether in a polite way.

'Look! How very odd! These hands seem to have been painted in afterwards, by somebody else. They look like real hands. I can't understand how hands like that could have got into such a picture.'

Ursula was polishing the brass bowl of the Sacred Heart lamp.

'You like them, do you?' she asked, smiling

'Oh, yes! They look sensitive and capable, a real surgeon's hands.' Ursula had come up beside her to look at the hands.

'So they do!' she agreed. 'I put them there, you know.' And she shot Breena a vivid blue look of gratification.

'You mean you painted them?' The words came out too quickly for Breena to be able to control her unflattering surprise. She hurried on, in an effort to cover it up, 'If you can paint like that, it's a shame that you've given it up. I mean, I never see you painting nowadays.'

'Now, Breena, I know you don't really believe that I ever could paint like that. No, I cut them out of a print of a famous painting of hands. Peggy and myself and Mamie (Kitty and Maurice's mother) made that picture long ago from cut-outs that we pasted together. What d'you call that kind of work? It's not done much nowadays, I know. It's considered a waste of time, I suppose.'

'Cut-outs?' Breena peered more closely at the picture. 'Yes, I can see. A patchwork saint! So that's not a saint's face at all. It's nobody's face. No wonder…'

'Oh, it's a saint's face all right. The right saint's face, too. Peggy found it in some volumes of the *Lives of the Saints* we had at the time, and cut it out most carefully. I remember…'

Breena was now staring so hard at the picture that she was able to make out all its component patches. She sighed with exasperation. What an irritating picture it was, with that dim face above those exquisite, alive-looking hands. She wanted to take it down, to throw it away. She knew that every time she passed by the altar during the next week or so, she would be drawn to peer at it and ponder grimly over it, rather than offer up a prayer for the dead man's soul.

Ursula had now collected the last of the altar things. As she placed them carefully in their box she shifted her position so that she was standing in the sunlight that beamed in through the south-facing window. For a few seconds then, a few seconds only, she lingered in the sunshine; against her will it seemed. There could be no mistaking the pleasure she found in standing there in the sun during that tiny fraction of time; and yet she was in it completely by accident. Her eyes wistfully sought out of their own accord the square of blue sky that could be seen through the window. Breena noticed that her eyes were like pieces of the sky, they were so blue; she, Breena, experienced again, as she had done many times before, a kind of fear or foreboding at the thought of the kind of life Ursula lived.

Then Ursula came forward with the box and placed it squarely into her hands: 'Breena, will you take this into my room, like a good girl? You can put it down on the table. One moment, I'll just take out this cloth to wrap round your Uncle John's pipe…'

Breena hurried off at once with the box into the narrow passage where Ursula's room was, exactly above her own, on the first floor. When she came back again to the landing Ursula was of course already out of sight.

CHAPTER 8

Breena hurried down the main stairs, intending only to go to her room and collect a warm sweater; the chill of the evening would have settled well in before she returned. She wanted to get quickly out of the house while the going was good. But when she reached her room she was drawn by the brilliant sunshine to go and stand for a moment in the bow-window. Thinking of Ursula, she stood there very still. Gradually a feeling of ease and restfulness came over her. What a jewelled, permanent quality there was in the blue of the sky! No need to fear today that the sunshine would fade with the morning. And from now on the day was all her own!

Suddenly, out of the corner of her eye as she stood there, she caught a glimpse of something black that fluttered for a moment within her line of vision and then disappeared behind the great tangle of climbing roses that could just be seen to the left of where she stood. Her instant conclusion was: a cat! Her hands moved automatically to raise the lower sash of the window. It had been well oiled for this purpose, and moved easily and soundlessly. Then she turned to look back into the room. Her glance roved with desperate haste from one object to another, seeking the blackthorn stick she kept in her room for occasions of this kind. She caught sight of it at last, down by the wall behind her violin case, and darted from the window to catch it up before she climbed out into the garden.

As she caught up the blackthorn and rushed back to the window she wondered yet again why such mean-souled, lazy creatures as cats had ever been invented. Just how dare they leap down into her garden and before her very eyes stalk down her songbirds? The birds who were always teaching her to be up and out, never to let the walls of the house close in on her…

She pulled a chair close to the window, so that she could easily step out. Then she peered cautiously round to the left, to find out where the cat was now. But what she actually saw out there made her draw back with furious haste, lift the chair and take both it and the blackthorn as far as she could go into the corner on the right. There she sat down, as noiselessly as possible, turning her knees in towards the wall. No time was left to make for the door.

What she had just caught sight of was an altogether unexpected and unprecedented thing: Dr Peggy, Dr Peggy herself; head down, black dress fluttering, arms purposely swinging as she made for Breena's window. The heavy warning sound of her footsteps must have been muffled by the turf and by Breena's own feelings of outrage against the cats.

In her corner Breena squeezed herself as close to the wall as she could. After her few moments of impetuous action the beating of her own heart sounded so loud in her ears that it distorted all other sounds. She could not tell if Dr Peggy had yet reached her window. All the time she was thinking wretchedly to herself; 'Oh what a fool I am, what a fool I am! Why didn't I get straight out of the house when I came downstairs?' But even then she could have remained standing at the window, and greeted Dr Peggy when she came up in a natural and polite fashion. As if that piece of idiocy last night were not enough to have to forgive herself for!

And now quite clearly she heard her own name 'Breena! Breena!' being softly called at the open window. Still her heart was beating so quickly, and everything inside her was so confused and miserable, she only flattened herself further back against the wall and gave up the situation.

Then her pulse quietened, she listened hard for every sound from outside. But she could no longer hear anything that suggested Dr Peggy still stood nearby at the window. Certainly the 'Breena! Breena!' that had lacerated her a minute or so before could no longer be heard. A wave of common sense washed over her then, and she jumped up and hurried to the window. There was nobody there.

It was obvious that only something very important could have brought Dr Peggy over here especially to see herself today, when she might simply have phoned through and spoken to her from the other house. The more she thought about it, the more uncomfortable she became. At last she decided that the only thing left to do was to seek out Dr Peggy at once and ask her quite simply, with an implied admission of her own guilt in hiding away, what she had come for. With that she drew the chair up to the window once more, climbed hurriedly out into the garden and ran across the grass to the back door of Dr Peggy's rooms. She found this door locked. Her knocking, her soft calls of 'Dr Peggy!' brought no response. She peered through the window and could see only the closed doors of the passage. She had no choice but to go to the front door of Dr Peggy's quarters.

This door also was locked; here too her knocking went unanswered. She turned away and started up the corridor. She went on into the kitchen where only the smell of her breakfast greeted her. It was being kept hot for her in the oven. She hesitated, hardly knowing which way to turn. Then she heard the yapping of the dogs. She ran out into the yard and was just in time to see the high wooden gate swing inwards. The sun was in her eyes; she gave herself no time to think but hurried forward crying:

'Oh, Dr Peggy, I've been looking everywhere for you. I…'

'Looking everywhere, have you?' The voice that cut her off was Thady's voice. She pulled up short, shaded her eyes against the sun and saw Thady standing just inside the gate; his arms outspread to ward off her headlong advance. She exclaimed somewhat irritably:

'Yes, can you put down your guard, Thady? I'm not going to run you down. Have you by any chance seen Dr Peggy?'

'Yes, I've seen Dr Peggy. Not only seen her, but passed the time o' day with her. She was just pulling in at the other house as I drove off.'

'Pulling in… ? Did she… did she give you any message for me?'

'No; no. Not the smallest whisper of the beginnings of a message did she give me.'

'I see… ' She turned away to go back into the kitchen, then impulsively swung again towards him. 'Thady, why have *you* come back here? I thought that today you'd stay for hours over at the other house – with Uncle John, I mean.'

'For hours!' There was a sardonic edge to both his tone and his glance. 'Well may you ask, young lady, what brought me back! I came back to fetch the pipe you took away from your Uncle John last night. 'Twas more than I could bear, to sit by over there and watch the way he was suffering without it.'

'Well, as a matter of fact… ' In a hurried, rather shame-faced manner she explained that she had already taken the pipe to Ursula.

'Well, well! If Ursula has the pipe, there's no help for it… Ah, what a God-given day! I'll just sit down here at my ease a moment and enjoy the sun. Then I can give Ursula a lift across to the other house when she's ready.'

Breena sighed to herself, very much at a loss. She watched Thady as he leaned back against the stone sill of the kitchen window and raised his face to the sun. If she were to tell him now how she had so stupidly hidden in the corner from Dr Peggy, would he understand it? Would he be able to advise her; to help her in some sensible yet subtle way?

She looked across at him with a kind of aching intentness. She saw how his eyes, the true hazel eyes of the Cappaghs, glinted pure yellow now in the sunlight. She noticed how much brown there was still in his cropped hair. She saw that his face, for all the time he spent indoors in the shop, had the healthy red-brown colour of a farmer's.

'Thady...'

'Yes... What is it? What do you want?' His voice sounded lazy with the sun.

'I... I wondered if you...'

She broke off and sighed hard. What was the use? How could she expect Thady, or anybody else, to listen seriously to her story about Dr Peggy? Such a tale could only be told as a joke. And yet for her, Breena, it was certainly no laughing matter...

But she had not quite given Thady up yet; she watched him still. In fact she had begun to stare openly at him without realising it. She seemed to see him more clearly than she had ever seen him before; to see him and to feel a kind of wondering compassion for him... She could remember very well that when she first came to live here at Uncle John's he had seemed to her a man on his very last legs – approaching eighty at the very least. But the older she grew herself, the younger he had come to look in her eyes. Now she was no longer quite sure what age he was. She studied him carefully as he leaned against the sill. Certainly he was very lean, active-looking. He might live twenty, twenty-five years. Yet what had he, Thady, to live for?

When had he reached that terrible state he was in now, that Ursula-like state with a sound like passing-bells in it, ringing out so very slowly; re-sig-nat-ion? Like Ursula, he had never married; but unlike her he had at least had the courage to go far away from the town in his youth and try what life was like in other places. Yet he had come back – to be what he was now. Of the life he led now in this house, so completely overshadowed, obscured by Uncle John, she only asked – how was it possible? But maybe, she thought now, it was his love of the sea that had drawn him back home. Maybe if

| 75

you had been born near the sea you could never forget it, you always hungered afterwards for the sound of the waves.

The dogs barked, a group of people passed the gate. Thady remarked: 'They're beginning to come in for second Mass.'

He shifted his position as he spoke; he had become aware of her intent gaze. But for the moment she failed to realise this. In vague unease, half-drugged from the sun, it came to her that in some strange way she liked and respected Thady – but why? Why should she like Thady when often her only impulse was to start running at the sound of Ursula's voice? Ursula, to whom she owed so very much!

All at once Thady stopped looking at the sky and turned a very steady glance on her face. He demanded:

'How much longer is this going to last?'

'What… what going to last, Thady?'

'This staring. Is there something you want to ask me? If so, go ahead.'

'I wanted… I wanted to ask, no tell you… I…'

It was useless. She sighed hard as she broke off once more. He said:

'For the past few minutes you've been staring at me hard enough to burn holes in me. And now you stand there sighing like a bean sídhe. 'Tis a good thing I'm not a vain man. I was beginning to hope…'

He paused to examine her face. She came in eagerly, 'To hope what, Thady?'

'To hope that you might want to come out to Maurcappagh with me.'

Maurcappagh! In worrying about Dr Peggy she had completely forgotten about Maurcappagh. So Maurice had been right when he said that Thady intended to go out to Maurcappagh today, in spite of the wake…

Thady had folded his arms and was saying very quietly as he

looked at the ground: 'You'll not remember this – 'twas before your time. But while you were eyeing me so hard just now I was thinking that all the family: Desmond, Hugh, Father Patrick, Jerry, all in their turn used to be wild to come out to Maurcappagh with me. Then one by one I've seen them all go away. Hugh, 'tis true came back, but he's not the man he was before he went away. Desmond and Jerry too, they're always back and forth; but they've changed as well. And now the time is coming when yourself and Maurice and Kitty'll be off like the rest of 'em. Then 'twill seem like a dream to me that there ever were so many eager youngsters who used to be so wild to come out to Maurcappagh with me.'

'Thady, you know that *I* will never change. I'll always love Maurcappagh, I'll always love the sea. Even if I do have to go away for a while I'm sure of one thing; nothing will ever have the power to change me.'

'Aw, but sure that's what they all say! But like the others you'll go away. And like the others… '

He broke off and made a visible effort to be more cheerful. 'But we haven't settled about today yet. I take it you do want to come out to Maurcappagh with me, then?'

'You know I do. More than anything. But it will make no difference, will it? You're set on going, whether I go with you or not?'

She could not afford to go, she told herself. She must not let herself be tempted. She must go after Dr Peggy and find out what she had wanted. In her life so far Dr Peggy was almost an unknown quantity; she could not tell what the consequence of not seeking her out now and explaining things might be… Besides, how selfish Kitty and Maurice would think her if she were simply to go off to Maurcappagh now!

Thady was saying: 'I'd like you to come with me, that's the truth. I don't such relish the notion of going out on the sea on my own. 'Twould be a downright senseless thing to do. You know what they say; only a fool takes on the sea single-handed.'

'But won't Sean Mor be there? And Young Jamie; isn't he still home?'

'Maybe. But have you no eyes for what kind of day 'tis, girl? They'll all be out saving the hay today after the week of rain we've had – Sunday an' all though it is.'

'I didn't think of that,' she admitted. 'So it isn't simply just a question of whether I want to go; you'll really *need* me… But Thady, what about the wake?'

'The wake? Faith, I'm easy in my mind about the wake. I spent all last night over there. And I'll be going back there again with Ursula, to sit with your Uncle John for a bit. And again tonight – to sit up all night if necessary. I deserve a few hours off, I think.'

'Oh, yes, *you* do without a doubt – so you're not leaving for Maurcappagh straight away, then… What time d'you plan to leave?'

'Not until around two, I'm afraid. That's a bit late for Maurcappagh, but it can't be helped today.'

'Well, if you're not leaving until two I'll certainly be able to go with you. There are some things I must do, but I can make it my business to be back here by two. Thady, when I asked you about the wake, I really meant… Uncle John. No doubt you've already told him that *you* intend to go out to Maurcappagh today, but… would you mind very much, Thady, when you get back to the wake again, just mentioning to Uncle John that… that you specially *asked* me to go out with you to Maurcappagh today?'

There was a little silence. It occurred to Breena then that Thady's desire to be out on the sea was as strong and in its way as irresponsible as her own. Perhaps right up to this moment he had not reflected how little in sympathy with him Uncle John could be today. Well, from now on the business of Maurcappagh was Thady's look-out. He must arrange matters with Uncle John as best he could. *She* would play it that Thady had asked her to go; that he had told her in no uncertain terms he needed her to man the boat.

The silence went on. She raised her face to the sun. Let Thady puzzle things out; let *him* rack his brains for a change. But all the time she was conscious of strong desires that played a painful tug-of-war inside herself. First of all, she passionately wanted to go to Maurcappagh. But at this same time she greatly desired to be able to rise to the unselfish heights of going across to the other house and spending the day with Kitty. Dear Kitty! Her friend of so many years' standing who today was so helplessly, so painfully sad, and who would make Breena herself equally sad as soon as she went to her. Then there was Maurice; she wanted very badly to skip going to see Kitty and to run off instead to hear what Maurice had to say to her; what he had come hurrying round last night to say. And finally, of course there was Dr Peggy. Rather, there was her own great need to blot out that sorry vision of herself hiding in the corner by finding Dr Peggy and coming to some understanding with her.

And all the time she felt the sun on her face, the sun very warm and soothing on her face and body. She realised how easy it would be to forget everything, to lose herself, to let herself drown in the happiness of this scented, sun-warmed day. Oh, how could anybody who had any freedom of choice think of doing anything today except being out in the sun!

Standing here she was very close to the nasturtiums that trailed round the fuchsia outside the kitchen door. She glanced down at their orange and flame-coloured faces. Their tangy scent was the very smell of summer to her, she had breathed it in on so many warm summer days. Their faces dazzled her, they were like small suns. They seemed to give off heat of their own. It was like double sunshine, standing here between the glow of their sun-like faces and the real sun above.

She was roused out of her sunny dream by the sound of Ursula's voice coming out of the stock-room. Hastily she straightened herself, shook off the drowsiness of the sun. She looked across at Thady, who was staring up with wide strong eyes at the sky.

'I'll see you back here at two o'clock then, Thady – give or take five minutes. Is that all right?'

'Yes…' The word came out very slowly. He added, as much to himself as to her, 'Your Uncle John might be against it. 'Twon't be an easy subject to broach to him today.'

Again as she watched him she felt a stab of pity for him. That she, at her age and in her circumstances, should be worried about what Uncle John thought was understandable. But Thady, at his age! A bright idea occurred to her. She said in an eager voice:

'Thady, you know Uncle John hasn't been out on his usual Sunday morning round to Filemoyn and Maurcappagh to count the cattle today. He won't be able to go later on either. So why don't you tell him that when we get to Maurcappagh we'll count the cattle first thing, most carefully? I'm sure he'll be very relieved to hear that *somebody's* going to count them.'

A small smile twisted Thady's mouth. But he kept his glance firmly on the sky. 'Yes, I could mention the cattle,' he agreed, as Breena turned away and slipped into the kitchen.

CHAPTER 9

What Breena had in mind now, while there was still time for it, was to summarily get rid of her breakfast, which was still stewing away in the oven. She jumped up and snatched some newspaper from the top of the press and opened the oven door. She was somewhat disconcerted to find several platefuls of breakfast sizzling in there with a faint sound like the chattering of teeth. After a moment's hesitation, and with the help of the newspaper – the plates were very hot – she lifted out the topmost one and carried it to the sink. She tipped the breakfast into the newspaper, folded this over and over, and put the plate neatly aside on the draining board.

Hannah came back into the kitchen. She began some good-natured remark then broke off to sniff the air suspiciously. Her questioning glance came to rest on the newspaper parcel, which Breena had just caught up under her arm. She moved in on Breena.

'What are you holding there under your oxter?'

Before Breena could reply she saw a brightness, a gleam of full understanding, leap like a living thing to the surface of Hannah's grey eyes. She felt no surprise. She had known since she was a child how quick Hannah was.

'Ah!' Hannah reached out for the parcel, and carefully unfolded it. There followed a little silence, while they looked one another full in the face. Then Hannah said in a queer tone, not a scolding one, but rather an awkward and uncertain attempt at playfulness:

'So you are going to take your breakfast in a newspaper parcel out to those lazy pals of dogs of yours. And you had great fun, didn't you earlier on, tip-toeing past me at the kitchen door?'

Breena judged it best to keep her mouth shut and simply look at the floor.

'May God forgive you! Wasting good food in that way! And don't expect any gratitude from those great lazy dogs. You've heard often enough, haven't you, of the dog that bit the hand that fed it? By the looks of those two pampered creatures out there I'd say you won't have long to wait until…'

But while Hannah let off steam in this way there was a very clear undertone of reproach in her voice. She seemed to sense that something more than a natural tendency towards clowning, or a mere selfish desire to be off and away among people of her own age, lay behind Breena's attempts to steal out of the house without her breakfast this morning. The truth was that Breena feared to be alone with Hannah. She feared certain experiences they had once shared together, which had not yet in her own mind become mere memories, but had to be lived through again each time they were recalled; had power it seemed to drag her bodily back out of the present into an immediacy of pain and regret. So that now she had to keep always on guard in her mind a tall sentry, who could sight the very shadows of these things in the distance as they moved in on her.

But now Hannah's bright look of intelligence assured her that these were things Hannah would never presume to speak of, no matter how closely circumstances brought them to mind. But it always went hard with Hannah to keep any grievance to herself; the next moment she stopped pretending to scold and broke into plain speech:

'Once and for all, girl – let me say it now and have done with it – you'll never find *me* trying to pull the scabs off old sores by my silly gabbling. I mean what I say and there's an end to it. You can believe me or not, just as it suits you.'

'Of course I believe you, Hannah. And I'm sorry for the way I carried on this morning. I should have come straight in here from Mass and… '

'Well, let's say no more about it now. Let's put it right out of our heads.'

Now, in sheer nervous frustration, Breena asked with an air of eager, indeed almost desperate, interest:

'Why are there so many breakfasts in the oven? Who are they for? Are you expecting the Dublin crowd so soon?'

'No. Can you credit it, I cooked breakfast for everybody in the ordinary way today! It didn't occur to me until it was too late that they'd all be off to the other house as soon as Mass was over. With all the hungry people there are in the world, God must be asking himself just now what he ever gave me a head for.'

'Perhaps the Dublin crowd *will* arrive in time to eat them all up,' Breena remarked in a hopeful tone.

'Well… ' came at last Hannah's cautious verdict, 'I s'pose they might eat them.'

Breena began to feel quite nervous now at the thought that this so-called Dublin crowd – relatives and friends from Dublin who were expected to arrive during the course of the morning to attend the wake – might turn up here at any moment. Among them could be numbered two quite important persons: Desmond, Uncle John and Dr Peggy's son, their only offspring; and Father Patrick, who came between Jerry and Hugh in that family. If Desmond and Father Patrick were to arrive now and find her here, they would naturally expect her to stay with them for some time; they would utterly ruin what was still left unwrecked of her morning. Very deftly therefore she helped Hannah to fork the breakfasts into the glass dish; picked up her newspaper parcel and made for the door. There her conscience pulled her up, she stopped to ask: 'What are you going to do now, Hannah? What d'you plan to do today?'

'Oh, there's one thing I'm never short of, and that's things to do!'

| 83

Hannah was a proud woman, who abhorred false sympathy. She also liked very much to have the last word. Breena therefore contented herself with smiling – not too widely – at this sally as she escaped into the sun.

And now, strong and sweet and urgent inside her, greater than any anxiety, curiosity or pity that up to this moment had plagued her, rose up her longing for, her hankering after the sea. She could no longer think of it as a mere selfish urge, so many things around her seemed to share it. Rather, it seemed an impulse from the sunny landscape. Even the nasturtiums glowing within their proud green leaves had an alert look about them, as if they too, and even the bushes of fuchsia amongst the bright grass, were moving with infinite, aching slowness towards the sea.

CHAPTER 10

Bran and Hippy gulped down the breakfast Breena brought them in something less than half a minute. Afterwards, as they stood under the top lapping up water, she looked them over in a somewhat impatient and fretful manner.

'Come along then,' she told them, and smiled in spite of herself at their joyful scamperings as they escorted her to the gate.

Outside, in Main Street and the square, the town seemed very quiet with all the people in at second Mass. Warmth was settling in between the houses. She looked about her as she walked with the utmost satisfaction. How wonderful to be able to feel at ease about the day.

On this July morning when she was nearly eighteen she could not help knowing that a great many people in the town were keenly interested in what would become of her. She knew that this was mainly due to Ursula's hunger for reassurance and confidences; that Ursula was forever consulting friends, neighbours and customers about 'what Breena's poor parents would have wished'. There was hardly a hope, dream or doubt, Breena suspected, ever expressed by herself about her own future that was not by this time well known to the whole town. This morning, when she noted a bright awareness of herself in the eyes of people she passed, or in glances that she caught through the open doorways of shops, she guessed that Ursula had been talking again. Lately one of the teachers at school had indiscreetly given her the label of 'brilliant' in Ursula's hearing, and Ursula had taken the word up with naïve satisfaction. It obviously gave her great pleasure to think that one of her household walked abroad distinguished in this way.

The results of Breena's final school examinations would soon be out. She knew that a good many of the gossips of the town were waiting to see what her 'brilliance' would result in. She believed that she had done very well, but found it easy enough, in this summer when she was nearly eighteen, to put off thinking about it all until she knew exactly what there was to think about. Ursula, however, did not help at all in this. It was strange that Ursula, who over the years had proved the very soul of kindness and good intentions, could yet be guilty of curious cruelty of the tongue. A mere hope expressed by Breena a whole year before could suddenly blossom out of Ursula's memory as certain expectation; a tiny wish could grow overnight into a mighty ambition. Breena had learned that great modesty of speech on her own part (indeed something like near-idiocy) was needed to counteract this.

Now she continued along Church Street until she reached the open road where, free at last of houses and pavements, she began to run. Bran and Hippy kept close behind her. They had sense enough to know that she was making for the open fields; they made no attempt to go off exploring on their own. Soon they came to the gate that opened onto the footpath to the lake, where they had walked last night. Here she could for a moment forget about the dogs. There were no sheep in this field; the dogs were therefore free to scamper where they wished.

A great hunger had come on her to retrace her steps; to walk again where she had panicked and stumbled in the dark last night, but now in the sunlight. With the sun on her face she began to climb the sloping track – slowly, practising her old trick of reining in her glance. There could be no question of looking freely about until she came to the corner of the orchard, where she had stood last night and seen below her that house from her childhood 'suddenly lit up from floor to top'. After some time – some fairly long moments it seemed to her – she became aware that the orchard fence cut off the view in front. She swerved to the right to get to the corner. Finally she halted and looked about her.

In that first moment she was struck by a mysterious sense of another presence that stood there beside her. It seemed to be holding its breath, yet she knew it was there. Behind the rustlings of leaves and grasses and the humming of insects and warblings of birds she sensed it standing there very still. She looked round, she stared at the house below. It was the same house that had caused her panic last night. But now she looked at it over the swaying green branches of apple trees, she saw it beyond a lush tangle of clover, meadowsweet, daisies, buttercups, speedwell, wild scabious. The windows that last night had blazed with light were now only spaces between the glistening green leaves of the Virginia creeper.

It was the same house, yet subtly altered. She drew a deep breath. A feeling of restful, yet intense and expectant happiness surged through her. She knew then it was summer, Nature's very self, that was standing there beside her. She stood very still to realise it, to impress herself with every sound, to savour deeply every scent and colour. She knew that this was the kind of worship that was summer's nature's due. Yet so generous was Nature, that all the benefits of it would finally accrue to Breena herself. Her lips moved, she repeated to herself:

> ... *Nature never did betray*
> *The heart that loved her; 'tis her privilege,*
> *Through all the years of this our life, to lead*
> *From joy to joy: for she can so inform*
> *The mind that is within us, so impress*
> *With quietness and beauty, and so feed*
> *With lofty thoughts, that neither evil tongues,*

Rash judgements, nor the sneers of selfish men,
Nor greetings where no kindness is, nor all
The dreary intercourse of daily life,
Shall e'er prevail against us, or disturb
Our cheerful faith, that all which we behold
Is full of blessings…

After that she remained standing there in exalted mood, looking happily about her. Before many minutes had passed, however, the dogs came back to her side. The day was so warm that they had no heart for running about. So far this had been a cool summer; few chances had been given them to get used to the sun.

She called on them softly, lazily, to follow her, and with some difficulty led them up the grassy fence and through the blackthorn hedge into the orchard. There in the lush tall grasses, under the lightly swaying branches of apple and pear trees, she walked very slowly. No need for now to persuade the dogs to lie down and take their ease. First Bran and then Hippy sat down uninvited in the shade of the old plum tree at the top of the orchard. There – more by way of a strong hint as to how they were to behave in her absence than as a serious attempt at coercion – she tied them up with the worn ends of an old rope that was stapled, only God knew for what original purpose, to the mossy trunk of this tree.

She went on, stooping under the wise branches of the plum tree to get out into the yard, when she suddenly caught sight of both Maurice and Hugh out there. Instinctively she drew back again to watch them a moment. She saw that each was surrounded by a small group of people, and that they were standing with only the width of the porch between them. From what she knew of them both, she had a very good idea that Maurice was out there only because Hugh was. She watched, and saw what kind of people made up the little group around Maurice; six or seven of those flickering entities generally called 'young lads' in the town. These Maurice could gather around him in small or large groups whenever he wished. She knew what he believed; that by standing there surrounded by his meagre group of followers he was holding a very powerful mirror indeed up to Hugh. These satellites of his own he considered more than adequate comment on the middle-aged worthies who had proved to be Hugh's fate since his return to the town.

Breena hated the effect Hugh had on Maurice. She understood that at the moment Maurice was doing his best to pay Hugh back for the way he had so publicly shouted at him and brought him to heel outside the church. She felt a very great reluctance now to go forward into the yard and so catch Maurice at his silly game of baiting Hugh. She wished to save both herself and Maurice from any discussions on it afterwards that might prove as foolish as the behaviour itself. She waited, drawing still further back into the shade of the old moss-covered tree; hoping moment after moment that Hugh, who was always the pace-setter in this asinine game, would finish his talk with his associates and go back into the house.

'Breena!'

She was rather badly startled to hear her own name being spoken in a low voice at her elbow; when she turned and found Kitty herself planted fair and square beside her she positively jumped. All her attention had been concentrated on that area ahead where Hugh and Maurice were standing.

Kitty exclaimed somewhat peevishly, 'There's no need to jump as if I'd just stuck a pin in you. I've been watching you from my window upstairs for the past five minutes. I was wondering how long it would take you to move from here. In the end I couldn't stand it any longer, and came down to help you make up your mind.'

Breena ignored Kitty's tone and as explanation of her behaviour she merely nodded in the direction of Maurice and Hugh. Kitty burst out:

'Don't you think I've seen the pair of them already? It's too bad of Maurice, today of all days. This is the second time since we came back from Mass that he's followed Hugh out into the yard like this. Will he ever grow up, d'you think?'

'Grow up?' Breena looked thoughtfully at Maurice and then from him to Hugh. She said as mildly as she could: 'Hugh *does* overdo it a bit. He's not an ambassador, you know. Look at him now, all that smiling and shaking hands. He tries too hard, that's the trouble. Just to watch him smile wears me out.'

Kitty turned an exasperated blind face towards her. She was still wearing the black dress she had worn at Mass, but now with a dark brown chiffon scarf – her mother's, it must be – pulled low over her forehead to hide her ravaged face. She retorted in a rush of speech:

'Whatever you say, Breena, and whatever Maurice says or does, I can't see that it's open to poor Hugh to behave much differently just now. You know how he hated working abroad, how badly he always wanted to come back home. And now he's been chosen as Head Doctor of the new hospital here – one of the youngest men in the whole country, too, to be given such a job. No wonder he feels he must keep smiling, whatever it costs him. I feel very sorry for him. Everybody in this town must think he's so lucky, I'm sure they'd sooner see a crack in the walls of the new hospital than a look of worry or bad temper on Hugh's face.'

Breena sighed. She sighed for her old friend, the Kitty of two years or even eighteen months ago, who would have hooted out loud in mockery at just such a speech as had now come out of her own mouth. What fun the Kitty of those days would have made of this Hugh standing before them here, with his grand 'post' right back in his 'home town' and all his hard smiling; the Kitty who used to make Maurice and herself gasp with her cynical comments on almost every subject that came up! Now the thought of how fast Maurice and herself were leaving that old friend, that most generous and loyal Kitty behind, made her say with sudden compunction:

'Yes, no doubt you're right, Kit. Obviously if Hugh were any different…'

She had to leave it at that. In her own mind the word 'different' had suddenly taken on a particular meaning: more self-doubting, more subtle and humble in his intelligence…

But Kitty was quite satisfied. She said in a softened tone:

'Well, it's only fair to try and see Hugh's point of view too. We're always inclined to take Maurice's part. But come on, I can't stay out here any longer looking like this. Follow me in; I'm going to streak across the yard like a hare.'

She turned and was gone. But Breena did not move after her at once. She knew from a certain woodenness that had crept into Maurice's attitude, and from the way he had drawn out into the yard, away from the porch and Hugh, that he had seen Kitty and herself. The zest had gone out of his game. A few of the young boys around him, moreover, had openly turned to watch Breena and Kitty.

Now Breena hesitated a moment, then made up her mind. As she stepped out into the yard she turned her head and looked straight at Maurice. He seemed to be expecting it. He looked towards her, their glances met full on. He half-smiled at her, acknowledging the foolishness of what he had been doing. Then, right under the eyes of his lanky disciples, he started across the yard towards her, an act that required some courage, she thought. But now she could scarcely bring herself to look at him; she knew all his friends were watching. She hated the thought of their sly, inquisitive eyes.

They drew together. She had only a vivid, heart-warming impression of the quick smile that passed from his eyes to hers as he said hurriedly, 'Don't stay too long with Kitty. I'll be waiting in the hut.' Then they both moved on. It must have seemed to the others that they had only exchanged a greeting in passing.

All Breena hoped for now was to get past Hugh without being seen. But as she came up to the porch Hugh stepped forward to greet some newcomer; suddenly he stood directly in her path. She stopped short, flustered. The next moment he turned, and she found herself looking straight into his eyes.

| 91

'Hello Breena,' he greeted her then very pleasantly. 'I suppose you're going to join Kitty? I've just seen her go in.'

'Ye-es,' she stammered. His extreme politeness, which followed so hard on his rudeness after Mass, only added to her discomfort.

'I know Kitty must be very pleased that you're here at last. By the way, Breena… '

She felt herself flushing as he put his hand on her elbow and drew her a little aside. She hardly heard him as he expanded on what she knew very well already; that Kitty was very upset today; that she needed to be soothed and calmed; that 'she needs sleep more than anything; if you could only persuade her to lie down and rest for some hours… '

She could not keep herself from blushing as he flattered her with his hands on her elbow, his meaning glances, his assurance that her presence alone could act like a tonic on Kitty. She felt sure he was as insincere now as he had been in his parade of grief as Mass, yet she continued to utter her inane comments: 'Yes, I agree'; 'I'll do my best'; 'Of course!' The fear, the knowledge rather, that Maurice was watching only made her blush all the more.

Then Hugh turned back to his own group and the men in it, no doubt spurred on by his example, were only too ready to smile at Breena in their turn. As she did her best to smile back at them she felt a most unpleasant squiggly sensation inside her. She hurried on into the hall and up the stairs to Kitty's room.

CHAPTER 11

Kitty opened the door. 'Breena, at last! What a long time you've been!'

'Oh, I'm sorry, Kitty.' She felt quite incapable of explaining the reason intelligently.

Kitty led the way to the window-seat. As soon as they were both sitting down she exclaimed impulsively; 'Oh, Breena, why did I have to cry like that at Mass? I let everybody down. They all kept a grip on themselves except me. I was the only one to… '

'It wasn't your fault.' Breena's indignation at the way the family had behaved in church revived again. 'They should have let you kneel by the door, so that you could have slipped away immediately after Mass. I can't understand why you all knelt together in the front like that.'

'Oh, Hugh wanted us all to be together. He said we *should* be together today.'

'Hugh!' So it was Hugh…

But she stopped herself. She reflected that criticism of Hugh would help nobody just now. 'Stop tormenting yourself about it. Don't think about it any more.'

'Don't think about it… ? Yes, that's good advice… Breena, just look at me. My eyes… I can hardly see.'

Breena glanced quickly away. The squint in Kitty's eyes – usually so slight that it suited the eager, headlong effect Kitty made, adding

| 93

to her looks – was now very pronounced. Every time she tried to focus her glance on Breena's face her pupils seemed to shoot towards one another, collide, and shoot away. It was very painful to sit beside her and watch her repeated failures. To relieve the situation Breena stood up and walked across the room to the gable window. The best way to help Kitty occurred to her then. She turned back to her and said eagerly:

'Kitty, you must come out for a walk with me. Come on, the dogs are waiting outside by the plum tree. Let's leave this place and get out into the fresh air.'

And then, a little more insistently, because Kitty made no answer, 'You mustn't let these four walls close in on you, Kit. A walk is what you need – look how beautiful it is out!'

She added the last words because Kitty had come drifting uncertainly after her to the window. They stood looking out over the heat-haze to where, far away towards the south-west, a small square of sea gleamed like a man's dark ring. Breena glanced at Kitty's bruised, blinded face.

In her heart there was a great desire to help and comfort Kitty. Only within the past year or two, since she became capable of reflection, had she come to realise how much she owed Kitty. She understood now that when she first came to live at Uncle John's, Kitty, who was her own age near enough, and the only girl in the two families, might have resented her, grown a dislike for her, carried tales about her to their elders, made her life very miserable. But she knew now that it had never even occurred to Kitty that she might have behaved in that way. Only quite lately had Breena been able to recognise how far to meet her Kitty had come.

'Kitty, darling, I can only help you if you agree to come walking with me, out and away from this place. While you stay up here, and nobody realises you're here, you're bound to think…'

'Think! I'm not *thinking*. Give me credit for knowing that. I'm only feeling, letting myself ooze out all over the place. And I've only stayed up here because my face looked so awful, I couldn't go down. I've been trying to read too. Look!'

She pointed towards the window-seat they had just left, where a small book with a brown paper cover lay open. Swiftly and gratefully Breena went back and sat on the edge of the window-seat and picked up the book.

'Go on, read it. There, that verse. I've read it I don't know how many times since I came home from Mass.'

Breena looked up at Kitty. And because Kitty was standing over her, glowering above her it seemed, she stood up again to be on a level with her.

'Is it going to bite you?' Kitty said. 'Is that what you're afraid of? You used to like it well enough not so very long ago. You used to ask *me* to read it to *you* then.'

'Kitty, we've talked about this before. There's no point in discussing it again – certainly not now. All I can say is that… that I went through a certain kind of phase, and now I… I've outgrown it.'

'A phase. I see. And you've outgrown it. Well, I'm nearly eight months older than you, and I'm still going through that phase. Isn't it strange? So will you please read it?'

Breena looked steadily at Kitty for a moment. But though Kitty tried hard, it was beyond her power to return that look. Her eyes were completely out of control. They kept shooting wild glances everywhere except where Breena was. And all around her face the tendrils of her hair were stuck by tears to her cheek and forehead, like a child's. She was very flushed. She looked as if she might break down and cry again at any moment. Suddenly Breena gave in; she picked up the book and began to read where Kitty pointed.

'*Lay not up to yourselves treasures on earth, where the rust and the moth consume, and thieves break through and steal. For where thy treasure is…*'

'*There is thy heart also!*' Kitty finished for her, and then went on to demand in a low strained voice, 'Can you say you've outgrown that? And if so, what grand new wisdom have you put in its place?'

'Kitty, please. As I've just said, we've discussed all this before. We've quarrelled about it all before too. It seems to me now that we've done nothing else except quarrel about it ever since I changed my mind about being a nun. This is certainly not the time to bring it up again.'

'No? You want to hold back, I suppose, to spare me? But isn't it a bit too late for that now? You've already let slip what you really think of me. You think I've got stuck fast in one phase of growing up, whereas *you*, you've already spun far beyond the phase that I got stuck in. Very complimentary to me, I must say.'

'Kitty, I refuse to quarrel with you today, no matter what you say. I don't understand yet what made me change by mind about becoming a Medical Missionary, so I can't talk sensibly about it. Or, rather… I think that I'm just beginning to understand. The truth is, I'm not half, no, not even a quarter, as generous as you are, Kit. I wouldn't have been accepted as a nun. If I hadn't changed my own mind in time, the Mother of Novices would have forcibly changed it for me, within two weeks of my entering. And, Kitty, the joke of it all to me now, looking back, is that I didn't want just to be a nun. No, that was far too meagre an ambition for me. I wanted to be a saint. A saint! Me! A girl who can't even bring herself to give up for the sake of others one day's fishing at Maurcappagh, or a swim in the sea, or a walk as far as the lake with the dogs!'

But now Kitty, with her usual impetuous generosity, came suddenly and completely round to Breena's side.

'Don't talk nonsense, Breena. You're not selfish. At any rate you're not anywhere near as selfish as I am, in my own stubborn way. And as for being a saint, who knows? It may be your destiny to be a saint out in the world, like Margaret of Scotland or Joan of Arc. I'm the one that's to blame, for not thinking of that before. I promise you now that I'll never, never again quarrel with you because you changed your mind about being a nun.'

Breena could not help laughing. She exclaimed with some satisfaction, 'Saint Breena! It sounds good, that. Or better still, Saint Breena of the Nuclear Era!'

'Don't make fun of it,' Kitty answered quietly. 'Come and sit here in the window, and we'll read these verses over again together.'

Breena sat down beside her, and this time Kitty read, rather slowly and painfully, while Breena closed her eyes and listened.

'*Lay ye not up treasures on earth…*'

Each word rang clear as a bell within what had now become the vast vaulted quietness of Breena's mind. It seemed to her that she was walking with noiseless tread past heaps of treasured things: all that man had ever coveted throughout his strange and lonely adventure of living in this world. Gold piled very high, bright baubles of precious stones. Rubies, diamonds, sapphires, emeralds – those savagely bright slivers of rock that were surely intended only to beguile the glances of a savage or a child. Then furs, great houses, glances of envy and hate deliberately provoked to enhance a sense of power. Power most fleeting, very soon to end as it had begun, in utter nakedness…

'Don't read any more.' Breena put her hand over the page so that Kitty could not go on. 'You have committed yourself to it, Kit, so it upholds and comforts you. But me, it only upsets me at the moment.'

'You're not alone in that,' Kitty came in quickly and unexpectedly. 'It upsets me too. This morning I've read it over and over again. I was thinking about this house. This house is my treasure. And now of course it will have to be sold. Breena, d'you think it's a very stupid thing to love a house?'

Breena hesitated. 'No, indeed. I can understand why you love this house, Kit. This room up here is not just a room, it's an extension of the sky and the mountains.' She hesitated again, then plunged on, 'What I *do* think stupid though, utterly silly if you don't mind me saying so, is the notion that the house will have to be sold. Surely

Hugh will want to keep it on now? And aren't you glad now that he and Mrs Hugh haven't yet started to build their own house?'

Hugh and Mrs Hugh had been living here, in Kitty's house, since they came back to the town. But they had already bought some land out at Filedearg, near the sea, where they intended to build a house of their own very soon.

'Hugh may want to keep the house on. But d'you honestly think Mrs Hugh would ever consent to live in a ramshackle old place like this?'

'Well, then, my Uncle John will see to it – sorry, Kit, I shouldn't speak of him as "my" uncle. He's your uncle, not mine.'

'No, not mine. Yours, yours. You can keep him and welcome.'

'What does that mean, may I ask, Kit?'

'Oh, honestly Breena! You must admit that I've always tried to have patience with you about "my Uncle John". But in this case surely even *you* can see that Uncle John will be the first person to advise Mother to sell the house? He knows that Father already had an offer for it, from those people who wanted to build that hotel.'

'But the last thing Uncle John would want is a hotel here. He has a great feeling for this house. How can you think… ?'

'How can I think? How can you be so blind? Who sold that land where they're going to have that pre-fab – what is the name for it – motel? Who sold the land for that?'

'Why, Uncle John did, but… '

'There you are! Pre-fabs, motels, in this town! If only it were some poor man who needed the money for his family… '

'But Uncle John didn't know. He thought… '

'Oh Breena! Everybody but you knows he knew very well. He got a special price for that land.'

But now Breena cried out in sudden awareness of the fresh turn their exchange had taken: 'What are we talking about Uncle John for? Like this! Today! I don't want to talk about him.'

'All right, then. If *you* don't want to talk about him, don't talk about him. But *I* do want to talk about him. Breena, somebody must wake you up soon, before it's too late. We all know here that Uncle John would do anything for money. You wait and see. He'll sell out Maurcappagh yet. That's what he's planning for. He's buying it up, field by field. He's already bought poor Thady's share. You just wait. I'll tell you frankly what *I* think of your Uncle John; I think he has the soul of a shopkeeper.'

'Kitty… Hush! Uncle John is a shopkeeper, 'tis true. And it's a good thing for… for me, at any rate, that he is.'

'You were going to say, it's a good thing for all of us. But it isn't, Breena, it isn't. Uncle John destroyed my father. Just because he had better luck with that legacy long ago, and was able to put Father through school and college. Have you forgotten the wild look that used to come into Father's eyes sometimes? You know the name we gave him, "Jeremy the Younger!" And how Uncle John saw to it, your Uncle John – let me make you a present of him – that Father remained younger all his life, that he never forgot who gave him his great chance. Yet Father was the kind of man who would have thoroughly enjoyed trying to get somewhere on his own. He didn't just die of a heart-attack like they said. That heart-attack was only the culmination of all the frustration and bitterness he suffered for years in this little town, under his brother's thumb.'

Breena saw clearly in her mind a picture of Uncle John bowed over the sitting-room table last night, during that moment's flashing of the light. It was on the tip of her tongue to tell Kitty about it. But she bit it back. Afterwards, for many reasons, she was glad that she had done so.

She made herself keep silence a moment. During that silence she fought hard for the forbearance to hold her tongue indefinitely, and so put an end to the argument, which she realised was getting more ugly every moment. But after only a very short pause she could not keep herself from going on:

'I know I've said that I don't want to talk about Uncle John. But in all conscience I must say this; *I* know how generous he is, and also what hard life he's had.'

'A hard life! How would you describe Aunt Ursula's life then, and poor soft-hearted Thady's? Not to mention dear old Hannah's! I wouldn't like to tell you want I've heard so-called friends of Uncle John's in this town say, making fun of those three for being such fools.'

'Look, Kit, I'm certainly not interested in the spiteful gossip of idle, stupid… '

'Of course you're not interested. That is, you as you are now, the kind of person you are at the moment, could not possibly be interested in that sort of thing. He has corrupted you Breena, with his masterful ideas, with his masterful ideas about all of us. And at the end of it all, what great plans has he thought up for you? What does he want to make of you? A shopgirl, that's what he wants to make of you. A shopgirl!'

Breena turned away to the window. Before she could help herself the hurt of that word 'shopgirl!' ached very deeply. She muttered, 'You know better than anybody Kitty, that I have no intention of being a shopgirl. I… '

'And of course you've already explained that to Uncle John? You've gone into your own plans in detail with him?'

Now Breena spoke almost pompously:

'No. I haven't yet explained my plans to Uncle John. And you know very well why! There's no point in going to a man like Uncle John, with his practical way of thinking, and telling him that "it's expected of me at school" or that "I feel absolutely sure in my own mind" that I'm going to win a university place. No; before I go and speak to him I must have in my hand the actual piece of paper… '

'Well, take care! Maybe it'll turn out yet that you've exchanged dreams of becoming a saint for the reality of being his shopkeeper.'

Breena made no answer. She was mastered at last. Besides, it had just occurred to her that silence was something she owed

Kitty, part of a debt that went back a long way. She looked out of the window and saw a queer vision of the sky, a glittering blue that extended over everything. Then she could not help asking, though in a strained, apologetic tone: 'Kitty, last night… Why did you all wait so long before you phoned and let Uncle John know?'

Kitty swung sharply round in surprise to stare at her. 'What makes you think that we… '

'You did, didn't you? You waited at least an hour. Uncle John must realise by this time that he was the last member of the family to be informed. And I don't think the knowledge will comfort him.'

Kitty drew a deep breath. 'Well, if you must know, and you've only yourself to blame, you asked for it, none of us wanted Uncle John here, taking us all over and telling us what to do. As if a brother's claim was stronger than a wife's, let alone the children's! We wouldn't have phoned him as soon as we did, even, except that Dr Peggy came on here from the hospital, and made Mother go to the phone.'

Kitty hugged her arm and continued. 'You mustn't blame poor Mother too much. You know she's always been jealous of Uncle John. When I was younger I was so impatient of the whole business… ' She broke off and sighed. 'But lately… Many's the time lately… I've stood upstairs behind the blind in Mother's room, by Mother's side, watching Mother and watching Father – watching her watching I mean. He'd be down in the yard below with Uncle John, walking up and down, talking, talking, talking. The expression on poor Mother's face… Oh, I pity her, Breena! If I were her I'd have fought Uncle John, fought him every inch of the way. By God, from the time I could talk I made sure he respected me! Poor Mother; she had to watch Uncle John break Father, she had to watch him go under inch by inch… '

Breena looked down at her hands. She gave only part of her attention to what Kitty was saying. It irritated her, with that peculiar irritation of a sad tale told from a very biased angle, and completely beyond one's power to help. At the same time, in some odd way, it also comforted her. She thought to herself, 'Why, I don't think Kitty has changed all that much after all. That old, reckless, contrary nature of hers keeps breaking out; she'll have a job to smother it under a nun's veil.'

With that she began to think back nostalgically on those halcyon days of extreme cynicism which she and Kitty had walked through in complete harmony at the age of fifteen or fifteen and a bit. In those days they could pick the whole world to pieces and only like one another all the better for it. There had been no nonsense then on Kitty's part.

But now Kitty took Breena's continued silence and downcast looks for acquiescence in what she was saying about her mother and even perhaps shame that she had defended Uncle John so strongly; as usual her reaction was a generous one. She suddenly broke off, pressed Breena's arm and whispered, 'Well, your visit has certainly done me good. I'll take a couple of aspirins and read for a little while.'

She crossed to the mirror and examined her face. 'Yes, thank heavens!' She began to tidy her hair, and while doing so asked with peculiar inflection: 'Have you already been in *there*? Was that why you were so slow following me up?' She meant, of course, had Breena been in to say a prayer at her father's bedside.

'No.' Breena said.

'Do you want to go in now?'

'Now?' But Breena knew well enough there could be no refusing.

And since she must go in, it would be as well to do so now, at once. She accepted the scarf Kitty held out to her. But she did not wish to leave until she had let Kitty know that she planned to go to Maurcappagh with Thady. It was important to her that Kitty should know. She began to tell her now, adding a quick, almost shamefaced way when she had finished: 'If you think I shouldn't go, if you think it's selfish of me, I can easily find Thady and tell him I can't go after all. Then I'll come back and spend the day here with you.'

'Here with me? But, Breena, I'll be asleep! Of course you must go… And for God's sake ask Maurice to go with you as well, won't you?'

'Maurice?' Breena had not expected that.

'Yes, Maurice. He'll be far better off out at Maurcappagh than carrying on here like he's been doing all morning. For his own sake, for Hugh's, get him away from here. And for your sake too, of course…'

Breena hesitated for a moment, not daring to venture a reply. It still embarrassed her whenever Kitty made one of her half-sarcastic, half-teasing references to the growing sympathy between Maurice and herself. Then in a lingering, rather dissatisfied fashion she left the room.

CHAPTER 12

At the door of the waking-room Breena had to stand aside for a group of girls who were coming out, and she used those few seconds to look carefully round the room to see which members of the family were present. Her heart gave a sickening thud to see Dr Peggy sitting there in front of the darkened window, side by side with her sister Mamie, Kitty's mother. But there could be no drawing back now. As soon as the way was clear Breena walked on tiptoe into the room.

Carefully and quietly she went to the bedside and knelt down to say her prayer. She made one attempt, and one attempt only, to look at the face of the dead man. But the glow of the seven candles at the head of the bed got into her eyes and blinded her. After that she looked only at the white bedspread, or at her own hands clasped in front of her. But her eyes were still dazzled from the candles, her pulse was beating strongly. Whatever she looked at seemed to jump up and down before her eyes.

Breena stood up, and for a moment tarried, dithered there uncertainly, nerving herself to go against all custom and leave the room without speaking to the members of the family present.

She turned to go round the bed. She felt awkward, and stumbled a little. She was very conscious of Dr Peggy sitting there beside Kitty's mother. She could feel herself flushing. The room seemed very crowded; it took her a long time to get round the bed, past people's feet, across to the window. But at last she reached the place where

Kitty's mother was. She saw that she was now standing up, that she was going to embrace her. She had time to catch only a glimpse of the widow's face, strangely bright-eyed and serene, almost smiling it seemed in the intensity of its pious submission and patience, before she was engulfed in that embrace.

Then Kitty's mother released her, she felt the candlelight beat once more on her face. No longer did it seem half-darkness. It seemed more like a glare. She bent over Kitty's mother, who still kept one arm around her, to help her back into her seat. She saw then that the look she had at first taken for glad resignation was a pitiful, fixed and trance-like effort at self-control, and all at once she lost all her self-consciousness, she forgot about herself. She caught the widow's hand impulsively and bent down and began to speak simple and heart-felt words of sympathy and regret into her ear. Then she looked round for an empty chair, so that she could sit for a few minutes here in this room and so express all the better her sympathy for Kitty's mother. She quite forgot Dr Peggy, who all the time was sitting less than nine inches away, in the next chair.

It was only when she glanced round for a place to sit down that her attention was instantly and forcibly recalled to Dr Peggy. She found that Dr Peggy was watching her very closely. Indeed, so intent was Dr Peggy's glance that it seemed to leap up at her the moment she turned her head. She was very much put out, it was beyond her power to return that merciless look for more than a few seconds. It was such a keen, assessing glance, there was such a shrewd concentration of interest in it, that she stood there transfixed, looking down, having quite forgotten her original purpose of finding a chair, waiting for Dr Peggy's lips to go on with the cutting words her eyes had already begun to say. Then the sound of Dr Peggy's voice came to her, and it jerked her glance upwards in fresh surprise, it was so kindly in tone. She could hardly trust her senses to find that Dr Peggy was now giving her the full benefit of her great smile, that seemed to split across her face from ear to ear.

'Hadn't you better go and have some tea rather than sit here?' Dr Peggy was saying. 'I'm sure they'll have some in the kitchen!'

Breena turned immediately and went very quietly out of the room. She paused for a moment in the corridor; the image of Dr Peggy's blue eyes as they examined her with bright, keen, insulting interest remained very vivid in her mind. She tried to persuade herself that it had only been a trick of the flickering candlelight. But, no. The keenness of that look had cut across the candlelight, it had not been an effect of it.

Out in the passage she was getting into the way of everybody who wanted to go in or out of the waking-room, and earning their puzzled stares; but now, instead of turning to the left into the back-kitchen, she turned the other way, into the sitting-room. As yet there was nobody in this room, though there were chairs and benches ranged all round the walls. It was too sunny outside; people preferred to stand or walk about in the yard. Since the room was empty, Breena decided to get out of it in a very handy fashion, by the back-window – as Kitty and herself had done so many times since they were children. She swung herself over the sill of this window now, into the wilderness beyond, which had once been a garden. Then she leaned back against it a moment, gratefully breathing in the scented warmth of the day.

Kitty... Her 'He has corrupted you Breena!' and 'A shopgirl, that's what he wants to make of you, a shopgirl!' were hardly comforting sounds to remember just now.

'Shopgirl!' Breena spoke the word aloud, in exasperation. What an ugly, ill-informed word it was, carrying undertones it had no right to carry. Then in spite of herself she smiled, repeating in a whisper the curious old-fashioned phrases, typical of Uncle John, that had been spoken to her so very often during the past month, since she left school. 'I have no wish to hurry your decision, Breena. But be assured of it, we won't wrong you. As soon as you make up your mind to join us, steps will be taken, proper steps, to ensure your future!'

'Proper steps!' she thought, her smile growing wider as she turned away from the window and saw before her the flight of crumbling, dangerous, not at all proper steps she must climb in order to reach the hut where Maurice had promised to wait for her. Comforting visions of the life she planned for herself, the life she was proudly confident she could win for herself by her own unaided talents, went through her head as she began carefully to climb these steps.

CHAPTER 13

She found Maurice waiting for her by the hut. He was standing with his face raised to the sun, so that when he turned at her step the sun was behind him and for a moment his face had the drowsy beauty of an ancient mask, the mask of the sun god, who was never going to die.

'Breena!' He came forward eagerly to meet her. 'Kitty has kept you a long time. How is she?'

'She's going to read for a while and then try and sleep.'

'That's good. Did she tell you that I went in to see her shortly before you arrived, to advise her to go to bed? But she wouldn't have anything to do with me then.'

'No. She was cross about… about that carry-on with Hugh. But before she went to sleep she sent you a message.'

In a rather hurried fashion then, to cover up her own interest in the matter, she told him what Kitty had suggested; that he should come out to Maurcappagh with Thady and herself.

She finished speaking. He made no attempt to answer, but only stared at the ground. He was standing out of the sun now, she saw how pale he was. She waited a while, patiently, even with some relish. She felt the warm wood of the hut at her back; she was aware of the various summer scents of the leaves and long grass around; she heard a thrush's song, pouring out clear and sweet above the summer warbling in the hedges.

'Well?' she prompted him at last. 'Don't you want to come with us?' Then she added, as if the name were a charm, 'To Maurcappagh?'

'Maurcappagh...' He repeated without looking up. 'D'you know, Breena, at the moment I hardly know where Maurcappagh is.'

She studied his face, not knowing how to take this answer. He looked up then and made rather a bleak attempt to smile at her. He said, 'My thoughts are in a terrible state. I'm sorry I can't work up any enthusiasm over Maurcappagh, but the fact is... Look, you've spent well over an hour with Kitty. You can't have enjoyed it much, the way things are today. I feel sure that all you want to do now is to go out into the fields with the dogs and enjoy the sun...'

His voice trailed off. Again she waited a moment. Then she said in a very low voice, to hide her hurt at his queer, abrupt, changeable manner:

'You want me to go away, is that it? You've decided that you've nothing to say to me after all; that you'd rather be alone and concentrate on your own thoughts?'

'For God's sake no. I'm half-afraid of my own thoughts. I certainly don't want to be alone with them any longer. All I meant was, can you bear another bout of talking? First Kitty, now me – d'you want to stay?'

She smiled at him. 'Of course I want to stay. I very much want to hear what you have to say.'

'Look, come into the music room, will you. On a day like today you never know who is walking about amongst these overgrown shrubs.'

Somewhere to their right the rustlings of leaves and the crackling of dry branches, as if they were being trodden underfoot, seemed to confirm his suspicions. But it was probably only the small wild creatures of the undergrowth. She followed him inside.

This hut, this so-called music room of Maurice's, had been an earth closet in the days when there was no piped water in Maurice's house. That was before Maurice's time, when the house stood a good

| 109

mile outside the town, or village as it had been then. Nowadays the older members of the family still choked on the word 'privy' when they referred to Maurice's music room; the younger members, including Maurice himself in his unguarded moments, called it by the name of their own childhood, the hut.

Inside, the hut was larger than it gave promise of from outside. The walls had been well whitewashed and the floor covered with a layer of rush matting. There were quite a number of musical instruments in the room, but they were all ranged against the walls, so that there was no appearance of clutter. Now Maurice pulled a table out from the wall to the left of the door, so that Breena could sit down. He himself sat down opposite her. Their glances met, they exchanged a quick smile of pleasure in one another's company. Then for a moment there was silence. Swaying to and fro across the wall was the enlarged shadow of a fuchsia branch, its bells like strange tropical insects as they moved back and forth.

At last Maurice asked in a careful voice, avoiding her glance, 'You've been in to see him?'

There could be no mistaking whom he meant.

'Yes, I went in.' She stared down at the table, an old, brown, scratched table. 'I… I wasn't able to make myself look at him.'

'Yes, I can understand that… But it's a pity all the same.'

She glanced up then and saw on his face an inward-looking preoccupied expression. This and what he had just said seemed to put a distance between them. The next moment she heard herself blurting out a question that had been preying on her thoughts since Ursula came into her room at dawn. She knew it to be tactless, but would not keep it back.

'Maurice, it won't make any difference to *you*, will it? You'll go back to school in September, won't you, and take your exams, as planned?'

Maurice had been off school since the November before, when he had been severely ill with an attack of rheumatic fever; so that both Kitty, who was his twin, and Breena, who was more than eight months younger, had by this time passed him out of school.

'As planned?' he echoed her now. Suddenly his glance was very bright and intent on hers. 'Is planned the right word to use? Wouldn't it be better to say "as taken for granted"?'

He paused for a reply. She watched him, but made no attempt to speak.

'Breena, last night was a very long night. I went round to see you, as you know. But I had to come back without seeing you. After that I had a lot of time for thinking. Not so much "thinking" maybe. Remembering… then Kitty came to call me into Father's room. He was laid out, they were going to say the rosary. I went in. Father Hennessey was there, the whole family. We said the rosary, and then Mother asked for those verses from St Matthew about the sparrows – you know them? "Are not two sparrows sold for a farthing? And not one of them shall fall to the ground without your Father. But the very hairs of your head are all numbered. Fear not therefore…"'

There was a short silence. They searched each other's faces. Then Maurice went on:

'Have they told you how Mother found him? He had fallen to the ground. Slipped down, rather, with his back to the wall. They say he tried to keep some control over himself to the end – if that's possible.'

'Yes. Ursula and Kitty both told me that.'

'And do you agree with what the verses say? That the very hairs of our head are all numbered? That nothing happens without meaning?'

'Well… We've been brought up to believe that, haven't we?'

'Yes… That's a rather odd way to put it, Breena… Last night, after those verses were read, do you know the questions I kept puzzling over? Why did Father have to die just now? Why did his health give way so suddenly? Do you know the conclusion I came to? Father died because he himself believed that he had come to the end of his time, of his usefulness, in this world. He believed he had nothing more to give to anybody – can you accept that?'

'Accept it? It's a very strange use of words… But apart from that altogether, there was a… a kind of loneliness about your father. It was like the promise of some development yet to come. He never grew fat, he didn't seem middle-aged. He was easy to talk to. I liked him very much.'

'Yes, yes. He was a likeable man. *Was*. Breena, you must go in again to see him. And this time look at his face. Have the courage to look at it carefully. I tell you, he's glad to be dead. Just lately he found the strain of living too much for him. All his great new ideas for me, his plans for his own future, they had come to weary him. He didn't believe in them any longer. Can't you see that? Otherwise he'd have lived to see them through. He was by nature a family man; his family meant a great deal to him. Yet when it came to my turn, do you know what he did? He died. Now, don't you think that a very significant thing?'

Breena did not answer at once. She was staring down at the table. At last she said in a disjointed, halting way:

'When my own father died… It's a long time ago, but I remember very clearly the face of an old woman… She was very old, she wore a shawl over her head… I didn't know her name. She came up to me at the wake and she said, "Life is for the strong. You know that now, don't you? Don't ever forget it. Life is for the strong." She said it three or four times. I remember what a bitter sound it had… They had to take her away. Yet I knew she was trying to comfort me. But she was so old… Maurice, your father is dead. What he could do for you he did. You can't accuse him of putting you out to work at the age of twelve; you can't accuse him of ill-treating you or neglecting you in any way. All you can accuse him of is dying and so breaking some wild promises about your music that lately, since you've been ill, he's been making in what I can only call a conscience-stricken, rather desperate fashion. He knew he should have understood before what your music meant to you. But you can't blame him, Maurice. He couldn't do more for you than it was in his nature to do.'

'Breena, keep it steady now. I'm not blaming him, of course I'm not blaming him. I'm only trying to make sense to myself of what has happened. The sudden death of somebody like Father, who appeared perfectly healthy… Oh, when I ran upstairs last night and saw him! Mother came downstairs screaming you know; my God, such screams… When I spoke to him and he made no answer, when I rubbed his hands and felt the cold, the silence he was caught up in… Kitty cried her heart out this morning, but last night she was so quiet, so white-faced, she did everything so methodically and well, phoned for Hugh, Father Hennessey, fetched blankets, pillows, hot water bottles. I pitied her with all my heart. After the first two minutes I knew it was all useless – and only a couple of hours before Father had been up here with me in this room, listening to me play, speaking enthusiastically of all the new plans he had for me; people he must write to, people I must certainly go and see, who would want to help me, exams I must take, and so on. Never had I seen him so bubbling over with optimistic projects. After I knew for certain that he was dead his voice kept coming back to me. It was almost as if he was saying to me, "Over to you now!" I sat for a long time in his room after we had said the rosary. They didn't think me a nuisance; I kept quiet in the corner. And, Breena, I talked to him all the time. I was afraid he couldn't hear me; for all they say, I got such a grasp of what death means, such a grasp, when I first bent over him and tried to revive him. But for all that I spoke to him. You see, since I was ill… When I was getting better and I was so weak, he was so patient… I got to depend on him; I suppose I became a bit childish again… Last night I promised him that, half-baked as I know I am, fool as Hugh and Mrs Hugh and that crowd rate me, I would try my best to be what I had lately told him I could be. I swore that I would take my life into my own hands and cherish the only kind of faith in myself that's worth having; that I am a workman worthy of my hire.

I promised that I would try to be great.'

Breena had leaned her elbow on the table so that she could shade her face with her hand. For a time there was silence. Then she took away her hand and said in a firm voice:

'Maurice, you're upset now, that very obvious. You're just as bad as Kitty. You're speaking under the influence of the first strong emotional shock you've ever had. What... what exactly are you trying to tell me, though? I don't understand you.'

'Breena, look... take me seriously, won't you? Nobody else will at this stage. I know what you're thinking; is it possible that I, spoilt and silly Maurice, could go off and do something hard? But can't you see, that's why I must go off. I must find out. If I stay here they'll beat me. They'll destroy me.'

'Who'll destroy you? Maurice, what in heaven's name are you talking about? And when you say go off, what do you mean? Go off where? I'm afraid I've completely lost the thread of your argument. You were telling me about your father, and now suddenly you're talking about going off. Could you... Could you please explain the change of subject?'

'All right. I admit I've made a leap. I was following my own thoughts; I took it for granted for a moment that things must be equally clear to you... Breena let me ask you a question. Which of the women in this town, or in our own family, since you know those better, do you most want to be like when you're, say, thirty?'

'Oh, Maurice, stop it! None of them, of course. I reject the very idea and well you know it.'

'You believe you can make yourself into a different sort of person, quite unlike these women? But how?'

'How?' she hesitated. 'By the exercise of my... my own talent. But I don't want to talk about it. I can't talk about it yet, I have no right. I must earn the right to talk about it by years spent learning my craft. I am not like you, Maurice. Your gifts overflow on the surface; everyone can see what your talents are. But I have only one talent, and at the moment that's buried, not under the ground, but deep inside me.'

'Well… that's fair enough, I suppose. If you won't come out into the open, you won't. But *I* must come out into the open; I must state my argument so that you'll understand me. So I'll go back to where I started, I'll say again what I said ten minutes ago; that Father's sudden death must necessarily have a greater significance for me than for Kit or Hugh or the others. I'm bound to miss him more than they do, for sheer selfish reasons. I'm bound to question what has happened, and to think very carefully about what I must do now.'

Breena considered a moment and sighed. 'I can accept that. Please go on.'

'Don't sigh. And don't say "Please go on" in that tone of voice. It makes me want to stop, not go on. Look, Breena, I'll do my very best to spare you any dramatic or hysterical over-statement of my case. I'll just say, as you've already said, that I have certain gifts, talents. I can play quite a few musical instruments the moment I pick them up. Tunes come in to my head, I play them. They may be just plagiarised versions of tunes I've heard. I'm not sure. I'll have to find that out. Also, I can easily scribble down words, lyrics, to match the tunes. I'm not saying that these talents I have are very wonderful at the moment, or better than anybody else's talents. They're just mine, what I can do. And with them, and by them, and through them, I want to earn my bread. Do more than that maybe, eventually. One day I might even write great music. And if I fail, what does it matter? While I'm alive, I'll never admit failure. And after I'm dead, the pundits can say what they like. Don't you agree?'

'Agree? Oh, Maurice, out of all that… But yes, certainly I agree with you in your estimate of your talents. But what has that to do with your going off? And off where?'

'Wait. Wait a minute. Give me time. I'm nearly nineteen years of age, as you know. Last November I went down with rheumatic fever

| 115

– rheumatic fever plus complications – and consequently missed out on my exams. You could call that bad luck, or you might say that it was my destiny. One of the first things you asked me a while back was if I would be returning to school "as planned" in September? But you know very well that Father's latest plans for me, though in a very woolly state, were certainly not mainly concerned with my going back to school in September.'

'If his plans were so woolly, all the more reason then why you should go back to school.'

'But why, Breena? Why should I, as I am now, go back to school? To compete with last year's chaps? To force-feed myself with facts that I'll certainly have forgotten by this time next year?'

'But you must go back to school; you must sit your exams, if you want to go to college. How can you get a university place if you don't sit your exams?'

'A university place? Yes… for a long time that was Father's one idea. He was so insistent that I must not be "wronged"; that I must be given the same chance as my brothers, in spite of the very obvious differences between us. And I must admit that up to the time I became ill I myself had not got beyond thinking of college as a very necessary step. I had no confidence in my own talents up to that time. But now this thing has happened; or, rather, these two things. I have been ill, and Father has died. D'you know what I honestly believe now? That for me, as I've developed since I was ill, any years spent at college would be an absolute waste of time.'

He said the last words rather tentatively, with his pressing, bright glance full on her face, showing clearly by tone and look that this was a point he still needed support on. But she was able to meet his glance only for a moment. She looked away, and stared at the shadows of the fuchsia bells swinging on the wall.

CHAPTER 14

A slow, sick fear of coming change was building up inside her: an apprehension, a realisation, a certainty, that this wonderful summer, this first summer of her complete freedom, was even now beginning to slip away from her. Oh, how strange it was, how terrible, that only now, with the first faint threat of its loss stealing up on her, was she able fully to savour the vivid, the yearning sweetness of this first free summer of her life… Or, the new, glad, stinging, growing excitement of her awareness of Maurice? Was it always like this, even with life itself? Last night when Maurice's father, with the death-pain already at his heart, did his best to control his fall to the floor, was it only then that all the strangeness, the sweetness, the mystery of his presence here in this world became clear to him, and overwhelmed him?

Outside the thrush was singing again. She forced herself to speak: 'Maurice, I feel… inadequate. D'you honestly think I'm the right person to be discussing this with? If you can't speak to Hugh, there's always Father Patrick or Jerry or Desmond, all more experienced members of the family. I don't think that I… '

Silence. She heard the swishings and rustlings of the leaves and long grass outside. She felt her dress stirred by the small gales from the shrubs. Then she heard Maurice's voice:

'This is a new kind of talk from you, Breena. Can you imagine Hugh sitting there where you are – having consented to come up here in the first place, mark you! – listening patiently to my soul searchings? As for Patrick and Jerry, they might want to help, but no, their prejudices are too strong. They've both done so brilliantly well at college, their ideas of themselves and of life generally are so bound up with the success they had there… You can see that, can't you? Can't you… Breena, look at me!'

In spite of herself her glance was drawn to his face. He was watching her closely, she knew. She half-expected his look to be demanding or challenging, willing her to agree with him quite regardless of what she felt. But the moment their glances met he smiled at her. So serene, that dark-fringed golden look, she had no choice but to hold it and try her best to respond to it. She said impulsively:

'I may not be as different from Patrick and Jerry as you give me credit for. Anyway, Maurice, we've discussed this matter of the value of going to college before. I'm sure you remember, I'm sure that's what you're driving at. Oh, I wish, I wish with all my heart… '

'Breena, can't you see that during those two months at the turn of the year, when I was lying ill in bed, I outgrew college? That's the best way I can put it. I must not; I cannot act as if I had not been given another chance. I have a trade to learn, I must be off on my travels. I must learn how to make music, and how to sing songs. But they must be music and songs about the people I meet on the road, my own kind of people. Breena, I must break out of this honeycomb of family concern that's suffocating me at the moment, that's already suffocated poor Kit. With Father gone… I owe it to him, I think, to be off on my way. And I must go now. Now. Some very deep part of my nature is warning me, "Act now! Now!" While the spirit of God is moving inside me. Breena… Don't you agree?'

'What do you mean by now, Maurice? Do you mean today, or tomorrow, or in a week's time?'

The bleakness in her heart came through into her voice. It was so low that the summer rustlings outside threatened to smother it and Maurice had to lean forward in order to catch her words. She could not bring herself to look at him.

'Well, of course at the moment – don't you agree, Breena? – I must give Mother every consideration. I must wait two or three days at least. Breena… '

'Maurice, is this all only talk? Wild, silly, heedless talk… ? Adolescent talk, like we've had so many times before? Or d'you mean what you're saying this time? Are you going to act on it?'

'Yes, Breena. I mean it and I'm going to act on it.'

Their glances met and fluttered away again in sheer, anguished inadequacy. There was a short silence. Then Breena said:

'Let me… let me get things clear. You're going to leave home, is that it? One day very soon you'll get up in the morning and set off? With no money, no plans, no clear idea where you're bound for, even? Is that what you've been saying?'

'Yes. But I implied of course that I would work for my money, and that my plan was to see the world, to see it while I'm still young enough to use my own eyes and not be influenced by other people's prejudices.'

'And what do you think the family will say?'

'I know very well what they'll say. They'll say what they've said hundreds of times before. That I'm talking nonsense. That I'm a fool and a clown. That I can't face the thought of going back to school and doing a hard year's slogging. Therefore, that I'm running away. That every family has some cross to bear, and at least one black sheep to put up with. Do you want me to go on?'

'And are you so very sure that they're all wrong and that you're right?'

'Yes, Breena. I'm quite sure. Don't you see? It's because they'll all oppose me that I must go very soon, within the next week at least, while I still see so clearly what life and death are about… '

His voice trailed off; the faint hissings and swishings from without took over again. She knew that he was put out by her reaction; that he had expected enthusiasm, or at least a very lively interest. Every time he spoke her name, his voice appealed to her to look up again, to look at him. But she knew the expression that must be in her eyes at this moment, there was such sickness at her heart. Change again, more change, change always and everywhere!

And then suddenly the gay, 'Look up, I'm here, I'm here!' of a robin's song trilled through the hut. The fuchsia branch on the wall swayed wildly. The blurring of the bird's shape could be seen where the branch thickened. Maurice, who was in no mood for silence, seized on the excuse of the song:

'Listen to that; just listen to it, Breena! You know what it always reminds me of? I've often told you. That poem, the first, no the second, poem I ever learned of my own accord. Under your influence, Breena. Say it for me now, go on, say it. It goes so well with a robin's song!'

Breena shaded her face with her hand. She said, 'You only like it because of the music. It was only after we read Shaw that time, and found out about Elgar, and then you got the music… It isn't because of the words you like it, so there's no point in my saying it.'

'How could I like the music and not the words? Don't be mean, Breena. Please say it. Go on, say it for me.'

Breena kept silence a moment, her hand still shading her face. And then, because it suddenly occurred to her that her silence might look like sullenness, she said, 'All right, I'll say it.' She started off very quickly.

> "'We are the music makers,
> We are the dreamers of dreams
> Wandering by lone sea-breakers,
> And sitting by desolate streams,
> World-losers and world-forsakers,
> On whom the pale moon gleams:
> We are the movers and shakers
> Of the world for ever, it seems…'"

That's all I can say, Maurice, because it's… it's all I can say at the moment.'

'It's enough. Now will you say that other one, the one you were reciting out at Maurcappagh on Wednesday morning?'

'Maurice… you needn't try to batten this kind of flattery on to me. I… I accept what you've just been saying to me. I respect it; I believe you're in earnest. I'll think it over until I can see things one hundred per cent from your point of view. There's no need to keep on asking me to say poems. I know they don't mean the same thing to you as they do to me, they…'

'This one did! Please say it for me. I do want to hear it, Breena, honestly…'

> '*God guard me from those thoughts men think
> In the mind alone;
> He that sings a lasting song
> Thinks in a marrow-bone;
> From all that makes a wise old man
> That can be praised of all;
> Oh what am I that I should not seem
> For the song's sake a fool?*'

'That's the line!' Maurice interrupted her in an excited tone. 'That's the line I was trying to remember. *Oh what am I that I should not seem, for the song's sake, a fool?* Last Wednesday morning you, you, were quoting that poem at me as the very epitome of wisdom! And now, don't deny it; because I can see it in your face, you're blaming me bitterly for taking that wisdom to heart!'

'No, Maurice. It's just that…. well, you must give me time… The way we've been brought up it's hard to approve of your going off, setting off in that wild way… It's hard to see that it's necessary. I…'

'Breena, you've had so much talk this morning; first Kit, then me, as I said before, it's not fair. Come on; let's go out into the High Field at once. You'd like that, wouldn't you?'

| 121

His voice, so gentle, so considerate of her hesitations, her holdings-back, only gave her a further pang. He was so sure of himself! Up to now they had both lived by talk; talk had been almost a way of life with them. But now he was ready to go beyond talk into action. He had passed her out.

She saw that he had jumped up. She too stood up, rather more slowly. She shivered as she stepped out of the cool hut and stood in the path shaded by tall fuchsia. She heard him ask:

'The dogs are in the orchard, aren't they?'

'Yes.'

'Would you like me to fetch them? You don't want to go through the yard just now, do you? You'd rather go straight into the field?'

'Yes,' she agreed awkwardly, not looking at him. 'If you don't mind…'

'D'you want me to help you over the hedge first?'

Still she could not look at him. She bit back the retort 'When did I ever need help over the hedge?' and said instead, 'I'll be all right. Thanks for getting the dogs.'

CHAPTER 15

Breena turned away and hurried, every moment more quickly, through the cloying, dank-and-sweet scents of the overgrown garden, until she came out into the clear sunlight on the other side of the hedge. She was vaguely aware of a sense of comfort from the sudden full blaze of the sun's heat, but she did not stop to savour it. She began to make her way up the field, brooding to herself. Strange how in one year, one year out of all the years of her life, she could have come to feel that Maurice was something like a poem or a mountain! A part of her life she need not bother too much about, because it would always be there when she needed it… Well, that was all changed now.

She reached the top of the field. In utter weariness she sat down, by the turn of the pathway where she had walked last night. The sun was heavy on her eyelids; she let them droop until only a small half-circle of vivid green, with cloudy, shiny edges to it, came within her line of vision. Then her attention was caught by the glint of another colour. She leaned forward and pulled. She found herself looking at a small sprig of toad-flax in her hand. She stared at it. A creation of such delicacy and complexity could only be viewed with simple wonder… She stroked it and saw, with an easing of a pang inside her, that she had pulled it up from the root. She bent down and began to scratch at the place where it had been.

'Oh, God help me!' she prayed in sudden disgust at the

selfishness of her thoughts. 'God make me clear-sighted, generous. Make me help Maurice, with true friendship… '

Maurice came up with the dogs. 'What are you doing?' he asked her.

'I plucked this piece of toad-flax without thinking. I want to replant it.'

He dropped on one knee beside her and began to pat it gently into place. She watched him.

'It will need some water,' he said. She jumped up. It was a relief to have that excuse to jump up and move away. She ran a few yards to the right to where the cumar tinkled its small summer notes between high banks, and climbed down and filled her cupped hands. She had to come back a little more slowly, keeping her hands cupped tightly together.

'Will you hold its head up?' she asked Maurice as soon as she reached him. 'A day like today, it would scorch away if we let its head get wet.'

He did as she asked. Then, watching the water which she let dribble down into the root of the plant, he commented:

'You brought back more water than Fiona brought Diarmuid. I think it will live.'

'Yes, I think so. It's… it's a tough little plant.'

They stood up. There was an awkward silence.

'Look! I've muddied my hands,' she blurted out in sheer nervousness. They both looked down at her hands, which were a little stained with mud from pressing the wet root into the ground. 'I… I'd better wash them. Let's go to the cumar.'

They began to walk side by side, in silence, towards the stream. Breena could have wept, they were walking so slowly, like two old, old people, and there was such a distance between them, though they walked side by side. On this balmy summer's day too, when all around them the companionable hum of bees and friendly chirping of grasshoppers only emphasised their silence.

But at last they reached the banks of the cumar. The dogs had made it before them. Below in the shade they could see Bran lying down and Hippy frolicking by himself over the slimy stones. Breena jumped down to dabble her hands in the water. Maurice waited above.

When she came up again she found him standing very still where she had left him. Her glance met his the moment she straightened up. He said at once:

'Breena, I've obviously made a mistake. I shouldn't have talked to you as I did in the hut. I'm beginning to see now how selfish my arguments must have appeared in your eyes. To spend the day of Father's death declaring that because he was dead, and could advance my interests no further, I owed it to him, to *him*, to go off at once and seek my fortune elsewhere! All the same, Breena, as I see it, I have no choice in the matter. Things have happened as they have happened, and I must go… ' He stopped and waited. But for the moment she could find no words to answer him. She could only look at him, and she experienced a queer pang at the sight of him there before her. Afterwards she would always be able to see him with the sun on his bright hair, and his face smooth again, polished into the curves of a pharaoh's mask: the mask of the sun god. She would remember how she thought to herself that he already looked quite grown up, quite master of himself, a person right in every detail. And she believed that this outward look of being complete, finished, was not deceptive. Because of the talents Maurice had, that drew people around him wherever he went, and because of his happy temperament and the long spoiling of his growing up, he knew nothing of the ferment of self-doubt that had tormented Breena herself since she was a child. Maurice could happily call himself a fool, a clot, a clown. These words carried no sting for him, for the simple reason that they were words and not music. He had never been troubled by that fluidity of personality that made Breena seem to herself not one person, not 'Breena' as people believed and called her, but a succession of strangers under her skin. 'Breena, don't put up a wall between us. Be on my side! You've been so for so long now that I forget it could ever be otherwise. Oh what a damn mess I made of my heart-to-heart disclosures in the hut!'

'Maurice… listen. I know that… that you had to talk to somebody about this, in order to clear your own thoughts. I'm very pleased that you chose to talk to me. I can't pretend that I'm not surprised… Shocked even. But if this is what you want, if you feel sure you can carry it through, then… I'm ready now to congratulate you… Congratulations, Maurice, on reaching a brave, exciting decision… It must be right for you, otherwise… otherwise you'd never have thought of it, would you?'

Out of pride she smiled at him as she said the last words. For a moment he only looked back with a very dark, searching gaze, and then he took a step forward and caught up her hand and kissed it. Last summer, before he was ill, he had often tried to do that, and much more, but always in a boisterous, puppy-dog fashion that she utterly disdained. After that came his illness, with its inevitable sapping of vitality. Yet here and now, after all his wild talking, a thing that had seemed past praying for had happened: he kissed her hand and he performed that complicated, grown-up gesture in such a way that it had seemed absolutely the right thing to do. Afterwards he kept her hand in his, and she no longer felt the slightest impulse to draw it away. Instead she felt his touch go tingling up and up until it made a vibrating sweetness in the very heart of her.

It seemed to her that freshness had come back into the day. The sun was still very warm, but it was an early-morning warmth, refreshing and gay. The fence that was there at the edge of the field, the orchard fence and the gate, seemed a very long way off. They walked towards it very slowly, hand in hand. She no longer regretted this slowness. They talked together, but now she hardly knew whether she was feeling or talking, so curiously had the various parts of her nature fused together. She listened to Maurice's voice. She felt what he said, rather than heard it. Yet she was clearly conscious of what he was saying; she knew he was flattering her, with a new delightful, grown-up sort of flattery, that he had never been able to command before.

'... It was you who taught me what words mean, Breena. Before I got to know you I used to throw them about like stones, the way children do. But then I got to know you a little, and I saw how you despised me. So I started reading, and trying to write a few songs on my own, to go with my music. If I hadn't met you when I did, I can't imagine how my life would have gone. D'you remember three summers ago, when you called me the Fiddler of Dooney, and I astonished you the very next day by quoting the whole poem to you?'

She laughed; she laughed that he should remember such a thing. It was easy to laugh now. He smiled in sympathy, but said, 'You needn't laugh, Breena. I can remember most of that poem to this day... I remember the effect it had on me: *The good are always the merry, save by an evil chance...*'

So he went on until they came to the moss-covered gate that overlooked the yard. They stood a little back from the gate and looked down into the yard.

'Up here,' Maurice whispered, 'we're like Adam and Eve... peering down over the rim of the garden.'

'Maurice, why don't you come to Maurcappagh with us after all? Do come! Kitty particularly asked me to tell you, I mean as you...'

'Yes. I have a good idea how old Kit put it. She said I'd be much better off out of the way, didn't she? Well, didn't she?'

Breena only smiled at him.

'H'mm... I can see she did. And she may be right at that. After all, what good can I possibly do around here today? I'll tell you what I'll do...' his face lit up with a quick smile of inspiration, 'I'll go and see Uncle John about it. I'll tell him straight out that I want to go to Maurcappagh, and ask him if he has any objections. Nothing pleases

Uncle John better than the direct approach. And *his* approval will protect me from any backlash from Hugh or any of the others…'

Maurice was a decided favourite of Uncle John's; his view of him was therefore necessarily very different from Kitty's. They discussed the matter for some minutes, Breena a little wistfully. Where was Uncle John now, she wanted to know: in what room, with what company? How completely she had forgotten him during her talk with Maurice! How pitiful was his present situation, with so much of what was best of his life behind him, so much lost! And how could she, Breena, with all her life before her, ever dare to feel sorry for herself?

Thoughts of him were painful. She made a resolution to do her utmost to help and comfort him as soon as the funeral was over and she could be with him again. In that way she was able to assuage her conscience, and put him out of her mind for the present.

Time was getting on. Breena had arranged to meet Thady around two; Maurice must seek out Uncle John. They parted, Maurice to go through the yard, Breena to run down the field with the dogs. Maurice's last words were:

'Don't start for Maurcappagh without me unless I phone. I'm sure Uncle John will give me his blessing. He's no dog in the manger. I'll be round to the house as soon as I can.'

CHAPTER 16

As Breena made her way back into the town the shops were just beginning to close. There were few people about. More than once, however, she noted some inquisitive body who stepped out to the edge of the pavement at sight of her, in expectation of a chat. But she made sure that the wind of her hurry reached these people before she did and blew out their curiosity. By the time she was sweeping past they had resigned themselves to a quick greeting only.

Indeed, the very idea of engaging in small talk or gossip with anybody at the moment sickened her. Her mind was full of conversation with Maurice. She thought too of Kitty, and it was a strange thing, she felt something like envy for Kitty. She could not help remembering that time, scarcely twelve months ago as yet, when she herself felt just as sure as Kitty did now that she had solved the whole problem of what life was about. She had confidently believed then that she would always be able to look about her and state happily: 'Life is beautiful; I have found it so, because I have had the courage to make it so!' But where was she now, where had all her certainties vanished to? All gone, swallowed up in the depths of the blueness of the sky. That same sky that had lured her senses on a summer's day hardly more than one short year ago, when she looked up from her desk in the stuffy classroom and saw through the open window, over the drifts of chalk dust, a blueness that filled all the upper part of the window. From where she sat it looked like a mountain, sparkling blue in its distance. Deep inside her she felt something stir to the challenge of it, and she knew then that she would never be a nun. She knew it at once and irrevocably, but not without a feeling of loss, and a sense of regret and loneliness. It was these same feelings, of loneliness, and uncertainty, and loss, that had been stirred within her again this morning, and that she wished to shake off now as soon as possible. She looked to Maurcappagh to do this.

She reached the house, tied up the dogs, collected her swimming things from her room, and went into the kitchen to get some food to take out to Maurcappagh. Hannah was nowhere about but alas! the bowl of breakfast left-overs, more shrunken and shrivelled than ever, was still simmering on the stove. There was no help for it; Breena had promised to take this food with her. She wrapped the bowl round and round in newspaper and then went into the dairy (a larder still called 'dairy' from the days when cows were kept at the Filemoyn farm) to get some home-made bread, butter, apples and milk to go with it. She heard before she was ready Thady's signal from outside, a quick 'Toot, toot, toot!' on the horn. She hurried out to tell him that Maurice also was coming with them, expecting some expression of surprise at the news. But all she got from Thady was a stolid, 'Is that so, now?'

Then Maurice came hurrying round the corner. Somewhere behind the high wooden side-gate a blackbird was singing. All the dreamy happiness of his song suddenly filled Breena's heart as she got into the car.

CHAPTER 17

The cove of Maurcappagh lay directly behind the town, divided from it by the range of the Maurcappagh mountains. It had to be approached, first along the main road north out of the town, and then by a white dirt track that branched off westwards through meadows, moorland, and bogland towards Oisin Pass. This Pass was the only way through the Maurcappagh range on level ground – the only possible way through for a car. But there were various other pathways and tracks that a hardy walker from the town could follow over the shoulders of the Maurcappagh range, between the highest peaks, up and up, and then down again, into the cove at Maurcappagh.

Today, as Thady had predicated to Breena earlier on, men and women and children of all ages were out in the small fields on either side of the road, tossing the hay in the sun. Most of these stopped their work and leaned on their forks for a moment to greet Thady as he passed by. Thady saluted them all with his usual regal gesture, slowly raising his right hand to the level of his ear. Once every five minutes or so he took the trouble to slow the car almost to a stop, lean out of the window, and shout an answer to some questions from a special old neighbour or friend. The others he acknowledged by merely waving his hand in the air – waving them back as it were to the dolts and numbskulls who had thought them up.

Now they were driving up under the curve of the mountain

| 131

range, along the edge of the valley, only a mile or so now from the Oisin Pass. Legend had it that the Fenians: Fionn himself with his two dogs Bran and Sgeoiling; his son Oisin; Osgar the poet, Oisin's son; loud-mouthed Cuculainn, down here on a visit to show off his skill with the long spear, and a great hosting of others, had often ridden through this pass. It was a dismal place, 'a place of stones', as it was often described in the old stories. Except at high noon in the very height of summer the twisted shoulder of the mountain above blocked out the sunshine. Now as they turned into the pass a cold blast of air came in through the open windows. Not so very long ago, only an hour ago the great boulders that lined the road would reckon it, a battle had been fought here.

The line from last night's poem came again into Breena's head; *All things remain in God*. She began to repeat to herself the second verse of the poem, all of which had seemed to burn itself into her memory by this time:

> *Banners choke the sky;*
> *Men-at-arms tread;*
> *Armoured horses neigh*
> *Where the great battle was*
> *In the narrow pass: Men come, men go,*
> *All things remain in God...*

But this had been no great battle, only an ambush. No banners, and horses on one side only. Not one of the men on foot had escaped. Breena, with the poem on her mind, tried nevertheless to put aside the grand imagery of the poem and think to herself what it must have been like to die as those cornered men had died.

The road widened. They came out of the pass and the cove of Maurcappagh lay before them; small green fields sloping away towards the heart-lifting glitter of the sea. Thady drew in under the shoulder of the mountain to the left, to the wide shelf of rock where Uncle John always parked when they came out here to count the cattle. They got out of the car. Breena breathed in deeply. The tang of the sea breezes up here, at the first savouring of it, always made her feel light-headed with happiness.

But now Thady, who was sniffing at the breeze like a suspicious animal, muttered abruptly, 'It has too much freedom in it!' Breena was struck by this remark. She took another deep breath and caught a sniff of that freedom. Wildness it was, the smell of the sea's wildness… It gave her an insight into the kind of life Thady led, into the kind of life she wanted for herself. She shaded her eyes with her hand to look out across the sea. Then the word Kitty had spoken came suddenly into her mind – 'Shopgirl!' On the instant she was back with Kitty by the window. The sea and the valley below her were blotted out.

'Breena come and sit here.'

It was Thady speaking to her. She started and turned round. Already Thady had settled himself on one of the boulders that the glaciers of a cold time, long ago had left strewn everywhere about here. Maurice was crossing over to sit down beside him.

'What are you doing?' she asked them. 'Aren't you going to come with me to count the… '

'We're counting as hard as we can,' Thady assured her. He gestured towards the left, where some cattle could be seen. 'I've got as far as six. How far have you got, Maurice?'

Maurice hesitated. He turned to look at Breena. It was a piercing look he gave her. His eyes looked very dark now against the glitter of the sea and brightness of the valley below. And though Breena realised that he could have no idea of this new strange darkness of his look, a mere darkness of contrast, yet the intentness of his glance was new too, and thrilled her. He began to pat the boulder beside him. He invited her, 'Come and sit here.'

But then all at once he seemed to become aware of the way he was staring at her. He blinked and turned away. She found herself pushing excitedly against an invisible current that swirled from him to herself and back again. The tensions of that current kept her quite still; she could not choose but remain where she was. She muttered, 'I don't want to sit down at the moment.' Then Thady's cheerful voice broke through the stress of her feelings and she looked towards him almost with surprise. It was a moment or two before what he was saying made sense to her.

'Ten. That's ten I've counted already. How about you, Maurice?'

Maurice could just about be heard murmuring in agreement, 'Yes… ten.'

Thady looked round and gave Breena a subtle smile. She looked back at him hard, and then looked towards Maurice.

'Thady! I believe you've no intention of counting the cattle. You're just playing at… '

But Thady was again consulting with Maurice. 'How many can you see now? Fifteen, did you say? Ah yes, over there – I can see him now… '

'What wonderful eyesight you have, Thady,' Breena commented. 'You can see round hillocks and through stone fences.'

Thady ignored her. 'Where did you say Number Twenty was?' he asked Maurice. 'Oh, yes! Up there at the very top of the field. Inside Diarmuid's bed.'

Breena looked up to the mouth of the cave where, according to folklore, Diarmuid and Grainne had spent their last week together. From here it looked like a diamond-shaped patch of shadow on the sunny, furze-covered mountain.

'There are no cattle up there,' she asserted.

'You're wrong,' Thady said cautiously and politely, but firmly. 'There's one beast lying up there under the lee of the rock, enjoying the shade.' He pointed to the exact place, very helpfully.

She looked up again, and this time thought she could discern a thickening of the shadow towards the right side where Thady was pointing. She sighed in exasperation.

'*He* can see us, at any rate,' Thady went on. 'He's watching us very closely. He's trying to stare us down, I imagine.'

At that moment the tears came into Breena's eyes, she was looking so hard. Maurice and Thady kept glancing at her. Now they caught her trying to blink the tears away.

'He's upset you!' Thady exclaimed. 'That beast up there has upset you, with the ignorant stare of him.'

She held her tongue. Her sight had cleared again. Now the passing of a cloud-shadow over the cave gave an illusion of movement. For a moment she believed in the animal up there. She blinked and dropped her glance before his glittering beast's stare.

Then she looked round at Thady. He had taken out his pipe and was stretching his legs, saying to Maurice in a tone of pious satisfaction:

'Well, that's the twenty cattle accounted for!'

Now Breena saw that Thady had turned back and was looking at her in a significant way. As soon as she met his glance he nodded in Maurice's direction. She looked more carefully at Maurice then, and saw that he had taken his flute out of his pocket and was putting it together. She was very surprised, and looked questioningly at Thady. But Thady, who loved music, was already leaning back against the boulder behind him. It was obvious that he, at any rate, thought no question necessary.

Maurice began to play. After a few moments Breena too was able to rid herself of her surprise. It no longer seemed wrong to her that Maurice should want to make music today, out here. Now she believed that he had begun to play not only because this was the gift he had – his best way of expressing what he felt – but also because he wanted to put them at their ease. He had no wish to spoil the day for Thady and herself. She selected her own boulder and sat back and looked up at the sky. The high, sweet music seemed as pure as the blue of the sky. It was as wild as the crying of the curlew and the plover. After a while, as she continued to gaze upwards, the colour of the sky gave way before her look. There was no longer any blue up there, only softness and light. She went into a dream then. She forgot that it was music she heard, a sound made by a flute. It was her own voice calling out freely as she soared and plummeted like a kestrel in that brightness above. She imagined that she was free at last; a wild, free creature circling up there beyond the reach of the keenest glance.

Then the sound changed. It was some moments before she realised that the music had stopped, and that it was only the memory of it that teased her. She sat up quickly. She ached to hear it again. But she was very put out to find both Thady and Maurice looking back at her and smiling. To speak became a necessity then. The words were like an armour she instantly put on. She cried at Maurice:

'Oh, I didn't want you to stop. I wasn't even sure, until I sat up, that you *had* stopped.'

'Listen to that, now!' Thady said. He turned to Maurice. 'Did you ever in your life hear such subtle flattery?'

'No, indeed.' But, flattery or otherwise, Maurice's bright look thanked Breena for it.

' 'Twould be impossible, of course.' Thady stood up. 'There's only room for one Breena in the world, and we have the good fortune of her here. Well… I think we'd best be going. We can't afford to waste any more time today.'

CHAPTER 18

From the Pass the road ran down a fairly gentle slope, the ridge of an eskar it was said, for a couple of miles or so towards the centre of the valley. From there it wound for about a mile beside the loops of the Maur river, on level ground, before plunging again for the last dizzy half-mile to the sea. But to get to the jetty and the level fields that formed a natural terrace behind it, where Thady's boat was kept during the summer, it was necessary to leave the road at this point, where it petered out amongst the cliffs and rock shelvings, and follow a track that climbed again up to the eastern slope of the valley.

Today, since they knew that young Jamie Cappagh was home from the States, Maurice wished to run up to the Cappagh house and ask Jamie if he wanted to come out fishing with them. Thady approved of this. He liked young Jamie. But in order to save time – 'Not to let the best of the day go by,' as he put it – he decided to drive Maurice up to the house. This suited Breena very well. She had fully intended to get a swim in sometime, either before they went out in the boat or afterwards. But what better time than now, when she felt so unpleasantly warm, and the tide was so full and smooth and blue around the jetty? She declined Thady's invitation to go with them up to Sean Mor's house.

'I'll be bound to see Sean Mor afterwards,' she excused herself. 'You know he always comes down to help us haul up the boat, and to have a look at the catch.'

Swimming was a passion with her at the moment. Hardly a day went by that she did not somehow contrive to get out to the sea; either here at Maurcappagh, or at the Yellow Strand or Filedearg. Now she leapt out of the car by the jetty, leaving Thady and Maurice to drive slowly up along the steep boreen to the house.

She ran down the grassy slope and leapt on to the level concrete head of the jetty; and then stood a moment looking about her with a feeling of the deepest, keenest, happiness. The sun so warm. The sea, so full, such a tamed, smooth-skinned, chortling creature, dappled with many colours. And everywhere silence – the deep silence of high summer, that the cries of the sea-gulls only intensified.

She climbed up into the hollow rock behind the jetty that she called her dressing-room, where she could hear the water groaning and complaining in the cave underneath while she undressed.

She pulled on her cap slowly, hesitating a little, knowing that the run she made when she turned and jumped down from the rock must end in a plunge from the jetty. She counted up to five, and felt her heart-beats keep time with her counting. Then she turned and ran. The shock of coldness when she dived seemed to jolt her right outside the limits of her own being, so that she became the milky, copper-green water that surrounded her on every side. As usual, she swam under water as long as her breath held. Then when she came to the surface and turned over, panting hard, and lay on her back and looked up into the sky, she still found it impossible to assess what she was; where the limits of her own being ended and all that she could see about her began.

She loved swimming so much, and knew a great many strokes. Now to warm herself she went into them one after another, using first her arms, then her shoulder and stomach muscles, then her legs, sometimes rolling over on her back and resting her hands on her hips and kicking as hard as she could, feeling perfectly at home and at ease here between these two immensities of sea and sky.

From where she lay she could see the trees around Sean Mor's house and Thady's car parked a little below. Every now and again she glanced up there. At last she thought she caught a movement between the trees. They were coming back! She turned then and made for the jetty, flattening herself in the water and reaching out as far as she could with her arms.

As she hauled herself up on the jetty, her numbed legs doubled up under her. Then as she fumbled with her clothes she could see her fingers moving, taking up her things, but had no feeling of what she was doing. Then as she picked up her dress her watch happened to slip out of the pocket. She caught it up and glanced at it and exclaimed in surprise. She had been in the water nearly three quarters of an hour! Three quarters of an hour, and she faithfully promised Uncle John that she would never stay in for more than twenty minutes at a time… She shook the watch and stared at it. It was certainly going. And it always kept good time.

It took her some time to dress, her fingers were so numbed. But she finished it at last. Then she walked out along the jetty to look up once more at Sean Mor's house. The car was still there.

She still felt very cold. She shivered in her thin dress as she stood there on the jetty. And then the idea came to her, why not run up to meet the car? Running up that boreen would certainly warm her! No sooner had she thought of it than she began to run, first up the grassy slope behind the jetty, and then along the sandy, stony boreen. She had climbed to within a field of the house; she was panting and stumbling with breathlessness when her blood came up. She felt the first surge of warm blood to her face and arms. Only then did the exhilarations of the swim take her over. At once she stood absolutely still. Every shape and colour of the valley about her she experienced with the vividness of pure joy. She began to run again. Only by a run that kept pace with that one drifting cloud above could she express her feeling of unity with everything she saw.

She reached the car as Thady came out of the house above.

Maurice followed behind him. As they came closer she studied the expressions on their faces.

'I know what you two have been doing!' She looked accusingly from Maurice to Thady. 'Sitting in there in the house, enjoying a delicious cool drink, with no thought at all for me waiting below on the jetty, half-dying of thirst.'

Maurice said rather too quickly, 'We've only just got back. We…'

'We had to go up to the top meadow for Sean and young Jamie,' Thady came in to explain ponderously. 'They were out at the hay like everybody else.'

'Do you want something to drink?'

This was a new voice. Breena looked up and saw Jamie, 'young Jamie', standing a little above them, at the edge of the flagged yard outside his house. She fervently hoped that he had only just come out. Usually she felt very much at ease with Jamie, and talked to him freely as she did to Thady and Maurice. But now she found voice only to refuse the drink (the icy waters of the cove had more than taken her thirst away) and to ask him, not without some awkwardness, if he intended to come fishing with them.

'You know there's nothing I'd like better,' Jamie said with regret in his tone. 'But I must go back to the hay. My father will be wondering already what's keeping me.'

'Oh, I'm sorry,' Breena sympathised with him, then she turned to Thady and Maurice and murmured sweetly, 'And you two must go back into the house and finish your drinks, mustn't you? Well, go ahead. Take no notice of me. I'll just sit here by the car and wait.'

They went. But they showed by their gait a consciousness of the moral victory she had scored over them. When they were out of sight she opened the car door and took out the bag of food she had so hastily prepared earlier. Then after a moment's thought she sat in the car to eat it. After the dig she had just given them, Thady and Maurice could hardly dare to be long. She may as well get comfortable in the position in which she would have to continue eating.

She had had no breakfast, and the swim had sharpened her appetite to the point where she could scarcely wait to unwrap the bread. Just before she raised it to her mouth she eyed it with the purest appreciation of its beauty. Then something prompted her to unroll the dish of breakfast left-overs out of its mummy-like bandage of newspapers. Strange! The savoury smell that began to ooze out from under the last of the newspaper wrappings quite astonished her. She plunged in her hand and pulled out a couple of sausages and sprinkled them with salt. She was chewing hard, with the utmost satisfaction, when she looked up and saw Maurice running down the path from the house. She reached across and opened the door for him.

She saw from his glance as he got in that he too found the bread and dish of breakfast food very attractive.

'Like some?'

He nodded very positively, she gave him some bread, and passed him the dish to help himself from, and put some salt into his hand. He took huge bites and chewed mightily for some time. She passed him a second piece of bread.

'God isn't it good?' he said at last. 'This is the first food I've tasted today, do you know that?'

It was on the tip of her tongue to make a similar boast, but she stopped herself in time. She had done and said enough for the moment. She passed him the last of the breakfast food. Then she saw Thady making his way down to the car and she picked up her bottle of milk and timed it so that she was having a long drink out of the bottle just as he opened the door. The somewhat unpleasant lukewarm flavour of the milk was completely compensated for by the gleam of guilt she caught in Thady's eye.

But then suddenly she became quite conscience-stricken.

'Oh, Thady! We haven't saved you any food. We've eaten it all up!'

Thady's glance met hers in the mirror. 'Don't worry your head about that, girl. I've just had something I like a lot better than food.'

Maurice leaned towards Breena, and mouthed: 'He's had *four* glasses of Guinness. Or maybe five. Maybe Jamie gave him another one after I left.'

Breena mouthed back in consternation; 'Four? Five? D'you think he'll be able to manage…'

Thady had sharp ears. 'Yes,' he came in now, 'I'll be able to manage the boat. And I'll be able to manage my crew too…'

CHAPTER 19

In summer Thady's boat was kept on planks in the level field about a hundred yards from the back of the jetty. Sean Mor shared Thady's boat with him. He had the use of it whenever he wanted during the week, and in return came down when rough weather threatened and hauled it further up along the fields, into shelter from the gales and far above the water line.

They reached the jetty. While Thady and Breena were getting oars and rowlocks and tackle and other gear out of the car, Maurice went up to place the rollers in the correct position in the path of the boat. Then they eased the boat along the planks until it rested on the first roller. Getting the boat completely off the platform and placing it evenly on the rollers required a few minutes' intense effort. Thady on one side was matched against Maurice on the other, with Breena pushing or pulling wherever Thady yelled at her to go. But once the boat had been balanced on the rollers it had only to be guided downhill into the water.

At the end they were all running. Breena felt keenly that moment of ease and relaxation when the bows of the boat splashed into the water and at last it was afloat. Then Thady clutched at the gunwale to swing himself in. The boat dipped almost to the water's edge, it seemed to be drifting away. Still Thady stood at an incongruous angle, both his feet still planted on the jetty. Only at times like this, in his indecision and clumsiness, did he show up as an old man. Breena held her breath. But then he had made it, he was in. She loosened her own hurtful grip on the stern of the boat. Now Maurice gave the boat one last shove to clear it of the jetty. Thady pushed the oars into place in the rowlocks and brought the boat broadsides round to the steps, so that they could both step down into it.

Thady's eyes were on the gannets circling around the point ahead.

'The place is alive with fish. Pay out the lines now, bit by bit.'

The jetty was half-way out along the cove, on the right as you looked in from the sea. Sitting in the bows Breena looked back at the small fields that made an uneven line of green along the basalt cliffs. She could see a footpath following the shelves and slopings of the rocks down to the water's edge. But it was only for an hour or so at low tide every day that the shingle on the beach was uncovered. Even on a hot day like today in the height of summer it looked dank and chilly down there.

They paid out their lines gradually under Thady's strict supervision. 'Easy now, there's weeds under us here!'; 'hand over hand, take yer time!'; 'Pull back now, ye'll be catching one another in a minute.' Maurice winked at Breena. The change in Thady's mild and reflective personality as soon as he stepped into a boat and there were only its flimsy planks between him and the sea, always called for a few moments' calm reflection on the part of his crew.

Thady had been born in this valley, and had grown up here. Both his grandfathers, his father, and his uncles has been fishermen. The sea was in his blood, not as something romantic and enjoyable, but as a discipline. He knew that the sea was a thing to be feared. You braved it in a frail craft for one reason only, to get food. You had to school yourself to indifference to all but the practical issues involved. Views were for the amateur, the holiday-maker, the habitual belittler of the sea. Stoicism was what you had to learn. You might admire the scenery, but only in silence. You might hope for a large catch; you kept the hope to yourself.

In a boat, Thady was always telling them, there could only be one master. And it was certainly that way. His mastership went far beyond the mere giving of orders. There was a mystique of the sea he made them practise. Everything that was pleasant to do was forbidden; trailing your fingers in the water, singing, gazing round at the landscape, and even counting the catch. Yet Breena respected Thady. There was something in him she knew she could learn from. In every small facet of his life he was upheld by ritual. Taking down the shutters in the shop, putting out the keys, entering a sale in his books, starting his car, rowing his boat, paying out his lines: all these were done in a well-tried, ceremonious way that gave them significance beyond the moment, and even a kind of beauty. He was a man very strong in himself.

Now while they paid out the lines Thady leaned back on the oars, sending them skimming over the water with slow, slow strokes that yet had a joyful rhythm to them. Breena counted to herself as she watched him: the dip, the pull, the pause, and then the dip again. She was trying to absorb the motions into her own limbs as she counted, letting the harmony of them seep into her until it became second nature. She was very keen to master this ancient art of rowing. So far her rowing was unrhythmic and therefore both bad work and ugly to watch.

Maurice sat rather tensely, arms outstretched to support his lines, waiting for the first bite. Always at the beginning there were some painful moments when they feared that the fish would refuse to bite that day. To reassure them, Thady looked round and repeated his first remark:

'The place is alive with fish!'

'Yes. But maybe they've all just decided to go for a siesta,' Maurice murmured.

Gannets circled over their heads, calling out to one another in their beautiful, free voices.

'It's swarming with fish,' Thady asserted again.

No breeze caught them here. The sun was directly overhead. It was very warm in the boat. When Thady stopped rowing they seemed under a spell, glued to the water. Then the line in Breena's left hand suddenly came alive, tried hard in fact to leap out of it. Almost at the same time her right-hand line did the same thing. Even while she instinctively tightened her grip the tugs came again, hasty, unmistakeable. She looked up to call Maurice to help her and caught on his face a peculiar expression. He had bent his head and drawn his two hands together; he seemed to be listening to the lines he held. Before she could speak to him he had turned back to say something to Thady.

By now Thady had boarded the oars and gone back to sit in the stern. He had begun to pay out his own lines. Breena heard what Maurice said to him, and gave up all hope of help from Maurice. She was already winding the left-hand line around her foot to keep an even pull on it, when Thady called to her:

'Tie up your lines, Breena, and pull in one of Maurice's.'

But she was too occupied even to attempt an answer. By the weight on her lines she knew she had caught something good: she hoped two fine plump pollock. But Thady expected obedience from his crew. He called sharply:

'Did you hear me? Damn it girl, he'll lose…'

All the hurry of the moment flared in her head. 'Damn it! How can I? With my toes?'

She saw them both swerve round in surprise. Then Thady had grasped it. In a moment he had pulled off his shoes. His bare shanks gleamed as he came down the boat, his feet gripping the boards sure and swift. 'No moving about in boats!' was a cardinal rule of Thady's. But of course he could always break his own rules. Maurice handed him one line, Breena another. He sat down by Maurice and began to haul in steadily hand over hand, with the same sure rhythm he had when he was rowing. Breena pulled impatiently and unevenly, spattering water over her dress, not winding the line on the frame but letting it fall in thin coils to the floor.

'What? What?' she cried to Thady, who was saying something to her, trying to get her to do things in a better way. She came to the end of the line and began to swing the fish in so high that they gasped and shouted out that she had lost it. But it was safe in the boat. It was a pollock as she had hoped. She was already paying out her line again and taking over the other one. The fever of the sea had come on her. It was on them all. Thady went back to the stern. Breena was fishing now with one line always around one foot while she hauled in the other. Then the heat of the moment passed. Quietness, a cessation of action as well as speech, came through to her, and she looked up. Maurice and Thady were no longer fishing. They were sitting in silence now, but from the angle of their bodies it was obvious that they had just been speaking together.

'What's the matter?' she asked quickly.

Thady gave a nod in the direction of the jetty. She looked round and saw Sean Mor and Jamie standing in there at the head of the jetty, looking towards them, obviously waiting. She exclaimed:

'Oh! It can't be time to go back already!'

Then she saw that the sun was quite low in the sky. Thady's glance met hers as she turned round again. He looked down significantly in the boat. She was astonished to see the whole floor covered deep in fish. They seemed to be heaped five or six deep in places. She had known of course that they were doing well, but only now realised the full extent of their success. There were almost as many fish as if they had used two boats and a seine. Then she realised that her own right-hand line was still out. She began to haul it in, doing her best now that Thady and Maurice were watching to be very steady and rhythmic in her movements. But as it came up to the boat she saw something at the end of it, making no fuss at all, a little mackerel. He panted in her hand as she freed him from the hook, as gently as he could. She looked down at him. He was slender and long, beautifully made. But he was bleeding from the mouth. As she looked at him some memory stirred, some blood-memory of menace and brutality. At once she understood intimately what it was like to be that fish. His plight became her own. Swiftly she leaned over the gunwale and placed him back in the water. He sank immediately out of sight. She could not put it to herself that he swam; he just plummeted like a stone. She sat up and asked Thady:

'Will he recover, d'you think?'

'Faith, I couldn't tell. I never yet met a man who understood the ailments of fish.'

There was no sympathy in Thady's voice. Whimsical actions had no appeal whatever for him.

'Oh, but he was such a skinny little thing!' Breena coaxed.

Maurice was smiling. Evidently he thought it best to change the subject. He remarked to Thady:

'I've seldom seen the pollock come so far in, why d'you think that is?'

It behoved any person who sought Thady's respect to notice such things. They discussed the matter at some length while they wound the lines carefully back on the frames, the way Thady liked them. Then, as Thady once more placed the oars into the rowlocks, he summed up their achievement:

'Faith, there'll be no hunger where we are for some time!'

Besides the normal pleasure in a good catch Thady also had the traditional fisherman's appreciation of fish. Fish was still for him the preserver of life, the ultimate repast after the harvest failed.

It was always on the way home that Breena and Maurice got a chance to practise their rowing. But today Thady made no offer to hand over the oars. Sean Mor and Jamie were waiting, and they had come out only a little way – just beyond the headland. Steering a straight course between here and the jetty was always the most difficult part of the journey back. They used no rudder. Tides and currents had to be judged. Only Thady did this well. Breena and

Maurice exchanged glances of disappointment when Thady leaned back on the oars, making it clear that he intended to keep them to himself today. But they kept quiet about it. This was Thady's kingdom.

In this pure sparkling light the water looked very clear and smooth as they neared the jetty. Breena could see the ridged sand far below when she looked over the side of the boat. She glanced at Maurice. By the absorbed look on his face as he leaned over and trailed his fingers in the water she guessed that he too was dying for a swim. Suddenly she gave up her own longing, it was a great ease to do so, and concentrated on his. She said to him over Thady's head:

'Why don't you go in? Nobody can quarrel with your going in today. You promised to wait for "exceptionally warm" weather. And maybe we won't get another day like today again this year.'

He looked up. In his eyes, as their glances met, she saw the eager light of acceptance and anticipation. He muttered so quickly as to be almost incoherent. 'I suppose... Yes, Jamie and myself could go in from the rocks... not more than five minutes.'

And then they both looked quickly at Thady, expecting some comment from him. But Thady only kept evenly on with his rowing. There was nothing in his expression to show that he had heard them. Breena found this very provoking. She said to Maurice:

'After all the lessons I've had from Thady on how to hold my tongue and mind my own business, it's a wonder I'm not a monster of reticence by this time!'

But Thady found this too unworthy of comment. He was looking over his shoulder, using first one oar and then the other, as he steered his course for the jetty. Every action made it clear that he had no time for any chatter or nonsense. Maurice put on a very serious expression and cautioned Breena in a half-whisper;

'Stop wagging your tongue so hard, girl! Can't you see that the tide's on the turn? A mere tongue's flip could upset the boat at this moment.'

Breena looked round. The jetty stood gaunt and high above them now as they came in. But still the waves swept the outermost, lowest verge of it. The jetty came too far out into the cove to rise clear of them, except during the spring tides. Thady brought the boat in smartly on the crest of a wave. Breena from her seat in the bows jumped first, then Maurice further down, splashing himself a bit. Then Sean Mor and Jamie came to their aid. All together they held the boat steady against the sucking-out of the tide while Thady lurched and floundered out. The next wave lifted the boat and they carried it as far as they could up the jetty.

In the ordinary way it was a hard struggle to get the boat from this position on to the level field at the back of the jetty. But today they had young Jamie's help and were buoyed up by the excitement of the large catch and the intoxicating quality of the day. Inch by inch they pushed it up. Breena and Sean Mor gave them all the help they could. Thady himself was red in the face from talking and pushing at the same time. At last the level ground was reached and they had to run to the bows of the boat and pull with all their might. Then the boat, water, fish and all, was back on the platform.

Breena's glance met Maurice's. 'Now, your swim!' she mouthed at him. But then another thought struck her and she cried out in sudden alarm, 'But no, no! You must wait a bit. You must cool off before you go into the water.'

Then she looked round self-consciously, thinking that everybody must have heard this outburst, and be staring at her now. But in the general hubbub it had passed unnoticed except by Maurice. Thady, with his sleeves rolled up to his shoulder, had plunged his hand in under the fish to raise the floorboards and release the plug. Sean Mor and Jamie stood side by side discussing the catch. Now and again one of them stooped down and caught up a particular fish and examined it more closely.

Reassured, Breena called across to Maurice, 'Let's fetch the bags.'

They went together to the car to fetch the pile of canvas bags they always hopefully brought for the fish. While they were there Breena handed over her towel. Maurice placed it round his neck. He said nothing. He seemed paler than usual, in spite of the hours they had spent in the sun. But the want of colour in his face was made up for by his eyes. They spoke to Breena in a language that was far more telling than any words. Suddenly she smiled, with whole-hearted participation in what he was feeling and looking forward to. She urged him:

'You must go off at once. This very minute. Leave the bags to me. I'll take them back. And I'll give Jamie the nod to join you.'

With that, and knowing that in his present mood he was only capable of doing what he was told, she lifted the pile of bags and ran off with them to the boat. There, Thady and Sean were already sorting out the fish. Large pollock in one pile, medium and small in another, the same with the mackerel, and the few white trout and flounders and so on in piles of their own. She went up to Jamie and said a few words in his ear. The next moment she had the satisfaction of seeing him slip away to join Maurice.

For some minutes Thady and Sean were too absorbed in sorting out the fish to notice that Jamie and Maurice were missing. Breena did her best to get the various piles of fish quickly stowed away into their separate bags. It was work she hated. The staring eyes of the dead fish, their coldness to the touch, the fine clean shape of them, made for quickness, for life, the smell of the bags, her own feeling of being over-heated; all of it made her head ache. And today there were far too many fish. She picked up a large pollock that was still alive and thrashed its tail and wriggled its body in her hand. She gave a small shriek and dropped it.

Thady caught sight of the pollock knocking itself about on the ground in terrible, futile spasms. He came quickly round to Breena's side, picked up the fish, and in a business-like, unconcerned manner, struck its head three or four times against the bows of the boat. And then, uncertain as to which bag it should go into, he passed it into

Breena's reluctant hands. It was bleeding, and still convulsed with the strange power of life that was in it.

She had had enough. This sorting out of fish, this putting them into bags, was what Thady and Sean enjoyed. Well, let them get on with it, then. Without any explanation she turned away and walked swiftly down the slope towards the jetty. Down there at least she could take off her shoes and paddle, she could dip her arms in the water as far as the shoulder, she could splash her face and neck. Soon she was making the last leap on to the dank, pebble-strewn sand below.

CHAPTER 20

Sometime later, when Breena re-joined the party by the boat, she found all the fish tucked neatly away within the proper bags, Jamie & Maurice sitting on the grass in high good humour, and Thady and Sean Mor just back from splashing their faces and washing their hands at the jetty steps. Sean Mor, his face still glistening with water, was rolling up the overalls he had worn over his Sunday suit while sorting out the fish.

It had already been arranged that Sean was to come in to town with them in Thady's car, to visit his wife Norah, who had recently been seriously ill. She was still in hospital in the town, Hugh's hospital, but now very definitely on the mend. And spend some time at the wake. Later young Jamie would also go in to attend the wake and later still, probably in the early hours of the morning, he would drive his father home. But now, as far as the immediate future, the next hour or so, was concerned, there were two hills that Thady's car took great exception to on the road that led out of this valley.

Usually when Breena and Maurice came out here to Maurcappagh with Thady they got out of the car and walked up those two hills. Quite often they also had to heave to and help the old car along with an encouraging bout of pushing, shoving, and shushing. Now today they felt sure that the old car would splutter out under the burden of Sean Mor, who was probably double their

| 153

combined weight, on the very first yard of the first of those hills. So they looked at one another, and with Sean Mor between them started off walking, determined to get as far as they could on the way to the Pass before Thady overtook them.

The sandy track sloped downhill for a while, as far as the bridge over the Maur river. It was quite pleasant to be walking now. The cool of the evening had set in. Breena as she walked plucked some of the young bells, that the bees had not yet got at, from the fuchsia hedge that bordered the track and sucked the nectar from them. She was very interested to hear Maurice ask Sean Mor the question that had occurred to herself earlier on:

'Jamie speaks as if he intends to settle down at home for some time. I suppose you're very pleased?'

Maurice spoke in Irish, the language Sean Mor could best respond to. In English he was awkward and slow, even clownish. The phrases he used, and his accent, took the dignity from his height and fine-boned face. But in Irish he was fluent and sure. He spoke a pure, aristocratic, sensitive language that made the history of their family – handed down by word of mouth only for nearly four hundred years, since the last Cappagh who could read and write – a thing to question and inquire into, rather than mock at. Now he said with supreme conviction in answer to Maurice:

'Yes. I'm certainly very pleased. He'll have no luck if he decides to go away again from the valley. None of the Cappaghs who've ever left it made good.'

Maurice laughed and said something light in reply. But Breena thought of Thady, and then of Sean's other sons, his brothers and sisters, his and Thady's uncles and aunts; all the Cappaghs who had gone away to different cities, how they must bake and broil on the pavements of those inland cities! Had they got what they went away for? And if so, why had none of them come back to boast about it? Only Thady had come back, and now Young Jamie.

This summer Breena had reached a stage in her life when she

found immense satisfaction in getting into conversation with a man like Sean Mor. When she was a child, after she first came to live at Uncle John's, this man Sean Mor had profoundly impressed her. She had thought him then a man addicted to silence. He had no command of small talk. Whenever she came out to Maurcappagh in those days, she found him always thoughtful and kind in such matters as taking her out in the boat with him or fishing from the rocks – matters of gigantic importance then – but always silent. It was this heroic silence of his against the background of sea and mountains out here at Maurcappagh that made her see him when she was a child as a figure from the old myths: a man of the same stamp as Fionn MacCumhaill, or Oisin, or Cuchulainn himself.

But now Breena was nearly eighteen. Her Irish had improved by leaps and bounds since she came to live at Uncle John's. Whenever she found herself in Sean Mor's company nowadays it became a very enjoyable challenge to make him talk. By now she had studied him well; she knew how to engage his interest. She was therefore able to seize immediately on his remark about Jamie and the bad luck of the Cappaghs to ask him an irresistible question about one of the Cappaghs of his grandfather's time. She was delighted to see his face light up at the mere mention of that long-dead Cappagh's name. The next minute she looked across at Maurice and gave him a quick little wink of triumph.

By now Sean Mor had warmed to their questions and was doing most of the talking. There was nothing modern about Sean Mor. He made no pretence of believing that Breena and Maurice, simply because they had spent more years at school than he had ever had a chance to, were anything except playful youngsters. For him wisdom, by its very definition, was something that came only with age – 'ciall le haois'. Breena's caperings on the bridge had not escaped his notice. As soon as they got going again he took care to put their relationship on the proper footing by remarking slyly:

'What a deal of book-learning you two must have in your heads by now! But I'm pleased to see that you're still well able to skip about. Ah, young people are the same in every age. Always up to some kind of antics! Wild for dancing and all kinds of excitement. How well I remember my own strength and high spirits. What is any kind of learning except another game to young people like you? It hasn't even scratched the surface of your fine opinions of yourselves.'

'But should it do that?' Maurice wanted to know in the gentle, wholly respectful tone he always used to Sean Mor. It was his manner to Sean Mor that had first made Breena take particular notice of him. 'What you call our fine opinion of ourselves is only self-respect after all. And self-respect is the beginning of respect for others.'

'Self-respect is a fine thing, I agree. But self-respect is one thing, and conceit is another. You know what the old monk wrote: *Conceit lets you know what books it has read; culture keeps quiet about them.* I know there's no need for me to go on with that poem. The gist of it, as you both well know, is that the more real learning a person has, the humbler he becomes.'

'Oh, I couldn't agree more,' Breena cried, breaking into English. 'It's only another way of saying… Maurice you agree, don't you? *God guard me from those thoughts men think | In the mind alone…*

'Of course, of course,' Maurice agreed, laughing. 'And now I'd better come in at once with some Latin or Greek quotation. Otherwise you'll both lose all respect for me. So here it is – the only one I can think of at the moment: *Homo sum; humani nihil a me alienum pute.*'

But Sean Cappagh disapproved of this levity. He turned to Breena, and asked her, 'Will you repeat what you've just said? It takes me some time to get the sense of those English words.'

Breena repeated it. Then Maurice did his best to translate it into good Irish. Sean nodded his head portentously after each phrase, and at the end gave it his whole-hearted approval:

'Yes. 'Tis easy to see that that poet must have studied the old writings.'

But Breena's thoughts had wandered back to the first poem. She said: 'It stands to reason that education must teach a person humility. The more he knows, after all, the more he realises there is still to know. And I must say, though my own education could hardly be said to have begun yet, that I'm a very humble person. In fact…' she paused to consider the matter, 'I'm the humblest person I know.'

Maurice burst out laughing. Sean Mor gave a slow smile. As soon as Breena got round to seeing the joke she put the best face she could on it and joined in the laughter. But she was anxious to have the matter forgotten. She asked Sean Mor to recite for them poems she knew he loved: 'Mise Raifteirí'; 'Bean na dTrí mBó'; 'Cill chais'; 'Fáilte don Éan'; 'Úna Bhán'. These were poems Sean had learned, not at school – children were punished for speaking Irish in Sean Mor's day – but from his grandfather, a man whom he still spoke of with great liking and respect.

In the middle of these recitations Thady drove up behind them. But there was no point in getting into the car just now. They had kept up a fairly brisk pace and already covered the mile or so of level road, as well as the first steep climb from Maur bridge. Sean Mor had long legs and even now in old age retained a sprightly use of them. They were within a few yards of where the road mounted again for the Pass. So they turned to Thady and waved him nonchalantly on.

'The Pass! The Pass!' Breena and Maurice shouted for encouragement as he swept by them with as much speed as he could muster. They knew, and he knew, that if they were to get in now they would in all likelihood never reach the Pass. They were all fond of Thady's ancient car, and wanted to put off its demise as long as possible. They thought of it more in terms of an aged and infirm man than a worn-out machine.

They watched the cloud of dark smoke growing behind the car as it began its climb.

'We'd better slow down,' Maurice said, 'or we'll be passing him out in a moment.'

| 157

Thady disliked it when they passed him out. And in fact they only did so absent-mindedly when they became engrossed in some conversation. Now for good measure, since they were all a little winded from walking quickly and talking quickly, and doing a bit of laughing and jumping about as well, they sat down on the fence to recover, and to save themselves from the tactlessness of passing Thady out.

Sean Cappagh had recited himself into a speech-making mood. Once he got going in Irish, some poem or proverb was bound to remind him of his sage's duty to instruct the young. Now, after a short, thoughtful pause, he began in carefully measured tones:

'Don't ever forget those poems. Remember what I've often told you both before. Those poems were written in the times of the great troubles, in penal days. Yet there were people in Ireland who found the courage to write poetry. And it's up to every Irish man and woman today not to make their labour useless. Keep those poems in your heads. Wherever you go, and both of you, by what you tell me, intend to go far afield, don't ever let it be said that either of you let those poets live out their days in vain. Keep alive the words they wrote. That's what I'm asking of you both now. And don't forget either that it was me that asked it. Old Sean Mor, on this lovely summer's evening. Take those poems with you, wherever you go.'

By the time he had finished, and they were getting off the fence to resume their climb, Maurice was ready to answer in a tone of powerful sentimentality:

'Yes, I promise you, we'll remember them. We'll never forget them. And we'll remember you, too. Don't ever doubt that.'

Breena thought this more than enough for both of them, and refrained from adding to it. She could swear that she caught the glitter of tears in Maurice's eyes. With this pair, evidently, sentiment was never out of place, even at its most mawkish. But you just got a little bit excited about humility, and you were pounced on at once… Still, some allowances had to be made for Maurice today.

And for Sean Mor too, she supposed, since he was so very old. As they continued their uphill walk, stopping every hundred yards or so to get their breath back, she took no part in the discussion – or the instruction, rather – that went on between them. Sean Mor was saying the poems again, and Maurice was repeating them, to show that he knew them by heart.

Breena listened to Sean Mor's voice, and the words he spoke no longer seemed to come from outside her. They were no longer words she savoured with conscious satisfaction in her head. They were sounds that seemed to lap to and fro inside her with the pulsing of her own blood. She felt rather than heard them. And now she answered to herself the question she had made fun of earlier when Sean Mor asked it. No, she had no desire to let those words lose their meaning… How many of the men who had written them went blind in the end? Beggars they were, too, blind beggars, as it was said Homer also had been. The wages of poetry is blindness – and rags. And also a queer kind of beggar's scholar's pride, that could make you include the word 'Dall' in your name, as an honourable title… No! Rather than let the poems of these men die out, she would become a teacher, she would spend all her life in some obscure school, striving every moment…

'Hurrah!' Maurice cried suddenly. Breena felt herself reddening as she turned towards him. Could it be that she had muttered something aloud in her sudden burst of enthusiasm for their language? But then she saw that they had rounded the end at the top of the second long, straight, uphill stretch, and were now on a level with the Pass. Thady's car waited for them by the rocky shelf where they had parked earlier.

From here the way lay mostly downhill. It was safe to get into the car. On the way into the town they stopped at many houses and left small amounts of fish. It was Thady's great pleasure to distribute bounty of this sort. But all the same it was no haphazard or eccentric gesture. The houses they stopped at were the houses of old friends and steadfast customers.

They had arranged among themselves to stop for only a minute or two outside Maurice's gate, so that Breena and Sean Mor could get out. Thady had more fish to distribute. Also, he would want to change his clothes before he came back to the wake. Maurice had decided to go with Thady. It would be better, Maurice thought, to sort out the fish at Uncle John's, and later bring back home, neatly and inconspicuously wrapped, some of the white trout and pollock his mother liked.

As they approached Maurice's house, Breena began to think more and more, and somewhat guiltily, of Kitty. She felt the need to run in and say a few words to her before she went home to wash away the fish-smell and change her dress. Almost certainly Kitty would be very surprised that they had stayed out so late. Soon the car drew up by the gate. Breena from her back seat jumped quickly out, Sean Mor eased himself out more slowly from the front. They went together into the yard.

CHAPTER 21

Almost as soon as Sean Mor and herself stepped inside the gate Breena caught a low rumbling sound from within the house. She paused and listened. It was the sound of voices raised in unison. They were saying the rosary. As they drew nearer the door, the sound of the prayer swelled into a strong murmur. Then she began to hear separate words quite distinctly, '... Lord is with thee... pray for us sinners...'

Rather hesitantly she went up to the porch door. There were some men standing round it in a trance of silence, their heads bowed, listening or maybe praying to themselves. Sean Mor slipped in amongst these. Beyond, within the porch, other men stood or knelt on one knee, coming in at the end of the responses in uneven gusts of sound. The doors into the rooms beyond were open and from them came the rising murmur and fall of the prayer. It was an unusual time to say the rosary, Breena thought, much too early in the evening. Then she heard Father Hennessey's lone voice leading it off from the back-kitchen. It was because he was there, she surmised, that they had decided to say it so early. He was a close friend of the dead man's, and indeed of the whole family.

She stood hesitating there by the door. Since Kitty was not free to speak to her just now, might it not be better to run off home at once and get washed and changed? She was on the point of turning away when one of the men at the door looked round and saw her standing there. He took it for granted that she wanted to enter the house. He jumped aside himself and cleared a way through the blocked passage.

Breena lacked the courage to set at nought such concern and gave up all thought of going home. She hurried through the connection in the porch into the big kitchen. There she found a place amongst the praying women, and knelt down quickly and bowed her head. The women were listening, concentrating, so that they could come in on time with the responses. After the first rather faint, 'Holy…' from the next room their voices came in to swell the sound. Then the wind seemed to catch the prayer, one room after another joined in. It became like the roaring of a gale. Monotonous, urgent, curiously obsessed, at last it was a force on its own that carried them all along with it. In the corner beside Breena a woman was crying, a very old woman with a black shawl over her head. The responses sank towards the end and merged into her crying, then in a couple of minutes rose, soared easily above it, thrilling it out of account. Breena closed her eyes and heard only the sound of a prayer. A sound that belonged to this time and this place, but also called to mind pictures she had seen or shadowy images her mind had formed in response to sentences read in books. Then she opened her eyes and the women were there before her with bowed heads. Women praying: in menaced times at Thebes, at Sumer, hooded figures crouched behind the walls.

The prayer ended and there was an uneven flow of muffled indeterminate sound, chairs being pushed back, the shuffling of feet, low whispers. Breena got to her feet. The woman beside her glanced at her and for some reason, probably because she knew her to be a friend of Kitty's, and presumed she wished to join her, stepped aside to let her pass. Out of politeness Breena moved forward. After that the women kept giving way before her. They wished to stay where they were, and saw her in movement so they naturally presumed that she wanted to get past. In a few minutes she found herself at the foot of the stairs. So, she thought, she was being urged upstairs to see Kitty quite independently of her own will… She was just about to go up the stairs when she heard her name being called. She looked up and saw Eileen, Jerry's wife, coming down the stairs towards her.

'Oh, Breena! Dr Peggy wants you. She's been looking for you for some time. She's on her way down now. Wait here… '

Breena stopped dead. Dr Peggy! An image of herself that morning came immediately to mind. Of course Dr Peggy had seen her! And now she wanted… What? After the freedom and light-heartedness of the day, all at once her wretchedness was very great. Oh, what an idiot she was!

But then Dr Peggy's black hat appeared at the turn of the stairs, above a couple of women who stood talking there. They parted to let her pass. She saw Breena.

'Oh, there you are! At last!' Her blunt, red-veined face had been frowning tightly with the effort of her quick descent of the stairs. But something, perhaps the expression of Breena's face, made her slow down. Breena could feel her heart beating quickly against her left arm as she stood there so demurely, waiting. Then Dr Peggy reached the bottom of the stairs. Breena heard her say:

'There's something I want to speak to you about. Will you just… ' And she nodded towards a door on Breena's left, behind the sitting-room. Breena went quickly to the door of this room and held it open. Now Dr Peggy hurried in past her and sank down on the first chair that came her way. Breena closed the door very slowly and carefully. But for all her slowness and care in closing it, she had to turn from it at last and face Dr Peggy. She stood still a moment just inside the door, looking about her vaguely.

But now Dr Peggy, who up to this moment had been trying to get her breath back, said quite gently: 'Breena, aren't you going to sit down? Come and sit here beside me.' Breena found out then that she felt weak; she wanted to sit down. So she went very quickly and sat down in the chair beside Dr Peggy's. Then Dr Peggy began to speak.

'Breena, have you ever wondered what a bachelor must feel, especially if he's no longer very young, when he hears of the sudden death of a man like poor Jeremy?'

This question astonished Breena very much. She turned in her chair to look hard at Dr Peggy. She met that dark blue glance now with only a very slight awareness of how acute and searching it still was. She heard Dr Peggy go on:

'Believe me, news of a sudden death like that gives a bachelor a dreadful shock. Especially if, as I've said before, he's no longer very young. It jolts him right out of his usual complacency, I can tell you. It makes him review his whole life.'

She stopped again, and this time she gave Breena a look that was a very definite invitation to make some comment. But Breena was still trying to gather her wits together. Not the smallest murmur of a reply occurred to her. She had no choice but to keep silence.

'Do you understand me?' Dr Peggy demanded then. 'Do you know what I'm talking about?'

This at least was very clear and precise. Breena looked Dr Peggy straight in the eye and told her bluntly, 'No. I… I honestly haven't the slightest idea what you're talking about, Dr Peggy.'

There followed a short pause, while Dr Peggy stared at the floor. Now with every moment that passed, the light dwindled under the window. It was getting dusk in the room. But Breena was near enough to Dr Peggy to be able to see quite distinctly the frowning, puzzled look on her face.

'Well, it seems Desmond was wrong, then…' Dr Peggy came in at last, in a much slower, more thoughtful way than she had spoken to begin with.

'And I must admit that I was very surprised myself at first. But then I thought, maybe you knew more about it than I did. I took Desmond at his word; he is my son. He convinced me that you must have some idea…'

'Desmond!' Breena exclaimed. And then the thought came,

Desmond was a bachelor. Other, wilder thoughts hovered on the brink of her consciousness. But the next moment Dr Peggy looked up at her and gave her one of her sudden, very wide smiles.

'As a matter of fact, just after Desmond spoke to me about it on the phone, for a second time mind you, but I'll tell you about that in a minute, I drove across to the house, in the hope of being able to say a few words to you in private. I looked in at your window. But you weren't in your room, though the window was open.'

Breena stared at the floor, and then stammered desperately:

'I… still don't understand. What did Desmond… I mean, why did Desmond… speak to you over the phone? Where… where did he speak from? I thought he was expected here about nine this morning?'

'No, no. Hoped for, but not expected. He was delayed, in the usual way. They only arrived a couple of hours ago. Exhausted, of course. They're resting now.' She said all this very quickly, and then paused to get her breath back.

Breena waited. By now she realised that the two extraordinary sentences that had been used to open the conversation must be the result of careful thought. Dr Peggy had planned this scene… But then as she sat there looking at the floor, in a very unpleasant nervous state, she felt the flitting of quick, dry, kisses all over her face. At the same time a torrent of words was poured over her head, no longer carefully planned or even in sequence. And all the time Dr Peggy's arms continued, every other minute or so, to clutch her.

The worst of it was that between the astonishment and exasperation of it, and the deafness that resulted from each successive squeeze, hardly a word of what Dr Peggy was saying got through to her.

A kind of fright seized her then. She jumped up.

'Dr Peggy, I… I didn't quite hear what you said. It doesn't make sense. Would you mind, please… sitting down, and telling me again?'

'You're astonished!' Dr Peggy exclaimed. 'I can see that... Well, as I've said more than once already, I could hardly believe my own ears at first. But Desmond thought you had some suspicion of it...'

Desmond! Again Desmond! Now she was able to give all her attention to piecing together the disjointed sentences she heard. Into her mind with Dr Peggy's next words came the image of a pleasant, tanned, rather fat face. It was not Desmond's face. It was the face of Mrs Hugh's brother from Dublin, who for years now had been coming here to the town, three or four times a year, for a few days' fishing or golfing. First, with his sister and Hugh, then later while Hugh was abroad with Desmond. It was the only possible conclusion there was before her.

CHAPTER 22

It was not Desmond, but Desmond's friend, Mrs Hugh's brother, who wanted to marry her. Unexpected as it was, unlikely, unthought of before this moment; preposterous: after her first idea about Desmond she was able to accept it with the utmost relief, and with only one very earnest and quietly spoken question:

'Dr Peggy, are you very sure about all this?'

'Well, as I've already said more than once, it was more than I could take in myself at first. Up to this morning I still thought of you as a child, a baby! I kept asking Desmond on the phone, "Is this a joke?" And it would have been a joke in very bad taste, you know, with poor Jeremy just gone from us. In the end Desmond just put down the phone. He said, "I'll give you half an hour to think about it, Mother. Breena is a big girl now. She's nearly eighteen. Think about it. I'll call you back in half an hour's time. So I did. I thought about it, I mean. You know, Breena, it had never occurred to me before that you're nearly eighteen years of age. Why, it seems only yesterday that you first came to us! And I thought, how often I used to pray when you first came to us that you would never have reason to regret that it was to us you came! You'll understand when you're older what a great responsibility it was. It's not like having a child of your own. With your own child you can think, "Well, God sent him to us, and we'll do the best we can for him, and that will be that!" But when it's a question of another person's child! You'll only understand when you're a lot older what heart-searching is involved. You keep thinking, what if somebody else had taken charge of her? One of her real aunts, or that uncle in Australia who wrote to say he was willing to come over and legally adopt her on the spot… You can't help asking yourself, but I'm wandering from the point. What I wanted to tell you was that Desmond rang me again as he promised. I was waiting by the phone. He gave me more than half an hour too, to think about it. Over an hour, in fact. He must have thought I needed a lot of convincing!'

Breena squirmed uncomfortably, and said hurriedly, 'What seems very strange to me is that… '

She came to an abrupt halt. What on earth was she to call the man, this brother of Mrs Hugh's! His name was Gabriel, she knew. Gabriel! The archangel! Dr Peggy had already used this name at least twenty times, but Breena just couldn't bring herself to utter it. Gabriel! A man so many years older than herself, whom she had always thought of as either 'Mrs Hugh's brother' or 'Desmond's friend'. Kitty and herself had often joked about his name; so that now it seemed rather sneering, in somewhat bad taste, to pretend to say it in all seriousness. So she began again:

'I can't help thinking it strange that Mrs Hugh's brother should speak to Desmond first, instead of waiting and speaking to me. You did say, didn't you – or at least imply, I forget which – that he had come down with Desmond for the funeral, that he's already… '

'Yes, yes, so I did. He's upstairs in the gable room now, with Desmond and Father Patrick. They were all exhausted when they arrived, as I think I've mentioned before. We put them all three into the gable room, as far out of the way as possible. I looked in just before the rosary and the three of them were sleeping like babies. But what was I saying? Oh yes – Mrs Hugh's brother – what a name to give him! He'll expect his own name from you from now on, be sure of that. As for speaking to Desmond first, you can set your mind at rest on that point. Don't give it another thought. Desmond explained it to me. As a matter of fact, Desmond – I don't mind admitting it – was a bit put out when he arrived and found that I hadn't yet told you what he'd said over the phone about Gabriel. He'd gone to the trouble of phoning me twice, mind you, so you can't blame him for thinking me a bit slow.'

Here Dr Peggy paused a moment, maybe quite by accident, maybe just to draw breath. Then she went on enthusiastically:

'Well, as I've just been saying, Desmond explained to me over the phone why Gabriel spoke to him first. Be sure I asked him that question, while I still thought he must be up to one of his tricks, you understand. And do you know what Desmond said about Gabriel? "He's the very soul of honour!" Those were Desmond's very words. You see, Gabriel knows your position in the family. He wouldn't dream of speaking to you without letting us know first what he intended to do. "You'll never find a more honourable man!" That's what Desmond said.'

She paused for some comment from Breena. But Breena was thinking about Desmond. What kind of faces had he been pulling at the other end of the phone when he made those grand statements about honour, and honourable men? 'He's the very soul of honour!' So this proposal, her first proposal, was a soul-of-honour proposal. And soul-of-honour proposals were received over the phone, at second and third hand? Of necessity, they must be very rare. Breena pondered on it. But Dr Peggy had got tired of waiting for an answer.

'I see you can hardly believe it at the moment. You can't take it in. Well at first, as I must have told you at least ten times by now, I found it very hard to believe myself. It never occurred to me that you were Gabriel's type somehow. But God's ways are strange.'

Breena felt that she was in an utterly ridiculous situation. But Dr Peggy was so enthusiastic, so truly unselfishly delighted for her, that she felt it would be intolerably crude and coarse – indeed, impossible – to state baldly what she thought at this moment of Gabriel and his soul-of-honour intentions. So, after a moment's hesitation, she only said, with the utmost seriousness:

'Dr Peggy, are you absolutely sure that Desmond… that you… over the phone… you know how easy it is to grasp at a word and draw hasty conclusions… And you know how Desmond loves a joke. Did you by any chance check with Desmond after he arrived? Did you ask him outright…'

'Yes, yes, I did. Believe me, Breena, it's all true. I had a few words with Desmond very soon after he came in. But bless you! You can't believe it, I see.'

Dr Peggy paused once more and leaned forward to study Breena's face. But fortunately the room was full of shadows by now. Breena knew that as long as she refrained from smiling broadly or bursting into tears she was safe enough. No finer shade of expression could be discerned in this light. She was trying desperately hard to think of something pleasing and meaningless to say; something that she could easily explain away afterwards to Desmond and that would give her the right to stand up now and leave the room. But she lacked both the wit and the composure to think up such a statement. Desmond! It was all Desmond's fault. If he hadn't consented to make those two calls… Sheer, cynical disregard of everything except his own comfort was what she accused him of now in her thoughts. How he must have grinned to himself when his mother caught up those two statements about 'honour' with such eagerness. No, Breena could not trust herself to say anything at all just now. To keep her mouth tightly shut was her only hope. But Dr Peggy was too excited to remain silent for long.

'You can't get over it, I see. Desmond will be astonished when I tell him how surprised you were. And just think of it! Gabriel is such a well-to-do man. And the very soul of honour, as Desmond said… That lovely house of his, too, just round the corner, in that lovely old square, so different from our poor little square down here… God's ways are certainly strange! Since Gabriel's mother died that house has been there waiting for you. And he has only one sister, and she's down here, well out of your way. You'll have nobody to interfere with you. You'll be like a queen. And you're not yet eighteen years of age! You'll have…'

Suddenly Breena stood up. Her unexpected action made Dr Peggy break off, and haul herself to her feet too, and reach out to turn on the light.

'Good God, Breena! How pale you look! The surprise has been too much for you. I'll take you home…'

Breena was at the door. It was all so absurd and preposterous, so irrelevant to the real issues of her life. And yet Dr Peggy was so well-meaning and kind, so truly delighted for her. Breena again tried desperately to think of something witty or humorous to say. But when Dr Peggy came up to her at the door with, 'Come on, I'll run you home. You don't want anybody to see you like this!' and Breena opened her mouth with some idea of placing the matter in a new light, what she heard coming out of her own mouth was the question:

'Have you told Uncle John about all this?'

'No, no! He's far too upset as yet. Besides, Desmond particularly asked me not to mention it to anybody except yourself.'

'But Uncle John ought to be told. Then he could speak to Desmond and make him…'

'Well, well, we'll have to wait. Tomorrow or the day after…'

But Breena already felt cross with herself because she had asked in that childish way about Uncle John. She certainly had not meant to do so. The question has just slipped out. Now she was afraid that if she opened her mouth once more she would blurt out something even more silly, perhaps about Maurice. Now at last she understood why Maurice acted so stupidly when Hugh became bossy or interfering. He just couldn't help it.

With her head down she followed Dr Peggy in silence out of the room.

'I had to leave the car outside the gate,' Dr Peggy was explaining to her. 'There wasn't room in the yard when I last came in…'

| 171

CHAPTER 23

When they got outside the wind had risen, the evening was turning cold. There were only one or two people about in the yard now. For a moment Breena mixed her sighs of exasperation about Gabriel with sighs of regret about the weather. By the look of the sky she knew that it would almost certainly be raining again tomorrow.

Even along the length of this yard a walk with Dr Peggy required some concentration. Dr Peggy had got into the habit of walking so fast that she found it impossible to set a straight course.

'Oh! Oh!… You must give me a minute,' Dr Peggy cried as she got into the car and sat back gasping for breath. Then she looked across and said something that touched and surprised Breena. It was the first remark Dr Peggy had ever addressed to Breena the grown-up, as opposed to Breena the child.

'Forty years ago I started walking fast like that out of sheer fright. I hoped people would mistake it for self-confidence… I can't give it up now, though it's killing me.'

'Yes, I… I understand.' Breena stammered uncertainly, but with quick sympathy, feeling more at ease with Dr Peggy after this exchange.

'Breena…' Dr Peggy's tone was all at once so lingering and sweet, so much more like Ursula's than her own, that Breena looked round at her in surprise. At once then she noticed the thin silvery streaks that gleamed here and there on Dr Peggy's age-darkened cheeks. It was the light from outside glittering on her tears, where they followed the dried-up courses of her wrinkles.

'Breena, my dear, when Desmond told me about Gabriel this morning, I can't tell you what relief I felt. I used to be so afraid, you see… I used to feel in my heart such foreboding, when I saw you so serious over your books. I don't mind telling you, I know you'll respect my confidence, that I was thirty-three years of age before any man asked me to marry him. That was your Uncle John; and he was the only man who ever asked me. Then because of my age, or my own worrying on account of my age, I lost my first two children. My little Mary, and my poor little John. It was a miracle that even Desmond survived. And nobody knows what a difference Desmond made to me. He taught me so many things! And he's still teaching me… When I look back over my life, it seems such a long, bleak trek until Desmond came. And now at last to be able to feel at ease about you, to know that you'll never experience the sorrow of such things! To feel pretty certain at last that you'll never have reason to regret coming to our house.'

'Oh, Dr Peggy, I don't regret it. I couldn't regret it. How could I ever regret it?'

'No, no, thank God. As it has turned out now, with God's help you never will.'

But now Breena's thoughts had become even less coherent than before. For Dr Peggy she could only feel, for the first time in her life, both affection and pity. But to be told that Dr Peggy had often felt pity for herself, Breena! More, that Dr Peggy had even feared the pattern of Breena's life would follow that of her own. Why, it was enough to take her breath away. Surely it was as clear as day that in anything you could name they were poles apart. As for Desmond's friend, Breena could quite understand that if Dr Peggy had met such a man in her youth, she would have found his proposals very pleasing. But that was such a very, very long time ago. How could Dr Peggy understand how wonderful life seemed for girls of Breena's

| 173

age today; how for them marriage to such a person as Gabriel could only be seen as the placing of senseless limits on vistas that stretched away into next year and five years from now? Breena had no illusions about marriage. Kitty and herself had discussed it too often. During that rollicking, gleeful phase of extreme cynicism they had passed through together at the age of fifteen or so they had dissected every marriage in the town at that time. The conclusion they had come to was that for women marriage meant housework, babies, and mental stagnation; and that therefore no woman in her senses would willingly choose to marry. Within six months they had both made up their minds to become Medical Missionaries.

And now this evening, Breena, trundling down Church Lane and along Church Street to the sound of Dr Peggy's eager voice, experienced a fierce and passionate nostalgia for that period of her closest friendship with Kitty.

CHAPTER 24

The fact that Dr Peggy was accompanying her into the house alarmed Breena. To be sure, the light was on in the kitchen. But she hardly knew whether to be pleased or only further alarmed at this. Then, they reached the door. Breena got there first and opened it. And there, thank heavens, sitting in her rocking-chair in front of the stove, suavely and imperturbably knitting another of those horrible garments, was Hannah.

Dr Peggy looked straight across at her. A glance full of meaning passed between them. Dr Peggy said:

'You'll look after Breena, won't you, Hannah? I had to run her home. She didn't feel at all well…'

'No wonder Breena doesn't feel well! Starved, that's what she is. Half-dead with hunger! D'you know that she went out of the house this morning without eating one bite of breakfast?'

Then, in answer to Dr Peggy's speaking look, Hannah got up and followed Dr Peggy out into the yard. The murmur of their voices could be heard all mixed up with a series of wistful or interrogative barks from the dogs.

Breena hurried to the sink at the back and discreetly began to splash her face and neck with cold water. Afterwards, when she turned round from drying herself at the roller-towel, Hannah had come back into the kitchen.

| 175

It turned out that Hannah had not yet had her own supper. She had, she declared now, been waiting for somebody – Breena, Ursula, Thady, Desmond even – to 'turn up and share it' with her. Now Hannah began to set the table. She brought out a dish of salad, some of yesterday's ham, a round of home-pressed brawn rich in its own jellied juices, a steak pie, a cheese, some apple cake and some brown soda-bread and butter. As each item appeared Breena's anguish over the events of the day seemed to merge into the shadows cast by the dishes where they were placed on the table.

When the table was ready, Hannah called to Breena to sit down, and sat down opposite her.

It turned out now that Breena's splashings at the sink had refreshed her wonderfully. She found the freshly-pressed brawn and the steak pie delicious, and told Hannah so in glowing terms. In that way she achieved her object, and was helped to some more. After that she felt so restored and strengthened that she could no longer hold back her curiosity. She composed her face and remarked:

'What were you talking about out in the yard with Dr Peggy?'

Hannah looked at her plate for a moment in silence. Then she said slowly, still with a downcast look:

'I'd ha' thought anyway that you'd have known what was on her mind tonight.'

'So she's told you, Dr Peggy's told you!' Breena cried. 'She said she wasn't going to tell anybody tonight, not even Uncle John…'

She broke off because Hannah had now raised her glance and was watching her with such bright, lingering interest that Breena could only pause to hear what she had to say.

'Do you think for a moment, girl, that the likes of Dr Peggy could keep such news to herself? She didn't mean to tell me. I'll give her credit for that. She won't mean to tell anybody. But the news will be all round the family by tomorrow all the same. You'd better be prepared for it.'

Breena picked up the well-buttered slice of brown bread she had been relishing a few minutes earlier and mechanically took a bite from it. She asked: 'Hannah, what d'you think of it all?'

'What d'I think? I think 'tis lucky for me my mind's not a clock. Otherwise this news 'ld have stopped it for good.'

Breena stared a moment at her bread and butter.

'Hannah, what *did* Dr Peggy say? I mean how exactly did she put it?'

'Well, to cut a very long story short, what she told me was that Mrs Hugh's brother Gabriel wants to marry you, and that when you heard the news you were so delighted, overwhelmed, that you were absolutely speechless. She could hardly get a word out of you, you were so utterly overcome by the surprise and gratification of it.'

'Oh Hannah, what nonsense, what utter rubbish!' Breena could feel herself reddening with irritation and helplessness. 'But you're only joking, I know. Dr Peggy didn't say anything like that at all… How could she?'

'Well, that's what she said. Those were her very words. "Speechless with delight!" – that's how she put it.'

Breena pushed away her plate of bread and butter. 'Well, it's true that I didn't say very much. But how could she take that for delight? I just didn't have the heart to tell her outright what I thought. She was like a child with a new toy…'

'So yer going to marry Mrs Hugh's brother just to please Dr Peggy? Is that what yer trying to tell me?'

Hannah's voice, that had sweetened of late years through constant association with Ursula, now broadened out with impatience into its old country accents.

Breena was tracing a pattern on the table-cloth with the nail of her little finger. She was troubled with the notion that to talk about Mrs Hugh's brother at all, to discuss him even like this with Hannah, was only a kind of boasting. If what she really felt inside her was distaste and something like mockery, then she had no right even to mention Gabriel's name. She thought a moment and said:

'You see, Hannah, I don't think that Gab – that Mrs Hugh's brother really *does* want to marry me. The idea is preposterous. It can't be true. It's just a… sort of joke of Desmond's.'

'And did ye tell Dr Peggy what ye suspected? Did ye tell her flat that ye thought it was all only a silly joke of Desmond's?'

Breena put her elbows on the table and shaded her face with her hands. 'No. I just let her go on and on… Of course you're right, Hannah. I should have stopped her and told her what I thought. I know that Kitty would have stopped her within the first three minutes. I can't account for it now… the way I just sat there and said nothing. All the time I was thinking that it was utter nonsense, and yet I just went on listening. I know it's because…'

She broke off, and finished the sentence only in her own mind: 'because my nature is in some way flawed. My wits desert me at critical moments. I can't even begin to put this right yet, because I haven't yet begun to grasp why it happens. But one day I'll find out, and then I'll do my utmost to put it right.'

At this point she looked up at Hannah, and found Hannah's warm glance full on her face, waiting for her to go on. So she continued hurriedly:

'Dr Peggy got very excited. She talked a great deal to me. For the first time ever she made me like and understand her. She made me understand too why… why she wanted me to do the very opposite to what she had done herself, and get married young.'

Breena paused here. She knew that she was on dangerous grounds. There was a little silence. Then Hannah said in the softened, gentle tones that were her ordinary tones nowadays:

'You know that I'd be the last person to speak up against getting married young. I was married young myself, and widowed young too, God help me…'

In the short silence that followed, it was not Hannah's glance but Breena's that wandered to the little altar beside the dresser, where a photograph of Hannah's husband always hung at a few inches' distance from the holy pictures. It always caused Breena a little pang, that photograph, the face was so young-looking. Hannah seemed to have no idea how far behind she had left that young husband of hers. To look at him now, he was more like her son than her husband. Breena collected her wits and said hurriedly:

'Of course I agree with you, Hannah. To get married young is a very good thing. Provided you want to, of course, and… and the man wants to. But in my case the man hasn't said anything at all that I know of. It's all come from Desmond, so… '

'D'ye mean to say,' Hannah broke in, getting excited again, 'that if Mrs Hugh's brother himself had spoken out, an' ye were sure it all came from him, ye'd be delighted as Dr Peggy took it for granted ye were?'

'Of course not Hannah. I was talking of *young* marriages. Mrs Hugh's brother isn't young. Why, he must be… '

Here she broke off, again at a loss. It had just occurred to her that Mrs Hugh's brother was certainly a good many years younger than Hannah. The next moment she heard the sentence being finished for her very smoothly:

'He must be at least twice Maurice's age, and maybe more – that's what you mean, isn't it?'

'Well, yes, Hannah, something like that. He's a great deal older than I am, that's really what I mean.'

'Exactly. My advice to you now, girl, is to go straight across to the other house – it isn't by any means late as yet – and speak to your Uncle John. You'll find that he'll soon put a stop to Desmond's nonsense. And as soon as Dr Peggy understands that it's only a joke, she'll do everything in her power to make it up to you.'

Breena looked down at the table-cloth. 'I can't always be running to Uncle John. I want to deal with this myself.' (And in her mind as she spoke there was a vision of herself in the sitting-room last night, only last night, hurrying oh so swiftly to Uncle John's side, with such little result.)

'And how are you doing to deal with it yourself, may I ask?'

'I've already decided on that. I'm going to speak to Desmond first thing in the morning. Just look at it this way. Maybe it is one of Desmond's jokes. But until I've spoken to Desmond I won't know for sure whether it's a joke or not. Sometimes now I think it must be a joke. It's all so absurd. And then again I think, maybe it's not a joke. But either way, Hannah, aren't we taking it all too seriously?'

Breena now appealed directly with her eyes across the table to Hannah to corroborate this statement. 'Well… maybe we are. Desmond likes his play-acting, 'tis true. But he'll not forget either, I fancy, that Mrs Hugh's brother is Hugh's brother-in-law, and as such worthy of respect – if not for his own sake. If it turns out to be a joke, the only person who'll look foolish I'll be Dr Peggy. And she'll be far too busy to have any notion how foolish she'll look. There'll be a few cracks made at your expense too, of course. But *you* won't mind that.'

'No, certainly not,' Breena said with an air of dismissing the subject.

Hannah got up then to clear the table and wash up. Breena stood up to help her.

'Talking of Hugh,' Hannah said, 'have you heard that he's arranged for the funeral to take place tomorrow?'

'Tomorrow? Surely not. The day after it must be, because… '

'No, tomorrow. They were saying across at the wake that it has something to do with Father Patrick having to be back at a certain hour tomorrow night. But nothing'll persuade me that it wasn't all Hugh's doing. I don't know how 'tis, but just like yourself I could never get to like or trust that Hugh. I believe he'd bury you alive if he got the chance. God preserve me from that hospital of his, that's all I can say. High-Jeannie, that's what I heard 'em saying today he calls it, shoving people underground, poor things, the very next day but one after they leave us. His own father too, may God forgive him! Only one full day's waking, that's what it amounts to. Whoever heard of so small a tribute to your own father? You'd think…'

For a moment Breena lost track of Hannah's voice. 'High-Jeannie?' she was saying to herself distractedly: 'High… Jeannie?' And then with a sense of enormous relief the word came to her, 'Hygiene! Oh, of course!' Then she was able to give all her attention to Hannah again.

She was saying:

'I heard a queer tale today about the Filemoyn branch of your family – the Cappaghs who used to live in that village on the eskar, where the roofs have all fallen in now. Well it's a queer tale altogether. It's about a pair o' twin brothers. You know how twins run in the Cappagh family?'

'It hasn't exactly escaped my notice.'

'Well these brothers were called Owen and Hugh. (Breena knew at once that Hugh would prove to be the villain of the piece. This was Hannah's technique; the unpopular man in real life always turned out to be the villain of the story.)

She set herself to listen. She loved those stories of Hannah's which were always ghost stories. She was in no mood for going early to bed, and she wanted to put off thinking about Gabriel until tomorrow. Within ten minutes Hannah had succeeded in capturing her whole attention. By the time she got to the end of the story Gabriel was far less real to Breena than the twin brothers Owen and Hugh, both of whom had died in sad circumstances, and one of whom, Owen, had been unable to rest peacefully in his grave. So real indeed had these brothers become to her that when she parted from Hannah for the night (to make her lonely way down along the corridor and through the high, empty hall, while Hannah went easily upstairs!) she had a very uncomfortable feeling that the ghost of Owen was interested in her movements. Never in the two years since she had begged to be given the big room on the ground floor as her bedroom had she so bitterly regretted the folly that had moved her then.

CHAPTER 25

Breena got ready for bed as quickly as possible then hurried to the table where only the morning before she had put down her latest, prized victory in borrowed books. And then, with the book already open in her hand, she remembered! Only that very morning she had made a resolution not to read for two days! For a moment she stood absolutely still, with her hands clenched around the book. Oh how in a life like hers could she be expected to keep her resolution? When it was possible to keep on living only if she held within her grasp the power to blot it all out at any moment? Oh think of Dr Peggy, of Desmond and his friend… But no, no! She had no desire to blot anything out… Only to be able to put things at a distance, see them for the small things they were. Yet… wasn't it against moments like this, when reading became a drug, that she had made her resolution?

She put down the book. It was Shaw's *St Joan*, which Father Hennessey had brought round only yesterday morning, after a number of requests on Breena's part, and a number of protests on his. 'Nobody reads that old pagan nowadays!' Because St Joan was her own age, seventeen, going on eighteen, she had been looking forward very much to reading this book. And now, that stupid resolution!

But the need for oblivion was paramount. Always when she made one of her resolutions against reading, there was one book that was understood to be excepted. It was her safety valve. And since by now she knew it pretty well by heart, its value was mainly soporific. She took it up now and got into bed to read it. The book was the Bible.

She had first begun to read stories from the Bible at an age when she had no grasp whatever of the sequence of time. It was not within her power to read about a number of events, and then mentally place them in order as they had happened. She had no idea that one was finished and done with, maybe for a hundred or a thousand years, before the next began. For her they were all happening at the same time, though of course in different places.

Whenever she read through the Bible as a child, her mind expanded into a plain so vast and variously coloured that it satisfied her most inward and secret desires. Here in one corner, under lowering skies, with the tide already washing about his ankles, and his wife and three daughters-in-law looking up into the sky nearby and wringing their hands, stood the indomitable Noah, with his mouth full of nails and a hammer that banged like clockwork in his hand. Yet only half an inch away – because the area of the brain is small, though the imaginings of the mind are limitless – the great golden sun of the desert beat down on burning sands. And there, secretly laughing behind the flap of her tent, stood Sarah. While outside in the sunlight an angel of the Lord spoke to Abraham, her husband… An angel, a dazzle of white garments, with a glinting light for a face… Yet encroaching on the sands where he stood was a shadow of the oak tree where Absalom hung, his face, his long hair, his beauty, all strange, shadow within a shadow, not understood. And only a clear voice calling, 'Oh my son Absalom, oh Absalom my son, oh my son…' A quarter of an inch further on, and Solomon's temple gleamed in the sun, and the flowers in his gardens glittered and glistened, and his circus of animals frisked about. And then the sky freshened, the wind rose a little, and there stood the rooftops and watch-towers of the hospitable city that had received Ruth and

Noemi. Yet turn your glance only half an inch to the left and the skies were bleak with thunder, forked lightening lit up in flashes the doomed white cities of Sodom and Gomorrah.

Turning over the pages now, Breena read a sentence here and a sentence there, and became drowsy. She began to think back on that first absorbing picture-story she had made of the world. The prickly fear aroused by Hannah's tale remained in so far as she felt no impulse to get out of bed and draw the curtains and open the shutters. But she had almost forgotten about Gabriel. Less than an hour after she got into bed she was reaching out to put off the light. Images from the Bible filled her mind, she drifted into sleep.

CHAPTER 26

Towards morning she woke; started up from a bad dream and jumped out of bed. She hurried to the window and drew open the curtains and unbolted the shutters. Never, never again would she sleep with the shutters closed! Outside, the first faint glimmering of dawn could be seen above the Tobar mountains across the valley. She raised the lower sash of the window and stepped out on the grass, relishing the coldness and wetness of it against her feet. Hugging herself, shivering in the biting air, she thought… a face, a face in a dream… A dream, moreover, that her own cowardice had brought on.

It was the face of Kitty and Maurice's father. In a silly mood yesterday, in a state of hysterical hyper-sensitiveness, Breena had carefully refrained from looking at it. How shameful to have behaved so that a poor dead face must be made the subject of a nightmare!

Dr Jeremy was dead. But what did that word 'dead' mean? Breena had not an iota of an idea what it meant. Yet she was afraid of it. Was it for an instant or an infinity of time that Dr Jeremy had trekked through that aloneness of the country of the dying? Breena had glimpsed that shadowed country once, a land where dusk was always thickening into night. And a short while ago in her dream had she just for one moment, yes… also inhabited it?

The pre-dawn coldness and wetness of the grass numbed her feet. But now on her cold face she could feel the scalding warmth of tears. Tears that welled up from where and brought with them what strange comfort? After a few minutes of them she was able to fight down her aversion to going back into her room. She promised herself that she would only stay in it while she quickly dressed, and then go along immediately to the other house.

In the other house the wake would still be in progress, the night-watchers sitting up by the dead man's bedside. Breena knew that she would find warmth and light there. And she knew too that she would also find an opportunity to face the dark and cold that she feared. She would be able to do what she had omitted to do yesterday: kneel down by the dead man's side, and look at his face while she said her prayer.

As she got back through the window the dogs barked their drowsy awareness of her. The sound comforted her. While she got dressed – hindering herself in her shivering hurry – her thoughts in spite of all her efforts scuttled back to her dream. She had suffered from nightmares at one time, after she first came to live at Uncle John's. Acrobatic nightmares, in which people she knew well performed very complicated antics enticing her to follow their example, until at last she had climbed so high and strained so far, there could be no hope of return. Then she had to scream out for help from some high tower or overhanging cliff or topmost branch of a tree.

When she dressed she went quickly out of her room and through the hall and out by the main door. This saved most of the dogs' excitement. She heard a few puzzled yelps, that was all.

Half-way up Fairhill she hurried across the Bradleys' yard and then through the ghostly garden path of the big house next door. In that way she came into Church Lane and finally to Kitty and Maurice's house. Even at this early hour there was a small group of elderly men standing by the front door, murmuring together behind misty blue whorls of tobacco smoke. As Breena came up to them she recognised them as men from out Filemoyn and Maurcappagh way; men who had certainly known Dr Jeremy as a child, and were now paying their final tribute to the man, boy and child they could remember. As soon as Breena came up to them and turned to greet them – in Irish, the language she could hear them speaking – they gave her back a grave, courteous, 'God and Mary and Patrick go with you!' that rang like a blessing in her ears. All at once, then, she saw them as men rooted in the atmosphere of this, their parish, as firmly as the hedge behind them was rooted in its soil; and for a moment she had a distressing vision of herself as a leaf that the wind was only blowing past them.

She went on into the house and straight on up the stairs. When she reached the top she heard a very low murmur of voices from the room where the dead man was laid out. She stopped a moment and leaned against the wall of the landing to get back her breath, then went on again. She knew from the door-shaped glow on the wall of the corridor that the door of the waking-room stood wide open.

The moment she stepped across the threshold of the room the shining of the seven candles on the small table beside the bed got into her eyes and half-blinded her. But she somehow made her way to the bedside and knelt down to say her prayer. The room seemed warm after the dawn coldness outside. Hot blood rushed to the surface of her skin, her eyes misted over. But she moved her lips to pretend to the people in the room, whoever they were, that she was praying. Then her sight cleared; she saw before her the dead man's face. At once all her silly agitation vanished. The nightmare – whatever it was that had drawn her here – no longer mattered. She thought to herself: only the most insensitive, the most selfish person could mourn or shed a tear over that face. The expression was so rested, serene, and at peace, she could think only of the deepest, most ease-giving sleep.

All the lines that in life had marred the cheeks and forehead of that face were gone. Youth with its smooth skin had come back. The keen, hopeful look of youth was there; all the intelligence of youth and the fine bones of it that disdained coarseness and the acquisition of flesh. All at once the confusion inside her resolved itself into the question: who was it that lay there? Those sharp cheek-bones, that nose, that mouth and forehead, surely she had seen them all before? Selfishly withdrawn into the same peace, caught up in the same way and lost in their own calm and restfulness?

A touch on her shoulder made her start and turn round. It was Uncle John. He whispered: 'You've been kneeling far too long… ' She felt his hand on her elbow, helping her up. But when she stood up and turned towards him the glow of the candles was still in her eyes. She was unable to see his face. She was aware of him only as a curb on her movements and a huge shadow thrown across the ceiling above. She twisted a little, to get free of his grasp. But his grip on her elbow only tightened.

'I want to sit down,' she whispered. 'I want to stay here for a while in this room.'

'You should be at home, in bed.'

He spoke in a whisper. But his voice sounded loud in her ears. She felt ashamed at being treated like a child before the other people in the room. She made no further protest, but allowed herself to be led across the room towards the door. The only light was the candlelight. She could see no face clearly, but was aware of about a dozen people sitting in groups of two or three here and there about the room.

Uncle John led her on past the doorway to the top of the stairs. He stopped there and freed her arm. He asked her in the same harsh, carrying whisper he had used before: 'What are you doing here, in the middle of the night?'

He was standing now in deep shadow. She got only an impression of the tired, firm lines in which his face was set. She retorted somewhat childishly, in a tone of mixed triumph and irritation; 'It's not the middle of the night. It's already dawn. The birds are singing.'

'Go down to the kitchen. It's warm down there, and you can

have some tea. And then go home.'

She said, 'Yes, Uncle John,' and turned away. But as she went down the stairs she was clenching and clenching her hands in an agony of dissatisfaction. What a glib word 'juvenility' was. But what did it mean?

A wave of warmth, rather too close and oppressive, came out to meet her as soon as she opened the kitchen door. She saw that the door of the range was open, so that the heat from the glowing, high-piled fire beat out freely through the bars. There were only three women in the room, and these sat grouped at the head of the table, intolerably close to the fire it seemed to Breena. She paused in the doorway, not sure at first glance who the women were, and waiting for them to turn round. But they were deep in some conversation, their heads together. She studied them a moment, and then with something like fright recognised Mrs Hugh as one of the group. The other two were half-strangers, part of the 'Dublin crowd' – friends of Hugh and Mrs Hugh from Dublin.

Breena hesitated in the doorway. Her quick, rather guilty and dismayed conclusion was that the three must be talking about herself. This was too much for Breena; she was on the point of closing the door again and stealing quietly away when Mrs Hugh looked up and their glances met. Breena gave one keen look into Mrs Hugh's face. What she saw there, the immediate, rather dazzling smile of welcome, convinced her that she had been wrong. It could only be that Mrs Hugh was sitting up at this late hour – putting herself out over the wake to the extent of staying up one whole night – simply because she had two old friends to talk to, and not because she had the state of her brother's heart, or the foolishness of his impulses, to discuss.

Now Breena heard herself being introduced with great politeness to the two friends from Dublin. She wondered whether or not she should remind Mrs Hugh and these particular old friends of hers that they had all met before. She judged, however, that it was too early in the morning to make any mention of such a trivial matter. She listened with sympathy while Mrs Hugh described how glad she was to see these two old friends again; how surprised and delighted she was that they had been able to get away for the funeral.

'There's some tea in the pot,' Mrs Hugh went on. 'You must have some. We've been bravely keeping it going all night, for all comers.'

At this the younger of the two friends, who had already got up to shake hands with Breena, jumped up once more and fetched the teapot from the range.

'I think we've met before, haven't we?' She said in a low voice to Breena as she filled her cup.

'Yes,' Breena said. The girl's name was Patsy.

'Let's all have some more tea!' Mrs Hugh suggested brightly. 'It will mean more washing up, but…'

'Oh, I'll do that,' Patsy put in quickly.

Now all the cups were filled. Mrs Hugh passed Breena some bread and butter to eat with her tea.

'We've taken the trouble to cut it, so you must take the trouble to eat it,' she remarked, smiling. 'Is there anything else you'd like? Please look round and take your choice.'

Breena felt very tempted by the spiced beef. For some reason she felt shamefully hungry, and she loved spiced beef more than anything. But after a moment's hesitation she smiled and nobly shook her head and went on eating her bread and butter.

Mrs Hugh received her refusal with a smile of particular friendliness, and immediately turned to look from one to the other of her friends.

'Breena won't mind if we go on with our chat; I know she understands my way of thinking. She won't be at all offended.'

Breena saw that this was a tribute to her own broadmindedness. She smiled, and fervently hoped that her smile looked less foolish than she felt. What had they been talking about, she wondered? Some intricate feminine mysteries… Breena arranged her face, and sat prepared for anything. But after all when the talk began it turned out to be nothing more than an account by Mrs Hugh of what an outlandish little town this was, and what strange customs were practised here.

Evidently Breena, when she came in, had interrupted a catalogue by Mrs Hugh of the shortcomings and downright shoddiness and weediness of this little town. When Mrs Hugh began to speak again, it was with a great deal of animation; her face glowed pink as she cast dark velvety glances about from one to the other. But Breena noticed something else about Mrs Hugh. Somewhere in the delicate etching of her face lurked a poignant hint of transience; a blurring that showed up now here, now there. Breena believed that in two or three years' time she would no longer look like she did now. Her beauty was too delicate, too flowerlike, to last. Like a flower it would be beaten down and bedraggled by the first harsh winds.

Now Breena found it impossible not to feel sorry for Mrs Hugh. What emerged from her bright malice was the extent of her loneliness and isolation down here. What was at last becoming clear was that Mrs Hugh did not see this town at all. What it was in itself, a small market town, rough-fashioned maybe, but the working centre of a community, in a landscape of sea and mountains, completely escaped her. Only as a clumsy, unfinished attempt at city amenities could Mrs Hugh even begin to assess it. Where Breena's world began, the petering-out of the little streets, Mrs Hugh's ended. All at once Breena grasped this; a vivid realisation of the difference between Mrs Hugh's vision of the town and her own took her over. She knew that Mrs Hugh had never learned to swim; that the mountains made her shiver and draw closer to the fire. It seemed obvious to Breena now that Mrs Hugh was made for city living, that her whole personality had been formed by cities. What kind of life lay in store for her down here? What the town needed more than anything, a young Dr Peggy or a young Ursula. And what if her great hopes to have a family failed her too? What kind of person would she become then?

Yet, strange to relate, all this time Breena was also listening hard for sounds from upstairs, and waiting. She could deal with what Mrs Hugh was saying, and with her own by no means absorbing reflections on Mrs Hugh, with the top layer of her thoughts. All the time underneath there was a tense concentration of waiting. Every moment she expected to hear footsteps on the stairs, Maurice coming down. Once or twice she thought too of Uncle John, how he had told her to go down to the kitchen and have some tea and then go home. But by necessity that had already become a shadowy, candlelit, half-forgotten episode. Because it angered her, with an obscure helpless anger that she had experienced before and was afraid of, she had succeeded in pushing it gradually to the back of her mind to be 'dealt with later'. All the time as she sat and looked about her and listened, and reflected, and waited, she was pushing that scene with Uncle John farther and farther back in her mind, until at last it fell over the brink of her consciousness.

CHAPTER 27

Breena was waiting for Maurice. It was like a test she was putting him to. This summer she had reached a stage in her life when she believed that there was power, actual motive power, in the feelings she had for him. This power she had carefully verified by experience. How many times lately had she not thought to herself; 'What's Maurice doing now, I wonder? Well, I wish he'd stop doing it, and come along here!' And then, a few minutes afterwards, when she looked up, Maurice would be there, making his way towards her, all unconscious of the fact that she had summoned him. On her own side, what she felt for him could make her gentle, generous, forgiving, considerate for others. It seemed quite natural therefore that it should also confer on her the power to summon him to her when she wished.

At last she heard footsteps on the stairs. The door opened, she looked up eagerly. It was, of course, Maurice. And even when he sat down beside her and told her that he had been sitting near Uncle John in the room upstairs when she went in; but had judged it best to wait for some time before following her down here, even then she saw no reason to question the power of her feelings. It seemed clear as day to her that it was some instinctive foreknowledge of the fact that she would be along at dawn that had kept Maurice sitting up there beside Uncle John until that time.

But now Mrs Hugh and the others were preparing to go to bed.

They had arranged to be relieved by other women around this time, and these could be heard stirring and whispering upstairs.

Maurice whispered to Breena: 'Let's go outside... I have something to tell you...'

They went out through the back porch, to the garden that Maurice's grandmother had planted. As they passed through the garden, Breena spared that dead woman a thought, gave up to her a few seconds in which she might exist again... Seventy years ago, four times Breena's age ago, she had come to this little town, planted her fuchsias, roses, azaleas, geraniums; given birth to her three children, and died. The garden had survived her. It was now a beautiful, strange jungle of a place, where the strongest of the plants had spread and intermingled. In some clumps four or five different kinds of flowers could be seen. Breena said to Maurice: 'Let's go out of here into the high field. It ought to be sunny out there pretty soon.'

She led the way so quickly that he only caught up with her, panting, when she had to pause to open the little gate. As they began to walk across the field together, he said very seriously; 'What's the matter, Breena?' His glance was keen as he asked it. She said:

'What makes you think that there's anything the matter?'

'Your face. You look... not like yourself.'

She hesitated. Did she want to tell him about Gabriel, about that proposal that had been passed on to her at second and third hand, and that now, at this hour of the morning, she lacked all belief in? All at once with a gambler's instinct, she decided to leave it all to chance. She would tell him about Gabriel, or not tell him, depending on the way subjects, silences, discussions, came up or were dismissed between them. Suddenly she became very light-hearted again. She turned round, smiling, to challenge him:

'But you said you had something to tell me? You'd better hurry up if you want to get your story in first. I might have a tale to tell you too...'

He sighed. 'Well... I thought this would amuse you, Breena, after what I told you yesterday. They have a job lined up for me.'

'A job? They? Who?'

'Why, the family. Hugh, Mother, Patrick, Jerry maybe, Uncle John...'

'Do you mean a job until September? Until you go back to school?'

'Go back to school? You know better than that, Breena... No, I'm not going back to school. The job they're thinking of is a job in a bank.'

'In a bank? As a clerk?'

'I suppose so. They all begin that way, don't they? I didn't ask.'

'For life? They want you to work in a bank for life?'

'For life!' That made him smile. 'That's about it! A life-sentence!'

'And what did they say when you told them your plans for the future?'

He made no immediate answer to this. By tacit consent, or perhaps by mere force of habit, they had changed direction a little, and were now making for a large flat rock where they sometimes used to eat their breakfasts in the summer, when they were children. The flushed eastern sky was before them, with the inky blackness of the Tobar mountain range below. Breena repeated her question; 'Well, what did they say? What did they think of your plans?'

When he still made no answer, she turned to look at him. She saw, with a great deal of surprise, that he was laughing. He was shaking with silent laughter. Indeed, she could see that he was quite unable to answer her for laughing. She said quietly:

'Maurice... could you please stop laughing in that way? I asked you a question. What did they say when you told them your own plans for the future? And when did all this happen? Where? What time last night?'

He succeeded in controlling himself. He said in apology; 'Sorry for that stupid fit of laughter. It's sheer nerves, I think. I haven't had a wink of sleep since Friday night. The answer to your question is, of course I didn't tell them about my own plans at all.'

She stepped up close to him then, and looked at him straight into his eyes. In this harsh dawn light there was no entry into the hard gloss of their brilliant surfaces. She could see only a reflection of herself in each. She said; 'Maurice, I think I'll go home now. I can see how it is... You have already left this little town in your imagination. All of us here already seem like comic figures to you. We don't seem like real people any more. You can only laugh at us... The hard polish on your eyes is a glitter of expectancy. You can hardly wait to leave us in body, as you've already left us in spirit.'

Maurice made some exclamation. They had reached the big rock, and he pretended to lean against it for support. The next moment he took her hand and gripped it, and then they stood side by side, leaning against the high rock. Breena was very conscious of the fact that for the first time ever they stood so close that their shoulders and hips touched. Maurice said:

'It's the glitter of sleeplessness, Breena. Never before in my life have I realised how much the human body cries out for sleep.'

'I'm more sorry than I can tell you,' Breena murmured, 'for saying those harsh things to you. Even if they were true, I had no right...'

'Yes, you had. Who has a right, if not you...? But don't you want me to tell you what happened last night?'

'Yes, of course.'

'Well, it all began with Kitty. Or, to be quite honest, with myself. When I came back from giving round the fish with Thady, I ran into Kitty, who was searching the house for you. Sean Mor had told her that you came in with himself and must be somewhere around. Then Desmond told us Dr Peggy had taken you off home. Kitty got very depressed. We went into the back-kitchen to have a cup of tea together. Kit and myself had a corner to ourselves. Just to cheer her up then, to take her mind off herself, I began to tell her about my plans – what I told you yesterday morning in the hut…'

'No!' Breena exclaimed, 'Maurice, surely you didn't think that Kitty, in her present state, could…'

'Well, I'm afraid I did. The next thing I knew, old Kit was pushing back her chair, with her handkerchief pressed to her eyes. She rushed out of the room. By the time I reached the door she was out of sight, so I took it for granted that she had gone to Ursula, or Mother. But as I found out afterwards, she had gone straight to Hugh. I went back to my tea. Within twenty minutes there came a summons, Mrs Hugh herself; speaking in her softest tones: would I mind just stepping into the sitting room for a few minutes? I stepped in of course – who could refuse Mrs Hugh? – and found that Hugh had got an intimidation board together to receive me; Mother, Aunt Ursula, Uncle John, Father Patrick, Father Hennessey, Hugh himself. And that's about all there is to tell, I guess.'

'All there is to tell?' Breena repeated blankly.

'What I mean is, you can guess the rest.'

Breena kept silence a moment. Then she said, 'I can't be very good at guessing. I'd like to hear exactly what happened.'

'Well, Hugh began by calling me names; on Kitty's account, you know, because I'd made her cry. And the way I so heartlessly went out to Maurcappagh afterwards on a fishing trip. At that Uncle John intervened. He made it quite clear to Hugh that he knew about the Maurcappagh trip. Then Hugh changed his tactics once more. He asked me, what did I think stood between me and the "most humiliating, the most degrading hard work? Work that would put an end to my fine speeches for all time?" Can you guess the answer to that one?'

'Your talents, I suppose. Your education…'

'Talents, education, nonsense! The answer is, my family! My family, that's the only protection I have…'

After a moment's silence she asked him in a gentle voice:

'I take it that no mention was made of your going back to school? And what *had* Kitty told Hugh?'

'Kitty had told Hugh a very distressing tale, the truth as she saw it, we can't doubt that. She told him I was planning to run away from home because I was afraid of another year's hard work at school, afraid of failing my exams – that sort of thing. You know my family has always suspected my… my academic intentions. Last night it was made clear to me, by Hugh and Father Patrick both, to go back to school. All that pampering nonsense has died with Father. Things are rock-bottom serious now. The problem now is to find me a respectable living; to save me from soul-crushing hard work or actual want. I can go back to school, yes. If I'm a good boy. But it was put to me, again by Hugh and Father Patrick, that I already had the right number of subjects for the bank. And Hugh and Father Patrick, both, with the help of the connections they have so laboriously built up over the years, are now prepared to guarantee that I will be interviewed "sympathetically" either in Glenmere or Castleboyne, whichever I choose.'

Breena waited a moment, and then said in a tone that must easily have matched Father Patrick's for carefulness:

'And, Maurice… weren't you tempted at all by this offer – by all these offers? Do you think it's impossible to earn your living, and work at your music at the same time, at home?'

'To earn my living? But I'll have to do that wherever I go. I don't intend to starve.'

He withdrew his hand, and moved a few paces away from her. For a minute or two there was silence. He stared at the ground. Then he broke out; 'No! I wasn't at all tempted by their offers, by their bribery. It's hard to tell you what I felt. I became very excited… '

He paused. But Breena, who for some minutes had yielded to the selfish hope that he would take the job, and stay at home; and knew that he knew that she had yielded to it, had no comment to make. Suddenly he turned on her and accused her outright:

'Breena, even you don't believe in me, you don't trust me. You don't want me to go away. You're almost as bad as Kitty. You think its cowardice about next year's exams, and not courage, that's driving me away.'

She stepped up to him:

'Maurice, you say that even I don't trust you? But do you trust yourself? And if you do, how is it that you didn't confront your family last night with your plans for the future? You've told me, haven't you, that you said nothing whatever to them about your great plans to go off and learn your trade the hard way? So all they've heard so far is some hysterical, garbled version from Kitty…'

'That's not fair, Breena. Why should I explain to them? Hugh's not my father. Last night he tried to step into Father's shoes, and I showed him up before the whole family as a pitiful failure in that respect. I refused to take him seriously. Can you guess what hurt me most of all last night, Breena…? It was that… not the smallest, slightest mention was made of my one real talent, my musical gift. I waited and waited for somebody to mention it. But not one of them did. And then I saw them looking at one another. I realised each one was afraid of the other. Nobody dared bring up the subject, for fear of somebody else's mockery. That's why I kept silence about my plans. Out of contempt, not cowardice.'

Breena sighed. She said, 'Maurice, I ask you again, are you in earnest? Is all this just talk? At the moment, it seems to me, talking is our way of life. We live by talk. But to talk about leaving home is one thing, and to leave home another. I'm getting tired of talk, as you know…'

With that he went up to her and swung himself up on the rock near where she was standing. Then he reached down and helped her up beside him. He might have kissed her, just when her face came up on a level with his. He looked at her mouth, and then looked straight into her eyes. There was a moment's silence. Then quickly, as if he could not quite trust himself, he jumped impulsively down off the rock, and began to talk in a breathless fashion as he walked about below.

'Breena, can you think of all the sitting I'd have to do, between now and the time I died, if I took that job as clerk? And what if a big bomb went off and I got blown out of existence in a sitting position? The shame of it!'

She sighed again. 'Yes, yes. I know how you feel about it, believe me. I… it's exactly the way I feel about the shop.' Then she shivered and murmured: 'It's cold up here. There's no warmth in the sun yet. I … I think we'd better, I mean I'd better go in now and see how Kitty is.'

She jumped down. He came up to her and put his hand on her arm.

'Don't go in for a moment… Listen, Breena, I… You understand, don't you. I must go. I explained it all to you yesterday, surely. And now my family has forced my hand. They utterly despise my one, my only talent. If I stayed here my soul would rot, I'd become hopeless… And what is sin after all except the actions of people without hope? And if it's possible to know any truth at all, how can you know until you've suffered for it?'

He ceased speaking, or, rather, pulled himself up abruptly on a tight rein. For a minute or two there was silence once more. Then they turned towards one another and almost at the same moment began to speak. It was one of those frantic, excited conversations they often had nowadays, when they interrupted one another and sometimes spoke together for the length of a couple of sentences, their tongues beating up and down like the hoofs of horses straining neck and neck for the winning post. After a while they were too excited to remain in the shade of the boulders any longer, but walked out once more into the open field, and began to stride back and forth across its whole width. Which of them said what no longer mattered. As their blood came up, and the beauty of the landscape and the morning seemed to increase accordingly, they found heightened satisfaction in one another's company, and their mutual harmony of feeling. What pleasure it was to be able to walk and talk like this, on this lovely July morning! As long as they kept on talking did it really matter what they said?

At last, when they had wagged their tongues into a fatigued state, and their throats were sore and their eyes blazed until they hurt, they looked at one another and smiled, admitting by their glances that they were exhausted. They began to walk down the field, but since they were both excited and over-warm, they walked very slowly. When they reached the yard, Breena glanced at her watch and exclaimed:

'Heavens! It's much later than I thought. I'd better go up at once and see Kitty. What about you? You'll try and get in a few hours' sleep? The Requiem Mass is at half-past eleven. That gives you well over four hours… '

And so they parted: Breena running up the stairs to Kitty's room; Maurice, as she thought, turning off to his own for a few hours' rest.

CHAPTER 28

As soon as Breena entered the room she saw that Kitty was asleep with her face buried in a huddled mound of pillows. Her eyes were closed fast and her breathing was restful and even and almost crooningly deep.

Breena surveyed the room. Around on the floor were scattered not only articles of clothing all jumbled up, but at least half a dozen cups and saucers and two cluttered trays. She made up her mind that it must be cleared up at once. With a rather solemn and self-righteous gait, she went quietly about the room, picking up all the stained and partially filled cups that were stationed about in such odd places that she was afraid of kicking one over any moment. She kept one eye on Kitty, as she stooped and straightened her clothes on a chair. Then she closed the shutters to lessen the noise from below, and stepped out into the corridor making sure that the door was closed. As she turned to go down the stairs, she paused a moment, and forced herself to listen.

Along the corridor, from the dead man's room, came the terrible rise and fall of the old keening. Breena listened; made herself listen. Her scalp tingled at the sound of it… terrors older than history were revived inside her. She understood now what the first dwellers on the plains had felt; what weird chills and tremors of the blood had warned them… Those ancestors of hers, who had first crept out from behind the shelter of the trees, and stalked in terror the fear-driven shadows that stalked them. These sounds were an excursion into pre-humanity. They made anything possible. They were an ache, an orgy, an expression of pure nostalgia for the freedom of dogs to bay and wolves to howl…

Then the wild ululation, the shrill cacophony of ill-matched voices, ceased. Now one voice alone took up the keen, a voice true and sweet, pouring out like a blackbird's song, yet matching each note with words of regret or appreciation that could be clearly heard. Breena's pulse beat strongly as she listened. She thought, so the ancient art of 'raising the keen' was not lost after all. She noted how in each word the soft vowel sounds were made to glide over and gather into themselves the harsher consonants. It was the old bardic poetry she was listening to, that Maurice was so interested in. Words and music were both improvised. All that was needed –a voice so true and pure that it thrilled with fresh meaning every word it uttered –was certainly here. Breena recognised the healing power of it. She hearkened to, and rejoiced in it. The soft Irish sounds no longer took her by surprise, but seemed to be words she had heard before, and was expecting to hear again now.

> *You have gone away from us now, but which of us will ever forget you?*
> *Your nature was strong, but there was no fierceness in it.*
> *Knowledge was your strength, and you used it gently.*
> *In your presence the bully became silent and slunk away like a wild beast.*
> *In the times of our sorrow we called on you to help us.*
> *Which of us ever had cause to doubt you?*
> *Our trouble now is that you went away so lonely;*
> *None of us helped you.*
> *We will never again pay heed to the sound of your voice,*
> *Or listen hard for the sound of your coming…*

The sweet voice, high and pure like the sound of a flute, soared so true over every note that Breena caught her breath at it. She went into a kind of dream as she listened. But soon, far too soon, she was harshly roused from this. The other women, evidently believing that the lone performer had had more than her turn, joined in once more. In the confusion of sound the words were lost again. There was no more music. The baying of wolves and the howling of dogs had begun again. The involuntary cries made by all animals in pain; the wordless moans of sheer hurt – these were all that could be heard now. There was nothing human in them, no effort to understand or control. They were pre-reason. Such sounds had given rise to the legend of the bean sídhe. They could not be borne. Breena rushed past the waking-room, and hastily plunged down the stairs – luckily there was nobody on them at the moment – and made her way out into the yard, now beginning to be crowded, into Church Lane.

CHAPTER 29

Somewhere inside Breena there was a small ache. She told herself it was only a very small ache, but it was there all the same. As she turned into Church Street, she could still hear the high, sweet music the lone keener had made. It was like a poem she had heard once and badly wanted to hear again. A poem that bewailed, not death, but the passing-away of friendship. *Sic transit amor mundi.* She could hear her own voice, Maurice's voice, talking so excitedly in that red morning field. About what?

She came up to the church. A few stragglers were still going in to First Mass. She stopped to watch them. There was something about them that even now gave her a joyful sense of the newness of the day. Walking briskly with downcast glances, intent on their own thoughts, in the early morning, they made her also want to hurry, with a feeling of urgency and excitement. What might not happen today! When she glanced up at the sky she saw that barred clouds had put a look of wistfulness on the sun's face. But the breeze was still warm and scented sweet with the morning. Life was still full of challenges, tremendous, terrifying… On impulse she went into the church and knelt in her usual shadowed corner, where the candlelit altar looked like a patch of sunlight in the distance. She knelt down and bowed her head and spent the first few minutes trying to fight down the ache inside her.

She realised that she was very late for Mass; so late indeed that there could be no point in pretending to herself that she was part of the congregation for this particular Mass. She decided to make it a period of private prayer instead. She bowed her head and began to recite the prayer her own father had taught her. 'Oh, incomprehensible creator, the true fountain of light, and the only author of knowledge, who out of the treasures of thy wisdom... ' She brooded on these once-resented words, finding now, through memory and association, layer behind layer of meaning in them. She could clearly recall the first time she had looked them up in the dictionary, and how she had puzzled to use them in sentences of her own. She considered to herself how her ideas of things had changed even in the past year, since that time she had believed she had it in her to be a saint. She realised that her idea of God was no longer that of the gentle, loving-and-beloved, Jesus-in-the-tabernacle figure of those days. It had expanded into a sense of mystery, a long, pleasurable, brooding awareness of the infinity of questions she might ask and never expect to find an answer for. What was life, and who was she, Breena? Why had she been born in this particular country, at this particular period of time? What meaning was there in the events of her life up to this time? Why was she, in contrast to so many other people of her own age in the world, so healthy, so unmarked by want, famine, the nightmare world of bombs, wounds, torture, fire? Could she, Breena, survive in a place of hunger or war? She closed her eyes even more tightly and imagined: a town on fire, flames belching wind-blown across a whole street, one house after another blazing out; children lost, screaming unheard in the ear-splitting din, bullets, vehicles, tearing, veering, screeching through smoke-maddened crowds... What was the value of life? Her own life, so cared for; so protected here whilst other lives in other places that even at this very moment, as she knelt here in this shaded church, were going out in agony? What meaning could be assigned to it all? Only to realise it was to be lost in feelings of helpless concern and awe, and to whisper with hope the ancestral word, 'God'.

All at once she looked up: the calling of her name, the whispering of it rather, had got through to her. Ursula was standing above her. In a kind of trance Breena got up, genuflected and waited for Ursula to lead the way out of the church.

They reached the outer door. As usual, the first thing Breena did was to glance up at the sky. She was surprised and delighted to see that the sun had broken through the dark cage that had imprisoned it earlier, and was beginning to beam through quite brightly once more.

'I have some things here for Jerry's children,' Ursula confided in a whisper as they stepped out on the gravel and went on in a coaxing tone; 'Will you take them round for me after breakfast? I'd take them myself, but Mamie's expecting me across at the other house any moment now.'

Breena consented at once. Even at the price of paying Jerry a visit she wanted to escape from Ursula's smiling insinuating glance as quickly as possible.

Then came the gentle inquiry: 'Breena, you don't look quite yourself, somehow. Are you sure you feel well?'

This was without doubt a gambit to introduce the name of Gabriel. But Breena countered it with a hasty; 'I… I slept very badly last night.'

'Ah, that's only to be expected,' she heard Ursula whisper. And when Breena looked at her there was such a glow and depth of meaning in Ursula's eyes that her own glance fell at once before them.

'I have a message for you from Dr Peggy,' Ursula went on. 'We've talked the matter over together, and she thinks it's best for you not to attend the funeral today. We don't want you to be upset. And you may be sure there will be such a crowd you won't be missed. And you needn't even slip across to the Requiem Mass, if you don't like the thought of it. You've already attended one Mass today. After the funeral, we'll arrange a little outing for you. Since it's the first time, Desmond will go with you, so that you needn't feel shy with himself (Gabriel). We can trust Desmond to find somewhere nice and quiet to go. We don't want people thinking that we mean any disrespect to the dead… Is that all right?'

Breena evaded the issue completely. Looking down at the untidy grey parcel, which for some minutes now she had been clutching to her bosom, she said politely; 'Oh, yes… Thank you. I'll do as you say. I won't go to the funeral, and I… I'll take the parcel to Jerry's now, at once, before breakfast,' and turned away to do so.

She knew that an abrupt departure of this kind was the last thing Ursula wanted just now. But she knew too that until she got rid of this stupid parcel, and then came back home and had an equally stupid conversation with Desmond, there could be no peace of mind for her.

CHAPTER 30

It was Jerry himself who had accepted the parcel. Out in the street again, Breena reflected that she had said too much about Maurice.

Maurice selfish... full of himself and his own affairs... never bothers to listen, only opens his mouth to talk about himself. And Jerry had said that 'sometimes he found himself wagging his own tongue to get his courage. Don't imagine that there's anything final about thinking you're in love with Maurice... there are certain aspects of Maurice's nature... ' he had added. Still, she'd had the last word. And now the fact that she had answered Jerry, that even in a small way at the end she had answered him, had been able to give tit for tat, cheered her immensely. She smiled to herself and winked at the sun.

'You and I,' she addressed it, 'we understand what life is.' She turned into Main Street, and crossed to the side-gate.

As she entered the kitchen her glance took in the two trays set out on the table. Hannah was standing by the stove on the right. Breena sniffed the air appreciatively; liver, bacon, onions – Desmond's favourite breakfast.

'Hello, Hannah,' she panted, 'have you cooked some for me? Is Desmond up yet? Who are the two trays for? Who else is staying in the house? Surely not Gabriel? Why are you taking them breakfast in their rooms? Didn't you say last time that you'd never... '

Hannah stopped her at this point by exclaiming sharply:

'D'you want to wear me out, girl, with your questions? Sit down, get your breath back. Ask one question at a time.'

But Hannah's grey eyes as she turned round gave the lie to the irritation in her voice. They surveyed Breena with such warm intentness that Breena could not help exclaiming:

'What's the matter, Hannah?'

Hannah seemed to hesitate. Then she said slowly: 'It's all true, Breena – what Dr Peggy told you last night. I've talked to… I've found out… I know for a fact that Mrs Hugh's brother Gabriel is tired of being a bachelor, and you're the one he wants for a wife.'

Breena sat down heavily on the nearest chair. 'Yes… Jerry has just been saying much the same thing.' After the excitement of her talk with Jerry it cost her a very positive effort to concentrate on Gabriel again. She thought for a few moments, and then added in rather a muddled way; 'Well Mrs Hugh knows nothing about it, I'm sure of that. And he's done it all so *clumsily*… '

Hannah had turned back to the stove. 'It's true all the same… And I've heard them saying that it's because you're young, and… not living in your own house, that it was all done the way 'twas.'

Breena made no answer to this. She stared at Hannah's back for a moment with great dissatisfaction, then asked abruptly:

'You've already taken Desmond a cup of tea, haven't you, Hannah?'

'I have indeed. If I didn't take him a cup o' tea first to wake him up, he'd drown himself in the teapot at breakfast.'

'Well, then… ' Breena darted sideways for the stairs and began to climb them two and three at a time. As she neared the white ceiling-boards that would take her out of sight of the kitchen, she glanced down to her left, astonished that Hannah had let her go without a word. She saw that Hannah had stepped back from the stove and was looking after her. It seemed to her now that Hannah was on the very point of warning her not to go ahead. She even thought she could catch the beginning of her name on Hannah's lips. Hastily she tugged at the banister on her left and hauled herself up on the landing out of sight. There could be no point in waiting for Hannah to speak, since she, Breena, intended to ignore anything that was said.

Desmond's bedroom was over the stock-room, only a little way down the corridor, opposite the sitting-room. It was always kept ready for his use, so that he could feel free to come home whenever he had even half a day off. The journey by car from Dublin, as Desmond drove, took only three or four hours. Now Breena quickly smoothed down her hair with both hands, pulled at her sweater and dress, and then knocked gently at Desmond's door. At first there was no response, no sound of life from within. She knocked again, rather more loudly and smartly.

'Hann, Hann, Hannah,' the voice squeaked shrilly, 'come in, come in. Hurrah-hay! Breakfast, Hannah.'

(Desmond had long ago adopted Breena's name for Hannah, and there could be little doubt but that Hannah liked it). Breena now pushed the door a little open, and was relieved to see that at least the daylight had been let into the room. Desmond had had his tea, the curtains were open; he would be in some condition to understand her.

'It's not Hannah,' she whispered into the chink. 'It's me, Breena. Desmond, I want to speak to you, please.'

'Breena, is it?' The tone was amazingly normal, even alert, considering first the silence and then the parrot chatter. 'Wait a minute, will you?'

Breena deemed it best to respond to that tone by withdrawing outside again and completely shutting the door. While she waited she heard distinctively some low-voiced muttering going on inside, and the question – was Desmond swearing to himself? – made her heart beat quicker than ever, out of all proportion to the occasion. She acknowledged to herself that in Desmond's eyes Breena with problems must seem a very poor substitute indeed for Hannah with liver, onion, and bacon. Yet, surely he ought to have expected… Then, quite suddenly it seemed to her, she had heard no sound of

| 211

footsteps, the door was pulled sharply inwards. Desmond stood there before her. Taller by a head than she was, his thick dark hair all in his eyes like a child's, he was covered as far as his bare feet in a striking pair of bright pink and tan pyjamas. After one glance at his face it was mostly his feet she looked at. She noticed how pale and long and straight his toes were. She was aware that he was rubbing his right eye with his right fist, and she said hurriedly:

'Desmond, excuse me for coming up like this before you've had your break… '

'Breena! Hello, hello! It's good to see you again.'

His greeting sounded so hearty that in a rather shame-faced and urgent manner she felt compelled to return it.

'Oh, hello, Desmond. I'm… I'm very pleased to see you too… I thought I'd just run up and tell you, I mean ask you… '

'Schh!' The warning sound interrupted her very softly. Her glance flew up from the pale straight toes to the sleep-flushed face. She saw that the hand that had been rubbing the right eye was now laid against Desmond's lips, in a dramatic call for silence. Then she looked down again and saw that the bare feet were tiptoeing out to her own side of the door. She saw that the door was being drawn to, softly, significantly. All the time the hand against the lips kept her in silence.

She watched the door close. 'I can't speak to you now,' she heard Desmond's whisper. 'I'm not alone. Guess who's sharing my room?' She saw that he was keeping his hand on the doorknob.

'Sharing your room?'

'Yes. I'm on the truckle-bed, and he's in mine. Guess?'

'Gabriel?'

It came out on the instant, even it seemed to her. There was a certain inevitability about it. Almost she believed now that she had been expecting it.

'Yes. So, schhh! about… you know what… '

All confused as she was, watching the door open again and the long pale toes go tiptoeing back into the room, she heard him go on to ask:

'Have they given you the parcel?'

'Parcel?'

The parcel for Jerry's children was what came first into her head. Then she realised that Desmond couldn't possibly know anything about that. Only then, in her anxious and bewildered state did she remember that whenever Desmond came home, he always brought her a present. That must be the parcel he meant. Coming home even this time, at such short notice to his uncle's funeral, he must still have remembered to bring her something. But oh how exasperated the mention of a present from him, another parcel, made her feel at this moment! She whispered desperately:

'No, I haven't been given any parcel yet. But Desmond, please come out again for a moment. Close the door. I want to…'

'Schh!… for now.' She glanced at his face and saw that the hand was up once more before his lips, in a play-acting childish, warning way. 'We'll have a long chat afterwards.'

The door was very gently closed in her face. She stood a moment staring at it, its colour a greyish-white haze in her eyes. Why had they put Gabriel in with Desmond? Was he really in there after all? She might, she thought, knock again at the door and this time directly challenge Desmond. Even if life was always a game for him, he must be made to understand that other people were not quite so lucky. She could knock again at the door, say to him outright; 'Even if Gabriel really is in there, you must come out and speak to me. Close the door, please. I must tell you…'

And yet, though she raised her fist and held it for a few seconds at the ready, she did not quite dare to knock at the door again. Or perhaps it was not so much that she did not dare to do it, as that she firmly believed Desmond would outwit her again. She was no match for Desmond. All right, she thought then. On Desmond's head be whatever happened. His dear friend and room-mate Gabriel would

| 213

find that he had wasted a few days out of what was left of his precious life, by coming down here.

As she began rather slowly to move away from the door, to return downstairs, she found that her hands were wet with perspiration. Impatiently she pulled off her sweater and rubbed her face and hands with it. She thought to herself; 'I need a long swim out at Maurcappagh.'

When she got back to the kitchen Hannah had her place set for her in her favourite corner behind the dairy door. As usual Breena, for all her troubles, felt extremely hungry; so that when Hannah passed her a generous helping of liver and bacon most of her irritation with Desmond vanished and gave place to the social impulse to discuss the matter with Hannah. Breena looked across at her and remarked in quite an off-hand way:

'It's a shame that Gabriel had to sleep in Desmond's room. I thought I'd be able to speak to Desmond, and ask him to tell his friend to leave me alone.'

Hannah sighed. 'I thought that's why you went up. But you ought to know by now that Desmond would be too smart for you.'

It was now Breena's turn to sigh. Hannah went on:

'Don't bank on any help from Desmond, girl, that's my advice. 'Tisn't that I don't like him – you know better than that. Who can help liking him, he's always so open-handed and pleasant? And if I was in a tight corner, Desmond would be the first person I'd go to for help – if there was nobody else in sight. But as I said last night this matter is just sport to him. If I was in your shoes at this moment I'd sooner put my trust in an eel than in Desmond.'

Breena considered this and sighed again. She chewed a while in silence and then put down her knife and fork.

'Oh, Hannah, why should I have to take Gabriel seriously? You know it's all ridiculous, Hannah. I'd give almost anything not to have to see him at all, not to have to face him…'

'Well, this is the way I see it, Desmond won't help you. They've kept your Uncle John out of the secret, or he's kept himself out – he can't get interested in such things just now. Dr Peggy is highly delighted with it all – she thinks you're made for life. And she's brought her two sisters, and with them I'd say Hugh also, round to her way of thinking. So now it's up to you. Either you go to your Uncle John, and ask him to speak for you – tell him all about it – or make up your mind to speak for yourself. You're always writing things down, aren't you? Well, then write down on a piece o' paper what you think best to say to Gabriel, then learn it off by heart.'

'Yes… that's good advice. Either go to Uncle John or face Gabriel on my own. Well… ' She stood up. 'I'll think over what you've said… ' But she knew that no member of the family, least of all perhaps Uncle John himself, would thank her for troubling him about Gabriel today.

Monday was a comfortless day in the house. Two cleaning women, Cathy and Sheila, came in to clean out the premises, and had to be supervised by Hannah. These women came in now, Hannah began to bustle about making tea for them. Breena was only too pleased to escape to her own room.

Her mood was confused. She felt shivery, excited, exasperated, full of indecision. Yet at the same time she was in some queer way vibrantly, joyfully aware of all the strange, woeful, glad, exhilarating surprises life held in store for her. She went to the window and pressed her nose against the large cool lower pane of glass and looked idly out. There was still some sunshine brightening the grass, though the shadows were creeping up on it from every side. Only the somewhat dreary 'cheep-cheep' of the sparrows could now be heard. Gusts of wind round the house; the rowan tree at the turn of the garden swayed and hissed. There could be no doubt of it, it was a time for Mental Discipline. She went to her table and sat down and pulled out her discipline notebook. She opened it at the page she was working at, and with her elbows on the table and her fingers in her ears tried to blot out all silly emotions in a bout of hard study.

CHAPTER 31

Some kind of sound from behind her made her swerve round, though still with her fingers in her ears. Hannah was standing in the doorway, her grey eyes giving off sparkles and glitters of annoyance. Breena took her fingers from her ears at once.

'Breena! Five minutes I've been calling you, and all the time you've been sitting there at the table, playing at being deaf.'

'Hannah, you know very well that I always put my fingers to my ears when… '

'It beats me what putting your fingers to your ears has to do with reading. Come on now, you're wanted upstairs in the sitting-room.'

'Wanted?' Breena jumped up. 'Who wants me, Hannah?'

'Who wants you? Every man who claps eyes on you, no doubt.' Hannah was obviously in no mood to impart polite information.

And she turned away from the door. Her hurried footsteps could be heard crossing the hall; a busy woman, indignant at being needlessly called away from her morning's duties with Cathy and Sheila. Breena took it for granted that it was himself, Gabriel, who waited for her upstairs. She hurriedly smoothed down her sweater and dress, and rubbed her sleeves across the front of her shoes.

When she got excited about anything it was her ears that went red first of all. She could feel her ears throbbing hotly now, in tune with the faster beating of her pulse. She combed her hair carefully over her ears, to hide them. There was a mirror on the wall near the bed, but she refrained from looking into it, fearing that something in her reflection might discourage her. She felt very excited; but she was surprised at the feeling of relief that was also there inside her. Yes… it was a very definite relief to be able to get the stupid matter over and done with.

She went up the main stairs two and three at a time, winking at the foolish, inquisitive face of the clock as she passed. 'Just think of it,' she whispered to the clock, 'when I come down these stairs again all that nonsense will be over!' She reached the sitting-room and as she pushed open the door caught the impression of a man's figure, in a needlessly thick greatcoat, standing by the middle window, looking down into the square. She withdrew her glance from that quarter at once, and turned to shut the door with great care. At last she had to look round, but she kept her glance on the floor as she took her first few steps into the room. Then she looked up, and at once she stopped short, very surprised and put out. It was not Gabriel, but Hugh, who stood there before her.

'Dia's Muire dhuit,' was Hugh's greeting. He said it in the most natural way in the world. He seemed to have no idea how astonished she was. Yet never before in her life had he called on her like this – nor had she ever expected him to do so.

She answered automatically: 'Dia's Muire's Padraig.' She saw that he was pulling out a chair for her at the long table that took up most of the breadth of the room to the left of the door.

'Suig sios, agus leig do ski,' he invited her pleasantly. She felt too much at a loss for the moment to meet his glance, and she pretended not to notice how he pulled out the chair. She remained where she was, standing. She hesitated, then took her courage in both hands and asked him in English, in what she hoped was a tone of polite astonishment, though she stammered a little:

'Do – do you want to speak to *me*, Hugh?'

'Yes, certainly, I do. Please sit down.' And he indicated the chair a second time. She could hardly pretend to be blind, and she lacked the wit to find an excuse. There could be no ignoring this second gesture, so she went quickly to the chair and sat down. Hugh walked round the table. As he settled himself into place opposite her their glances met. His eyes, blue like the three sisters', were deeper and warmer in colour than she had ever seen them. He smiled at her. Of its own accord then, her face jerked itself into an answering smile or grimace rather, that induced him to say:

'Well, well! It's a good thing I'm not a vain man. I came here thinking that you'd be very pleased to see me. But here I am, and I've never had a cooler welcome in the whole course of my life!'

Quickly and foolishly she protested then, 'Oh, no!' The upshot of this was to make him say:

'I had no idea I was beginning to have this effect on young girls. Marriage! Three short years ago they were not like this with me. But I was a bachelor then.'

Hugh ended his little speech with a sidelong look that was so arch and at odds with the dignified image of himself he had been trying to build up since his return to the town, that her slight awe of him faded and she was able at least to look up and meet his glance. He smiled at her again, and this time she was able to smile back with something of a genuine smile. This obviously pleased him. He leaned towards her, letting his elbows slide on the polished surface of the table until they were nearly half way across, and told her briskly:

'I'll come straight to the point. You know Maurice had just been to see me?'

'To see you? Maurice? No. I thought he intended to get in a few hours' sleep.'

In her surprise she had said too much. Hugh's glance became at once so keenly blue and interested that her own fell before it. She understood then that Hugh must have been talking to his wife about Maurice and herself; that he must have gathered how she and Maurice had been together in the kitchen earlier on that morning, and then gone out of doors together.

'So he didn't tell you that he was coming to see me? Hmm… it adds up. He must have acted on impulse – as usual. His impulses get wilder and wilder. Well, not three quarters of an hour ago I was called into my office, and there he was. The moment I put my face in at the door he jumped to his feet. Then he began to stride up and down the room. He flailed his arms at me and hurled words and sentiments at me as big as boulders. I can't tell you half of what he said.'

She was holding his glance now out of sheer nervous inability to look away, though it was extremely painful to her. He lowered his voice and went on in a more confidential tone.

'As you may well imagine, I said as little as possible. A few vague protests here and there, just enough to encourage him to go on… You see, I think it's essential at this stage to let him get it all out of his system. But do you know that in the end he went away very quietly? It was obvious that he felt sorry he had said so much. And, of course, he was more than a little baffled by my attitude.'

Now Hugh was smiling directly at her. She was dying to ask him, *what* had Maurice said? Yet she knew that to ask him any question whatever just then, or even to continue to hold his glance, would be to conspire with him in making fun of Maurice. She had no choice but to drop her glance. There followed a moment's silence. Over the polished surface of the table shadows passed, faint images of Maurice, shapes that his red mouth had made yesterday when he pronounced certain decisions, his white wistful look when she left him in the field…

Then Hugh drew away, leaned back in his chair and began to speak again. She saw immediately that he had decided to change his tactics. He had suddenly become very serious. His eyes when she glanced up once did their best to look with trust and confidence in her. But mostly she kept her glance on the table. She did so out of embarrassment, because of what Hugh was saying. He was telling her now, in so many bald words, and in a low, emphatic, confidential tone, that what he had really come here this morning for was to *ask her advice.*

At this Breena was imprudent enough to look up. She found herself meeting a full significant look, a look of… ? She could only call it in her own mind by that hoary old name, 'secret understanding'. But secret understanding of what?

All at once she felt very depressed and chilled. Right up to this moment she had taken it for granted that what went on between Maurice and herself, concerned themselves alone. But now she understood quite clearly that it was a matter the whole family was interested in. She saw too the far-reaching consequences of what Dr Peggy had told her only last night. An hour ago she had been discussing it with Hannah as if it were exclusively her own business. Now the realisation came to her that Hugh was paying his visit not to her, Breena, but to the future wife of his own wife's brother. How slow she was, not to have grasped this at the very beginning! The prospect of marriage with his brother-in-law had raised Breena, whom he had publicly shouted at and rebuked like a naughty child in front of the church yesterday, to absolute equality with Hugh. At one bound she had drawn level with him, had become overnight an adult, respectable person, whom he could come to *for advice.*

All this time, of course, Hugh was talking. He was still leaning towards her across the table, and saying in a soft, intimate voice, rather slowly and carefully; and looking down at the table in his turn, as if to stress the delicacy of the matter under discussion:

'I know you'll agree with me that Maurice has been very spoiled. He's had nothing but soft words all his life… He has a certain aptness and deftness as far as music is concerned, a gift for pleasing people. Everybody praises him and spoils him wherever he goes. He makes himself welcome anywhere.' Hugh paused once more; his voice became even more low, confiding and intimate. 'As I've just said, Maurice has always been very spoiled. With all due respect for the dead, I must say this, that Father often used Maurice as a mouthpiece for his own attitudes… From the time Maurice was a child, he was encouraged on his most extravagant notions. I know you won't misunderstand me, Breena, when I say that Father was in some ways a very disappointed man. You yourself have heard him say, as often as I have, that he had wasted his life in this obscure little market town. "Any old fool could have done as well down here as I've done!" How often have we both heard him make that remark? And you know how he used to go on, just like Maurice in a way, as if he were trying to goad us: "It's time one of us went out and made some stir in the world!" and "I think Maurice will be the one to do it!" that sort of talk. Maurice has been brought up on it. No wonder he doesn't know whether it's on his head or his heels he's standing at the moment, poor boy. If poor Father could only have foreseen the consequences of what he was saying. As I see it now, it's our plain duty to restrain him… '

Hugh's voice died away. For a moment Breena felt something like intense compassion for him. She acknowledged to herself that there was a great deal of truth in what he said. Poor Hugh had inherited a situation that she, Breena, had never bothered to inquire into fully, simply because it was such ancient history. As for Hugh's reactions to Maurice's plans – if plans they could be called – why, there could be no point in pretending to herself that yesterday morning in the hut, when Maurice first spoke to her, she had not bitterly condemned him as 'irresponsible' and 'unstable' in her own heart. She therefore understood what Hugh was feeling now. What she must do now was convince Hugh that first reactions were not always to be trusted; that they were often mere prejudices, which reason and – yes, generosity and affection too – must be brought to work on straight away.

CHAPTER 32

For the first time in her life Breena looked very kindly at Hugh, where he sat opposite her staring gloomily down at the table. For the first time too she conceded in her own mind what she had so often denied Kitty: that Hugh was really quite good looking, a pretty-faced man. It was just that he looked too much like Ursula. A face that was very right for a woman somehow did not do at all for a man.

Now Hugh was obviously waiting for some comment from her side of the table. He had no intention of going on, it seemed, until he had heard what she had to say. Now she clasped her hands firmly together in her lap. She could feel them trembling with the effort it cost her to control her impetuosity, and speak in the balanced, slow and serious fashion she understood Hugh would respect. She leaned across the table and said very earnestly, but rather breathlessly:

'It can't be denied that Maurice *appears* to be talking very wildly at the moment. And he seems to be conceited too, and big-headed, as you say, Hugh. But that's only because he thinks we're all against him. He talks faster and wilder but that's a sign of nervousness and humility, rather than conceit. He knows he has ability, talent, but he's not at all sure what it amounts to. Yesterday when he first spoke to me, I felt exactly as you do – that he was talking like a fool. But now I believe that Maurice, being the kind of person he is, has no choice but to put himself to the test. People want to be what they're able to be. I've… I've thought about Maurice, and I feel sure of that now. Just look at Terence O'Shaughnessy, he's been Maurice's friend for years. They've been at school together since they were five. They used to talk – we all used to talk, Terence and Maurice and Kitty and myself… ' Here Breena paused and smiled with direct appeal into Hugh's face, 'You know, I suppose, that Terence liked Kitty, still likes her, very much? We used to talk, all four of us, about our grand ambitions. But look at Terence now… All he wants to do is settle down and work in his father's garage. He knows that that's all he can do well, that's all he's fit for. So after all his ambitions and dreams, that's all he wants to do now. Whereas Maurice has moved on, he has kept to his first ambitions, and improved on them, he has… '

At this point she was interrupted by Hugh's voice, cutting in on her with the brutal sharpness of a blow; 'You know, you sound so exactly like Maurice, I hardly know whether it's you or he who's speaking at this moment.' He gave her a quick stab of a glance, looked down at the table, and then she heard him say in an anxious conciliatory tone:

'My dear, you must guard against taking Maurice too seriously. You must not allow him to influence you in judging a young fellow like Terence O'Shaughnessy. Terence is the only son in that house, you know, and that garage of theirs could hardly be better situated for business. They're planning to add a restaurant very soon. Has Terence told you? In ten years' time Terence will be, if not a rich man, at least well on the way to becoming one… But we were talking about Maurice. Oh, I know he spends hours in that… converted hut of his, engaged in what he calls "work". But I ask you in all common sense, Breena, how can such time-wasting be termed work? I admit he has some kind of talent, both as a music maker and a word spinner. For years now he has been encouraged to neglect his ordinary schoolwork in favour of these… these unknowable and indefinable mysteries. But I suppose you view them in a different light?'

Breena, who was still looking down at her hands, heard his voice die away, and glanced up. She saw that he was smiling at her. She smiled back quickly. Anything to get this visit over! Evidently he wished for some kind of answer, response, from her. He seemed to consider her smile response enough. He went on slowly:

'Maurice seems to entertain some idea that I'm insulting him – merely because I suggest that he makes an honest effort to earn his bread and butter – for the time being at least. Just for Mother's sake, even. He was there when Father died; he knows what a dreadful shock it was to her. Yet he selfishly persists in tormenting her with this new worry. How can you account for it?'

He paused again. But this time Breena's powers of pleasing failed her completely. She found herself unable even to look up. As for any kind of answer, she was utterly incapable of it. Now she could feel her cheeks as well as her ears begin to throb dully. The next moment she heard Hugh's voice saying apologetically:

'My dear Breena, you mustn't think that because I lost patience a few minutes back, and interrupted you somewhat rudely, I have no respect for your opinions... Believe me, Breena, I'm a busy man. You wouldn't find me here this morning, unless I thought you could help me...'

He paused, to give her time to digest this, and then his confiding, near-tender voice came a little closer. He must, she thought, be leaning nearly half-way across the table by now.

'As I see it, Breena, Maurice is just going through an adolescent phase of what appears to himself to be the most idealistic, self-sacrificing, noble search for the truth. But he'll outgrow this phase. And it's up to all of us, every one of us, Breena, to make sure that he does so without prejudices to his future development and happiness. In my view that's what families are for, to guide youngsters over these bad patches.'

At this appeal, Breena gathered up her strength and smiled quickly once more. Oh, would he never go! To think that Hugh should turn out to be such a talker! Up to now she had always thought of him as a mere smiler. He began to speak again, now in a trusting, good-humoured tone. What he had come for became clear at last.

'You must talk to him about this, Breena, make him see the reality of the situation. When I said just now that I came here to ask for your help, Breena, what I meant is this: I know Maurice talks to you, confides in you. What you must do now is encourage him, to talk as much as possible. Let him rant and rave about everything. Listen, and keep listening. Ask him questions, get him to tell you what he feels about every single person and every situation. In that way you'll help all of us and Maurice himself, most of all. You see, Breena, my experience of Maurice's type of mentality is that the more he talks, the less likely he is to act. At the rate he's going on, he must soon reach a certain feverish pitch of excitement. Then he'll effervesce. After that he'll be very quiet for a time, depressed maybe for a week or so, but then he'll buckle down and consent to listen to us at last. Believe me, Breena, it's our duty to… '

And so Hugh continued for some moments longer. The more she listened to him, the more puzzled she became. What she could not grasp at all, what she could not even guess at, was how Hugh considered Maurice would react as soon as, or if ever, he heard that she, Breena, was engaged to Mrs Hugh's brother. Was it possible Hugh could believe Maurice would go on confiding in Breena, and exchanging opinions with her, after she had introduced herself to him as Gabriel's future wife? That, she thought to herself, was the blind spot in Hugh's perception. His absolute lack of knowledge of how people behaved when strong feelings, rather than self-interest, guided them. No – for all Hugh's easy speaking about 'Maurice's type of mentality', there was a great gap in his own experience.

But now Hugh seemed to consider that he had accomplished what he had come for. He stood up. Then began to walk round the table. He made, not for the door, but for the upper end of the table, so that he had to come round by Breena's chair. As he came up to her he held out his hand with a manly-seeming impulsive gesture. Surprised, blushing again, she jumped up and placed her hand in his. He gave it a hearty, prolonged squeeze.

'I feel far more easy about Maurice now that I've spoken to you,' he assured her. 'You'll see, between us we'll manage to tame him yet.'

Then, still holding her hand, and giving her one of his blandest, brightest smiles, he remarked; 'I've never seen you looking so well. You've always been a very picture of health. But now there's an added glow and brightness. What's the reason for it, I wonder?'

With this he released her hand and turned away. But at the door he stopped and looked back. He raised his hand in a gesture of farewell, and before he closed the door gave her the same sidelong, smiling glance he had given her at the beginning of his visit, when he was trying so hard to put her at her ease.

After the door closed she walked mechanically across the room to the middle window-seat, and sat down on the edge of it, well back, so that nobody below in the square could see her. She felt almost sick with a feeling of self-hatred, heartache. Oh, what a puny-brained, useless creature she was! How first Desmond, and now Hugh, had scored over her! Why hadn't she spoken up to both of them? The shame of it, to have allowed Hugh to get away with so much. What was it he had said…? Then for some unknown reason, she remembered Thady's nostalgic speech of the morning before: about the young boy, Hugh, who had begged so hard to be taken out boating and swimming at Maurcappagh…

CHAPTER 33

A figure had come into her line of vision below in the square, where she was staring out vaguely. She had been looking at it absently for some moments before she realised that it was Hugh. To see him walking down there in the square was the last thing she had expected. He was always so busy: this morning of all mornings she had taken it for granted that he would already have driven off somewhere in a great hurry. Now she watched him across the sunny, blustery square, stopping once or twice to exchange a few words with other wind-blown figures there; turning his head now and again to answer a greeting called out from some doorway. She asked herself, what did he go away thinking he had achieved?

She could not help watching him with great interest. As he drew level with the church he stopped and half-turned, sweeping the eastern and southern sides of the square with his glance. She saw him standing there by the big gates of the church, scarf and coat ends flapping in the wind. A cheerful, sunlit figure as he leaned back a little on the bright wind, as on a friend. Then she saw him go through the motions of greeting somebody he had just caught sight of, obviously within the church gates to his left, behind the trees.

As she watched now, she saw, first, Hugh's aunt Dr Peggy, then Desmond and finally Gabriel, come out from beyond the trees onto the gravel path that led from the Presbytery to the church gates. They had evidently been in to see the Canon about the final arrangements for the funeral. The group had a peculiar fascination for her. She had no choice but to continue there, peering uncomfortably at them, intending every moment to go, yet staying minute after minute.

She saw how Hugh stepped forward to greet his brother-in-law Gabriel with a hearty slap on the shoulder. Then she saw him put his arm about his aunt's shoulders, and then, still with his arm about her, look across and make some smiling remark to his cousin Desmond. For a moment at least, he was the centre of the little group. Obviously something of importance was being arranged. At last she allowed her glance to light on Gabriel. Desmond and he were standing side by side. The difference in their ages was perceptible in their figures. Desmond was about as thin as he could be. Gabriel was stout. Breena stared at his solid figure, and experienced a vivid sense of his complete difference from herself. Even across the square she could see that he was going a little bald in front… She stared and stared at him.

Now the little group by the church gates had begun to move; they were making their way round the corner into Church Street. She saw them stop by a cream-coloured car; she saw Gabriel fumbling in his pocket for the keys. So it was Gabriel's car… It must be quite new. At Easter, when he was down before, he had been driving a dark-blue, old-looking model.

She watched Dr Peggy, Desmond, Gabriel climb into the car. Hugh remained on the pavement, talking to his aunt through the window. A kind of wistfulness, a kind of envy of the four of them, came over Breena then. They were so sure of themselves, so pleased with one another's company! At least three of them, and the fourth also, with little persuasion, could with truth recite at any moment their own peculiar Credo. 'I believe in the holy Catholic Church, in the Cappagh family, in the husbanding of all Cappagh resources, in the eternal damnation of all Cappagh rebels, and in the triumphing of all Cappagh values on the Day of Judgment. Amen.'

Suddenly she stood up, pushed with her hands against the window-seat and jumped to her feet. The car had swung round into the square. They were coming here! She knew it! Dr Peggy, Desmond and… Gabriel. Oh, why hadn't she guessed it ten minutes ago? Well what now? Was she going to run to Uncle John now? Slowly and thoughtfully she walked across the sitting-room and down the stairs.

CHAPTER 34

Breena met them in the yard, where the sun had once more broken through. She had already released the dogs – for moral support. Dr Peggy and Desmond smiled at her, and passed quickly in the house. Gabriel advanced towards her.

'Hello,' he said. 'Hello, Breena…'

He would have shaken hands with her but she took a quick nervous step backwards, which she tried to justify almost on the instant by catching hold of Bran's collar – Bran had come wandering inquiringly back to her – and tying him up once more. Poor Bran was surprised. As for Gabriel, he pretended not to notice how she had stepped away from him, and went on to ask in a companionable, suave tone; 'The dogs are your charge, then?'

That summer, a trough of water, in actual fact a cattle trough, was always kept full under the tap in the yard for the dogs' use. From where Breena stood now, a few steps away from Gabriel, the sun seemed to be directly above the water; its reflection glancing off in beams and flashes of brilliant light. Gabriel stood between her and the water, a little to the right. By contrast with it he seemed a darkened, shadowed figure.

Now she expected that her flustered 'Oh, hello!' and her hang-dog failure to answer the question he had asked, would send him quickly into the house after Desmond and Dr Peggy. But it was quite otherwise. He remained where he was, completely at his ease. At a loss for something to do – for by now she had succeeded in catching and tying up Hippy too – she took down the bucket of dog-biscuits from behind the door and began to fill the dogs' bowls with the old cup that was always kept in the bucket. From behind her, Gabriel remarked:

'I asked you a moment ago, but you didn't hear: do you always look after the dogs?'

She forced herself them to stand up and face him. The glittering of the water made him still a shadowed figure to her, whereas she knew that she herself was spotlit by the sunshine. She felt like a child being questioned at school. She answered carefully:

'Hippy is my dog, Bran's Uncle John's. Uncle John likes to feed them, but I usually take them walking, except on Sundays. Uncle John takes them out on the mountains on Sundays…'

She had to leave it at that. Her voice seemed to have sunk to the bottom of a well-shaft inside her. In her efforts to draw it up, she began to squeak. But he noticed nothing, or at least pretended to notice nothing. As soon as she stopped he took up the subject of dogs in a general and easy way. He admired Hippy's shape and high spirits, asked what breed he was; talked of Bran's shining coat and obvious good training; and then went on to tell her about his own dog, a 'beautiful creature', a golden retriever. For her his voice issued strangely from the dark figure that stood between her and the blaze of reflected sunlight over the water…

At last he had finished describing his dog.

'I think we had better go in,' Gabriel suggested, and she knew by his tone he was smiling at her, though no smile could be distinguished in the shadows where he stood. 'Desmond is going to make us some coffee and he really *can* make coffee, you know. Even you and I may be able to learn something from him.'

That 'even you and I' was enough to make Breena assent immediately to his suggestion. She slipped past him – he gallantly stepped aside to make way for her – but then controlled herself and moved more slowly, but still ahead of him, towards the kitchen door.

As soon as she put her head in at the kitchen door she saw that Desmond, Dr Peggy, and Hannah were grouped round the cooker. Desmond, being Desmond, was not satisfied with merely making coffee; he was going to teach them all how to make coffee. Now he stood holding a coffee-pot in one hand and an asbestos mat in the other. Hannah held the box of coffee, Dr Peggy a number of spoons. The moment Breena stepped into the kitchen all three turned and gave her a big smile. As she glanced quickly from face to face, herself unsmiling, determined now to meet this situation head on and conquer it, she saw at once that she had never been smiled at quite in this way before. For the moment even Hannah had gone over, perhaps without knowing it, into Dr Peggy's camp. Breena saw in every pair of eyes a glad, bright interest in her.

She willed herself, forced herself, to look back at them, glance from one to the other, with the utmost seriousness. And in view of the initial heartiness of their smiles, she was astonished at how quickly they grasped the fact that she wished them to be serious, and adjusted themselves to her mood. Apparently the desire to please her was uppermost. One by one they turned back to the stove. Dr Peggy called to her; 'Breena, come here. There's room for you here between Gabriel and myself.'

Breena nodded, but went to stand on the other side of Hannah, near the wall. Now that they had all turned away from her again, and she no longer had to contend with their stares, she realised that she was a little shocked at the frolicsomeness of Dr Peggy's manner. Considering what day it was, and that the Requiem Mass for Dr Peggy's brother-in-law was to be held in little more than an hour's time, Breena had certainly not expected to see her here this morning at one of these holiday-time coffee sessions. But then, Breena reflected, Desmond's effect on his mother was always to make her suffer a lapse of responsibility. She was always blithe and gay, when Desmond was home.

CHAPTER 35

Breena took up her station by the wall, across the way from Desmond. She intended to stare at him hard, to shame him into at least acknowledging by a glance that he understood what she felt about Gabriel, and would call him and the others off. Breena stared and stared. But shame, apparently, was something Desmond had no acquaintance with. When eventually he looked Breena's way it was only to give her a wide smile and a wink. He smacked his lips at her and told her: 'You're in for a treat, Breena. I'm glad we caught you in time, before you'd gone off to the dogs. Sorry – off *with* the dogs. You ain't never tasted coffee like the coffee Hannah and myself are going to make in a minute. We've put a whole jug of thick fresh cream by for it, and I have a pint bottle of uisge beatha upstairs. Ah, the water of life, that our ancestors…'

'The kettle is boiling,' Dr Peggy interrupted him.

'I'll get it!' Gabriel stepped forward obligingly. Now Gabriel held the kettle, Dr Peggy an unlikely number of spoons, Hannah the box of coffee, and Desmond the coffee pot and mat. Breena was the only idle onlooker.

Under a cover of nonsensical chatter Desmond, very quickly and slyly, with his deft, surgeon's hands, made the coffee, and put it down on the asbestos mat for the grounds to settle.

While the coffee was settling, there was a great to-do. The usual ritual of the glasses had to be gone through. The jug of cream was brought out of the dairy with great ceremony; a bowl was filled with moist brown sugar. Then Desmond had to run upstairs for his proud new pint of uisge beatha. There was nobody present in the kitchen by now who was not keenly looking forward to the treat in store for them.

Desmond came back and went from glass to glass, pouring into each a full measure of whiskey. Hannah followed behind with the coffee. Then each person had to take a glass, and Desmond, who during his so-called lesson had carefully refrained from communicating any knowledge whatever of coffee-making, now came in again to instruct them:

'Sugar's a very important point; you must always be sure to use brown sugar. Remember that, won't you? Coffee has no liking for white sugar, especially, I may add, white cube sugar. A colour problem, you understand.'

Finally, when the coffee was sweetened, Desmond made the rounds once more; this time to pour cream delicately over an up-turned spoon until the coffee-streaked, succulent, inner-nut richness of it rose high above the rim of the glass. Then he returned to his own place, picked up his glass, held it out towards Breena, who was, he must surely be aware of it, watching him closely. He gave her a quick smile, then looked round at the others.

'Today there can only be one toast,' he raised his glass. 'To Breena, who has only just left school. May the rest of her life be as happy and successful as her schooldays have been!'

'To Breena!' they all joined in. Breena looked down at her glass, and then willed herself to look up again and smile round at them by way of thanks. Then she took a sip of her coffee and looked across at Desmond, who was now murmuring softly; 'A speech, a speech! I want a speech from my cousin Breena.' His glance met hers: wise, blue, and if not innocent, at least blank. Breena met those eyes, flushed, nearly lost courage, then held up her head. She said quietly:

'You know a speech would be beyond me. All I feel up to is a comment... This coffee is delicious, Desmond, thank you. But

I must add, it's only what I expected. You have given me what I expected, *in every way.*'

Desmond smiled and murmured, 'My cousin Breena is hard to please. The knowledge that I have pleased her, even in this small matter of making coffee, pleases me far beyond my poor meagre powers of expression.'

At this point Breena realised that Hannah was looking at her. She turned; Hannah's grey eyes beamed forth a message as plain as words. It counselled Breena to hold her tongue, to say no more. Bandying words with Desmond was a dangerous game, Hannah's glance warned. But Dr Peggy had already come in with her usual kind, blunt, positiveness:

'Yes. Breena *is* hard to please. She sets herself very high standards. But she's right in saying that this coffee is delicious. That is, if it can be called coffee at all. What name does it go by, Desmond?'

'It's called "Deoch Beatha Desmond" – Breena will explain that to you... Well, Hannah, what about you? D'you like the coffee as much as usual, now that you've made it yourself?'

'Made it myself! As for liking it, I never realised what a poor word "like" was until now.'

Then Dr Peggy, who stood beside Breena, leaning against the warm stove, edged a little closer to her and asked her in such a well-intentioned attempt at a whisper that it nearly came off:

'By the way, have you fitted on the dress Desmond brought you?'

'No. I haven't even seen it yet. I... '

'Ursula has it. Don't forget to ask her about it after the funeral. Otherwise Desmond will be hurt.'

'It may not fit me, you know, or suit me.'

'Of course it will!' At the very idea of such a thing Dr Peggy forgot herself and raised her voice. Desmond and Gabriel turned at once to look at them. Hannah, who had been looking, glanced away. Dr Peggy's face split across in another smile, an apologetic one this time. She resumed her painful whispering:

| 235

'You ought to know by now that Desmond never makes an error of taste. I'm willing to bet that you'll think this the nicest dress you've ever seen.' She patted Breena's hot hand with her own surprisingly cool one. Breena's ears throbbed hot and painful under her hair. ('I'll not touch that dress, I'll not touch it,' she vowed to herself.) Dr Peggy went on:

'Of course you're not going to the funeral. If you think it will depress you, there's no need to come to the Requiem Mass either.'

'I… I haven't made up my mind yet. Maybe I ought to… and I like the singing… '

'Anyway, don't go too far up the mountain, will you?'

'Up the mountain?'

'Yes, if you take the dogs out. You must be careful, or you'll easily be seen by the people below in the… '

'Oh, with the dogs! Yes, I'll be very careful.'

At this point Hannah came up to them and said in a whisper to Dr Peggy; 'With the Mass at half-past, isn't it time we started to… ?'

Dr Peggy interrupted her by exclaiming, 'Good heavens!' as she swung round to look at the clock and saw what time it was. 'Come on!' she called to Desmond and Gabriel. She boomed kindly at Hannah, 'It's a good thing you're here to keep us up to the mark!' In a minute all was commotion; the regretful, quick swallowing-back of the last of the coffee, the glasses being gathered together, exclamations, compliments to Desmond on the coffee, more smiles. Breena was the first person to escape from the room. She slipped away while the others were still standing by the sink talking.

What a chummy, cosy future they were holding out to her! But now her blood was up. She felt sufficiently angry with both Hugh and Desmond to *want* to act on her own. It was her first chance to act independently as an adult. She had not wanted things to turn out this way. But now that they had done so, there must be something she could learn from them.

CHAPTER 36

All at once the Angelus bell began to ring – but no! It must be long past the time of the Angelus by now… It was the tolling of the funeral bell that she heard. Tears started to her eyes at the sound of it. A keen sense of the reality of what had happened took her over. Her imagination seized on the grim fact behind all the ceremonies: all the comings and goings, the wake, the rosaries, the keening, the Requiem Mass, the funeral… Kitty and Maurice's father, Uncle John's brother, had gone from them forever. In the place where he had sat and stood and walked there was now only to be a memory of him, a shadow within the shadowed brains of other people. For a moment she felt utterly wretched. A familiar figure, a man she had always liked and who had always liked her, a human being, was very soon to be hidden away under the ground; to be put out of sight because sight could no longer stand what it saw, banished of necessity, by the very people who loved him… How could it be borne? And Breena felt incapable of bearing it. She felt that if she were to allow her thoughts to dwell on it for one moment longer her brain would burst. She too must die. Thoroughly frightened she quickened her pace, tried to get away from the sound of the bell, so that by the time she turned the corner into Main Street she was running.

With the dogs at her heels Breena ran along the lane, and then along the road and across the meadows and moorland, until only the present moment, the sheer joy and light-heartedness of running as fast as she could, had any meaning for her. Nothing else could touch her any more. As she ran, the shower of rain that had been threatening for some time came sweeping against her, and she held up her face and threw out her arms to welcome it. Running as fast as they were, they soon got back to the open moorland which they must cross in order to reach the road and the lane behind Main Street that led towards home. By now, however, Breena felt exhausted. As soon as she had helped Bran under the barbed wire fence and scrambled clear of it herself she threw herself down on a thick patch of rough grass. It was damp from the rain and seeped through with the good, good, smell of the freshly washed earth. Bran came quickly and lay down beside her with his head on his outstretched paws, very glad of a rest it seemed. But Hippy launched himself straight at her face and licked it enthusiastically until she ordered him sternly to go back and sit beside Bran.

Then she clasped her hands under her head and stared up at the sky. The exhilaration of her run was still there inside her. It transformed the day. Now she could feel the heat that throbbed behind the grey blanket of clouds above. A flight of gannets passed low overhead, tacking, careening against the breeze in the direction of the Yellow Strand. Watching the spread of their powerful wings, hearing the occasional sharp, flapping sound as one or the other of them corrected course, she stood up, yawning and stretching, to follow them with envious glance out of sight. Then from the marshlands beyond the railway, at the foot of the Maurcappagh range, came the lonely cry of a curlew. For a moment she stood absolutely still, haunted by the wildness and strangeness of the sound, longing to hear it again. The cry was repeated; a second curlew answered. Once more it came, then again, and again.

As Breena listened, the question 'Where can I be?' formed in her mind as she glanced about. It was followed by confusion too quick and deep for thought; which stemmed however from the certainty that wherever this was she should not be here. She should be standing on the grassy hummock at home, beside the clump of ... *at home*? Within seconds understanding came, and she thought again with some kind of surging restlessness or regret, 'at home'! How strange, today, that such an expression should come into her head... Now the cry of the curlew came again, fainter, utterly alien once more; wild and lonely as when she first heard it...

> *O curlew, cry no more in the air,*
> *Or only to the water in the West;*
> *Because your crying brings to my mind...*

She started running again, with concentrated purpose now, watching only the ground before her; across the meadows, along the road, down into the lane, through the garage gate and across the grass into the yard.

The kitchen door was open. She could hear voices from within. At least she had judged the time well; the funeral was over. But the sound of voices surprised and alarmed her all the same. Who was she to expect when she went in? She had taken it for granted that everybody would go straight from the funeral to the other house, to join in the funeral meal. Such was the custom.

CHAPTER 37

Breena felt very pleased and relieved to find that after all it was only Hannah in there, and, of course, Ursula…

She stepped into the kitchen. 'Hello!' she greeted them.

'Breena! So you're here. Are you upset? Are you coming along then, to the stock-room?'

'To the stock-room?' Breena echoed, with no comprehension whatever.

'Yes; to fit on the dress Desmond brought you. I've just set it out for you in the stock-room. Your Aunt Peggy would like you to wear it later. Desmond will want to see you in it, you'll understand that. Or would you prefer me to bring it up here?'

'No, no. Of course not.'

'Well, come on down, then… The mirror in the stock-room is certainly better. And there will be time to fit it on, and get used to it, before they come back and see you in it… We'll go down by the main stairs, then we'll be able to stop by the altar and offer up a few aspirations for poor Jeremy.'

This last sentence Ursula spoke over her shoulder as she moved off briskly down the corridor to the left. Breena realised that it would be simple kindness to let Ursula get busy and concerned about the dress and so forget herself. And yet the thought of the wretched dress was now more distasteful than ever. She, Breena, cared as little for Desmond's present as she did for Desmond's friend. However, she followed unhappily after Ursula, who was going at a great pace and had already reached the landing where the altar was. There Breena caught up with her, and stood by her side until she had finished her prayer. Then as they made their way down the stairs together, Breena became aware that something was wrong, something disturbed her. All at once she stopped and turned sharply round to look up at the old clock.

'Why, Aunt Ursula!' she cried, very excited, 'Look! The clock's stopped.'

Ursula was so struck by her tone that instead of glancing up at the clock, she stood still at once and looked anxiously round at Breena. Then she said quickly in the bright, comforting voice that used to soothe away Breena's troubles when she was much younger:

'Your Uncle John forgot to wind it, that's all. It's an eight-day clock. It should have been wound up yesterday, Sunday. We must remind him to do it tonight… Come on, now. The dress is lovely. Just your colour. You'll be delighted when you see it.'

And while she was still speaking she went on down the stairs, rather too quickly, sounding more as if she were stumbling than taking deliberate steps. But Breena remained standing as before, clutching both banisters now, staring up at the round yellow face of the clock. The old childhood fancy came back. She found it easy to imagine that the clock inclined towards her where she stood. But with its familiar wheezy voice it had also lost its foolish, good-natured look of concern. It seemed hostile and strange… It wore a blank, snubbing look – like the face of an old friend that had grown tired of you – yet it approached, slowly, in the old way. And now it was close enough for Breena to make out its expression clearly. She saw that there was more than the blank vacancy of insult or contempt on that face. Its look was worse than that: completely void, meaningless. It was the face of a friend that was dead. Breena turned away from it and launched herself downstairs two and three steps at a time after Ursula – who in her noisy progress had not yet noticed that Breena was not behind her, and was still talking in glowing terms over her shoulder about the dress.

They reached the door of the stock-room. Breena had already made up her mind to loathe and despise the dress. It seemed clear that to loathe and despise the dress was the only honest course open to her. At the same time, some curiosity about it had by this time entered her head. It would do nobody any harm, she thought, if she were just to look at it - indeed, it would certainly do Ursula a great deal of good. To pretend a lively interest in the dress, fit it on, make believe that she was considering it, get Ursula immersed in the subject – what greater kindness could she do Ursula at the moment?

Then Ursula threw open the stock-room door. The scene was already set; all the lights on, the shutters opened well back. And there in the middle of the room, carefully arranged over one of the brown-leather armchairs, Breena saw the dress. It lay across the dark old chair like a splash of sunlight. A yellow dress, yet not harshly or crudely yellow. Glowing subtly, rather, so that Breena had to bend over it to understand how this effect had been achieved. Then she saw that there were a hundred different shades; the overall colour of yellow was only a first impression. The dress was the colour of summer; of a field of ripe wheat that you walked into late in the evening, with the great red-gold sun low in the sky over against you, so that every tint of richness shimmered in the field and sky around you.

Breena whispered, 'It's lovely! It's the loveliest dress I've ever seen.'

She heard a chuckle from Ursula behind her. 'Well, what did you expect? Has Desmond ever brought you a present you didn't like?'

And then when Breena made no answer, but only continued to gaze at the dress: 'I knew you'd be delighted with it. Desmond has taste hasn't he? It's a model dress. It must be. Feel the material. Silk, of course!'

Ursula lifted the dress in the tender way some women lift up a baby, and gave it to Breena, whose arms went out of their own accord to support it. 'Go on, feel it! Light as a feather, and yet it will wear forever. Silk! That word itself is so lovely, I've always thought… It has such a cool sound. There never was a more suitable name for a material.' Ursula's eyes shone. Tears and bitterness were all forgotten now. 'Come on; get a proper feel of it! Don't be afraid of it. It feels cool, doesn't it, just the way it sounds? Yet it soon warms to the touch… Silk has a sheen all of its own – look! Glossy, yet so delicate… There's no mistaking one of the new fabrics for it…'

Breena, holding the silk dress in her arms and staring at it fixedly, wondered to herself; what should she say now? *Go behind me, Satan; thou art a scandal unto me!*? But Satan was already behind her, holding her by the elbow and escorting her to the cubicle in the corner, all the time insinuating into her ear many pleasing facts and inferences about the yellow dress… At the entrance to the cubicle, however, Breena was pulled up sharply by a horrified cry from Satan-Ursula: 'Your shoes! Wait! You can't keep those shoes on. Heavens! The whole effect would be ruined…'

While a more suitable pair of shoes were being hunted out, Breena stood stock-still at the cubicle door and stared at the yellow dress. With all her heart now she coveted that yellow dress. She waited in a dream until a faint licking sound on the floor by her feet and a satisfied exclamation of, 'There you are! Try those on!' made her look down to see a very fine pair of yellowish-brown leather shoes just waiting to be stepped into. Automatically then, still tenderly holding out the yellow dress, she kicked off her walking shoes and looked down with the utmost pleasure at the new shoes now on her feet.

'Those shoes go so well with the dress, and they're so becoming to you, you mustn't part with them again,' Ursula-Satan whispered at her elbow. 'Let them be a present from me… We needn't say anything to anybody else about them.'

'Oh, no…' Breena protested feebly. But somehow she was already inside the cubicle, setting the yellow dress down with anxious care over the screen in the corner until she had pulled off the sweater and dress she was wearing. Then when she turned eagerly back again to the yellow dress she found Ursula standing beside her. After that Ursula's fingers were always there to assist her at the right moment; to smooth her arms' way into the sleeves, adjust the collar, secure a fastener. But the fingers had no weight to them. Their touch, skilled in helpfulness, was also exquisite in restraint: hypnotic, yet barely felt. It was like a sacrament, 'the laying-on of hands.' Over the years Breena had had many dresses from the stock-room, but it had always been Kitty's habit to help her on with them and discuss how they suited her. Until today Ursula had been given little chance to show more than a second-hand interest. Only now did Breena get an insight into the secret satisfactions of Ursula's life. What she had thought of until this moment as unrelieved grimness, 'working in the shop', could now be seen to have its own moments of elation and escape.

Every few seconds Ursula's touch, suspected rather than felt, experienced mostly in its effects – the closing of a zip, the smoothing of waistline and shoulders into place – seemed only an emphasis, an exterior, palpable outcome. Ursula's voice, which all the time in low, subtle tones, in phrases that hardly seemed more than the letting-out of breath, exulted in the beauty of the dress.

'I always think that silk is like your own skin… When you wear silk you *feel* what it's like to have skin. You feel the satisfaction of not being hairy, or furry, or having a thick hide like an elephant… Silk makes you more *human*, somehow… See how it seems to cling to you; how it seems to know how *right* it is… I never wear anything except silk myself, you know…'

Breena's fingers reached out and stroked Ursula's dress. 'Mm-mmm,' she heard herself purring, 'Mm-mmm…'

'Now let me see. Turn round – no, more slowly – let me just…'

It had never before occurred to Breena that there might be any art or enjoyment in the work Ursula did. She had always thought of Ursula rather as one of the serfs of ancient times; bound to the shop, constrained to it, a prisoner. This was her first intimation of the peculiar skill in salesmanship Ursula had, the exercise of which must surely be enjoyable. And of course she might have known that Ursula's life as she herself had pictured it would be impossible. It could not be borne – even by such a resigned and religious person as Ursula. There would have to be a stronger colouring to it than up to this minute she, Breena, had been able to imagine.

At last the dress was fitted and smoothed on precisely to Ursula's satisfaction.

'Now we must just arrange your hair… ' Ursula reached up to a shelf. The next moment Breena felt her hair being patted and combed very gently into place, with another 'laying-on of hands.'

'Well!' Ursula stood back to survey her handiwork, 'I can't think there's anything else – oh yes, of course – gloves!'

Breena found that a pair of white gloves were being thrust into her hands. But it was no longer in her power to put them on. Under Ursula's touch the very core of herself had melted away. Somewhere inside of her she was aware of a questioning; 'What am I doing? What am I doing? Why have I accepted this dress?' But she had to push it aside. Only a swooning, easeful satisfaction could hold its own within her being. She looked into the glass and saw a yellow dress and above it a face, neck, hair. But there was no kind of personal vanity, no idea of, 'How well I, Breena, look!' in her thoughts. There was only a sense of rightness, of the utmost suitability. It was a whole picture she saw before her in the glass. No part of it, face, dress, legs had the power to draw her special attention. It was like a yellow flower that bloomed there in front of her. She allowed Ursula to put on the white gloves for her and smooth them into place, and all the time she stared at the yellow flower of herself blooming there in the glass. She heard Ursula say, 'First of all, we'll have to see what Hannah thinks of you...' and a very pleasant, languid feeling, a kind of gladness, went through her. She allowed herself to be propelled towards the door, into the corridor, to the left in the direction of the kitchen. The next moment she was standing in the kitchen doorway; she heard Ursula say:

'Now, Hannah! What do you think of this young lady?'

Hannah, who had been standing at the sink, with her back to them, when Ursula pushed open the door, turned quickly round. The moment she caught sight of Breena she flung down her teatowel and stared a moment in silence. Then with an excited, indeed, half-alarmed, 'Breena, is it yourself?' she hurried across the kitchen towards them. In front of Breena she stopped short. Surprise, it seemed, made her speechless again. Breena looked into her eyes and saw twin pictures of the yellow flower blooming on their shining surfaces.

'I can hardly believe my eyes!' Hannah exclaimed at last. She turned to Ursula. 'Isn't it the cailín og herself has suddenly become?'

'Don't you like the dress, Hannah?' Breena asked politely, knowing very well that everything in Hannah's looks and gestures – most of all her silence at the first – expressed a very wonder of admiration.

'Like it? If you were to live for a hundred years you could never find a dress I'd like better! The colour of it! Who'd ever have thought, before you put on that dress, that there were yellow lights in your eyes and hair? Yellow... yes!' She had drawn a little nearer to make quite sure. 'Yellow and no mistake! To tell the truth, yellow eyes don't sound right. But just to look at them, at this moment, you couldn't think of a better colour of eyes!'

This made Breena laugh. Hannah went on: 'Yellow eyes that disappear when you laugh, too! Only God knows what he was about when he made eyes like that. Indeed, if anybody else but God made such eyes, what a to-do there'd be!'

But now Ursula, who had stationed herself beside Breena like an artist beside a prize exhibit, began to name one after another all the excellences of the dress she had already named to Breena. Hannah listened with an appearance of great attention; then as soon as Ursula finished gave vent to a very passion of enthusiasm:

'Oh, I agree with you, I couldn't agree more! The sit o' the dress, the style o' that little collar, the cut-back sleeves showing just enough arm for a young girl like herself! And it isn't a skimpy dress – there's plenty material. Look how it flares out at the bottom – yet it gives such a slender effect! And the length is just right, not too short, not too long. Just what I like to see on a youngster; showing just enough to make you think to yourself, "There's promise there!" yet giving nothing away on the cheap. And I must say again, the colour of it! If ever I've seen…'

Breena was aware of their open-heartedness towards herself, of their generosity towards her youth, of the kindness behind the extravagance of their praises. It seemed to her that their intentions were too good to accuse them even in her thoughts of any kind of exaggeration or grossness or flattery. As they went on she believed that everything they said was in a certain sense true, or at least became true immediately they said it. She could feel herself relaxing; could almost know herself to be growing petal-soft, rose-lovely, as they praised her. Yet the more she listened, the more chastened and sensitive became her mood. She looked at the marks of tears that still showed on their faces and knew that it would be a cruelty to stop them short, to cut off the generous flow of their expiation towards one another and herself. She listened for quite some time; then at last thought it safe to break in, to comment, laughing, on Hannah's last speech:

'Now, Hannah, who's letting her tongue run away with her? You must stop it, you know, or you'll have me growing vain and thinking that I'm good looking. And you know what a serious sin that would be.'

'Good-looking, is it?' Hannah did not scruple now to make a right-about turn. 'Who ever heard of a good-looking girl that had yellow eyes? 'Tis a cat God must have intended you for. And then at the last moment he changed his mind, in a mood o' stubbornness I imagine – such as even God himself must get into sometimes – what with all them seraphim and cherubim and saints and so on up there, doing nothing day or night except playing on the harp and telling him he can do no wrong – anyway God changed his mind at the last moment and instead of a cat turned you into a girl.'

'And I'm very glad he did, too,' Breena said. 'Being a cat wouldn't suit me at all.'

CHAPTER 38

It was then, at the moment when she stopped speaking, that she heard, very sharp and clear, the click of the latch of the side-gate. Instantly, of itself, her whole being froze into a concentration of listening. At once she heard, above the chuckles and exclamations of Ursula and Hannah over the last exchange, the sound of voices. Many voices, surely? For a few seconds her consciousness, the very soul of herself, seemed to leave her body stranded there on the kitchen floor - all her awareness went out towards those voices at the gate. She noted that as yet the sound of the voices lingered by the gate, that it had advanced no further inwards, across the yard, towards the kitchen door... So there must be a number of people out there, waiting for one another to get in by the gate... Dr Peggy – surely she could hear Dr Peggy now? There were certainly many voices, but they were very subdued in tone; far too subdued for any party that contained Desmond and his infatuated mother... Unless – could it be that Uncle John was with them this time? Uncle John? Was it possible? She thought of Uncle John's face this morning – only this morning – in the room where his brother was laid out, and in the corridor outside when he made her leave the room; the quick impression she had caught of the grim, fallen-in lines of his face, whitish-grey in colour like concrete, and like concrete, rigidly set.

She heard an exclamation from Hannah; 'They're back! Already!' and came to herself, returned to full awareness of herself standing here in the kitchen in her new yellow dress, shoes, and white gloves.

A yellow dress! 'What in God's name am I doing standing here in this… This wretched present from Desmond?' she was asking herself, before, the next moment, she was half-thinking, half-praying; 'They mustn't see me in it! Oh, God, they mustn't see me in it!' And now the fierceness of her greed earlier on, the lust to possess the dress that had taken her over, seemed like a fit of madness. No, it was more like a dream that was passing away, that she had just woken up from and vainly groped after as it already faded from her mind.

She heard Ursula say, with an excruciating slowness to grasp what was happening: 'Are you sure, Hannah? Can they be back already?' Then she saw that Ursula was stepping out beside Hannah; had passed Hannah; was making for the door to see who was coming. This was Breena's chance. Her way back to the stock-room was now clear.

With a muttered, barely audible, 'I'd better… ' She turned away, only just in time. Four or five pairs of feet already sounded urgent outside the door, the beginnings of shadows were being cast across outside the doorway.

She heard Desmond's voice '… rooted in every crack of the wall. One day they'll… ' That he could only be talking about the nasturtiums she knew and yet did not know. Some part of her understanding could contain only one impulse; to get rid of this yellow dress; to get it off and throw it somewhere out of sight before any of the people out there had time to catch a glimpse of her.

A tumult had begun inside her that went far beyond her own comprehension. Like all moments that are intensely lived through, the awareness even of what she was thinking left her. Now she was capable of only one thing: action. She raced down the corridor into the stock-room and once inside, with the door closed, reached backwards with both hands to pull down the zip of the yellow dress. But she found that the top of the zip was somehow hidden and hooked under a fold of the material. Her hands fumbled in vain. Ursula had helped her on with the dress so expertly and delicately that now she had no idea where the fastenings were. She had to run to the long mirror and look over her shoulder and first stare hard and then search under the collar with her fingers before she could find the little hook at the top of the zip. She had only just discovered how the fastenings worked when she heard the door from the kitchen open, voices in the corridor outside.

'In the stock-room?' she heard Desmond's voice, then a laugh, Dr Peggy's, and again the sound of many pairs of feet. She ran in a panic towards the door of the stock-room. She could see, of course, that it was closed; she knew that she had closed it when she first came in. But it was not locked. Now it seemed of the utmost importance, of a scale of importance against which all the values of her life were weighed, that she should find some means of securing it against the people out there until she had pulled off this yellow dress and got back again into her old dress and sweater. (Kitty's voice resounded through her head; '*Where thy treasure is, there is thy heart also!*' and she could only ask herself if this paltry silk dress was the only treasure her heart was capable of.) She reached the door, with some hasty, unthought-out idea of turning an easy key in a lock. Then she was up against the door, staring at its smooth, blank, white-painted surface. Of course there was no key... There was no keyhole, even. Three bolts there were, and two bars secured by padlocks, but they were all on one other side of the door, the corridor side... And while she stood there, baffled, helpless, she could hear the footsteps bearing every moment more strongly and loudly down the corridor towards her. The silly thought came, could she possibly keep them out by throwing all her weight against the door? Then she heard the first of them come to a halt on the other side of the door, with only the wood of the door between herself and them. In her own person, she had now become a beleaguered city.

'Breena is it all right if we come in?'

It was Dr Peggy's voice. With the sound of it still in her ears, Breena looked down in anguish at the yellow dress. In the few seconds before she answered she experienced what she had often heard it said drowning men experience: all the mistakes she had made flew through her head in lurid daubs of images, ten and twenty deep: not only the mistakes she had made since last night when Dr Peggy first spoke to her about Gabriel, but all those she had made during the whole course of her life. At the same time, hardly knowing what she was doing, panting in haste, she had turned away from the door and noiselessly, in long stealthy strides, was making her way back to the fitting-on cubicle. Arrived there, she faced the door once more.

'Oh yes, come in,' she called out in a high, false voice.

She watched with a kind of horror the door swing inwards. Then their faces were there. Dr Peggy in the lead, then Ursula, Desmond, Gabriel. And Hugh! Hugh was there too. Of all people, she had not expected Hugh. The busy, important Hugh, what was he doing here?

They crowded the doorway. They smiled at her, but not as she had been smiled at this morning in the kitchen. No, their smiles were beamed discreetly at her face, with a certain ambiguity: a quality of silence, yet intended speech. Knowing that she was very flushed – knowing even that across her eyes, most likely, were scuttling the shameful fears of a leveret at bay – she stood her ground and looked back at them with the doggedness of absolute hate. After a few moments however their silence diverted the stream of her animosity. She became puzzled. Why did none of them speak? Had they all lost their tongues? She had heard Dr Peggy laugh as they left the kitchen. That laugh seemed very much at odds with their silence now.

Then her attention was caught by a movement behind them, in the comparative darkness of the corridor. She looked beyond them and understood at once why nobody had yet spoken. Standing back there, taller than Desmond, taller by a head than Hugh and Hugh's precious brother-in-law, towering head and shoulders above Ursula and Dr Peggy, was Uncle John. He stood there quite still, looking in at himself. His face was very grey and unsmiling. But she thought at first that he simply felt very tired and sad; she expected his look to soften as it usually did when it met her own. Within a few seconds, however, she realised that he was searching so intently for something in her face he was hardly conscious of the fact that she was looking back at him. At this moment all her glance meant to him was the greater opportunity it gave him to study her face. 'They've told him!' she thought, and a second later, '*What* have they told him?'

It was the first time since she knew him that his face did not change in response to her own glance. (Except, of course, for last night, and that was in the shadows of candlelight, in the grim room where his brother was laid out.) As her glance fell before his she told herself in a sick, anxious way that she needed his help badly, that she could no longer trust herself in any way, that everything she said and did seemed only to involve her more deeply in the soul-of-honour farce of Gabriel's proposal. And since she had lost all confidence, for the time being at least, in her own power to extricate herself, surely the best thing she could do now would be to blurt out here in front of them all some such words as:

'Uncle John, don't take any notice of what they've told you! I don't like Gabriel. I hate this dress. Please ask them all to go away. I badly want to speak to you alone.'

And when she looked up once more she probably would have cried out to him in just such a way; she was whipping up her courage as she slowly raised her glance from tier to tier of the faces before her. But when it reached the highest place, above and to the left of Desmond, there was no Uncle John standing there. He had gone.

'Oh!' she heard herself wailing, 'Uncle John! He's gone.'

But she saw at once from their relieved glances, from the sudden burst of exclamations and admiring remarks about the yellow dress that came from them, and the way they were all now advancing into the room, that they had noted his going before she did, and were glad of it. Ursula came up and said in a low, kind, confidential voice right into her ear:

'Don't be upset. It's not that your Uncle John doesn't like your dress... But, apart from everything else, he's almost sick with exhaustion. He has hardly slept since Friday night. It's no wonder he can take no interest in you at the moment.'

But Breena knew very well that what she had discerned in his glance was not a lack of interest, but an interest far too vivid and comprehensive. So that now, while part of her mind took note of the fact that Ursula had again stationed herself beside her – just as she had done in the kitchen a while back, as if to claim credit for all the various beauties of the dress she was able to point out – the rest of her attention was turned inwards, to the torment of two questions that repeated themselves over and over again in her head: 'Does Uncle John know?' and 'Can it be possible that he does *not* know?' From the tone of the remarks Ursula had just whispered into her ear she realised that it was highly unlikely anybody had deliberately set out to tell him about Gabriel. But why then had he looked at her so strangely? Was it just the yellow dress on its own that had disgusted him? The fact that he had caught her here preening herself in this wretched silk dress on his way back from his brother's funeral? Or had he learned about Gabriel in some casual way, from some off-hand remarks that nobody but himself would be able to piece together?

Dr Peggy had now stepped up beside Ursula. Evidently she had something to say, both to her sister and to Breena. She began in a low voice, and Breena had no choice but to turn towards her and give her her attention.

'Desmond has planned out a little trip; he thinks it best not to go very far today. Only to Maurcappagh, in fact. We all think his father might be upset, otherwise. But nobody will be surprised if you, Breena, and Desmond – and Gabriel with you – should go out to Maurcappagh today. They'll all take it for granted that you've gone out to see Norah (Sean Mor's wife), who must just about have arrived home by this time. So…'

'Why!' Breena interrupted in a glad voice, all her selfish concerns forgotten, 'you don't mean to say that Norah has been discharged from hospital so soon? Today?'

'Yes, indeed. An hour or so ago. Much against Hugh's wishes and my own advice, I may add. But you know Norah. 'Twas hard enough to keep her on her bed even when her legs refused to support her, and now that she's able to walk about again…' But Young Jamie, they tell me, is as handy as a woman about the house. Somebody – it could only have been Bessie Cronin – was saying to me the other night at the wake that he can even bake a very good cake of wholemeal bread. And you know that Sean Mor won't eat any other kind… So, all things considered, Norah will no doubt be better off with him than… What is it, Desmond? What did you say?'

And at that first half-hearing of a question from her son, Dr Peggy abandoned Ursula, Breena, Young Jamie, Norah, Sean Mor, all in one go, and took a few eager steps sideways in Desmond's direction. Desmond now stood a little apart with Hugh, talking something over with him in low tones. Gabriel had turned away towards the window, out of politeness, Breena presumed, and was pretending to be staring hard at some object out in the yard… But Breena had barely enough time to glance after Dr Peggy and take note of what the others in the room were doing when she heard Ursula's reproving whisper in her ear; 'Oh, you've undone the hook! You've pulled down the zip a little! – Why?'

Breena hard herself stammering, 'Because I… I was going to take off the dress. I think I… I'd better take it off. It… it's too good to keep on any longer…'

Her voice came out much louder than she intended. She could feel a new, stronger flush sting her cheeks as she realised that she had caused the others to stop talking and turn towards her. Then she heard Dr Peggy's voice booming kindly at her across the room.

'No, no, you must keep that dress on. I've rarely seen you in anything that became you better. It's a very lovely dress. Desmond has excelled himself this time. He'll feel quite insulted I'm sure, if you…'

Breena, with some trepidation, some clenching of her fists and steeling of her nerves, turned slowly round – steered herself full into the blast from that assertive voice – with every idea of keeping up her protest, of insisting that she must take off at once this priceless triumph of Desmond's taste. But it was Hugh's glance she met as she turned. He gave her immediately the same arch, roguishly conspiratorial smile he had given her this morning in the sitting-room. From this she swerved away as from a blow. And at the same moment she felt on her neck Ursula's delicate touch pulling up the zip until it clicked into place and retying the little hook. She bowed her head at that and submitted. So clearly, so very clearly she understood then that it was too late for any insistence, any rejection of the dress. The time for rejecting it had long since gone by. The only comfort she could find was in a heartfelt prayer. 'Oh God, let me learn from this moment! Let me at least learn from this moment!' And she thought of all the centuries, the millennia, of lusting after gaudy finery that she must be carrying about with her in her female blood, and prayed again, 'Oh God, don't let me blame myself too much! Don't let me blame myself too much, and lose hope!'

As Ursula set the dress to rights once more she whispered into Breena's ear that Gabriel was feeling a little disappointed, perhaps even a little sulky, at the moment. He had wanted to take them all out to dinner at a lakeside hotel in a town about fifteen miles off, where they could eat salmon fresh out of the river. But somehow Uncle John had got wind of this project and sternly declared it to be 'quite out of the question'. Now they must make the best of going out to Maurcappagh. After that they must come back here for dinner. Ursula and Hannah must do their utmost, dinner-wise; rustle up the most tasty dinner that was in their power. It was a pity, indeed, that Gabriel, being city-bred, should so utterly fail to understand why his generous suggestion to take them all out to dinner had been immediately rejected by Uncle John and received by the others with sympathy rather than gratitude.

'Just look now!' Ursula whispered. 'I think Hugh and Desmond are asking your Aunt Peggy to speak to Gabriel… I'd say he has been sulking a bit all right. Look how he's standing there on his own, away from the others. But your Aunt Peggy will soon make him see reason.'

Breena glanced round and saw that Dr Peggy, Hugh and Desmond had now joined Gabriel by the window. She could hear the persuasive murmur of Dr Peggy's voice, though not, for once, the exact words she used. Within a very a short while, however, everything was settled. Dr Peggy looked up, smiling, to call across the room; 'Breena, are you ready?' Afterwards, what Breena remembered most clearly about the minutes that followed was her own uneasy, growing realisation that first her ears, and then her cheek-bones and her nose, were becoming more and more stingingly hot and red. She dare not look into the glass… She heard Dr Peggy wish her a very pleasant outing; she got another smile from Hugh. Somehow she gathered that Hugh and Dr Peggy were expected somewhere even now - she saw them go off together in a great hurry… Then she felt her white raincoat, from the press behind the kitchen door, being placed over her arm by Ursula. She felt her white gloves being smoothed on once more, her dress and new high-heeled shoes being finally inspected. Then she followed Desmond and Gabriel, who had been given some hint or nod by Ursula, out of the room.

CHAPTER 39

Gabriel's car was parked by the garage, behind Dr Peggy's. As they came up to it all three stopped short in surprise to find Uncle John walking back and forth between the cars, obviously waiting for them. His glance swept over them in a blank, unfriendly fashion.

'Which car are you taking?' he asked Desmond.

There was a moment's silence. Then Desmond asked cheerfully, 'Oh, have you decided to come with us? I'm very glad.'

Breena felt more ashamed than ever of her gaudy dress; she dropped behind Desmond, doing her best to hide herself. She guessed that Uncle John had decided to come with them in order to keep this little outing of theirs within bounds; yet up to this moment she had had no idea that he knew anything about it.

It seemed that Gabriel was none too pleased at the prospect of Uncle John's company. He rattled his keys rather fussily as he went up to his car. It took him some time to open the door of the front passenger seat, then he turned to Breena with a significant smile. But when instead of Breena Uncle John stepped forward with a grave 'Thank you' and got into the seat, he swerved round and shot Desmond a look of such sheer outraged astonishment that Desmond could not keep back a smile as he explained:

'My father has to have a front seat, y'know. Legs too long for the back. Look, Gabriel… ' his eyes gleamed and glanced with mischievous waywardness, 'why not let me drive? Then you can sit

258

in the back with Breena with nothing to do except admire the view.'

So it was arranged. They got into the car in silence, and in silence drove through the town. Then as they were passing Dempsey's, the last little grocer-shop in the town, some raindrops spattered against the windows. Desmond said, 'It's begun to rain, thank God. Now we'll have something to talk about.' Gabriel roused himself at this and turned to Breena and began to compliment her on her dress. Then Desmond, a quick and sure driver, who knew every turn of this winding road, tried to draw his father out and get some general conversation going. He asked questions about the various families they passed, about the quality of the hay, and so on. But it proved hard going.

Once Uncle John had a bad bout of coughing and Desmond stopped the car and took him out into the fresh air to recover. As they got out of the car Breena's glance met Desmond's; a significant look passed between them. Breena knew then that Desmond, for all his air of insouciance, had already noticed and was worried by his father's cough.

They came up to the Pass. Breena stared out hungrily at the harsh, gaunt lines of it. Only to be out there now by herself, strolling along with her face raised to the rain! She went into a kind of dream, with her eyes closed. She was thinking of the last person who had left the eskar. She remembered him very well, and for many reasons; because his name was also Maurice; because it was barely eighteen months since he had gone; because he had stayed on for over a year after his mother's death so that people were beginning to say that he intended to get married and stay on for good; because he had danced with her at the very first dance Uncle John had allowed her to go to; because he had danced with her twice at that dance, and she had seen in his merry look, and heard in his teasing voice how fast and with how many hopes his heart was beating, what giant *mirages* were beckoning him away. After she had danced with him that night she no longer believed the rumours that he intended to marry a girl from Filemoyn and settle down at home. And she had been right. Five weeks afterwards he was gone.

'Breena…'

Suddenly recalled from her reverie she noticed that the car had stopped. They had reached the top of the sandy track that led from Maur bridge up to the dunes above the jetty, and beside her was sitting Gabriel. She turned a little in her seat and saw that Uncle John and Desmond had already started walking up the valley.

'Don't those waters look arctic?' Gabriel was saying now. 'So different from… You don't want to go out there? We're better off in here, don't you think? In here we can talk…'

'Yes,' she agreed in a low voice. And she thought: in the name of sanity let's talk then, let's find out what we have to talk about…

But evidently he saw no need for hurry. He took out his cigarettes in a leisurely manner. 'You don't smoke?'

'No.' She shook her head emphatically, thinking of Uncle John's cough. Little details of this sort tended to escape him, however. He lit up and drew on his cigarette with satisfaction.

She looked down wistfully at the sea. Never before had she come out here to Maurcappagh and not gone fishing or swimming or both. And today the sea was the way she loved it best, grey maybe but lazy and full, moving not in the restlessness and splashing of waves but with a powerful coiled motion of the whole of itself, lithesome and smooth. It seemed to heave itself up with soft purring sounds as it rubbed against the rocks. She knew from long experience how enjoyable a swim in the water would be today. Across its rain-sprinkled surface you could glide with the ease of a fish. And it would be cool, cool… Her face still glowed, her arms burned…

'Do you know…' Gabriel stretched his legs and turned to smile at her. The voice that floated over his knees was sonorous yet low. (He was very good with his voice.) 'Do you know that when I was down at Easter I used to sit in the middle window-seat upstairs and watch you running across the square with the dogs? I used to time you.' He smiled again. 'It made me laugh to see how quickly you could get from one side of the square to the other. I remember once you got right round the corner by the church and out of sight in just over half a minute… That was your best speed, of course!'

'Oh!' Breena said. He watched her, his lips pursed in an indulgent smile. He seemed to be waiting for further comment from her. But she could only think; 'Good heavens!' For a few moments she sat very tense, fighting down a foolish smile that threatened to break her face in two. When she was able to listen again she found that he had gone on to talk about Portugal, where he and a friend of his had been going for holidays for some years.

Now Breena knew very well already that Gabriel had lately, that is during the course of the previous winter, acquired some kind of cottage or villa in Portugal. Gabriel now was describing how delightful it was to swim in the warm waters of the little cove just as the bottom of the slope of his 'villa'. This had spoiled him, he admitted, for swimming at home.

'I know how much *you* like swimming,' he remarked. 'You'd love it there… '

She found what he said interesting, in that it was quite outside her experience up to the present time. But in some queer way too it made her feel very depressed. Then as he continued talking it occurred to her, more charitably, that he might be 'wagging his tongue to get his courage', as Jerry had expressed it that morning. This view of things cheered her up. After all, if Jerry sometimes needed to take courage, why not Gabriel? So she merely glanced at her watch and then sat back with naïve patience to wait for some words such as 'Breena will you marry me?'

He went on talking. He went on and on and on. He talked about his house, his housekeeper, his work, his 'dear mother' who had, as she knew very well, died the October before; then again about his dear mother, his house, his housekeeper, his work, his place in Portugal…

Then, so suddenly that she could not at first believe her senses, he stopped talking. She turned wearily to look at him. Had he just paused to light another cigarette? No, he had definitely stopped. He was watching her with a careful kind of smile.

'Breena…'

The something that had been in his eyes was now in his voice. Instinctively she turned and made some sort of involuntary jerking movement away from him. The next moment she realised that he was smiling at her; he was saying with his first hint that he had any kind of charm:

'I'm afraid Portugal goes to *my* head. We must leave it strictly alone until… Look, the rain has stopped out there. Shall we go for a little stroll?'

She got out quickly and stood waiting for him on the sandy track, with her face to the freshening wind. She felt sure of one thing; he had been on very point of committing himself, of speaking out at last, when she made that awkward movement away from him. To think of it! At this moment she might already have spoken her 'No!' and been free of him.

All the same her feelings towards him had softened under the influence of that first gleam of charm he had shown. She no longer thought him such a graceless, heavy, self-satisfied creature; she was willing to concede that people of his own age and inclinations might find him interesting…

He came round the car towards her. He was smiling, but there was keenness and shrewdness in his eyes that warned her he would guard himself against a too hasty 'next time'. He said in a brisk voice, 'We're going to have visitors, I think. Look up there.'

She followed the direction of his glance and saw two figures striding downhill from the high fields to the right of the valley. 'Oh, that's only Desmond and Uncle John. They're coming from Sean Mor's, they must have been in to see Norah.' She turned to him impulsively: 'If you want a walk, let's walk up to meet them.'

His glance remained fixed on the marshy-looking high fields.

'Are they following a path? I can't see it from here. Those tiers of stone fences look formidable.'

'Well, there is a path, quite a wide one, but it winds round a bit. They're not following it. They're… '

'Yes, I see what you mean,' he interrupted in a dry tone. At that moment the two figures had reached a fence; Desmond vaulted it effortlessly and then turned back to help his father over.

Breena said quickly; 'The fences are quite low in places. They're very easy to climb. I know exactly where to climb them.'

'But we're not what you might call dressed for climbing fences, are we?'

It was the very gentlest of protests, or seemed so at first hearing. But there was an after-tang of dryness to his voice. Breena had only to glance at him to see that a ruling had been made. All at once she understood perfectly what marriage to Gabriel would be like. In her female blood the knowledge of it ebbed and flowed with the age-old tides that washed her bones. The very notion of it frightened her.

From beside her now came the gentle chiding of Gabriel's voice. Though she did not look at him she knew that he was smiling again.

'There's no need to stare so wistfully up at those fields. There's more to life than climbing stone fences, you know. For instance, let's go up and look at that boat.'

It was, of course, Thady's boat he meant. Breena followed him listlessly up the steep hummock to the platform. She found it hard to walk uphill in her new high-heeled shoes. When she reached the platform she found Gabriel walking round the boat, poking at it here and there, tapping it with his fists. She stood by the stern and watched him. It turned out that he had a boat of his own. He had to describe it in order to illustrate what he found wrong with Thady's boat. With every word he spoke the vessel under his hands seemed to become lower, broader, darker; more awkwardly fashioned in every way. Yet as Breena listened the almost intolerable depression

| 263

of spirits that had settled on her earlier began to lift. She had never before considered this boat of Thady's as a thing it itself, apart from its uses. To her it had always been a vehicle of delight, a means of getting out on the sea. Gradually, with every word she heard him utter; her own bright, happy confidence in her own values came back to her.

Without doubt Gabriel knew a great deal more than she did about a great many things. He knew about makes and styles of boats and cars she had never heard of. He owned, possessed, incomparably more of everything than she did. But what did all his knowledge and all his owning amount to after all? Wherever he went he would take what he owned and what he knew along with him, and they would come between him and where he was so that he remained always in one small space. What was he seeing now of Thady's boat? Yet up here on the platform the breeze tugged at them on its way round the headland, like a child trying to draw them into a game. And below them the shining, large-bodied, smooth-skinned sea chuckled and purred as it coiled itself against the jetty and the cliffs. A perfect sea for swimming in…

She watched her companion, who became more eloquent and smiled more often as he saw her there, listening intently in complete silence. Every moment she felt more happy, more confirmed in her own values. Tomorrow or next week, she thought, the stranger would have to go away, back to the city girls who would no doubt find him very charming. Yet always from now on she would be pleased that she had met him. She would know that she had learned a great deal from him.

'Breena! Gabriel! Where are you?' Suddenly, with infinite relief, she heard Desmond's voice calling from below. She ran to the edge of the platform. Desmond and Uncle John were now walking across the sand dunes in the direction of the jetty.

'We're up here!' As she spoke she yielded to the temptation of the inviting slope before her, and began to run down as fast as she could. Only when she was already on the way, with no hope of stopping, and she heard Desmond cry out, 'Not so fast!' in a tone of some alarm, did she remember that she was wearing high heels. She stumbled and plunged forward, barely succeeding in saving herself. She came to a breathless halt a couple of feet past the spot where Desmond and Uncle John had turned to stare after her. Desmond was laughing.

'Talk of flying projectiles!'

Breena looked from him to Uncle John. She saw that now his eyes were very kind. He smiled at her and said:

'Desmond has just been telling me that it's his fault you're wearing that yellow dress today. It never occurred to me that he'd bring you such a present, coming down as he did on the spur of the moment.'

Breena opened her mouth to protest that it was her own fault she was *wearing* the dress, but Desmond winked at her, so she said instead, in an awkward voice: 'I haven't thanked you yet for... For such a lovely present, Desmond... Thank you very much.'

She felt herself reddening. She smiled quickly, shyly, from one to the other and then turned away and began to wipe the heels of her shoes on a patch of long grass. So it was her gaudy dress that had made Uncle John look at her so sternly in the stock-room... Did that mean that, so far, he knew nothing about Gabriel? As she puzzled over the matter she saw Gabriel come up to join the others, who still stood about two feet back, where she had overshot them. Only at that point did she reflect that back on the platform she had abandoned Gabriel in mid-sentence, and she began to creep stealthily downhill towards the jetty, still pretending to wipe her shoes on the tufts of long grass.

CHAPTER 40

She reached the head of the jetty. 'Arctic' was the word Gabriel had used to describe the way the sea looked today. But now she saw with delight that a patch of blue was opening up to the south, out over the bay.

She stood looking down into the water. She thought of yesterday, of the fishing, of her swim… Then suddenly as she stood there she thought she heard the name *'Maurice'* being called out loudly behind her. She turned sharply about. But the slope above the jetty was too steep; she could not see beyond the top. For a moment she hesitated. Surely only her own longing could make her think that Maurice had suddenly arrived out here and that they were calling on him by name? Then she had begun to run; in her high heels, taking ridiculously short steps, she hardly seemed to move at all as she struggled up the slope. But at last she was far enough up to be able to see what was happening. And there coming towards them was Maurice, already crossing the sand dunes, bearing down on them rather more quickly than he wished as his bike skidded and slithered over the sand and tufts of grass.

She saw that they were all staring at him. She ran to the place where they were standing and reached it almost at the same time as Maurice. He jumped off his bike, his face bright red, and glistening with perspiration. Desmond stepped forward and put out a hand to support the bike. So far Maurice had approached so quickly and with such an air of purpose that though they were all obviously very surprised to see him, nobody had said anything. But now Desmond glanced at his father and then asked Maurice:

'Well? Have you come to fetch me? I thought that my luck was too good to last. Have they phoned for me to go back?'

They all waited for him to speak, to answer Desmond's question, but all he did was to stand there panting, the sweat creeping down into his eyebrows, his face even redder than before. It was evident that he had envisaged no such reception committee as was standing here to greet him. Desmond spoke again; his voice was restrained, but his eyes sparkled with lively interest:

'Come on, come on. What message have you brought?'

'Message? I... I...'

In face of the almost comic watchfulness and impatience of the three men, Maurice broke down into a stammer. Then in his meagre clothes – he wore corduroys and a sleeveless navy blue sweater, with old plimsolls on his feet – he drew himself up and asked with a great attempt at dignity: 'Why should you think that I've come out here to bring you a message?'

'Why? Why? Man, because...' But here Desmond checked himself and after a moment's silence asked in a patient, persuasive tone, 'Why *have* you come? D'you mind telling us that?'

Maurice suddenly let go of his bike. Breena knew he did it out of nervousness, but it made them all jump. Desmond, who already had his hand on the saddle, was quick enough to spring forward and take its whole weight. Maurice muttered: 'Sorry, I... I wanted to...' And stepped round to the carrier-bag at the back. He lifted the flap of this and pulled out what seemed to be a large bundle of old towels.

'Look!' He held himself so straight and spoke with such dramatic effect that he might as well have said 'Behold!' He raised the bundle. 'These are my swimming things; I've come out here just for a swim.'

| 267

The anti-climax of this statement, and the rather swaggering way in which Maurice was now clutching the old towels to his breast, proved too much for Desmond's sense of humour. He burst out laughing and put his arm around his cousin's shoulder:

'Maurice… Maurice! So you've cycled all the way out here, and got yourself into this state, just for a swim. You put us all to shame. Here we are, conveyed in a car to this most inviting swimming ground in all Ireland, and every single one of us is frightened of getting our big toes wet. I think we'll have to review the whole situation.'

At this point Uncle John stepped forward, not altogether to Breena's surprise. She knew that the way Desmond was holding Maurice's bike, letting it fall now this way, now that, was certain sooner or later to drive a man of Uncle John's orderly habits half-crazy. 'Give me that bike,' he said now quite curtly to his son. Desmond yielded it up without a word, but turned with his own comic brand of surprise and interest to stare after his father as he bore the bike off and propped it safely against a sandy hummock nearby.

Maurice used the interruption to edge up to Breena and tell her in a hurried yet triumphant voice, not a whisper but by no means a shout either: 'I've brought *you* your swimming things as well. Hannah hunted them out for me.' He stood now with bent head, fumbling with the bundle of towels, hindered by his own impetuousness as he tried to detach Breena's part of it from his own. Preoccupied with what he was doing, he failed to notice that Uncle John was coming back to re-join the group.

'Here you are!' At last he had found Breena's swimsuit. 'Take any towel you like, I can't make out which is which.'

'What's this?' Uncle John demanded. 'Breena, what's going on now?'

Like a thoroughbred horse Maurice started as this question was spoken in a loud tone close to his ear. He turned and stared wide-eyed and speechless at Uncle John, astonished at finding him so near. Breena looked round. She saw that Desmond had turned away; his father's bouts of heavy-handedness always embarrassed him; but Gabriel stood nearby as he had stood right throughout the scene, saying nothing but looking on with a peculiar watchfulness. In Breena's eyes at that moment Maurice seemed so much in need of support that she did not hesitate at all; she smiled at Uncle John, putting every trick of juvenility she knew into her face and voice as she said:

'Maurice has brought me my swimming things, Uncle John… I must go in for a swim now, mustn't I, since he's taken all that trouble?'

All the harshness melted away from Uncle John's looks. He glanced at Maurice. 'Yes,' he agreed, smiling, 'since Maurice has taken all that trouble, I suppose there's nothing else for it. You must go in for a swim.'

Desmond turned back to the group. He announced: 'If you two youngsters are going for a swim, I'm going in too, even if I have to wear m'scarf for decency.'

But now Gabriel, who had not spoken a word since Maurice arrived on the scene, suddenly turned and addressed Desmond.

'A few minutes back you spoke of reviewing the situation. If that means going in for a swim, I can accept a challenge as well as anybody else. I always keep two or three pairs of swimming togs in the boot, you know that.'

'Good man, good man! I knew you wouldn't desert an old friend. Now that I look at it again, I think m'scarf is too cumbersome to make a good loincloth.'

Breena turned to Maurice. '*You* shouldn't come in just yet, you know. Not for a quarter of an hour at least. You ought to wait until you've cooled down.'

Maurice, she knew, would not argue about this matter. All she had to do was remind him, and his love of swimming would give

| 269

way. But now Desmond's voice came in to support her; the voice of a Desmond no longer on holiday, but back on duty again.

'You're damn right, Breena. Of course Maurice can't go in yet. Here, Maurice, take this coat and wrap it round you; it'll help you to simmer down…'

Breena left them to it. She pulled off her silly high-heeled shoes and then in her stockinged feet ran down the grassy slope and jumped onto the concrete head of the jetty. She climbed up into her dressing-room, the rock-opening at the back of the jetty, where she could hear the waters sighing and crooning in the cave underneath. Today she was so dressed-up that getting into her swimsuit proved a major operation. Some minutes before she was ready she heard the men coming down the slope; she heard their exaggerated 'Ughs!' and 'Ooohs!' at the water's coldness as they reached the jetty's head and bent down to dabble their hands in the water. Then, her towel round her shoulders against the sharpness of the wind she stepped down, shivering, to join them.

Desmond saw her first. He cried at once, 'Here comes Breena. Three cheers for Breena, she'll lead us in. Breena abu!' At that the others also turned towards her. She became aware that Gabriel's eyes were taking in every detail of her appearance. Her response to his glance was to pull her towel proudly from her shoulders and walk slowly past him to join Maurice and Desmond.

She said in a consoling voice to Maurice: 'You look considerably less red than you did. In a few minutes I'm sure you'll be able to go in.'

A cry of 'Watch this, watch this!' from Desmond made them both swing around. They were just in time to see Gabriel spring in a graceful arc from near the head of the jetty and skim through the water in a beautifully controlled surface dive. For some minutes after that he held all their attention. Uncle John, who had strolled to the end of the jetty, came back to stand beside Breena and Maurice.

In the water Gabriel looked different again. He was every bit as graceful as Kitty, and far more versatile. Breena watched him go into one after another of the strokes she herself had tried too hard to master, and execute them all with effortless grace. She looked on with no friendly eye as, with an air of finishing the show, he circled round in a low luxurious crawl and finally hauled himself up on the jetty. Then he stood before them, tanned, glistening, smoothing back his wet hair with both hands, smiling, accepting their compliments with modest glances at the ground.

'Cold!' he exclaimed as soon as they gave him a chance to speak. The next moment he had turned and dived in again. He repeated his surface dive which carried him skimming far out over the water.

'God! Can't he swim!' Maurice exclaimed in generous admiration.

'Yes, he's good. He's like a porpoise,' was Desmond's comment. 'But we can't have a one-man show. Now watch me, all of ye!'

With out-thrust jaw and resolute step he marched to the top of the jetty steps. He had never learned to dive; now he could only lower himself step by step into the water. As the tide washed around his ankles and then reached his shins he gritted his teeth and began to groan in a very painful way.

'It's torture, pure torture,' he called up. 'Diving can't be worse than this.'

Once more he gritted his teeth. Then he closed his eyes and suddenly flung himself forward on the water. Breena winced at the whacking sound the water made against his chest and shoulders. Then she saw him thrashing about like a puppy. His eyes still closed, his hands pawing rather than cleaving the water. She glanced round at Uncle John, who she had been very conscious of for some minutes past, standing there within a few inches of her, a silent witness of all that was going on. Very pleased to have something to say to him at last, she remarked: 'Desmond's getting better, don't you think? At least he's attempting to dive now.'

To her astonishment Uncle John gave a helpless snort of laughter. 'Dive!' he exclaimed. 'He looks more like a man intent on committing suicide. Dive! Why, a h-h-hen could do better than that.' Breena and Maurice could not help smiling in sympathy. 'If… if there weren't some good swimmers about, I'd forbid him the water.'

All at once Breena felt very fond of Desmond. At least he never lacked courage, or the wisdom maybe, to make a fool of himself. Suddenly she felt she could wait no longer; she moved to the edge of the jetty and dived in. As usual, she swam under water as long as her breath lasted. She kept very low, holding herself down by grabbling with her fingers into the ridged sand at the bottom. She loved the colour of this sand and the broken shells that gleamed in it. Finally, as her breath was giving out she turned over and saw the cloud-coloured ocean above her. At that moment, the colour was not to her something she saw with her eyes. The subtle tones of it pervaded her whole being, she had become what it was.

CHAPTER 41

Breena surfaced and, with her own peculiar but very fast crawl, made her way to her sunning-shelf. She reached the ledge and scrambled back and sat down on the shell-encrusted rock that already felt warm from the sun. She leaned forward, clasping her hands on her knees, and look about her. But the brightness of the water made a haze out of the curving headlands. The Boar Rock and the other larger rocks and islands further out were blurred at the edges and refused to stay put. They seemed to sink out of sight and reappear like whales some distance to the left or right. Then she saw somebody swimming far out, doing a slow, effortless-seeming crawl in the glittering water. It could only be Gabriel. Well, he could certainly swim… She closed her eyes, lifted her face gladly to the sun… When something prompted her to open them again it was to see Maurice coming towards her, his head low and smooth in the water like a seal's, hardly rippling the surface as he swam. At once she sat forward and watched. Maurice kept his head low until he felt the ledge under his fingers. Then he looked up, smiled at Breena, and waited for one of the small waves that washed the rocks out here. On this he glided in, again like a seal. Within a few seconds he was far enough in to clamber nimbly to his feet.

'What d'you think of that?' he asked with a wide grin. '*An té nach bhfuil láidir, ni foláir dó bheith glic!*'

'Maurice…' She gazed at him lazily from under her lashes…

'Has anyone ever told you that you look very like a fish?' And then, seeing his expression, she laughed in his face, daring him to resent it. With Maurice here beside her, her present happiness was all the more intense for the depression, the questioning of her very right to be happy, that had preceded it. Still laughing, she said to Maurice:

'What I mean is, you swim like a fish. It has nothing to do with your face.'

'Thank God for that.' He sat down beside her. She turned to him eagerly: 'Maurice, who'd have dared an hour ago to bet on the sun's chances? Yet now the sun holds the whole of the sky. Just feel how hot that rock is up there! Let's move a bit further up…'

They moved further back, as far as they could, right to where the outer sandstone ledge came up against the high thick edge of basalt that protected the sand-dunes from the ravages of the sea. Breena gave a sigh of delight as she settled back into this sun-warmed rocky seat. Relaxed though she was, half-dreaming in the sun, she was vividly aware of everything around, both what she saw before her and what she felt inside herself. Oh how carelessly, achingly blue the sky was…

A shadow crossed her face; the warmth of the sun receded.

'Breena!' Maurice's golden face hovered above hers. He was smiling. 'I was beginning to think you had dozed off.'

'No, I…' She found it difficult to talk, to think of words.

'You haven't asked me yet why I came out, have you?'

'For a swim, you said, surely?'

'No… That's only half the reason. Hannah told me…'

He paused to brush off, very gently, a piece of dried seaweed that had floated down on her hair. She stirred restlessly, her dreamy mood left her. She waited only a moment.

'What did Hannah tell you?'

'Why, that they'd hurried you off out here, all dolled up in a silk dress Desmond gave you, and that not one of them thought of giving you a chance to go and collect your swimming things. So I decided to bring your things out to you. I knew it would nearly kill you to come out here and not be able to go for a swim.'

She leaned back once more against the rock. For a moment she felt desperately, appallingly disappointed. Oh, what a hypocrite she was! She badly wanted Maurice to know about Gabriel, and for the very worst, the meanest of reasons. She wanted him to know that a man like Gabriel found her attractive. Yet she wanted him to hear the story from anybody except herself. And why, why, why, hadn't he already heard it? They must have been discussing it around him all day. He ought, surely he ought, to have heard it by now… Could Jerry be right after all? Was Maurice so utterly taken up with his own affairs that he was deaf and blind to everything except his own direct interests?

Maurice was still, with a queer kind of absorption, plucking the fragments of seaweed from her hair. He said in a thoughtful tone: 'Of course I wanted to get in a swim for myself as well.' Then his voice changed. It almost melted away. He said:

'Breena, I'm very glad I came. This is the way I'll always think of you all the time I'm away, sitting here with your hair wet, in your swimsuit. D'you know, you're by far the best part of all this landscape out here at Maurcappagh? Breena, you should always… '

'Thank you!'

Again a shadow crossed her face. His lips were on hers a moment before the realisation came that he was kissing her. She felt his warm shoulder against hers. Then she felt his kiss and his touch go thrilling deeper and deeper inside her until they exploded in eddies of vibrating sweetness. She was still feeling these when she heard him speaking again, and knew that he had drawn away from her.

'There! That's a pledge. I, Maurice, pledge myself unto thee, Breena… From you, Breena, I ask for no pledge. I haven't the right. And as soon as I can I'll send you a beautiful, beautiful ring with all your favourite colours in it, all the colours of Maurcappagh. They won't be real stones of course. But nobody except you and me will ever know that. Wear it always until I come back. Will you promise me that?'

'I promise.' She smiled and sat up and stretched with exquisite languor.

'And by the way, I've brought you a message from Kit. She says it's most important… '

'Kit! Oh, dear Kit!' She started up. 'I promised to go and see her after… After the funeral. And here I am… '

'Don't feel sorry for Kit, Breena. Believe me, there's no need. She's stronger than any of us. She wanted me to come out here like this. She knew you were here. How d'you think I'd have got away today if Kitty hadn't been behind me? If anything, *she* feels sorry for you at this moment… '

'Sorry for me?'

'Well anyway she's sent you a message. It's short and sharp. It's this: force him to show his hand.'

She glanced at Maurice. He was watching her with a soft, roguish smile, as if… as if she were very dear to him. Suddenly, she had no idea by what means, she understood. She asked in a quick surprised way. 'You… you *know* about Gabriel?'

'Sure I know. I'm not deaf. The whole town knows about him by now, I imagine. To be quite honest, I feel grateful to Gabriel. He's taken old Kit out of herself; he's taken her mind off *me*. I haven't seen her smile for two days, but she laughed out loud when they told her about Gabriel and you. She was quite her old self just before I left, telling me what to tell you.'

'What does Kit really want me to do?'

'Lead him on; force him to the point. Get him to speak out, to ask the question. The sooner he speaks out, the sooner you can say "no!"; the sooner you're free. Right? Kit tells me she's been listening round. She says he's serious all right, but also that he's more than likely to take his time. The family's behind him, he knows that. And he knows too that they all feel he shouldn't rush things. Also, he has no sense of humour and there's no shaking his belief in the benefits he can bestow; ever since Hugh married he's been Desmond's bestest best friend. Desmond has been reported as saying that he'll soon be forced to take divorce proceedings. So with a man like that to deal with you've no need to feel any qualms of conscience whatever. So Kit says. He could keep you on a string for months. Kit says you must decide at once whether you're going to be a victim. So far, she claims, you've been pure victim. Now's the time to take your courage in both hands... '

They examined one another's faces and suddenly burst out laughing.

'D'you know I think I'll try it,' Breena said. 'It's certainly better than being a victim. Which is exactly what I felt like a while back, when Gabriel was speaking to me.' She paused and added in a low voice, almost to herself: 'I'm sure Kit is right about his taking his time. There was a moment in the car, but I spoiled it.'

'Try it. Remember; practice makes perfect. *Perservando vinces.* If at first you don't succeed... Race you to the jetty!'

His sudden challenge took her by surprise; she scrambled to her feet in such an awkward way, that he could not help laughing at her. Once in the water, however, he had reason to regret his laughter. He flopped his dive. She shot past him as he rose to the surface, spluttering and gasping for breath. She skimmed over the water with joy, feeling sure that she would keep her advantage.

Within a very short time, it seemed, her fingers struck rather sharply amongst the limpet-roughened concrete of the jetty. She had won, she had won! As she raised her head out of the water she glimpsed hands that were reaching down to help her on to the jetty.

She felt astounded; she stared at Maurice, just barely able to stammer out: 'Why, you – you got here first!'

Secretly she was very riled. To have failed after such an all-out effort; when for once she was so very sure that she had won! But she put the best face she could on it and smiled brightly. She could not bring herself to look directly at Maurice, however.

He seemed to see behind her smile. He said gently: 'Remember that I've had five or seven years' start on you as a swimmer. And think of all the practice you'll get in while I'm away. When I come back, all grey-faced and worn out from the cities, you'll have to teach me to swim all over again.'

'I'll enjoy that,' she assured him, smiling straight into his eyes.

'Look!' he cried suddenly. 'Gosh! Just look!' She followed his upward glance. All above them the sky was black. The clouds had crept up on the sun. As they stood there streams of rain began to lash the jetty, slantwise, driven by the wind. Breena laughed in sheer joy as she turned her face to the rain for a moment before following Maurice in his dash for shelter.

CHAPTER 42

When Breena stepped out from under her towel, turned into a shawl over her head, the rain had abated. As she climbed the slippery grass she saw that the greater mass of cloud had been blown inland by the wind and now hung darkly over the mountains, blotting out the peaks of the Maurcappagh range. Even the wind itself had passed on. Over the sea there was now only a high glow, with gauzy ribbons of cloud trailing down from it here and there. The water was grey and quiet once more. Emerald gleams sparkled on the dark whalebacks of the islands far out.

The four men stood around the car, securing Maurice's bike to the luggage-rack with a length of nylon rope. So Maurice was coming back with them in the car! She stood happily at some distance to watch operations, shivering a little at first, then gradually warming up as she felt the benefit of her clothes. The pleasant murmur of the men's voices as they adjusted and tied up the bike drifted across to her. 'It's touching on this side… '; 'Yes, it must go back a bit there… '; 'I'll hold it firm, you lash it down… '; 'Over a bit here. That's better…'

The swim had effected a change in everybody's mood. As they got into the car even Gabriel spoke with satisfaction and surprise of the 'bracing and invigorating' quality of the water out here, and of the delight of the short period of sunshine. They compared notes on how hungry they felt. Breena had often before noticed how a walk on the mountains, or a swim, or a few hours out on the sea improved people's tempers and induced in them friendly and serene feelings towards one another. But never had it been so marked as it was today. Even Uncle John seemed happy again, though he had not been in for a swim. Breena gathered that it was he who had suggested tying Maurice's bike on the rack and giving him a lift back in the car; and he was the kind of man who immediately became cheerful as soon as anything practical had to be done.

Gabriel had elected to drive his own car home. Uncle John's right to sit beside him was disputed by none of the others. Desmond, Maurice, and Breena settled happily into the comfort of the back seat. Breena, sitting in the corner behind Uncle John, with Maurice beside her and Desmond beyond, and feeling Maurice's rain-chilled hand on hers, listened in dreamy silence as Desmond commented generously on the progress she and Maurice had made in swimming and diving over the past year; and then went on to ask in an exaggerated tone of despair what in the world he himself could do to improve his own swimming... ?

Already they had passed the winding of the Maur river. Gabriel's car, with powers of acceleration that seemed magical compared with Thady's, seemed to fly over rather than circle round the high road that led up to the Pass.

As they came down into Filemoyn nobody seemed to take note of the passage of the car. No face could be seen looking out of any window; the storm had cleared the fields. Yet Breena knew, and knew that Uncle John knew, that from some point of vantage in every house the passing of the car was being watched. And wherever they went today – north, south, east or west of the town – it would have been the same; the car would have been noted, the route they had taken discussed and finally settled, and their identity established. Maurcappagh was about the one place they could go to today without being blamed for it. It would be taken as an act of kindness to Norah and Sean Mor. Breena had no need to be told that Uncle John had come with them on this outing to make sure they went to Maurcappagh and nowhere else. He knew that Desmond could not be trusted in this matter, because Desmond had no idea of the issues at stake.

Breena was very sensitive to Uncle John's concern to be thought well of by people in the town, especially by these people out here around Maurcappagh, neighbours of his and his family for generations. She knew his full sympathy with their standards, and his desire not to outrage them in any way. It was a great bond between her and Uncle John that the large, instinctual, never-ceasing curiosity of the country was second nature to them both. Even Desmond, quick as he was in many ways, had lost his jungle wariness when dealing with these old neighbours of the family. In Breena's opinion, life had narrowed by just that much for him, therefore. When he looked out of the car window and saw only people going about their farm business, he had no idea of the vivid interest and inquisitiveness that extended toward himself from these people and connected him with them in spite of himself; life had lost some of its richness for him, forever.

They were approaching the town. Maurice asked to be put down by the gate below his house, the gate where the footpath to the lake began. Desmond made an effort to persuade him to come home with them, and Maurice certainly looked eager to do so. Nevertheless he found the strength to refuse, in a muttering, steadfast sort of way. Desmond got out to help him down with his bike. Then as Maurice was about to leave them, Desmond tried again; he seemed to be affected by some kind of compassion for his cousin as he stood shivering there, very pale now in his meagre clothes, his tall frame almost skeletal in its thinness, certainly in need, as Desmond must think, of a good meal, which he would not get at home this evening.

'Aw, come on, Maurice! You know Aunt Ursula is bound to have the usual fatted-calf dinner ready when we get back. What ails you, all of a sudden? I've never know you to need so much pressing before. After that bike-ride and swim you must be famished. Are you afraid there won't be enough to go round, or what?'

Maurice smiled at this, almost shyly. He looked at the ground;

evidently he could not trust himself to look anywhere else. It was obvious that he wanted very much to come, but for all that he kept up his muttering refusals: 'Mother... I didn't tell Mother that I was going out to Maurcappagh... Only Kit knows... And I... I gave Kit to understand that I'd be back before this... They'll probably be wondering what's become of me...'

Uncle John suddenly decided to put an end to the agony. 'Good lad, good lad! It's right that you should think of your mother today. You go on home now, since that's the way you want it. Tell your mother that Desmond and myself will be along to see her after dinner. In a situation like this, each of us has his own duty to perform...'.

Gabriel drove up Church Street with the right skilful mixture of dash and caution. He set them down by the side-gate and drove off round the corner to put the car away.

The kitchen was warm and, as soon as they entered, crowded. Dr Peggy was there as well as Ursula and Hannah; as always when Desmond was home Dr Peggy had come down herself to oversee matters and try the patience of Ursula and Hannah. There was a great clutter of pots and pans about.

Uncle John and Desmond stopped just inside the door to exchange a few words. Breena paused beside them, suddenly almost delirious with hunger, savouring the mouth-watering fragrance of herbs and spices from the cooking dinner. It was a moment or two before she could listen to the talk. When she did so she found that it centred round Norah and Sean's family, as she had expected. But the important thing now was the change out of the yellow dress, which had become hateful to her, before it was time for dinner. Carefully therefore she arranged an intent and abstracted expression on her face and sidled round Desmond in an absent-minded sort of way, hurried behind the back of the others, opened the door into the corridor, passed through it, closed it noiselessly and went to her room.

CHAPTER 43

There was nothing unusual about tonight's dinner. A great fuss was always made of Desmond when he came home, whether he came alone or brought friends with him. Perhaps this evening's dinner was somewhat later than usual, but Breena herself and her 'little trip' rather than Desmond must be held responsible for that. Over the years, for convenience's sake, because of the shop and because of Dr Peggy's work, it had become the rule of the house to have dinner – the only meal of the day they could all have together – rather late in the evening. It was nearly always a very enjoyable meal. Ursula saw to it that the food was plentiful, and Hannah had her own particular gift of never overcooking food. When they gathered upstairs at the long table they were all hungry; for most of them the day's work was over; happy talk flowed with the rich scents and savours of the food. Hannah had her own place beside her friend Ursula for this meal, Thady lower down side by side with Dr Peggy. Indeed, Dr Peggy never looked more likeable (more human, Breena would have said once), than when she sat beaming broadly in response to some story Thady was telling her.

This evening, however, Breena had no great hopes of enjoying her dinner. The extraordinary task of Gabriel lay before her; the thought of it came between her and her usual pleasure in food. When she returned to the kitchen her dress changed, her hair coiled in a grown-up way behind her head, she found Dr Peggy, Hannah,

Ursula, gathered round the table, all intent with a very lively bustle and chatter in giving a final polish to the trays of cutlery, plates etc., that stood ready to be taken upstairs. A bottle of sherry, already half-empty, occupied a prominent place on the table before them. All the fragrance of a now-ready dinner was suddenly cut off for herself, however, by one little circumstance; as soon as they looked round and saw who it was they suddenly stopped talking and started smiling at her. She understood at once that they had been talking about Gabriel; the idea of Gabriel and herself, so preposterous even to Dr Peggy a short twenty-four hours ago, was beginning to take hold on all their minds.

All at once Dr Peggy gave up smiling to exclaim: 'Oh! I see you've changed out of Desmond's dress! Well! Well!'

Still in the doorway, Breena cleared her throat and asked: 'Can I help?'

'You can come and have a glass of sherry with us.' Ursula, who was surveying her change of dress with a kind smile, turned to pour her out a glass. 'Yes!' she approved then, reaching out to smooth down the shoulders of Breena's dress, 'I think you were wise to change. That's a cool pretty colour. And I like your hair done up behind in that way. It goes with your appearance…'

'Can I help?' Breena asked again.

'No; finish up your sherry and then go upstairs and talk to the men, they'll be expecting it. Besides, there isn't room down here for four of us.' And Ursula's hands came down once more on her shoulders, this time to turn her round and urge her in the right direction, upstairs.

Breena felt she had no choice but to go. They were all smiling at her; she just didn't feel up to standing there one moment longer and smiling back. The last thing she saw as she climbed the stairs was Hannah's face grimacing at her from below, cheeks puffed out, mouth elongated, in a fairly good imitation of a bonabh.

Upstairs Desmond was playing chess with his father in the

second window-seat down. Gabriel was seated nearby, watching with every appearance of interest. Uncle John gave Breena one of his old bright, full, kindly looks. 'Sit down and watch your cousin make an even worse fool than usual of himself,' he invited her.

Breena sat down. Desmond was indeed losing badly; he could play chess only in two ways: brilliantly, or abominably. Today was one of his excruciating days. His father threatened him seriously at three separate points. He could only lean forward and desperately intone; 'Now you must keep your head, for I am losing mine and blaming it on you.'

His father, who was advancing with inexorable slowness along his left flank, never making a move that he hadn't made hundreds of times before, and knew the consequences of, far beyond Desmond's patience for reckoning at the moment, suddenly lost his temper.

'Pull yourself together. We're playing chess, remember? D'you want to resign, or what?'

'Resign? Me and m'men? Never!' Desmond bent down once more. With a rueful glance he surveyed the board. 'There's only one thing for it!' He lowered his voice: 'My friends remember this; you can always take one with you!'

With that he set his two knights, his only remaining pieces of any value, galloping back and forth between his father's ordered lines in a way that made Breena burst out laughing. Uncle John shot her an exasperated glance. It was only a matter of minutes before 'Mate!' was called. But the melee at the end thoroughly upset Uncle John. He began to scold Desmond in such an excited way that Desmond, laughing, positively ran across the room to fetch him a stiff whiskey to improve his dinner.

Downstairs there were two bottles of wine on the table. The very sight of them depressed Breena. She knew from experience that they meant a prolonged meal. Nobody liked good food – and yes, her glass of wine too to go with it – more than she did; but food for her was only the beginning of the enjoyment of a meal. The talk, the company, were every bit as important. And this evening she sighed heavily to herself as she glanced round the table; Desmond and his mother, with Hannah between them, talking shop, to the obvious delight and horrification of Hannah; Ursula, on Uncle John's right, seeing to everybody's needs, and particularly seeing to it that 'John… John' had everything he wanted; Uncle John addressing himself to Gabriel, Gabriel addressing himself mainly to his dinner… what could she hope from such company? How she longed for Maurice, for Kitty, for dear old Thady who liked to talk only about boats and the sea. (Thady was absent tonight; probably knowing full well what was in store for him he had chosen to go off for a walk over the mountains with the dogs.)

As far as talk was concerned, Uncle John was at his most tiresome worst. How, if she were only sitting beside him, she could with a few apt questions coax him into a charming, boyish, reminiscent mood! As it was, he began with the hoary old riddle, 'When is salmon poached twice over?' and went on to long speeches that she knew by heart and could repeat ahead of him word for word. Gabriel made no attempt to interrupt. Probably added to the deference which he had first begun to show Uncle John on the way home from Maurcappagh, there was now the conventional attitude that Uncle John at his own table must be allowed to run on as he wished. Alas! The length of Uncle John's speeches increased with his intake of wine. Very soon it was:

'My judgment on the people in this town is not a harsh judgement. I make every allowance for their history and circumstances. Yet, as you must have noticed by now, I am not a popular man in this town. No, I am not a popular man. However, thanks be to God, I have been able to make my own life here, I have my own wide family circle… '

And then: 'I have travelled right round the globe, as no doubt I have mentioned to you before. The conclusions I have reached have not been reached easily. In my youth… ' here he paused to take a bite, 'in my youth I went twenty years or more without coming to one conclusion. Anybody who calls me an opinionated man is a liar. For more than half my life I have looked about me with a sharp eye, observed what there was to see, and kept my mouth shut. Maybe I thought all the more because of that. When I finally did come to my own conclusions about life, they were conclusions based on long, and may I call it, scientific observation...'

Breena got tired of saying it ahead of him. She remembered the immense, the incalculable amount of boredom she had patiently endured when she was a child, when she first came to the house, listening to long speeches such as this. All that was over at any rate, what should be worrying her now was that she was getting nowhere with her vamping. With Uncle John to compete against as well as the food... She needed inspiration.

Desmond, with a white napkin tied around his waist, had just got up to carve the prize dish of the evening, two 'fat capons' as he called them; two chickens stuffed very round and brown with potato and onion stuffing. There was also a baked ham to set off the flavour of the chickens, and a lot more food. Breena did not like even to look at what was being brought in: her own appetite, what there was if it, had been completely satisfied by the salmon. She was glad all the same of the excuse to jump up and help. At the sideboard when nobody was looking she swallowed a large dose of whiskey. She had to take it neat; there was no time to water it down. It did something for her. No sooner has she swallowed it than she hit on an idea that at first only amused her and then, as the whiskey began to work inside her, seemed good enough to act on. It was a simple idea; why not confide in Gabriel, flatter him by letting him in on her thoughts? She glanced sideways at him where he sat at the table, and for once found it easier to keep looking at him than to tear her glance away. His eyes met hers through the steam above the chickens. He smiled at her and she realised that this was the moment to act. He had no food before him as yet, and Uncle John had turned aside to listen to Ursula – she was giving him a more or less whispered account of how she had managed to get the salmon at such short notice, over which they were both giggling like children.

Breena made up her mind. She went quickly back to the table and sat down beside Gabriel. She started talking at once because she knew that was her only chance. She began by repeating verbatim for him Uncle John's speech: 'I have travelled right round the globe…' She had to keep her voice low; Uncle John would hardly understand that this was the best possible use that could be made of his speeches.

Gabriel's first reaction seemed to be one of astonishment. She was aware of his fixed, puzzled glance on her face. But she kept right on to the end; and perhaps it was the whiskey and the wine, but she found herself laughing quite naturally as she finished with: 'There! I know it by heart. Can you guess why?' And she hurried on to tell him how she used to deal with this particular speech when she was a child; by dancing her feet noiselessly under the table to the tune of a reel and singing under her breath: 'I've been round and round the… world; I've been round and round the… world; I've been round and round the… world; and come to no conclusion!'

Their plates were set before them. For some reason – whether it was Ursula's doing or Desmond's Breena could not tell – Uncle John kept on speaking to the other side of the table when they started eating again. She had Gabriel to herself, and she had the satisfaction of seeing him gradually enter into the spirit of what she was telling him. First it was a half-finished remark, uttered with a cautious smile: 'Yes, I can see how tiresome…' But soon he was responding in sheer human sympathy; 'Tell me a little more. I suppose you had a song to go with every speech?' She only picked at her own food; she concentrated on talking. The more she told him, the more he smiled at her. Finally he seemed to imagine he was her own age again; he even put forward some suggestions for lines of songs.

All the same it was hard going. She had a pain in her cheeks from the effort of smiling. Dinner seemed to go on and on. Then the clinking of cups on a tray caught her attention and she looked round with sudden hope. Yes, at last! Hannah and Ursula were coming in with the coffee. She watched with some fascination the raw, puce hillocks of Hannah's knuckles against the dainty coffee cups... Poor Hannah! Then her own cup was put before her. She stared into it and caught the eyes, as it were, of one enlarged brownish-black grain of coffee that seemed to wink at her as it bobbed up and down and swirled merrily round on the surface of the liquid as she stirred. Then suddenly she was sitting with clenched teeth in the utmost torment of anxiety, feeling her knees shake with helpless giggling, feeling the ripple of it gradually and irresistibly mount up her body. Oh, God! One thing at least she had felt fairly certain she had outgrown – those giggling bouts that used to make her life so wretched a year or two back, when she was fifteen and sixteen years old. But now at last dinner was over.

As she stood up, and said, 'Excuse me' with great politeness to Gabriel, she felt a touch on her shoulder. It was Desmond.

'Breena, a word with you.' He walked over to the window, then remarked: 'Gabriel wants to take you for a drive. To Castleboyne, I think. Is that all right?'

She smiled at him. This morning she had gone to him for help; now she only said in what she hoped was a bored voice: 'Of course I'll go. I'm dying to go, as you must realise... Provided, of course, Gabriel gets Uncle John's permission first... '

'Good girl!' was his unexpected reply to this. He smiled and went on, 'At last you're beginning to see the funny side of the situation. I knew you would eventually. I was watching your antics at dinner; I had a fairly good idea then that you'd come round to my way of seeing things. And as for going for that drive, quite frankly, Breena, I'd be obliged to you if you'd take Gabriel off our hands for the evening.'

'Why should *you* want Gabriel off your hands?' she asked him.

'Breena... I think I had better mention this to you... I noticed in the car going out to Maurcappagh how you looked at my father when he began to cough. Well, Mother and Aunt Ursula, as well as yourself, are worried about that cough. It's certainly getting no better. They want me… '

She leaned eagerly forward. 'To persuade him to give up his pipe? I think he should give it up, and the sooner the better. That old pipe always brings on his cough. I've noticed it time and again. He must give it up, like he gave up cigarettes.'

'Well, perhaps you're right. Perhaps if we can persuade him to give up his pipe… At any rate, you'll go out with Gabriel and clear the field for us?'

'Yes… and the sooner we get off the better!' (And, she thought to herself, I'll never respect myself again if I don't put an end to this silly business tonight.)

'That's the spirit!' He winked at her; it was almost as if he had read her thoughts. 'I'll go up and tell him, then… We'll wait for you by the garage. Good luck!'

Breena went to get ready. As she let herself out by the front door she saw that there was nobody about in the square. A strong cold breeze had risen, and the greyness that often came with it was on everything around; on the houses, on the Tobar mountains across the valley, on the Maurcappagh range that rose up behind the town. Breena rather relished this greyness; she knew how she could put colour into it from inside herself by running into the wind. It was an evening for walking up to the lake, she reflected.

CHAPTER 44

Desmond and Gabriel stood talking by the car. Gabriel made a great show of walking round the car to open the door for her. She glanced at his face as she stepped into the car. She did not pretend to herself that she felt at ease with him. In fact, for a few moments she allowed her whole being to melt into longing for the end of this drive, for the time when this completely false situation would be behind her for good.

Desmond winked, smiled, waved them off. Then there was only Gabriel. She sat beside him, staring out into the dusk. She was intensely aware of the dark bulk of him, rising up on her right. Now he smiled a great deal, turning his face towards her so that his teeth glinted in the dusk. His voice, as he questioned her about where she wanted to go, was almost playful. She tried to puzzle out how much of the softening of his manner was due to the food and wine he had just consumed. He asked her a great many questions; it was not necessary to attempt to answer them all.

'... What about that new hotel at Castleboyne? – You must want to see it? Everybody's talking about it... The right kind of choice for tonight, I should imagine? About twenty-five miles off? Is that far enough? But I know that you don't enjoy just sitting and having a drink? I know the kind of things *you* enjoy; swimming, climbing fences – everything that's exhausting! You love dancing, of course?'

She had to answer this. 'Yes. But tonight we couldn't possibly...'

'Of course not. The funeral and so on; I understand. I just wanted to know, for the record… You leave it to me then, where we go?'

'Yes…'

His good manner seemed to increase as she refrained from putting forward any suggestions of her own. Evidently it pleased him very much to find her so tractable. Then she felt his hand on her arm, she felt the crispness of his glove through her sleeve.

'You trust me… Breena?'

When he released her arm she curled it behind her on the seat, so that he could not reach it again.

They were travelling along the main road north out of the town. She took it for granted that they were making for the new hotel at Castleboyne after all. But he surprised her. They were now coming up to the white track that branched off towards Maurcappagh; the next minute she realised they had turned into it. For some minutes the last gleams of daylight and the brightening moon made the white track glimmer. Then Gabriel turned his headlights on full beam. At once the day was banished; the moon, just rising above Filedearg, became a lustreless white disk in the sky. Instead of fields and moorland, they were surrounded by a darkening and dismal landscape.

He was saying: 'I've brought you up here for a little private talk. I know you're very fond of this place… Afterwards we'll go on to Castleboyne, I'll treat you to your first martini. By the way, I hope I'm right in calling it your "first"?'

She nodded quickly, 'Yes, yes!' She wanted to hurry him on at once from this uninteresting subject to the 'little private talk'. She was now listening intently; she thought with joy, 'It's coming! It will soon all be over!'

'I'm glad… Breena. I want you to have your first martini and a lot of other "firsts" with me. You enjoy everything so much; I know that every one of *your* firsts will seem like a first to me too, That's your particular gift. But there are ways of sharing it…'

She sighed very quietly as she listened. He was asking her now:

'The Cappagh country is beyond the Pass, isn't it? Let's wait to have our talk there. It seems appropriate. In the meantime, I want to ask your opinion of a certain plan that I've already broached to Hugh. *He* thoroughly approves of it, and mentioned in passing that I might safely discuss it with you. He tells me that he depends a great deal at the moment on your good sense and influence over young Maurice…'

'"*Young*" Maurice?' She was surprised into making that exclamation. But Gabriel, who only wanted to be telling her about his plan, took no heed of her tone and continued:

'After Hugh exclaimed to me this morning how much trouble he is giving just now, I put on my thinking cap. And what disturbs Hugh most, you must understand, is that young Maurice speaks as if there were thousands of pounds to be spent on him. Instead of which…'

His reiterations of '*Young* Maurice' exasperated her. She could barely keep herself from protesting, 'Maurice is his name, not young Maurice. And he has no illusions about thousands of pounds. All he wants is to go off and give nobody any trouble!' But she pressed her lips together, she was silent. Nothing, she swore to herself, would induce her to discuss Maurice again.

He was saying now: 'No doubt you understand better than I do how worried Hugh is about young Maurice's health. So I've put it to him that if he were to return to Dublin with me…'

Gabriel went on to outline his plan. It would, he claimed, give Maurice 'token freedom' and 'an illusion of getting his own way' until he had passed safely through 'his present phase of adolescent rebellion'. It had to do with a friend of Gabriel's in Dublin, a television personality, a household name – though of course until the man was consulted no names must be mentioned. He felt certain that this man would, on his recommendation, give Maurice 'some kind of unusual, interesting job; something to do with his music…'

Breena listened in silence. She realised that Hugh and Gabriel must have discussed this matter pretty thoroughly. And again she experienced a chilling sense of the insignificance of her own, or Maurice's, 'adolescent' views.

At last they were coming up to the Pass. As they drove between grey boulders, with the darker cliffs looming above, Gabriel interrupted himself to ask: 'Well, what do you think of *our* plan?'

She hesitated; curiosity overcame her. 'Has Maurice been consulted about it yet?'

'Perhaps by this time, yes. Hugh promised to speak to him this evening.'

Hugh! Then there was a fat chance of Maurice's taking a favourable view of it!

At this point Gabriel had to give all his attention to his driving; he was backing on to the flat shelf that overhung the valley. 'Cappagh country!' he exclaimed as soon as she had achieved this. He switched off the lights, and began to speak briskly:

'I had a long talk with Dr Peggy this morning. She gave me a very graphic account of your surprise and delight when she spoke to you last night. She told me…'

And then in a queer kind of way he proceeded to describe her behaviour last night as seen through Dr Peggy's eyes; her 'modest disbelief', her astonishment, her 'speechless delight'. Strange to say, her first reaction to this was not embarrassment or resentment, but simple surprise. Had he brought her all the way out here to 'Cappagh country' to say what should sensibly never be said at all? And then it dawned on her that he had spoken to her as he had done on the dunes this afternoon because all the time he believed he was speaking to the girl who had agreed by proxy to marry him – to his future wife. For a moment she almost pitied him. She remembered what she had heard about his great devotion to his mother, who had died only the year before. She began to understand him. Some glimpse of his true predicament was vouchsafed to her.

She was hardly aware at what precise moment he finished speaking. The touch of his hand on hers roused her. He had taken off his gloves. She drew her own hand gently away and rested it against her dress. It cost her some effort to keep her voice steady, to speak without excitement or exasperation, as she replied:

'I can see that you have great respect for Dr Peggy. So have we all. She has one big fault though; all the family admit that. She is inclined to take up an idea and run away with it. I must tell you now that last night she just ran away with the idea that it would be a good thing for me to… to get married. But I want you to know that she has misled you badly about *my* reactions. I had no idea that you'd put such faith in what Dr Peggy told you. I most certainly never said that I…'

He laughed. 'That you wanted to marry me? Breena, you're a very modest girl. And you mustn't wrong Dr Peggy; she did *not* say that you told her in so many words you wanted to marry me. No. What she said was that there was no need for you to speak out. You have a very expressive face… Breena, my dear, *I know* that you like me; you like me far more than you yourself realise at this moment. When you came into the sitting-room this evening, and all through dinner, something showed in your face. I knew then that Dr Peggy had got her essentials right…'

This matter took her breath away. 'Oh God,' she thought, 'I'm a fool!'

Gabriel had begun to smoke; it was getting stale in the car. Impulsively she pushed down the handle of the door and stepped out. At once her heart leapt up; she saw what she had been unable to see from inside the car. The cove below had become a place of glitter and dark shadows. Down there the moon reigned, though here where she was standing, in the lee of the mountain, everything was in deep shadow. The moon could not be seen from here; the shoulder of the mountain hid it from view.

She stood very still, drawing strength from the loveliness below her in the valley. She thought to herself; all right, I'm a fool; therefore why not have the courage of my foolishness?

Why not be simple, foolish, artless? She looked back towards the car. She could just make out Gabriel's shape. By this time he had got out of the car and was coming towards her, hugging his coat around him against the freshness of the wind. She began to speak impetuously, calling him by his name for the first time:

'Gabriel, please tell me. Why *exactly* did you bring me out here?'

He stopped short. He seemed to hesitate; his tone softened: 'Breena... I want to explain to you... Dr Peggy asked me not to hurry you; she asked me to give you all the time you needed. She suggested we should wait a year. I want you to know that I agreed to wait... But if Dr Peggy was wrong, if she misread the situation – Breena, you know I want to marry you. Will you marry me soon... very soon?'

It had come at last! She felt the blood flowing away from her heart. Her lips trembled; she had to speak in a slow, pedantic fashion:

'Gabriel... I do not want to marry you. Now... or in a year's time... I do not want to marry you.'

There was a silence that seemed to her to last a very long time. Then he said in a tone that astonished her by its lightness, its near-gaiety:

'You see! Dr Peggy was right. I should have waited. The idea of marriage is very new to you ... you cried last night, didn't you? Well, let's say no more for the present, let's go on to Castleboyne at once. Dr Peggy warned me to be gentle with you. And you mustn't stand out here any longer in this cold wind.'

She broke out in an impatient voice, she could not help herself. 'I can't understand why you set such store by Dr Peggy's advice. Surely, in view of what *I've* just *said*... '

'Yes, yes! Now don't get excited. Let's go back to the car. Remember that martini I promised you?'

'I don't want a martini. Gabriel, I've been waiting all day to tell you this; I *do not want* to marry you.'

'I see. You don't want a martini, and you don't want to marry me!' She could not make out his expression in the darkness, but his voice sounded as if he were smiling. 'My dear, you're very young. You don't understand yourself yet, you don't understand your own feelings. That's enough for me for the present. It will take you some time to realise it, but all our friends will help you there. I think I can wait. I'm even beginning to like the idea of waiting. I'm an old-fashioned man.'

Breena felt breathless. She had a childish impulse to shout out, 'I hate you, I've always hated you! Can't you see… ' What could she say to him to prove that she was in earnest?

He was coming nearer, she saw that he was smiling. In the faint light his tanned face looked dark. It was a stranger's face; the face of a person she did not and could not know. He began to speak again:

'Yes, I'm looking forward to waiting! You must trust me, Breena. That's the first step. Come now, we'll go back to the car and… '

She saw him put out his arm; in a moment that arm would be around her, he would be leading her back to the car. She stepped quickly aside.

'Breena, come! This cold and dark is making you nervous. I assure you that when you're sitting in a warm room once more, having a drink, you'll feel quite as happy and as ready to talk as you did at dinner.'

But in stepping aside her foot had struck against the base of a boulder. On impulse she turned about, felt swiftly round with her hands, then clambered up onto the boulder.

'Breena, where have you got to? Oh you're up there, are you?'

'I want to make it quite clear… ' she heard him chuckle and broke off. Suddenly she was keenly aware of the absurdity of her position. What in the name of heaven had induced her to leap up here? Anything she could say from up here was doomed to sound ridiculous in advance.

'Breena, come down. Let's not waste any more of the evening.

Here, take my hand, I'll help you down. Can you see me? I'm over here.'

But having once jumped up here, could she now meekly take his hand and climb down again? Could she allow herself to be won over by that coaxing voice? Above all, what was she to say and do when she reached the ground? Burst into tears if he refused to take her straight home and insisted on going on to Castleboyne? And once inside the car, *his* car, would he take notice even of her tears?

'Breena, here I am. Take my hand. Don't be afraid. Come on…'

Again the sound of his voice floated up to her. Evidently he felt flattered by the thought that she was afraid of him. He was incomprehensible to her. How could she deal with such a man? She had an impulse to put a quick end to it all by jumping down and running past him, running, running, running – where?

CHAPTER 45

She looked down into the valley. The serene moonlit waters calmed her and lifted her spirits. Then she glanced up at the dark shoulder of the mountain behind her and the bright sky beyond. All at once she was possessed by a kind of exaltation; she knew where she could run to. The lonely and impulsive thing, the utterly foolish action…

Below her Gabriel was still urging her down, still manfully keeping his temper. But she had turned away; she was looking up over the mountain. She scarcely heard him. There was a pathway over this part of the mountain, a short-cut into the town, beaten out by the people who had once lived in the village on the eskar. She had walked it many times: with Kitty, Uncle John, Maurice, Thady, Desmond…

She turned back to Gabriel. He was saying, 'Is that agreed, then? I'll back up the car, you'll jump in, and we'll drive off at once to the lights and the warmth… '

Now that she knew what she must do; now that she knew she would soon be free of him, she was able again almost to pity him. No doubt, according to his own lights, he was being very patient with her. She called down:

'I've spoiled your evening, I'm very sorry. Why not go on to Castleboyne on your own; you have friends there. I'm going home now. I'll speak to Uncle John tomorrow, I'll ask him to talk to you. Good night.'

Silence for a moment; silence and near-darkness. She could not see him now, even as a dim shape. She had very quietly climbed on to the next boulder, higher up. Then she heard his voice, loud, authoritative; paying her at least the compliment of being angry with her:

'You nonsensical girl, what are you up to now? Come down here at once. Come down, I say. Don't you realise that I'm responsible for you? I'll give you two minutes, and then I'll go up and fetch you.'

She smiled to herself in the darkness. By now she had climbed even higher. She shouted down, 'You can't come up here. I know every inch of this ground, but you'd quickly lose your way. You might fall, hurt yourself…'

Again silence. 'Don't worry, I'll be all right,' she called down. 'I'll be home before you are.'

She turned then and began her climb in earnest. Behind her, already muted by the wind, she heard angry shouts and protests. Had she listened to what he was saying, he would no doubt have succeeded in intimidating her, have drawn her back downhill, a shamed and shrinking girl. But she knew that she could not afford to listen. That part of her nature that was deeper than thought told her that she had either to think or to act; either to reflect on what she was doing and stop doing it at once and go back to Gabriel, or to go ahead. She chose to go ahead, and in doing so moved out of her own human world into the animal world of simple endurance, where there was no longer any time, only a task before her.

Afterwards she could remember very few of the details of that climb, she could not think back and say, 'The hardest part of it was that, or that…' She had only a faint memory even of the one or two tricky places; the place where she had to ease herself down between two boulders and feel along under the right-hand one until she came to the opening that led out again to the heather-covered path; the place where she had to climb a grassy hummock and so reach a narrow track, with a ridge of rock on her left to guide her hand, above a fairly steep cliff face...

What remained in her mind was a vivid recollection of some sixth sense that had taken her over. She was able to recall a strong animal pride in herself as she moved along with skill, exactitude. She had a picture of herself with her head turned into the wind, listening intently.

She had a more distant memory of the moment when she reached the windy top of the ridge and crossed from the shadowed part of the mountain into the moonlight above Filemoyn. Joy was what she felt then, and joy was what she remembered. But later came the long strength of railway track in from Filemoyn; a track that in memory had no turning, but only sleepers blanched by moonlight going on and on forever before her. Finally she had a picture of herself in the lane behind Main Street, loping along in the light that streamed here and there from back windows, exhaustion kept at bay by the thought that she was nearing home, that now she must be very wary, very alert; that somehow she must keep the dogs from barking and creep to her room unheard, unseen. Explanations must come, but not tonight! Tonight she wanted only to sleep, to forget in sleep this interminable evening, and so recover from it.

But for all that she kept calling out to them softly, the dogs did bark as she was climbing the garage wall. She had neglected them all day; they wanted attention now, not blandishments. She cried out to them to be quiet; as she did so the lamp over the kitchen door was switched on, the yard was flooded with light. She heard her name being guardedly called, 'Breena...?'

It was Desmond's voice. She stared into the yard with eyes half-blinded from the sudden glare. She saw that Desmond was coming towards her.

'Breena, come in this way, will you? I've been waiting up for you...'

She slid down off the wall and leaned over the gate. She said, 'I'm not going in. I don't want to explain anything. I don't want to explain…' Then he was beside her, she felt his arm around her shoulders, supporting her, guiding her. His voice came and went in her ears. He sounded amused, he sounded anxious. Then she was in the kitchen, blinking at the light. She saw that Desmond was staring at her gloves, which she had pulled off mechanically. She too stared at them in wonder. They had been new only a few hours before; now they were filthy and in tatters. Suddenly she heard herself asking 'Have you seen Gabriel?'

'Yes. He's gone across to the other house. He has some idea you might be there. I asked him not to say anything to anybody. It was as much as I could do to stop him from summoning the fire brigade, the life-boat, the ambulance…'

She stood up. 'I think I'd better go to bed.'

'Drink this first.' He put a glass into her hand. It was hot, it was delicious. It was punch. He topped up the glass. Then Hannah was also in the kitchen. Hannah's eyes were very bright; they were brighter than the lamp. Breena could not look at them.

'I'd better go to bed,' she said again.

'Have some more of this,' Desmond said.

'No, thank you, Desmond. All I want now is sleep. And Desmond, thank you…'

He took her glass, lightly clasping her hand as he did so. His fingers seemed ice-cold against her hot skin. He said, 'Sleep well, Breena.' In spite of her great tiredness, she was struck by something new, something strange yet familiar, in his tone and look. The thought went through her head, 'He's very like Maurice. Why have I never noticed it before?'

She spoke this thought aloud to Hannah as they went down the corridor together. Hannah made no comment.

CHAPTER 46

That night Breena had a strange dream.

In her dream it was a summer's day and she was a child again, walking through the woods at the back of the house where she had lived as a child. She was walking very fast and she was crying. She was frightened. At first she had no idea why she was frightened, but the impression of fear was so strong that she began to run, pushing her way through the rhododendron bushes and darting wild glances upwards where the sun dappled the leaves of the beech and larch trees, and made slivers of light along their branches. She could hear a queer rustling of leaves all around her, though there was now wind in the summer wood. Then in one of those upward glances she discerned the cause of her fear, and she stopped dead in her tracks. Perched in every tree around her were things that at first sight seemed like great bats, but when she looked again, a cry bubbled up inside her, suddenly terror-stricken at the thought of what new dangers it might bring.

Everywhere she saw faces peering down at her through the branches. Hundreds of dull eyes gazed at her, half-blind it seemed as they strained to see her. She saw mouths that moved, champed, like the mouths of old women except for their colour, which was very red. She caught glimpses of strong, evenly-spaced, gleaming teeth.

She stopped crying; suddenly she realised how useless tears were. For a few moments she stared upwards, hearing nothing except the beating of her own heart, not daring to move. Then a kind of desperate courage came to her. She knew that she must act at once if she were to escape. Already she was shaking with fear of the half-human things above; soon she would be utterly unable to move. It came to her that her only hope was to turn back, to turn and run as hard as she could back the way she had come. She swung herself round and all at once the queer rustling in the trees grew into a strong hiss, hiss, hiss! She saw the branches quiver and once more she stopped dead. The winged, half-human things above must be preparing to come down and surround her…

'Help!' she heard herself screaming. 'Help! Help! Isn't there anyone…'

And then, striding out of the green gloom in front of her, came Maurice's familiar figure. She gave a cry of joy, courage came back to her. She bounded towards him. But as she drew near him she saw that he was enveloped in a black shroud that flapped about him wildly, as in a breeze, though there was still no wind in that summer wood. Terror-stricken once again she stopped short and watched him. As he came nearer and nearer her fear of him increased until the menace of the things in the trees became as nothing. Half-crazed she turned from him and began to run, back through a hail of half-bat, half-human tree-things, that were now falling heavily to the ground all around her, like wounded birds. But she took no notice of these; she hardly saw them, so great was her terror of the black figure behind. All the time, however, they were piling up around her. At length she stumbled over them in her wild running and fell to the ground. She knew she was helpless then. She had no more strength left. She could only press her face into the dry moss between the trees and wait for the shrouded figure to catch up with her. Then she heard a low, hurt voice asking her; 'Breena, don't you know I've come to help you?'

It was Maurice's voice. Dazed with relief, she raised herself quickly from the ground and turned to face him. But it was still the shrouded figure that stood there before her. She reeled away from it, she willed herself to lose consciousness, to faint...

'Breena, look!' Maurice's voice said. 'I've caught them all for you. Won't you take them?'

It seemed she had no choice then but to open her eyes and look. She saw that the shrouded figure held all the tree-things bunched together in its hands. Their aspect had changed; they had shrunk very much in size and they no longer had any faces, only small branches that swished to and fro with the sound of leaves in the wind. As the figure held them out to her they began to look more and more like small shoots of trees.

'Take them, Breena!'

Maurice's voice sounded so full of reproach, so hurt, that she made herself reach out to take them. But then she found herself staring at the figure's hands, which so far had escaped her attention. Some kind of loose, gauzy stuff hung about them; she could not see the fingers. She was afraid to touch them.

'Breena, surely you're not afraid of me?' The figure raised one hand and began to pull the shroud from its head. A sudden frenzy of horror seized her. 'No!' she screamed, 'no, no!'

Then she saw that the figure had begun to fade away from her, back into the sun-dappled gloom of the wood. The next moment she was sitting up in bed, feeling intense relief that it was only a dream taking possession of her mind and driving out the sense of horror that still lingered. She looked about the room. It was morning, though very early as yet. In the upper part of the window the sky gleamed bright, but below there was dusk; not the thickening dusk of evening, but the shifting, brightening dusk of pre-dawn. The piping of the first birds could be heard in the garden. She jumped out of bed and ran to the window. The image of her dream was still very vivid in her mind and distorted what she saw outside. The tangle of rose and fuchsia bushes against the wall opposite seemed to crouch like animals in their own shadows. Then somewhere at the turn of the garden a drowsy blackbird began to practise his first notes, and her heart leapt up. Morning and a blackbird singing! She was just about to push up the sash when she caught sight of a whitish object glimmering palely at her feet. With the quickness of surprise she swooped down, felt at it a moment with her fingers, then snatched it up. It was a letter. The first touch of her fingers had established that.

A letter. She gazed at the long white envelope, feeling the thick wad of paper within. Even in the half-light she could see that there was no writing on the envelope, no name or address, nothing. She turned it over in her hand, with a mind highly sensitive, over imaginative, as a result of her dream. She struggled to account for it. Suddenly she glanced up at the window. Open at the top! That would explain… But who had thrown it in? She could think only of two people, Gabriel and Maurice. The thought of Gabriel made snatches of events from last night go tumbling pell-mell through her brain and she prayed, oh not Gabriel, not Gabriel! – But if Maurice, what then? Why should Maurice send her a letter in this way?

She hurried to the table and switched on the lamp. Then, quite suddenly and shamefully, she was very much afraid. What if the person who had thrown in the letter still lurked outside in the garden, if he were standing out there now, watching her? Hastily she switched off the lamp, and now the soft dawn light outside could no longer be distinguished. Only a dimness that gradually thickened into blackness could be seen through the window. As she watched she fancied that something, a shadow, a part of the darkness, moved. She darted forward, pushed up the window, fastened it, bolted the shutters. But even then she had no desire to remain in the room. What a fool, what a fool she had been two years ago to make such a point of getting this downstairs room! And what a coward she had become since then! It cost her a decided effort of will to move calmly and noiselessly as she shrugged herself into her dressing gown and hurried from the room.

The kitchen with its glowing night-stove and bolted shutters was welcoming and safe. Leaning against the stove, she opened the letter. The moment she saw Maurice's handwriting her heart turned over. What could this mean? And yet it seemed to her that she knew already, before she had read one line, what it meant.

It was a long letter; three foolscap sheets closely written on both sides. She read it with painful concentration. There was a great deal of crossing out and scribbling over. In places the writing was so feverishly hurried that she could only guess at the meaning. All the same the message of the letter was very clear, sometime in the middle of last night Maurice had made up his mind that he must leave home at once, that, as he put it, 'I have just made the greatest decision of my life; I am going to leave home now, this very night. I can't trust myself to wait any longer…'

From the very first line it became obvious that by means of the dramatic phrases of this letter Maurice was lashing himself into the belief that he must go away at once, 'make a break for it', or be talked or tricked by 'them' into resigning his own personality. He wrote: 'To you and you only, Breena, I'll admit that Hugh's latest plan to save me from myself, a plan put forward by the way, by your friend Gabriel, had me sorely tempted. I repeat, I can't trust myself to hold on to my own viewpoint much longer. The courage that came to me unasked is beginning to run out. I must *act now*. I wouldn't be just a coward if I failed to go; I'd cease to be Maurice. I'd hate and despise myself so much that after a while everybody else, *including you, Breena* would begin to hate me too.'

He wrote a great deal about his father, most of it a repetition of what he had said that first morning in the hut. About his mother he wrote that in the long run it would be best for her if he went now, while his going would still seem only part of the shock of his father's death. 'Hugh will be with her, Hugh will always be there now. He's her favourite, and I admit with gratitude that he is a very good son. He'll smooth things out for her, tell her what to say to people in the town. I've included a few lines to her in a letter I've just left under Kit's door.'

In the last page he made a casual and confident reference to the future. 'You'll be hearing from me again within a few days. I'll write to you openly at Uncle John's, the family must learn to accept that. And what I promised you yesterday at Maurcappagh I promise you again now. Breena, I know that whatever they say to you, you won't give me up, you won't lose faith in me. Last night, after Gabriel came here looking for you, *I* knew that you wouldn't fall or lose your way on the track home from Maurcappagh. God bless you and me too.'

She read the letter through once, then again. She was just on the point of reading it a third time when suddenly she folded it up and pushed it into her pocket. No! This letter would make her mad if she went on reading it. She began to walk up and down the kitchen. She was conscious of the trembling of her whole body… It was an effort to walk. Yet to sit still was impossible. In the course of a few short seconds she thought of many things. The chief part of the pain she felt was regret. Regret all the more intense because it was so futile! To think that she had been suddenly asleep when Maurice came to her window, when she might have talked to him, even persuaded him… Oh why hadn't he called to her, why hadn't he tried to wake her up? But… but perhaps he *had* tried to wake her, and failed. The resulting sound of her dream came vividly to mind. In an effort to wake her, had Maurice swished something – the letter – across the window pane? And that louder sound of the tree-things falling to the ground? Could that have been Maurice knocking at the window? Then his voice – surely his voice had called her by name many times in the course of her dream?

Yes, yes; without a doubt he had tried to wake her. She found some comfort in being able to believe that. And then she realised that she had no idea where he was bound for; that he had made no mention of his plans in the letter, and this uncertainty sharpened her pain to the point of anguish. The question, 'Whither, friend, whither?' to which she could give no answer, kept repeating itself in her mind.

'Breena!' The voice came from the doorway; from the darkness beyond her own small circle of light. It was, surely it was, it must be, Maurice's voice! She shaded her eyes and saw, striding out of the shadows before her, a figure that for one moment might have been the shrouded figure of her dream. She shrank back. She felt no fear, only a sickening blankness of mind. Then the figure came closer and she saw that it was Desmond. He was wearing a dressing-gown that swept the floor and his long hair was tousled into a cowl about his head. He was saying:

'I see I've frightened you. I'm sorry. But you frightened me too. I came down with my courage screwed to the sticking point. I thought it was a burglar I could hear moving about down here.'

For some reason she felt guilty, she found it necessary to stammer out an excuse. 'I... I couldn't sleep. I... I came in here because...'

His smile stopped her. 'I know. Your intentions were honourable. You came in here not to burgle the kitchen but to make yourself some tea.'

'Tea? Oh, yes. I'll... I'll just...' She snatched up the kettle. But as she was filling it under the tap it slipped out of her unsteady hands and fell with a great clatter into the sink. He was beside her in an instant.

'Here, let me do it. You look... Sit down, come on, sit down here!' He pulled a chair up beside the stove for her. 'Didn't you sleep at all? After last night I thought you'd sleep soundly for a week. But over-tiredness sometimes works the other way...'

He went on speaking and she felt grateful to him; she felt truly grateful for his cheerful presence. For a while she even listened to what he said. It was a welcome change from the round of her own thoughts.

'Do you know that my father didn't close an eye until an hour or so ago. And by that time I myself was wide awake. I wanted him to take some sleeping tablets, but no; that would be sinful pandering to human weakness. We had punch instead, and with my father punch means talk, as perhaps you know by now. Talk about the past was what *he* wanted, but I had other ideas. To keep things on the light side I told him about yourself and Gabriel. He knew nothing about it, did you realise that? And he certainly relished the tale, especially the end of it. He's very proud of you. I can tell. You're a real Cappagh, he claims, though you're a foreigner by birth. He got very cross with Gabriel. "Does he think that his slick car and city gab would impress a Cappagh woman? Well, he knows better now!"'

The tea was ready now. He handed Breena her cup and went on talking. 'You realise of course that Gabriel has abjured me forever, that he's sworn never to darken the grimy door of my flat again? Don't get me wrong though. I'm not complaining. That man has been like a wife to me lately. And I'm determined on one thing; if ever I do take unto myself a wife, it's going to be a woman. Anyway, I know now what to do with the next friend I want to get rid of. I'll bring him right down here to propose to you. I'll... '

'Desmond!' Breena interrupted him in an excited tone. Her thoughts had reverted to Maurice and all at once she was struck by an entirely new aspect of the matter. 'But how could he have gone? Surely he didn't walk. And at this hour of morning... '

She broke off before Desmond's stare of surprise. 'Breena, you're not talking in your sleep, are you? You haven't dropped off to sleep on me?'

'No, No! I meant Maurice. Desmond... '

She hesitated. There was so much to explain and she felt very excited and impatient. On a sudden impulse she reached into her dressing-gown and pulled out Maurice's letter. She told herself that but for the accident of Desmond's being awake and joining her like this she would never have shown Maurice's letter to a living soul. As it was, now that Desmond was here, she badly wanted his opinion, his advice.

He read the letter carefully, some passages more than once. At last he looked up. 'So *this* is why I found you awake and wandering about down here? Maurice had been round earlier to deliver this letter? I hope he rang the front-door bell and handed it over in formal fashion?'

The sudden levity of his last question struck her all the more painfully because of the unusual and most welcome kindness he had been showing her up to the moment she gave him the letter. She stammered uncertainly:

'No, no… of course not. As a matter of fact… ' She explained how she had found the letter under the window.

He gave her a keen look.

'And why have you given it to *me* to read? Just because I'm there, like Mount Everest? Or because you want something from me? Well, please tell me exactly what you want. I shall find it far easier to oblige you, I assure you, if I know in advance exactly what's required of me.'

She could feel herself reddening. His sarcastic tone hurt her, she could barely keep back her tears. Yet in all honesty she had to admit to herself that he was right; she *did* want something from him. While she hesitated, she heard him go on:

'One piece of advice I do feel inclined to give you. Don't go about giving Maurice's letter to people to read. I assure you he wouldn't thank you for it. It's a letter of a highly personal nature. Probably already he regrets having committed himself so foolishly on paper.'

She was stung into a reply.

'Regrets having committed himself! How little you know Maurice! He's not calculating and cold-blooded, he… And you needn't think that I'll show his letter to anybody else, you needn't think that I… ' Suddenly she was very angry, and somehow this was a relief. 'But I know what I'll do. I'll tear the letter up, I'll tear it up this very minute, then I'll burn it.'

She reached for the letter and as she was tearing it into little

| 311

strips went on passionately: 'I only showed it to you because I thought… I thought… '

She had to stop herself; she had to clamp her lips together. If she went on like this she would be crying in a moment, and she knew she must not cry. She did not understand why this was so important; she only knew that it was. She rose abruptly from her place, gathered up the torn scraps of the letter and pushed them into the stove.

'Breena, my child, you make me feel very old – you and Maurice between you. Such drama as you're both capable of! Well, go on, finish your sentence. You only showed it to me because you thought… ?'

She turned from the stove and found his blue glance full on her face. For two reasons, because she had kept herself from crying and because she had burned the letter, she now felt quite able to stand up to him. She met his glance steadily. But when she began to speak the words came out in rather a muddle, too quickly:

'I thought that after you had read the letter you wouldn't mind going over to Maurice's house – that is, after I had asked you, of course, to see if he is still there.'

'Still there?' He stared in surprise. 'You mean you think Maurice capable of writing a letter like that and then… But if there's one thing that stands out a mile about that letter, it's Maurice's determination to go. He's been working himself up to it for days. Even I could see that.'

'Yes, I agree. But I know a bit more than you about… about the circumstances of the case. I think I'm right in saying that Maurice has hardly slept a wink since his father's death. You've read the letter. It's so excited it's almost mad in places. He must have been out on his feet when he wrote it. I think the very writing of it, and Kit's letter too and his mother's may have helped to… to exorcise his excitement. Then he came over here, he threw the letter in at my window. I… I had a dream, at least I thought it was a dream, but it might have been Maurice trying to wake me up. And afterwards, after I found the letter and switched on the light, I could swear I saw something, somebody, move in the garden. It frightened me then, now I think…'

She broke off, she knew that she was becoming incoherent. She glanced at Desmond. There was something in his face… could it be a look of pity? She turned away. She tried hard to keep a tight rein on her voice as she went on:

'Anyway, what I mean is, if Maurice was as exhausted as I think he was… After all, he must have been planning to hitch-hike out of the town, and he must have realised that his chances of getting a lift at this hour of morning were so slight that he'd be much better off going back home and snatching a few hours' sleep, then starting off fresh later on, rather… rather than trudging along the road for miles and miles until he was on the point of collapse. With the chance of being overtaken too by Hugh, and at least some attempt made to bring him back. Also Desmond… you have no idea how lonely and tormented Maurice is at the moment. He misses his father very much. I honestly think he wouldn't find it in him to go off on his own in the middle of the night, without hearing some human voice say to him "Go neirighid do bothar leat!"'

'Well… I suppose there's some sense in what you say – as far as I can understand it. Look, if you think you have the right to interfere in Maurice's affairs, why not phone up the other house at once and ask if he is there?'

'Phone up? How could I do that? Desmond… if Maurice is still there, I'd only be giving him away. It would be like showing his letter to everyone to read. They'd know I had some reason… And the people at the exchange… if they listened in… Desmond, please get dressed and go over. I'm not interfering, try and understand that. It's just that Maurice wrote me that letter, now if I can help him I will. I know he can't possibly have much money. I could give him a bit, and I know that Aunt Ursula… Do go, Desmond. Hugh must have told you that Maurice's health…'

'Maurice's health must take its chance. That's what Maurice himself seems to think, it appears to me. However…' He stood up abruptly, he did not look at her. 'I'll do as you say. I'll go across to the other house. Rather against my… but as well as Maurice, there's also my friend Gabriel, our mutual friend Gabriel, to be considered. He swore last night that he'd be off home around this time. It's only charitable to go and see him off and give him a chance to retract some of the very hasty statements he made to me last night. D'you want me to give him your regards if I happen to run into him?'

'I… I… Desmond, I'm very grateful to you. If you could at all manage it, would you… would you try very hard to speak only to Kitty? If Hugh…'

'Now, now, my child! Don't load me down with ifs and buts. Don't expect me to take sides. Don't expect me even to know which side is which. It puzzles me beyond expression, this fuss that has been going on in the family for the past day or two. As far as I'm concerned, if Maurice wants to go, he goes. He's old enough to know his own mind. Fence him in in this little town, or in another town like it, and one day he'll hold up the local bank, shoot the bank manager, and set off on the run. Then what a pickle the family'll be in…'

And with that Breena had to be satisfied.

CHAPTER 47

When Desmond came back she was waiting in the kitchen, fully dressed. She had risked very little thinking while he was gone. She had waited in a haze of hopefulness, feeding herself on daydreams. Perhaps another day, another half-day, another few hours even with Maurice! Perhaps only one hour, then again perhaps two, three, four… Who, from the viewpoint of half-past five in the morning, could foresee the end of this day?

Desmond barely glanced at her as he came in. He walked past her to the stove, where he made a great show of warming his hands. He said with his back to her:

'Well, he's gone all right. Gone too in such a way that nobody'll get a chance to stop him or bring him back.'

She was silent a moment. She had sprung forward to the door when she heard him coming; now she went back to the table so that she could pull out a chair and sit down and shade her face with her hands.

'How did he go?' she asked.

Desmond told her; Maurice had driven off very comfortably in his father's car, which Kitty had helped him push down the drive and out beyond the gates, for fear Hugh or his mother would hear him starting up.

She was silent again, digesting this piece of information. Finally she said in a disjointed, puzzled way:

'You mean he… he *stole* the car? And how did Kit happen to be awake? Why… why did she help him? She was dead against his going.'

'Well now… ' He still spoke with his back to her, 'to take those points in order. Maurice did not, I repeat *not*, steal the car. He merely borrowed it. He arranged with Kitty to leave the keys with the owner of a certain garage in a certain city – after nine o'clock tonight, but not until then, Kitty will be free to divulge names and places. As for Kitty's being awake, it seems that Maurice made such a noisy business of pushing a letter under her door that he woke her up. It turns out that you were right in your analysis of Maurice's state of mind; he didn't after all find it possible to go off uncheered by the human voice. As for the little matter of Kitty's helping him, I believe she did so for the good old reason that blood is thicker than water. She found him determined to go, so determined that as soon as he reminded her she had given him away already, that as short a time ago as Sunday evening she had brought the bloodhounds down on him, she began to realise that she had to choose between helping him and being despised by him. After that, for a girl like Kit, there appears to have been only one thing to do; help him with all her might. She maintains that his taking the car was all her doing; that she had to work hard at talking him into it; that up until the moment she suggested it his only plan was to set off on foot, with a bundle on his back. And oh yes, she was able to persuade him to take a little money as well. She's very pleased about that, though she's not yet sure as to the money; her mother will have to confirm that later. Anyway, it was money that by good fortune was lying on top of her father's papers on his desk, "lying about" you understand. And now have I covered all the ground? Are there any more questions you want to ask me?'

'Kitty was still up when you got across? You had no trouble getting into the house?'

'None whatever. The second door down was open. Kitty was sitting in the kitchen with the range well stacked up, bracing herself like any early Christian martyr to face Hugh and her mother. She was reading *The Imitation of Christ*. She seemed very pleased to see me – regarded me as good material to practise on, I suppose. She took it for granted that my first intention in coming across was to straighten things out with Gabriel, who by the way is still in bed.'

'Did she say what time Maurice left?'

'No. She was very free with her general statement, but names, places, times she kept to herself. Agreed policy between them, I expect.'

'Did she… did she say anything about me?'

'Yes. Says she'll phone you up after she's spoken to Hugh and her mother. I gather that silence and meditation are to be the rule until the great confrontation is over.'

Breena thought all this over for a few moments. At last she asked in a low voice:

'Desmond, you're about the same age as Hugh, aren't you?' Do you agree with him that Maurice is an extremely silly person? Not silly just because he's still only the age he is, but inherently, incurably silly? By that I mean selfish, conceited, self-dramatizing… ?'

'My dear Breena, I may be as old as Hugh, but that still doesn't make me five hundred years old. I refuse to become your oracle; I refuse to make pronouncements on Maurice. Though I can honestly say that there's one action of his I thoroughly admire.'

'What's that?' She looked up hopefully.

'His making his getaway in a car. I'm not saying that a helicopter wouldn't have been better. Nowadays one cannot help thinking a car a bit old-fashioned. But who knows? One day soon he may become the troubadour of the jet age. His fortunes will be made forever… '

Breena stood up. She said abruptly: 'Desmond, thank you very much for going across to the other house for me. I was too much of a coward to go myself, and I know now that Kitty wouldn't have

| 317

said anything over the phone. So thank you, Desmond, I'm truly grateful. Now... now I must get out of here, I must go for a walk.'

'Oh no, not another walk! Breena, let me tell you quite frankly that you haven't yet recovered from the last one. You look... Come on, sit down again.' He put his hand on her arm. 'Look, what d'you feel about some breakfast? Before Hannah and Aunt Ursula come down? I'm a dab hand at bacon and eggs... '

She shook her head, she couldn't look at him. 'Thank you very much, I'm not hungry. I must get out into the fresh air. But I won't go very far. Only up to the lake.'

'Only up to the lake! Breena, Breena, for anybody else that would be a two days' walk! You won't forget that my father is coming to Dublin with me? You'll be back in time to see him off?'

'Yes, of course I'll be back. It's not half-past six yet. I'll be back well before eleven.'

Outside she had to harden her heart against the dogs, who began to frisk about at sight of her, whining in a beseeching way low in their throats. But she knew that today a walk with the dogs would give no pleasure, either to herself or to them. From where she stood by the kitchen door she could see the sheep dotted all over the high fields leading up to the lake. Today she lacked the carefree quick-moving spirit that would keep the dogs interested in the walk and make sheep seem mere sluggish mounds in the landscape to them.

CHAPTER 48

Breena turned up Fairhill, intending to skirt the town and join the footpath to the lake further up, about half a mile beyond Maurice's house. Just now she neither wanted to see the house nor risk being seen herself by any member of the family.

She walked blindly, doggedly, with no sense of exhilaration or joy. She realised that she was very tired. Once she sat down on the low mossy wall that bordered the path, but it took her so long to get up again that she did not risk a second rest. 'Don't brood, don't brood!' she kept telling herself. 'Look to the future, not to the past. Those who look backwards are turned into salt.' But as always when she tried to take control of her thoughts she had to give her mind one image, one image only, to feed on. Today the Great Wall of China suggested itself. She had been reading a book about it lately; it seemed to suit her mood.

She stared down at the grey footpath and thought, according to the style of the book she had been reading, here I am, pacing the Great Wall, a sentinel by name, in actual fact a slave. My term of duty is over; from the watch-tower I can hear the snores of the man who should have relieved me. But I have no money to bribe our commanding officer. I must keep on walking. I can hardly hold myself erect for hunger; I can hardly keep myself from howling with rage like a wild beast. But if I stop, if I faint, if I reveal myself as useless, what mercy will be shown me? They know I could not afford to pay for medicines, or even find my own food while I was ill. They would not hesitate to throw me down over the Wall into some wild gully, where I might lie for days, not quite dead, not quite alive, before the wolves came. Then my name would be sent to the Governor of our province. They would tell him that I had deserted my post. My family would be disgraced, my brothers pressed into the service. My father would be shamed, made voiceless, among the village elders. My mother, with no sons of hers left in the house, would draw her veil over her face…

She turned off the path at the usual place and climbed the ridge that overlooked the lake. When she reached the top tiredness overcame her; she threw herself down on the damp heather and closed her eyes. Why had she bothered to trudge all the weary way up here? Then she opened her eyes, she made herself sit up.

In this thin, early-morning light there could be no imposing her own fancies on the scene below. She had to accept what was there before her. Ah!… but how readily she accepted it, how suddenly her heart leapt up to rejoice in what her eyes could see! The crimson flaring of the strangled sun above the black cliffs behind the lake, the lake-water itself, that in the shadow of the crags gleamed jet black, but took on as it emerged from the shadows all the hues of fire and blood – how well these suited her mood! Her thoughts went out to them; what she saw became confused with what she felt. Lonesome, angry, savage, grand! Oh, if only she herself could take on the character of this wild and hidden place. So proud it was, so careless of being noticed or admired… Suddenly her heart cried, teach me! Here and now, after I have trudged so faithfully up here towards this moment, teach me your proud secret of knowing how to be alone…

Not a breath of wind stirred down there; no long morning shadow was cast by the encircled sun. Heather and furze, even the slender fern, were motionless; they might have become rock or metal, such strange tints of red and black as they took on in this savage landscape. At the lake's edge the upright blades of fairy grass glittered like green daggers. At the back the water fell into its underground channel with echoing thunder, a voice composed equally of strength and despair. And in that voice this morning Breena heard words, echoes of words, echoes of tormenting words: *... went... went in the morning light, whether I would or no; me, men go... come... and go... All things remain in God...*

She sat for a long time at the top of the ridge, very still. Gradually the lesson that only this secluded place could teach her began to seep into her heart. She began to realise that life demanded no such stern discipline of her as to learn to be alone. All that was asked of her was that she should learn to be herself; first of all to know and then follow the laws of her own nature. In the same way she gradually began to understand that Maurice had not only been right to go; he had had little choice but to do so. In going he had obeyed laws of his own nature which he had been given no hand in drawing up, but which it would be death now to disobey.

Gradually as she sat there it came to her how Maurice's childhood, her own childhood, the years that had made them what they were now, were as much beyond their power of influence as the millions of years that had formed the lake, boulders and crags around her here; she began to understand how up to this moment all her thinking about Maurice had been warped by that sly and distorting word 'if'. If only he hadn't fallen ill last year, if only he had gone back to school last term, if only his father had not died just now! She might just as well sit here and begin lamenting, if only lake-water could flow upwards, if only crags and boulders would walk about! As far as Maurice was concerned, could it now be expected of him, after the way he had been brought up, that he should begin to labour seriously at 'fumbling in a greasy till, and adding the halfpence to the pence'? For her own part, it was not the past that she must brood over or bother about; it was what she could be, what she had in her to become and help others to become, from this moment of consciousness onwards that must concern her now.

All at once she looked up. The sun had broken through the clouds; it beamed down on here where she sat and slanted in bright rays over the steep fields below. The lake, and the cliffs behind it, were still in deep shadow, but when she turned she caught her breath to see how far, far below, the little town at the foot of the Maurcappagh range had suddenly acquired the flush and radiance of dreamed and painted cities. She leaned forward into the morning glow, and she too, became part of the mirage.

Dingli
Malta
1974